Fic   Mancini, Anthony
Man   Godmother

DEMCO

10 1993

Godmother

Godmother

ANTHONY MANCINI

DONALD I. FINE, INC.

NEW YORK

To the Italian immigrant

In each individual the spirit has become flesh, in each man the creation suffers, within each one a redeemer is nailed to the cross.

—HERMANN HESSE

ORDINATION DAY

The Archbishop of New York lay his pale marbled hands on the head of Angelo Falcone on June 18, 1950, the fourth Sunday after Pentecost. As the organ groaned in Saint Patrick's Cathedral the prelate gave him the chalice and paten that were to be the tools of his trade.

Thus did Father Falcone and sixteen other candidates join the ranks of some 360,000 Catholic priests in the world, a world where a failed haberdasher named Harry Truman occupied the White House, a self-named "Man of Steel" (Stalin) ruled the Kremlin and a hack politician named Bill O'Dwyer kept a precarious hold on power at City Hall.

In the first pew knelt the new priest's mother, Maria Croce Falcone, beaming with pride and satisfaction. She was a dignified-looking woman of forty-seven years to whom God gave the twin benedictions of beauty and brains. The glitter of jewelry at her wrists and throat could not match the luster in her dark eyes. Her back was ramrod straight as she knelt in a cloud of silk organza. The sequined handbag at her side contained one of the tools of her trade—a lightweight Beretta Modello 1934 with seven rounds in the magazine.

She knelt under the vaulting stone and stained glass, a rosary of pure ivory beads wrapped around her right hand, *La Cumare*, as she was known to one and all. Godmother. A woman of respect. Now more than ever.

Plenty of big shots filled the pews behind her. So-called respectable people. Union bosses, councilmen, lawyers, business executives, even judges (hoping to escape but willing to risk the notice of newspaper reporters who might be around). *Personaggi*. People who would not have stooped to spit on her as a girl in the old country. In times antique.

On the other side of the aisle sat many of La Cumare's associates in the world she ruled—the bookers and button men, yeggs and

3

runners, counterfeiters and bodyguards, fidgeting with their starched collars under the stony gaze of all the saints in heaven.

But by far the biggest contingent in the congregation was made up of common folk—tradespeople, shoemakers, bakers, tailors, seamstresses, waiters, errand boys, carpenters, masons and ditch diggers. Not to mention the old biddies in black muslin who like to lean out of the tenement windows or sit on folding chairs on the pavement, gold teeth glinting, acting like they owned the world as they commented on everything under the sun and panned nuggets of gossip from the people who streamed up and down Mulberry and Mott streets. The whole neighborhood, it seemed, had turned out to witness her son's ordination, to pay their respects to him and to her. Especially to her. Hey, they knew which side of the *pan dolce* had the sugar.

La Cumare made a pious tent with her hands. In the June heat a light dew of perspiration coated her upper lip. She felt the eyes of many people on her. It didn't faze her. She was accustomed to admiring eyes.

One set of eyes belonged to her son, to whom she appeared serene and beautiful, a madonna of flesh rather than fresco. The fumes of sacramental wine rose to his nostrils from the chalice that he held, reminding him that he was finally at age thirty a priest, a priest in the age of the atomic bomb. Doctrine said that Holy Orders printed an indelible mark on the priest's soul, but Angelo Falcone didn't sense any drastic or essential change in himself. The Archbishop was delivering a homily but the new priest heard little of what he said. More than anything, he craved a cigarette. He smiled to himself. Too bad the man in the red hat didn't hand out haloes with the chalice and host. He had merely been ordained, not canonized. His eyes again were trained on his mother.

She was radiant. She shone like silver with satisfaction. This was the day she had been waiting for most of her life. It was her crowning moment, making all the struggles and suffering fade to insignificance. And it made some sense of the orders, holy and unholy, that she had given and taken on the long rocky road from girlhood to womanhood to matriarchy.

She twined the beads around her nimble fingers. If only Pepe could have lived to witness this day! And Ottavio and Lisabeta and the gentle Balbi and the rest of her fellow pilgrims. Did their spirits hover here among the marble angels, martyrs, virgins and saints? Had they entered through the stained-glass transom on the breath of the summer wind? Yes. La Cumare was firmly convinced of their presence.

Auguri, family and friends. Welcome to Fifth Avenue and the ordination of our beloved son.

The Godmother lifted her gaze to the crucifix that hung above the altar and scrutinized the holy convict who was nailed to the tree. He reminded her of the suffering peasants of her wretched homeland.

As Angelo Falcone received into his hands the tokens of the ministry, his mother mumbled the rosary and communed with the ghosts of her past.

MAIDEN

On the night of the birth of Maria Croce—September 7, 1903, in the reign of Vittorio Emmanuele III—Vulcan grumbled in the bowels of Vesuvius, sending a shiver through the earth. The lantern swayed in the doorway of the room.

The midwife rolled her eyes, crossed herself and prophesied that the infant girl would grow up to become a woman of substance, one who would rule over men.

Soon the lamp stopped swinging.

The villagers of Miseno, shadowed from cradle to grave by the wrath of the old firegod, were used to tremors beneath their feet. But they were not used to women who ruled over men. The baby did not cry, lending credence to the prophecy.

But the infant's father, Ottavio Croce, merely spat on the dirt floor of the stone hovel. Like his father, grandfather and ancestors before him, the young fisherman put no faith in predictions of greatness. He heeded only the prophets of doom. And there were plenty of those around. Glancing at the buffalo horns mounted over the front doorway as a talisman against the evil eye, he sighed. Another mouth to feed.

The baby was bundled on the mother's breast. As her child suckled, Lisabeta Croce gave a wan smile. This one was the first of three to survive. "Maria," she said, noting that the calendar marked it the great feast of the Madonna di Piedigrotta.

The village lay a few kilometers west of Naples in a region called by the bards of Greece and Rome the Phlegrean Fields, stretching in a semicircle along the Gulf of Pozzuoli from Cape Posillipo to Cape Miseno. Across the eerily beautiful and forbidding landscape yawned volcanic pits hissing with sulphur springs. On the north side of the valley lay the harbor and a lake they called *Mare Morto*, the Dead Sea, a crater that the ancients believed was the River Styx, where the greedy ferryman Charon plucked coins from the mouths of the dead, setting an example for all the landlords, proprietors and tax collectors to come.

Indeed, the place where Maria Croce was born provided Homer and Virgil with a model for Hell. And hell on earth it was for many of the inhabitants down through the ages.

The land was cursed by God and Man. Drought, famine, malaria, volcanic eruption, earthquake, invasion, tyranny, every conceivable calamity came in its turn. And came again.

But this was no history lesson. This was La Cumare's story.

Ottavio paid the midwife with a string of fish and bushel of mussels. He should have given her the back of his hand. She had bungled the job. As it turned out, Lisabeta could have no more children. Ottavio cursed his luck. What good was a single girl?

But the Croces did all right for a while. Ottavio worked hard for the *padrone*, catching fish and mending nets, and he managed to put a few *soldi* aside, hoping someday to buy his own boat. And Lisabeta helped stock the family larder by cultivating a small plot of hired land on the promontory that overlooked the sea. The volcanic soil was very fertile but she was allowed to keep only one third of the wheat and tomatoes that she harvested. The rest went to the fat *latifondista* who owned the land. But every little bit helped. They also had to feed Ottavio's widowed old mother and mentally defective sister who had no other means of support.

Every morning at daybreak Lisabeta would strap the baby Maria to her back and make an hour's climb up Mt. Miseno to the terraced patch of land that for so many years she would irrigate with her sweat. On the way she passed the ruins of a Roman theater and spa, belled donkeys hauling goods and peasant women walking erect as they balanced huge ceramic jars of water on their heads. When she reached the summit she would place the baby in the shade of an olive tree and get her tools from the shed near the stones that once formed the foundation of the villa where Tiberius Caesar died. Haunted by the ghosts of imperial grandeur, she bent her back and hoed the ground. And little Maria slept.

Soon the baby would wake crying for nourishment. Lisabeta, tasting the salt of her own sweat, would put down the hoe and hustle over to the wailing child. She would brush away the buzzing flies, undo the strings of her bodice and lift Maria to her aching breasts. As the baby snuffled greedily Lisabeta would sit on the ground, resting her back against the tree trunk, and drink water from the pigskin flask. Then she would reach into her stiff muslin apron for her breakfast of bread and onion. If the weather was clear as she savored the food and rare moment of rest, the young woman would gaze out to sea, a mirror of blue glass jeweled with sunlight, and try to make out the outlines of the islands of Procida and Ischia even farther offshore. Then Lisabeta Croce would do a rare thing for someone of her time, place and position. She would daydream and hope.

Her dreams and hopes, of course, were not for herself but for her daughter.

Most of the *paesani* had ambition for nothing beyond the next scrap of bread. The people of the region had been bred like donkeys to haul and bray, not to think and plan. Like colonies of insects, they were predestined to work and die. But the augury of the midwife about Maria had struck a resonance in Lisabeta's heart. Her child, though just a female, would be different. She would amount to something.

Where did Lisabeta Rondine Croce, herself an orphan of Benevento, get such high-flown notions? The cicadas chirruping in the olive groves seemed to mock her thoughts. Why, she would be lucky if Maria at least escaped her own fate of having been auctioned in the piazza of Benevento for farm labor at age nine. She pictured herself at the time—a skinny, frightened, hazel-eyed girl. She remembered the disappointed look in her Aunt Luisa's eyes at the few *soldi* that she had fetched. She was not even worth much as a slave. But as the years passed her figure blossomed and her hands grew strong from hard work. She was thirteen when she met and married Ottavio Croce, who was twenty-three at the time. *Zia* Luisa arranged the whole thing through her godfather, a charcoal-burner who traveled far and wide and became acquainted with the Croce family.

At first Lisabeta regarded her husband as a savior. He was handsome, strong and treated her well. With the passage of time, of course, as she tended his hearth and slept in his bed and became acquainted with his faults, she saw him in a more realistic perspective. He was just a man, better than most, worse than some. His chief quality was also his main fault, she thought. He had an asinine streak of stubbornness, a total inability to compromise with the harsh realities of the world of tufa and scorpions that he inhabited. This same hardheadedness made him a good provider and a loyal friend. But somehow he lacked his compatriots' ability to bend with the winds of misfortune, oppression and poverty and stay alive one day longer. How did he get that way? she wondered. Maybe it came from having had to be a breadwinner since boyhood. His father, also a fisherman, drowned at sea when Ottavio was five. His older brother Enrico died soon afterward when, improbably, an eagle dropped a tortoise on his head. His sister Giacometta was stung by a tarantula and lost her mind. His sister Cara eloped with a Serbian sailor to Buenos Aires. His mother, once a spinner of silk, developed arthritic hands. Yes, the Croces had had more than their fair share of bad luck. That's why in a funny way Ottavio Croce's wife felt she had a license to dream. Surely the spinners of fate had reached the end of this skein of bad cloth. His daughter would have good luck, Lisabeta thought, kissing the horn of coral and cross of pewter that hung from her child's neck. No sense taking chances.

For a while it seemed that Lisabeta's optimism might be vindicated. The family enterprises prospered. The nets teemed with a variety of fish from sardines to swordfish, and Ottavio's cache of sovereigns grew. When Maria grew big enough to help her till the soil Lisabeta added crops of grapes and red oranges to the little farm on the mountaintop.

Soon Maria was transformed by the alchemy of time into a pretty and healthy young girl whose creamy complexion and almond eyes made all the young male heads swivel in the *piazza*. And not only the young ones.

Spying her walking over the stones of the village square one day, Pepe Falcone the carpenter smooched the joined fingers of his right hand and with a flourish sent the kiss flying in her direction.

Maria, balancing a wicker basket of laundry on her head, stopped by the fountain and gave him a withering look. Along with beauty God had given her proud ways and a tart tongue.

"*Weh, nonno*," she said, disparaging the thirty-six-year-old carpenter by calling him "grandpa," "save your kisses for the old widow who lives on the Via Carità." She was referring to the village prostitute that bachelors like Falcone (and some of the married men too) were known to visit whenever they had a few coins to spare in the rutting season (which ran twelve months of the year).

Giuseppe Falcone put his hands on his hips and laughed. She was a spunky girl, all right. He liked that. Then a sad look glazed his blue eyes and he shook his head. Falcone, stocky build and fair hair, was a sentimental man who deplored his bachelorhood, longing for the comforts of wife and kids. Before the war he had had plenty of chances to marry, as would any man possessing all his limbs and physical faculties in this region where the male population had been decimated by having to serve in foreign wars from Ethiopia to Austria, or had been lured away by the Circe of immigration. But in his youth Pepe had relished his freedom and turned down all offers of marriage that came his way. And now, after the war, it was too late.

His fellow villagers said at thirty-six he was still young enough to start a family. Many of the single women would bat their eyes at him in the village square or put an extra wiggle in their walk as they climbed the winding roads balancing burdens on their heads. Pepe paid no attention to them, prompting gossip that he was ''a stalk of fennel.'' But some of the females who had had trysts in the hayloft with Falcone before the war knew this wasn't true. So the village women concluded that he was blinded by his love for a sixteen-year-old girl named Maria Croce.

Maybe this was so but it didn't entirely explain his behavior. The real solution to the puzzle lay locked in the carpenter's heart.

Falcone first had noticed the girl with the blooming figure and sassy manner a year earlier when, festooned with medals, he had returned to the village from the Battle of Vittorio Veneto, where he had served the Kingdom of Italy under the House of Savoy as a corporal. He saw her coming out of church and was struck with the thunderbolt. But it was impossible, not because he was almost as old as her father, May–September unions being fairly common in Miseno and environs.

She called him *nonno,* and the name stung him like the thorn of a rose.

In spite of her acid tongue Maria did feel some affection for the lovesick fellow. He wasn't such a bad sort. She liked his gentle humor and was flattered by his attentions. After all, he was a war hero. But she certainly wasn't in love with him. Nor did she picture herself someday as the slatternly wife of the village carpenter. No, her mother had done too good a job on her . . . she had misty visions of future glory.

As she washed clothes in the spring-fed fountain that served as a communal laundry she didn't gossip with the other women and girls but kept to herself, building castles in the air. Of course her aloofness made her something of a pariah in this little village of the south, the kind of place where conceit was a mortal sin. Maria heard the sarcastic whispers behind her back. *Mene frega*, she thought to herself. Who gives a damn?

Her attitude matched the climate of the time and place—Italy too in 1919 was in a vainglorious mood. Bernardo Liguori, the schoolteacher, each evening read out loud in the village square the gazettes of Naples so that the mostly illiterate villagers could keep up with the times. This was how Maria learned that the nationalistic poet D'Annunzio and his band of quixotic followers had occupied the Adriatic port of Fiume, claimed by both Yugoslavia and Italy. And how she heard of a black-shirted orator named Mussolini who was striding toward power like a modern Caesar. The events in Rome and farther north fired her imagination and kindled her ambition. Though she knew she was merely the unlettered daughter of a poor fisherman she felt a spark inside herself that could not be quenched. She didn't know where it came from. She also didn't know how she would realize her dreams. But Greater Greece long had been famous as a place where the deities singled out mortals of humble birth for noble deeds. Somehow, without ever having read the old stories, Maria Croce saw herself in this Homeric light.

It was July now and the scent of jasmine and bergamot filled the air. Municipal workers from the country seat of Bacoli had been sent down to decorate the piazza for the upcoming celebration of Santa Maria di Carmine. As the workers festooned the balconies, balustrades and lamp posts with bunting and vines, children squealed around them, tugging sleeves and asking questions about food and fireworks. Then the kids scattered at the sudden rare appearance of a sputtering motor car in the piazza. As curiosity overcame fear the children inched back, gathering wide-eyed around the marvelous machine.

Then out from under the canvas canopy two men stepped. One, the driver, had a soft cap on his head and a bandolier of bullets strapped across his chest. A carbine was slung over his shoulder. The driver's eyes took in the *piazza*. The other man, an obvious big shot, wore a linen suit and a straw hat. Although he rarely came to Miseno everyone knew his name—Don Virgilio Corrado, the local Camorra chief.

He was tall for a southerner and his expression was kind, cheerful, an effect enhanced by the turned-up tips of his black mustache. People cleared a path for him as he walked across the now-silent *piazza* brandishing a gold-tipped ebony cane. The men who had been drinking in the cafe stood up and held their hats in their hands, their eyes fixed on the cobblestones. Most were silent, though some muttered inaudible words of anger. The women, hands plunged in laundry water, remained motionless as the marble statuary in the village church.

As for Maria, she felt a deep-down thrill at the smell of power the man gave off.

The villagers watched Don Virgilio enter the shop of the wine merchant Don Ernano, whose vineyards had done well lately. As the Camorra boss disappeared inside the shop the hum of voices and creak of cartwheels resumed.

Don Virgilio's visit surely meant trouble for the wine seller. Usually the boss dispatched underlings to collect the *tangenti* from merchants and proprietors. A personal visit must have meant he was very unhappy. No doubt Don Ernano was in arrears with his kickbacks. If so, he was very foolish, villagers thought. Why bang one's head against a wooden post? In the area around Naples, paying tribute to the *malavita* was a fixture of life, like the sun and the bays. Didn't the holy book say render unto Caesar what belonged to Caesar? Well, today Caesar wore a panama hat. The people of Miseno, as usual, shrugged their shoulders and looked the other way.

Don Virgilio reappeared at the wine seller's door along with Don

Ernano, face red as a plum tomato, hands caught in his apron. Ernano bowed low as the Camorra chief climbed into the motor car and drove off. Then, as the dust clouds settled in the *piazza*, he twisted up his face like a gargoyle on the cathedral spire and jabbed his middle finger up to heaven.

Maria laughed and scrubbed the clothes. No doubt the wine seller had been persuaded to pay up—with interest. She carefully noted this lesson in power politics.

Lisabeta Croce bent over the stone fireplace and removed the pizza. She carried the food on the broad iron spatula to the pine table, where the family gathered for the nightly meal. The ingredients for the pizza that bubbled fragrantly on the table were entirely produced by members of the household. The wheat, tomatoes, basil and oregano came from the farm on Mount Miseno that Lisabeta and Maria cultivated. The mozzarella came from the udders of the buffalo that Giacometta kept in the stable behind the house. And the anchovies came from Ottavio's nets. Thank God, times were good.

At first the four family members ate quietly. Ottavio gave a contented sigh as he uncorked a flask of Lacrima Christi from the slopes of Vesuvius that he had bought from Don Ernano. He then filled everybody's glass.

The wine reminded Maria of the visit of the Camorra boss. "Did you hear about Don Virgilio's visit today?" she asked nobody in particular. "I saw him with my own eyes. He came all the way from Posillipo. In a motor car!"

Her father grunted in disgust. "What was that stinking octopus doing in these parts?" The comment was not without a certain irony, since Don Virgilio's village was famous for *polpi alla Posillipo*, octopus cooked in hermetically sealed pots, and, of course, the Camorra chieftains were famous for the reach of their tentacles.

"He came to collect from Don Ernano," Maria said.

Ottavio spat into the fireplace. "*Ladrone*! I'd beat the thief with his own cane before I'd give him a lead *soldo*." Over the years Ottavio had picked up some vaguely socialist opinions from his fisherman pals. And he always had had a sharp sense of personal injustice.

Lisabeta quickly poured her husband another glass of wine.

" 'Who has iron has bread,' " Maria quoted.

Ottavio frowned. "Where did you learn that?"

Giacometta, in a world of her own, slurped wine and sang quietly to herself.

Maria answered, "Don Gabriele. He taught it to me." To her father's chagrin, Maria had been learning to read by taking lessons from the young village priest. "It's the watchword of *Il Popolo D'Italia*," she added, referring to a newspaper edited by Benito Mussolini.

Ottavio gave his wife a black look that said, Look what comes of wasting a girl's time with reading lessons when she could be doing useful work.

Actually Lisabeta had encouraged the lessons. They took place only once a week on Sunday evenings when even the beasts of burden rested, she had argued. Still, she had had to reach into her bag of female tricks to win the point. Not very deeply, though. Ottavio had a soft spot for his women.

The shutters of the window were open to let breezes filter into the stone house. The gray evening had yielded to black night. Down the winding road to the port a square of yellow light marked the inn, from where you could hear raucous laughter.

Ottavio was still grumbling. "You should use the time to sew linens for your dowry chest."

Maria shook her head. She had no interest in marriage right now.

"You're already sixteen, by God!" He glanced at his sister. "Do you want to wind up an old *zitella* spinning silk?"

Maria shrugged. "This is 1919, not 1819."

Ottavio raised his hand. "I'll give you a slap so hard . . ."

Maria ate calmly. It was an idle threat and she knew it. The man had never struck his daughter and never would. And she forgave his impatience because she knew that he only wanted the best for her. It wasn't his fault that he had such an old-fashioned outlook on things.

"I have no prospects anyhow," she said, hoping to close off the talk.

"Are you off your rocker?" her father said. "Pepe Falcone would marry you like that." He snapped his hook-blistered fingers. "Before the rooster crows again."

"He's an old fart," Maria said.

Ottavio gave his wife a look. "Listen to how she talks!"

Lisabeta stifled a smile.

Ottavio said, "I've got ten years on your mother."

"The carpenter has twice that much on me."

"So you'll be a well-off widow," he said. "He has a good trade."

"I don't want to be a wife or a widow."

"She's gonna be a schoolteacher," Lisabeta said.

"Don't encourage this," Ottavio told his wife, then to Maria: "Besides, I'm sure lots of other men would be interested too if you didn't always go around with your nose in the air." He raised his snout, mimicking what he considered her haughty attitude.

Maria laughed. "You look just like Donna Carmela's pig," she said, comparing him to the animal owned by the priest's mother.

Everybody except Ottavio laughed. The ice was broken. Maria went over and kissed her father. He turned his head, trying to disguise his affection. A life of mostly misfortune had made him wary of such moments. Awake or asleep, he wore the horn around his neck.

"Anyhow," Maria said, "I have no *dote*."

"That wouldn't matter to Falcone," he said. "And who says you won't have one soon?" His leathery face brightened. He had some news.

"I saw the old man's boat today. He moors her at Bagnoli under the crater. She's a fine-looking bark. Name of *Santa Lucia*. He's tired of working and wants to retire. He'll let me have her cheap."

"How cheap?" his wife asked skeptically.

"Cheap enough. She needs a coat of paint and a new mainmast, that's all. Me and the Pignataro brothers can fix her up good as new. They promised to work for me." He drained the glass of wine, basking in the glow of the grape and good fortune.

It pleased Lisabeta to hear her usually pessimistic husband talking and acting this way. She didn't want to do anything to damp his spirits. She patted his arm. "So you'll be *padrone* now," she said. "Good, good. You worked so hard to see this day."

Ottavio put a clenched fist to his mouth, defiance of the spirits who played dirty tricks in this luckless land, then drank another glass of wine before going off to bed.

After helping her mother clean up, Maria also lay down on her cot beside the hearth. Beyond the strings of lemons that hung in the window she could see the full moon that looked like a gold sovereign in the night sky. She heard the moaning of cats prowling the flagstones, and silently said her prayers, but instead of having sacred thoughts she thought of the young pastor in a much less than sacred way. She couldn't help herself, he was so beautiful. His fair hair and pale skin made him look like an angel dressed in black. She knew these thoughts were sinful, but how could she confess them? He was, after all, the only priest in the village. She would have to go all the way to Baia for absolution. That night she was awake for a long time.

Maria's father bought the *Santa Lucia* and he and the Pignataro brothers fixed her up as planned. For a while it seemed the *jettatori*, those creatures half-demon, half-clown who cast the evil eye, looked the other way. The *Tirraneo* teemed with cod, silversides, cuttlefish, eels, dogfish, oysters, razorshells, herring and sardines. The fig tree that Lisabeta had planted years earlier in the back yard finally bore fruit. At harvest time the landlord gave her a bonus of five bushels of tomatoes. And Maria won two hundred lire in the lottery.

With part of the proceeds her mother allowed her to buy the material for a new silk dress to wear to mass on Sundays. It was a blue dress trimmed with white lace and she was wearing it on the Sunday that Pepe Falcone finally got up the courage to ask Lisabeta for permission to walk them home after mass.

He had approached them on the terrace before the Church of San Rocco, a vantage that had a pretty view of the beach with the brightly colored boats drawn up on the shore. Pepe was one of the rare men of the village who attended mass on Sunday.

As the bell rang in the tower the carpenter's heart beat faster. "That's a lovely dress," he told Maria.

"Thank you," she said, head erect, eyes fixed on the stony path where they walked a few paces behind Lisabeta and Giacometta, who kept sneaking glances over her shoulder.

"Did you make it yourself?"

She hesitated. Was he inventorying her wifely skills? "No, Mamma did," she said a bit frostily.

"Yes? She is very talented."

If occurred to Maria then that the man who was courting her was about the same age as her mother. She glanced sidelong at him, noting how he perspired under the morning sun. His obvious nervousness moved her, a little. "Yes, I have a wonderful mother," she said.

"You do, you do," he agreed. Pepe's own mother was long dead, as was his father. But in Italy the mother ruled the heart and her husband was no more than a puppet prince in a Punch-and-Judy show.

When they arrived at the *piazza* Pepe invited the women to have ice water and coconut slices at the cafe. Maria, who had a sweet tooth, was quick to say yes. Lisabeta protested that it would cost Signore Falcone too much money.

"*Per carità*," the carpenter said, acting offended.

They took seats under a parasol with the name of a Sicilian marsala. In her new dress, spooning the sugar water, Maria felt like a duchess sitting in the Piazza Plebiscito of Naples, where she had never been but only heard about.

Giacometta made a big racket eating the *aqua gelata*.

Maria, basking in the envious attention of her neighbors, was in no mood to resist when Pepe asked, "Will you do me the honor of accompanying me to the band concert next week?"

She looked across the table at her mother, whose eyes said it's up to you. Maria then nodded at Pepe, who nodded in return and began to nibble a coconut slice. He couldn't believe his good luck.

Soon word got around that Maria Croce was keeping company with Pepe Falcone, and the prattling of the busybodies annoyed Maria very much. Why were they making such a big deal over a band concert and a few Sunday promenades? She had made the man no promises and had no intention of doing so. She just didn't want to hurt his feelings by turning him down.

The talk even reached Don Gabriele.

"So, young lady," he said one Sunday evening as they took a break from a reading of Dante, "are the rumors true?" They were outdoors by the ruins of the old castle. The setting sun cast a reflection on the sea below.

"What rumors?" she said, knowing what he meant.

"That I'll soon be including your name in the announcements of the banns."

It pained Maria to think that the priest might think this. "Nonsense," she said. "Falcone and I are friends, that's *all*."

Don Gabriele wondered about that. Platonic friendships between male and female were almost as rare as igloos in these parts. "Be careful, Maria," he said. "Don't toy with him. You'll break his heart."

"Who's *toying* with him? We have an innocent friendship. I gave him no reason to believe otherwise. I gave him no encouragement. So what if we went together to a band concert? Does that mean we're engaged? Just because a few tongues wag . . ."

His look had silenced her. The fading sunlight brushed the waves of his hair with gold highlights. She thought he looked so handsome. Why, she wondered, would God waste such beautiful clay on a parish priest? The Lord's ways seemed more than mysterious, they seemed pointless. But such thoughts were sacrilegious.

"Maria," the priest said, "you are young and pure. I don't believe you're aware of the powerful effect you might have on a man . . ."

Maria's bold stare had stopped him. Wasn't he a man too?

"Well, anyhow," said Maria, "I don't plan to marry the old carpenter."

"Let's get back to the lesson, eh?" Don Gabriele opened the book. They had been reading Canto Five of the *Inferno*, which described the descent to the second ring, where the poet and his guide encountered sinners of the flesh before the infernal pit. The damned included the souls of Paolo and Francesca. The priest asked Maria to read the lines of Dante quoting Francesca explaining her illicit love.

" 'One day to pass the time,' " Maria read, " 'we read the book Of Launcelot, and how love conquered him. We were all unsuspecting and alone: From time to time our eyes would leave the page and meet to kindle blushes in our cheeks.' " At this point she couldn't resist letting her own eyes' attention stray from the page and go to the priest's.

He didn't blush. Instead he praised her reading and urged her to go on. "Excellent, excellent," he said, "you've made great progress."

She continued: " 'But at one point alone we were o'ercome: When we were reading how those smiling lips were kissed by such a lover—Paolo here, Who never more from me shall be divided. All trembling, held and kissed me on the mouth. Our Galeot was the book; and he that wrote it, A Galeot! On that day we read no more.' "

Maria's cheeks felt like they'd been touched by a branding iron. She couldn't look at the priest. Through this poetry, desire sparked desire. Books were tinderboxes: Launcelot's illegal love for Lady Guinevere kindled Francesca's incestuous love for her husband's brother Paolo; then Dante's rendition reached across the centuries to make a peasant girl in Campania desire an angel in the cassock of a priest. No wonder some churchmen would burn books and outlaw verses.

Maria was aware of Don Gabriele's breathing and tried to look him in the eye.

"That's enough for today," he said.

Had she seen desire in those eyes?

She nodded, gathered up her skirts and started down the dusty road wedged between rows of poplars. For the time being, Maria thought as she went on toward the sun-bleached towers of Miseno, they had escaped the gnashing teeth of Minos.

The *Santa Lucia*, painted red and green, had been blessed by Don Gabriele on a broiling summer day, and the Christian charm seemed to work. Time after time she sailed back to the mussel-shell-encrusted moorings of Miseno with bulging nets.

As usual, village life proceeded in a slow, pantomimic rhythm.

Bent peasants followed plows drawn by brawny oxen. The school-master read gazettes in the square detailing the wonders of the world outside, of sightings of Fata Morgana in the Straits of Messina and of pistols brandished in the Chamber of Deputies in Rome. Men as muscular as Florentine statues strung up fish nets at murky river mouths. Adulterers trysted at night in the ruins of the Acropolis. Men, women and children celebrated the feasts of their patron saints. And spinsters like Giacometta pushed the shuttle of the loom to the right and the left.

In September disaster struck. The blood of San Gennaro kept in a flask in the Cathedral of Naples failed to liquefy on schedule. People shouted and jeered at the reliquary of the Saint but it did absolutely no good. Everybody went around "making horns" with the second and third fingers and touching the horns of bone and coral that they kept in their pockets and wore around their necks. They feared the worst, it would be a season for the *jettatura*, the evil eye.

Maria didn't believe it. Harvesting wheat in the shade of olive trees, she told her mother, "People make their own fortunes, good or evil."

One day not long afterward Ottavio was playing *scopone* with some cronies in the outdoor cafe overlooking the port. As the fisherman squinted to see his cards in the gathering dusk a man known as *Il Spagnuolo*, the Spaniard, approached the table. Il Spagnuolo was an agent of the *malavita*. Without being invited he grabbed a bentwood chair, turned it backward and sat down, resting his elbows on the back. "*Auguri*," he said. "Greetings."

The men grunted, chewing on their cheroots and pipes. The air was fragrant with tobacco and brine. Il Spagnuolo signaled at the innkeeper, who reluctantly came over, knowing the man would drink on credit and never pay the debt. These bogus big shots were all alike.

Il Spagnuolo made a circle with his forefinger over the group. "Let's have a bottle of *grappa* and glasses for everyone," he said.

These sons of bitches thought that a carbine transformed a peasant into a baron, the innkeeper thought as he went inside to get the bottle.

Soon after, Il Spagnuolo was getting drunk and poking his nose into the game. Although none of the men invited him to play they didn't complain either, even when he ridiculed their playing strategies, his stomach shimmering like gelatin when he laughed. They didn't complain because they knew that the drunken blowhard had iron in reserve. More than once Ottavio had had to bite his tongue and curse the thug under his breath.

Although it was Saturday night the game broke up early as one by one the fellows made excuses to go home. Only Ottavio and one or two others refused to budge from their chairs. Why should they let this lout ruin a rare night on the town for hard-working men like themselves? As he sipped a glass of local wine, Falerno, Ottavio's lean brown face betrayed his anger. The Camorra man looked at the fisherman. "Don't you like my grappa?"

"Thanks all the same, but I prefer the meat of the grape to the skin."

Il Spagnuolo slurred his words. "Are you implying that brandy is not a good Christian drink?"

"No, Gomez," Ottavio said. "But wine is gentler on my stomach." The fisherman was stubborn but not suicidal.

Il Spagnuolo vacillated, considering whether to take offense. He decided to laugh the comment off. "Can't hold your liquor, eh?"

Ottavio forced himself to smile. He noticed that Gomez had tomato stains on his cravat. All the other fellows had drifted off and the two were alone. Ottavio also decided to call it a night, drained his glass, mumbled good-by and got up from the chair.

Gomez manacled the fisherman's wrist. "Where you think you going?"

Ottavio thought he knew what was coming. "It's late, *paesano*, and I'm a working man."

"You work on Sunday too?"

"Very often."

"Doing well for yourself too. Or so we've heard."

Ottavio's throat clogged with anger and fear. You got a little ahead and they knocked you down. Flat on your ass. Thinking of Lisabeta and Maria, he made a special effort to control his anger. "Thanks be to God," he said. "Some days we do well, some days not so well."

"The sea is a fickle mistress, eh?"

"Exactly."

"But all in all . . . ?"

"I can't complain," said Ottavio.

"Right," said Gomez, reeking of garlic and alcohol. "You can't complain. But we *can*. Don Virgilio is displeased with you."

Ottavio looked down at the cracked paving. "How much do you want?"

Il Spagnuolo mentioned a figure that amounted to a quarter of the crew's monthly income. "A little nectar from each flower keeps the hive buzzing," the Camorra henchman said. "If you have bad times we would consider taking less. Don Virgilio has a heart of gold."

Ottavio's face had turned the color of baked brick. "That's pretty steep."

"You should have approached us sooner and made an offer. You know how things work in these parts. Don Virgilio gladly gives his patronage and protection to honest fellows. But you can't go around acting like a Mameluke or a socialist. You set a bad example."

Ottavio was no bachelor, he had to think of his wife and family. His hands hung at his sides, clammy and useless. Again swallowing his pride, he decided to haggle.

"Give me a break, *paesano*. I have to feed my family."

"And a lovely family it is too, God bless," said Gomez.

"Thanks."

Il Spagnuolo clapped the other man on the shoulder. "Ah, I've seen that daughter of yours." He kissed his fingers. He gave Ottavio a wink. "Maybe we can make a deal . . . ?"

Ottavio, no longer able to suppress his anger, cocked his fist and smashed it into the man's mouth, sending blood and bits of flesh and teeth flying over the courtyard. Gomez reeled, then toppled backward like a big tree, hitting his head on the moss-covered flagstones. Blood came from his head. The fisherman pounced on him and continued to pummel his face and head until the innkeeper and another man dragged him off. They held the struggling Ottavio while another man went to check Il Spagnuolo.

The villager put his ear to Gomez's chest. "He's still breathing," he announced.

The innkeeper let Ottavio go and made the sign of the cross. "Wake my wife," he told a serving girl, "and tell her to bring hot water and bandages." He gave Ottavio a look.

Ottavio stood there breathing hard, his knuckles bloodied and bruised.

"You better get out of here," the innkeeper said.

Ottavio was dazed, his feet seemingly rooted to the stones.

"I said, get out of here!" the innkeeper shouted.

Ottavio snapped out of the stupor and went across the cafe courtyard, stumbling over a chair. In the pale and merciless glow of starlight he ran up the narrow road toward his house.

Don Virgilio had his hair cut and mustache trimmed and waxed in the barber shop on the main square of Posillipo. Then, trailing the scent of cologne and raw power, he walked over to the seafront cafe to eat his favorite chocolate nougat and to hear a report by one of his lieutenants on the case of Livio Gomez, his enforcer in Miseno and Baia. Too bad the cretin had survived his beating at the hands of the fisherman, the chief thought as he sat down at his usual table overlooking the Bay of Naples. From this spot on the tip of the cape's finger the Camorra boss had a fine view of the water and the volcano. Yes, too bad, he continued to reflect as the waiter anticipated his order, setting the *torrone* and coffee in front of him. Gomez had always been a Neanderthal and a buffoon. It was his naked brutality that made him a valued member of the gang, but now he would be useless to the organization.

Savoring the tastes of hazelnut and honey on the chocolate wafer, Don Virgilio thought that he didn't blame Croce for what he did, if the rumors he had heard were true. The man had exploded in anger when Gomez made a remark about the fisherman's virginal daughter. What else could Croce have done but beat the daylights out of him? What man worth the salt in his pores and the blood in his veins could do less? Was chivalry dead? No, Don Virgilio was very sympathetic to the man.

He wiped his mouth with a linen napkin and pushed the plate aside with a sigh. Thinking about the matter had robbed him of appetite, the burdens of leadership lay heavy on his shoulders. In spite of his sympathy for Croce, Don Virgilio also knew he couldn't let the matter rest there. Slowly, he revolved the carved lion's head that formed the knob of his walking stick. Gomez was, after all, an agent of The Society. Croce had put a stain on the shield. Though he had a legitimate grievance he shouldn't have taken the matter into his own hands. He might have lodged a complaint, and Don Virgilio would have dealt a fitting punishment to Gomez. What if every hotheaded peasant in the region behaved this way? Anarchy, defiance would result. Besides, the fisherman, though he must have known better, had bought his own boat without informing The Society and offering fair tribute. He had not respected the code and this compounded his error. He must be made an example of. There were no two ways about it.

The deputy finally arrived at the cafe. After hearing the man's report on the condition of Gomez—he would be laid up in the infirmary for at least two months and would have impaired vision and speech for the rest of his life—Don Virgilio whispered instructions in the aide's ear, then sat back to finish his coffee, taking in the idyllic view.

Everywhere he went, Ottavio now carried the knife that he used to clean fish. He didn't tell Lisabeta what had happened but she knew something was wrong from his grim manner and from the way the villagers looked at them and stayed away from them. She knew that something serious had happened to her husband and that an account was waiting to be settled.

Finally, she broke the rule of wifely reticence and demanded to know the truth. "Tell me," she said one night as they sat in the one room of the house that served as kitchen, living room, work room and sleeping space for their daughter, "your trouble is my trouble too."

Maria lay asleep while Giacometta sat at the loom weaving wool. Piles of hemp were stacked on the floor.

Ottavio was at the table using his knife to slice bits of melon that he ate with dried goat's milk cheese. He looked at his wife. "If something happens to me, sell the boat to the Pignataros. They can pay in monthly installments. Then when you have enough put aside take Maria and Giacometta to my cousin Fabio's house in Gaeta. He's an old bachelor with a good stipend, he'll gladly marry you . . ."

Lisabeta was stunned that the trouble was so serious. The sounds of the loom's shuttle and treadle clacked in cadence. The fire in the hearth was reflected in the burnished copper pans hanging on the wall. "What on earth do you mean?" she said. "By God on high and Mary His mother, what's happened?"

It started to rain then, making a dog bark. Ottavio gripped the knife. "Last night I beat up Il Spagnuolo."

"*Why* in the name of all the saints did you do that?"

"He was disrespectful toward your daughter."

"Did you hurt him badly?"

"I hear they took him to the infirmary."

Lisabeta began to cry, biting her fist. Just when things were going so well, she thought.

"Shhh," Ottavio said. "You'll wake up the girl."

Regaining some control, Lisabeta asked, "What are we going to do?"

The rain made music on the roof and on the leaves of the nut and fig trees in the yard. Ottavio stared at the knife and morsel of cheese in his hands. "What can we do? I will try to protect myself as best I can."

"Shouldn't we leave here?"

"And go where?"

She thought a bit and said, "Maybe we could go to my Aunt Luisa in Benevento. Last I heard she was still alive."

"Too close. They'd track us down in a minute. Anyway, I would suffocate in the interior. I need the sea air to survive."

"You should wear bells, you're such a donkey. What good will the salt air do you when you become a ghost? Tell me that, eh?"

He lit his pipe. "I'm not running, I'll die where I was born."

What was one to do with such a stubborn man? This was the attitude that mired them in their backward ways. This was what turned her husband and his ilk into a bunch of victims. And this was the atmosphere that she prayed with all her might her daughter would escape.

Well, even if her husband was willing to give in, Lisabeta was not. Then and there she decided to take the bull by the horns, so to speak. She decided to hitch a ride with the next carter going to Posillipo and appeal directly to Don Virgilio for mercy. People said he was a just and honorable man. Surely he would listen to reason . . .

Maria was kept in the dark about the trouble. Next morning in the wheat field her mother came up to her and told her that she had to visit the hermitage in the hills to make a special devotion to Our Lady to fulfill a vow. She swore the girl to secrecy and promised to return before nightfall, then she hailed down the cart of a man and wife hauling goods to Marechiaro. From there it would be a short distance to Posillipo.

Maria waved at the cart as it clattered around a hairpin bend in the hard lava-covered road. At first she was puzzled and annoyed by her mother's sudden departure. It meant she would have to work twice as hard and, worse than that, she would be alone all day with no one to talk to. But then she told herself she was being selfish. She began to worry about her mother, who must have had a very good reason to make the long trip to the monastery.

Before long she began thinking about Don Gabriele. As flies droned around the sweet-smelling tomato vines and the sun ascended the pastel morning sky Maria grew warm and agitated with her thoughts. Stooping to pick ripe love apples and deposit them in the basket by her side, she felt her large breasts, unhindered by a corset or undergarment, moving free under her muslin blouse. Sweat trickled from the crevices of her young body, soaking through her clothes and kerchief. She grew light-headed with heat and work and the way she felt in her private places. After a while she had to sit down in the olive grove. The shade cleared her mind . . . What if an earthquake were to suddenly strike this place, as has happened often before, and she were to die on the spot? Her soul would descend directly down the crater to the underworld.

She made up her mind to confess her sinful thoughts in the Sacrament of Penance to Don Gabriele, the man who inspired them. And she had to do so or risk eternal damnation. Life was precarious in the *Campi Flegrei*! One couldn't dillydally over such things. Maybe she could phrase the confession in a general way to avoid his catching on that the object of her lust was himself. She rehearsed various ambiguous ways of putting it—

"You are either praying or plotting," came a voice that made her jump with fright.

The voice belonged to Pepe Falcone, who had approached quietly from the main road. "I'm sorry, I didn't mean to scare you."

"You almost gave me a stroke."

"I'm sorry—"

"It's all right."

He jerked his thumb toward the east. "I was just on my way to Balbi's patch to build him a new shed. Would you have a drink of water?"

She nodded, fetched the flask and handed it to him.

"Thanks." He drank, smacked his lips and handed back the goatskin. Leaning against the tree trunk, he appraised her. "So which is it?"

"Which is what?"

"Were you praying or plotting?"

"Neither. I was talking to the birds."

"Ah, a female Saint Francis." He touched the side of his head. "Better watch out, they'll put you away."

"Let them try."

She looked up at the position of the sun. "Well," she said, "I must get back to work."

"Wait, please, let's talk awhile."

"Talk won't fill our stomachs." She went over to get her basket.

He touched her arm. "I have something to tell you."

She put a hand on her hip and waited, curious and impatient.

"When the new year comes," he said, "I'm going to America."

The news seemed to surprise her. Sure, there was an exodus of adult males leaving the impoverished south for places like Brazil, Argentina, South Africa, Australia and the United States, places that gave hope for a future. Especially since the economic collapse that followed the war. But Pepe seemed rather old to pull up stakes.

"You're a lucky one," she said. "Where are you headed? New York? Buenos Aires?"

"*Ben Silvana.*"

"Who?"

"No, it's a place. A state of America. You know, *Filadelfia, Pizza-burgo. Ben Silvana.*"

"Ah, Pennsylvania!"

"Yes, my brother sponsors me. He works in the steel mills."

"God be with you, Pepe." Her dark eyes glittered with envy, which gave way to irony. "Mark my words, old man. It won't be long before an American girl snaps you up."

Pepe was looking out at the sea below. "I doubt it," he said.

"Mark my words," she repeated.

Suddenly he reached over and took hold of her hand.

His felt like sandpaper. She looked around nervously. "Please, Pepe, don't."

"I want you well," he said, using the ancient expression of love. "I'll miss you."

Blushing, Maria looked at the ground.

"I wish I could take you with me," he said.

The idea didn't wholly displease her. Wouldn't it be fine to escape this place where the farms were too small to be measured in acres and the bread was as precious as gold. Where people worked like mules and died like dogs. She faced west, where the cone of Vesuvius reared, where the landscape had a chimney that led straight to Hell.

She looked at him. "You're kidding, aren't you?"

"Am I?" He took off his hat and revolved it in his hands, then said, "Sure, I'm kidding."

She pretended to be insulted. "Why?" she said coquettishly. "Am I so repulsive?"

His clay-brown face was etched with longing. "*No,*" he said, and clearly wanted to say more.

She recalled the priest's words about not leading the carpenter on, and tried to change the subject. Looking toward Vesuvius, she asked, "Is there a volcano in Pennsylvania?"

He put the wide-brimmed hat back on his head. "Not that I know of," he said.

She studied his coarse red face dappled by the tracery of leaves casting shadows. He was holding something back, she thought.

"And olive trees?" she asked.

He shrugged.

"And girls as pretty as me?"

He looked at her squarely. "Nowhere in the world." He took her hand again, briefly, and then walked away. As he followed the worming road toward the plot of land tilled by his client Balbi, he was observed from a distance by the landlord's wife, Mrs. Barbalunga, who had been picking cherries and figs in a nearby orchard. She had been watching for a while and had seen the carpenter follow Maria into the secluded olive grove. Now she clucked her active tongue, drawing the only conclusion possible. She smiled through her disapproval. Would she have a tale to tell at coffee time after the midday nap!

Meanwhile Maria returned to work upset with herself. She should not have said such flirtatious things to Pepe. It was cruel and unfair. Sinful. More grist for the confession box.

The sun was a mottled orange about to melt into the sea when she noticed another cart coming up the road from the direction of the Roman cistern. She straightened up and massaged the small of her back. She shielded her eyes to peer at the occupants of the vehicle. Was her mother finally returning? The cart carried only two people and as it came closer Maria saw that they were the peasant and wife who had let Lisabeta ride with them.

The girl waved the cart to a stop and questioned the peasants about her mother, but the man shrugged and told Maria that her mother had not arranged to meet them for the return trip. He clucked his tongue, gave a snap to the reins and the cart wobbled down the road.

Maria, left in the gathering dust, finally decided that Lisabeta probably had hitched a ride back with something else that followed the route by the lagoon. She was no doubt home already, helping Giacometta prepare supper. Still, as she gathered up her tools and replaced them in the shed, she felt uneasy.

That morning Lisabeta had tried to pass the time on the trip to Posillipo by making idle conversation with the man and wife who were hauling orange preserves and tobacco from Cunae to Miseno to Marechiaro. But the couple, whose family name was Giordano, was uncommunicative. The woman, either an idiot or a mute, sat by her husband's side fingering rosary beads and biting her fingernails. The man smoked a pipe and confined all answers to Lisabeta's questions to one or two words.

"What's the donkey's name?" Lisabeta had asked once before she gave up trying to be sociable. Riding in the rear, she had to direct the question to the back of the man's head, watching wisps of tobacco smoke curling above his hunched shoulders and battered straw hat.

"Nobody," said Giordano.

"He has no name?"

"Nobody's his name."

Lisabeta shook her head. An apt name for not only the donkey but also the people of this region. She shrugged, trying to enjoy the ride and the time off from work. The animal was young and strong and dragged the cart fairly quickly over the bumpy road, and Lisabeta drove any doubts from her mind about her mission to Posillipo being a success.

The two-wheeled vehicle soon reached Bacoli, where Giordano stopped to water Nobody by the *Piscina mirabile*, the so-called magic pool, a huge cistern supported by forty-eight pillars, which the Romans used to supply water to the imperial fleet. The man offered Lisabeta a drink of orange juice, which she accepted.

They proceeded on the road past the thermal springs of Baia and the strangely silent volcanic Lake Avernus, where folks said Sibyl's Cave was located. Passing the cavern, Lisabeta wished that she had the power and coin to consult the prophetess. Approaching Pozzuoli, the road climbed to give a view of the sea and the hovels of country people clinging like hives to the hillside. They passed a herd of goats that stopped and raised their beards, frozen figures in a pagan bas-relief.

It was early afternoon when the travelers came to Solfatara, a village with an active crater belching foul steam and hot mud, where they stopped to eat preserved fish and tomato. Lisabeta had little appetite sitting here at the entrance to the underworld. She considered it a bad omen to have lunch here.

They then took the old seacoast road to Marechiaro, arriving at one o'clock. Lisabeta thanked the Giordanos and continued on foot to Posillipo.

She stopped at the Church of Santa Maria Bellavista to say a prayer, then walked down a steep road past beautiful pink villas to the fishing hamlet where Don Virgilio had his headquarters. She stopped and asked an old man standing in front of a livery stable under the ox horns attached to the portal to ward off the evil eye. He had a mustache that looked like wheat, a black beret and a hemp belt, and eyed her suspiciously at the mention of the Camorra boss's name but directed her to a villa nearby on the outskirts of the park. She thanked him, took a deep breath, and walked the few yards to the Villa Murat, a grand eighteenth-century mansion that served as the gangster's command post.

A guard carrying a carbine on his shoulder stood at the gate. She told him she had come for an audience with Don Virgilio. He looked her over with hard eyes, took her name and told her to wait, then disappeared inside the villa.

The sun beat down on her kerchiefed head as she rested against one of the pillars that supported the gate. She was fairly confident that she would be admitted, since the Camorra leaders still fancied themselves as champions of the people. Robin Hoods, so to speak. Was The Society not created to help the victims of Bourbon tyranny? But that, of course, was long before the *camorristi* themselves became the tyrants.

The guard came sauntering back, and a few moments later she was ushered into a large room that looked like the office of a postal official or a notary. The shutters were closed and the room was lit by an electric chandelier that hung from the high ceiling. Sitting behind a huge desk that had nothing but a bowl of fruit on top was a dark lean young man whom she had never seen before. She did know he was not Don Virgilio.

"With all due respect, Signor," she said, "I requested to see Don Virgilio."

The man smiled pleasantly. "Is that so? Well, Mrs. Croce, I am Lorenzo Mazzo, his assistant. Maybe I can help you."

Mazzo was the aide Don Virgilio had given instructions to in the cafe where he took nougat and coffee. His role was regional second-in-command and chief enforcer.

"Excuse me, but I've never heard of you," she said.

He smiled again. They were alone in the room. He had curly black hair and the sweet beardless face of a cherub. Using a knife with a long blade, he cut a pear. "Come closer so I can see you better. The light is dim over there."

She moved closer to the desk, frowning. What a discourteous lout! Why didn't he get up from the chair and pay his respects to a good Christian woman? Did his mother teach him no manners?

"May I be allowed to see Don Virgilio?" she asked again.

"Would you like some coffee?"

"No, thank you."

"I'll be honest with you, Mrs. Croce," he said, pouring coffee for himself. "I am the man assigned by Il Commendatore to handle your husband's case. If you want something I am the person to see."

She kneaded her hands nervously, said nothing.

Gesturing with the point of the knife, he added, "Your man is in a very bad fix. Gomez was a useful and respected member of The Society."

"But my husband was provoked!"

Mazzo shrugged. "How would it look if we allowed violence against our confederates? No, your husband sets a poor example." He surveyed her from head to foot. "Why do you peasant women bundle yourselves in so many petticoats?"

Lisabeta ignored the remark. "What were you ordered to do to my husband?"

"What do you think? Beat him to a pulp, of course. An eye for an eye. It's the only way." He ate a piece of fruit and washed it down with coffee.

"If you hurt my husband it will ruin us, he is just a poor fisher-man—"

"A fisherman whose nets have overflowed lately. And still he doesn't pay his respects to The Society that protects him. He must be taught a lesson."

"Please, sir. Don Virgilio is known up and down the coast as a man of reason. Of mercy."

Mazzo sipped his coffee. "Of course, for a consideration we might go easy."

"A consideration?"

"Well, we couldn't let him off scot-free. That wouldn't look right. But I could tell the boys to go easy." Mazzo got up from the chair and came around the desk. His long legs made him taller than he appeared sitting down. "For a consideration," he repeated.

Up close Lisabeta saw that the man's face was slightly pock-marked. His eyes looked drowsy, odd. "What do you mean, consideration?"

"Well, did you bring money with you?"

"Not a cent."

He clucked his tongue. "You came all the way from Miseno. How did you get here?"

"Some carters were kind enough to give me a ride."

"And how did you expect to accomplish this mission of mercy?"

"By appealing to Il Commendatore's sense of justice and honor."

He laughed. "And how do you expect to appeal to me?"

"The same way."

He laughed again, this time from deep in his throat.

At first Lisabeta had allowed herself to be blinded by her sense of purpose to thoughts of the danger she was walking into. Now panic took hold of her as she realized that she was totally at this man's mercy. She shouldn't have come, she should have worked harder to convince Ottavio to go into hiding. Too late for that now. She had to think of a way out of this.

Mazzo put the tip of the knife under her chin, prodding her to raise her head. He looked at her body.

"All those skirts," he said.

Her heart pounded. "Please . . ."

"How do I know you're not carrying a weapon under all those petticoats?" he said.

"I am unarmed, I'll just leave."

He shook his head ever so slightly and kept the point of the knife where it was. "I'll have to search you."

"Please don't," she said, "I beg you."

He put his free hand on her right side, pretending to search the garments. The hand roamed lower to her hips and thighs.

She whirled away from him but he grabbed her wrist, pulling her back against his chest.

"Don't play-act," he said. "You want this or you would never have come here."

"You're out of your mind—"

"What honorable woman would come here alone like this, empty-handed, and expect to be treated otherwise? No, you wanted this." He tried to kiss her.

She turned her head away. "You don't want a woman of my age," she said, her eyes filling with tears.

He smiled. "I like older women, women with experience."

He had pinned her against the desk with his body while his free hand was undoing the stays of her bodice. The knife at her throat glittered in the light of the chandelier.

"And I like peasant women," he said. "Field work makes their bodies nice and firm."

"You disgust me," she said through her sobbing.

He stepped back, unbuttoned his trousers and exposed himself. "How do you like this, eh? Does your husband have one as beautiful as this?"

She spat in his eye.

Furious, he slashed at her, cutting her left shoulder, then threw her against the desk face down. The blade flashed to her throat. His breath was a sirocco on the back of her neck as he began to raise her skirts. The bowl of fruit was all she could see as she opened her mouth to scream and scream.

On the way home from the fields Maria stopped by the church to ask Don Gabriele to hear her confession.

"Come later," he said. "I was about to have supper."

"But, Father, this can't wait. What if I'm struck by lightning?"

He made a sour face. "It's not even raining."

"The volcano might erupt. Then my soul would go straight to hell. It's your job to save souls, isn't it?"

He sighed. "All right," and led her to the confessional. After the formulas had been recited by penitent and priest, the girl said, "I've had impure thoughts."

The priest caught his breath, apparently unsettled by the subject, but his voice was calm when he asked, "Yes, how many times?"

"Who can count? Day and night."

The reply pinked Don Gabriele's usually pale cheeks. He crossed his legs nervously. He could not see the girl on the other side of the lattice but he could picture her flushed with the ardor of guilt and passion and he could smell the sweat on her body. "You must avoid the near occasion of this sin," he said.

"I can't."

A fly had found its way into the confessional stall and was buzzing around the priest's head. He swatted it away as he considered how to counsel the girl. In a village so small it was hard to avoid certain objects of desire. The formulas he had learned in the seminary at Capua had little real meaning to these poor folk who were more attuned to the rhythms of nature than the rules of priests. What could he tell a girl about sex who had observed rutting animals since childhood? How could he preach about fast days and days of abstinence to people who often saw seasons of starvation? In this place both the benign and the cruel God needed no formal introduction. His theological education had been designed for the puritans who resided in *palazzi*. It was of little use here.

"Well, then, you must make a novena to the Immaculate Mother," he said. "Satan can't enter a heart where the Blessed Mother reigns."

"Yes, Father," she said. Her voice sounded doubtful.

Don Gabriele finished hearing the girl's confession and gave her absolution, then went next door to the house he shared with his mother and ate a bowl of fish soup with beans. Lines of worry etched his face.

Donna Carmela Ugolini, noticing the worried expression, put her hands on her broad hips and scolded her son. "Don't you like my soup?"

"Yes, Mamma, it's very good."

"Well, you don't act like it. That look on your face would make one think the bowl was full of bitter herbs instead of delicious food from God's bounty." The woman crossed herself with broad gestures, like an actress on stage. Unlike her beautiful son, Donna Carmela was ugly. She had frizzy ginger hair, a big turned-up nose and skin as brown and creased as the volcanic earth. Naturally the woman (who called herself a widow but whose husband actually had flown the coop to Brazil twenty years earlier) doted on her only son, the parish priest. She had worried about his fragile health ever since his boyhood when the doctor in Naples had diagnosed him as anemic. And she ruled him with an iron fist.

"I'm sorry, Mamma. I don't have much appetite."

She bent over to inspect his face more closely. "Do you feel sick?"

"No, just tired. I think I'll go upstairs to my room."

"There's fresh cantaloupe. Won't you have some?"

"No thanks, Mamma."

She put her head on his forehead. "You're warm," she said. "Let me fix you some lemon and sugar . . ."

He told her no and got up from the table. "I just need rest," he said, his hand on the stair post.

In his room he lay down on the bed. His face burned, but not from any illness. Could a priest perform an exorcism on himself? He looked at the crucifix on the wall, then turned away. Had the eyes of the effigy that resembled an afflicted Italian peasant been filled with recrimination?

Don Gabriele had his own cross to bear: he was a twenty-eight-year-old virgin.

Usually the country curates of southern Italy put little stock in the vows of celibacy and poverty. Many were renowned for the tables they set and the children they sired. They took to heart Saint Paul's dictum that it was better to marry than to burn.

But Don Gabriele was an exception to the rule. As the son of an opportunist who had married his mother for her dowry and then broken his nuptial vows, the priest had a great incentive to respect sacred promises, hard as it was for him to do so. He tried to follow the example of Christ, who when tempted in the wilderness said to the Devil, "Get thee hence." But Christ had fasted only forty days and forty nights beforehand. Gabriele Ugolini had been fasting all his life.

Maria Croce posed a hard test for him. She was young, pretty and shapely. And whenever she was near him sparks were ignited. Or was he imagining things? The situation was not helped by her confession of sexual urges. It was pretty clear to him who was the subject of her impure thoughts. Did she take him for a man of stone? Well, he was made of flesh. And vulnerable too.

The evening was cool. He got up from the bed to close the shutters and light the lamp, then began to remove his cassock, unbuttoning the many buttons down the front. He wagged his head: priests played a daily masquerade. He sighed. Maybe everybody did.

He went over to make sure the door to his room was locked. He sat in a chair. His blond hair was disheveled and in his underwear he looked more like a rawboned schoolboy than a priest. A schoolboy was what he still was in many ways. He might tutor Maria Croce in reading but she could certainly teach him a thing or two about other subjects. All women, in fact, seemed to be born with knowledge that men, priests or laymen, had to struggle to grasp. While masculine heads were in the clouds, feminine feet were planted firmly on the earth. He stared at his naked knees.

Maria Croce's sensuality and beauty had stirred up a dangerous fire in him. His mother would say that he had been bewitched. Maybe that was true. What could he do about it? Certainly he knew the formulas. They were his stock in trade, reciting paternosters and beating the breast. But he did something else, something he habitually did to avoid or postpone a greater transgression of God's law.

He committed the sin of Onan, spilling the seed upon the ground.

When Maria entered the house she found Giacometta at the loom but her mother was nowhere to be seen. She gave her moonstruck aunt a look. "Where's Mamma?" she asked the woman who had been babbling an incoherent ditty.

Giacometta replied by singing an old song in praise of mothers as the shuttle moved back and forth.

The girl shook her head. It was no use trying to pry any useful information out of the woman. What could have happened to her mother? Surely she couldn't have been waylaid by bandits, they didn't prey on peasants. Maybe she had decided to stay in the hermitage to make a religious retreat. But Lisabeta wouldn't do such a thing without telling her family. Maybe she had been kidnapped. Maybe she had had an accident. Maybe she had fallen into a gully or drowned in the Dead Sea. Her leaving had been so mysterious . . . what was the reason for the pilgrimage in the first place?

Maria went outside and scanned the dim black line that formed the horizon where the night sky met the sea, its surface marked by pools of orange light cast by the fishing boats. Ottavio, out on a night fishing trip, was not expected home before daybreak.

Gathering up her skirts, Maria climbed the path toward the village square, where she might at least find someone who had seen Lisabeta or knew something about her. She was panting when she reached the fountain. She looked around. Since it was supper time the area was fairly deserted, but she was ogled by a couple of idlers in the cafe. Finally she saw the ironmonger's wife hanging wash from the second-floor balcony of her house.

"Have you seen my mother?" Maria shouted up at her.

The woman stopped flapping a damp shirt. "Not since yesterday morning when the knife-grinder came. Don't tell me she's missing!"

"Yes. Since early this morning."

The woman crossed herself, kissed the coral horn that she wore around her neck. "Where could she be?"

"*That's* what I'm trying to find out."

The ironmonger's wife seemed stung by the sarcasm.

It was obvious that Maria didn't care two beans what the woman thought as she rushed around the square, pounding on doors and questioning everyone she encountered, including children and the deaf-mute who stood guard over the post office. She might as well have questioned the belled donkeys who nodded drowsy-eyed in the livery stalls. Nobody had seen hide nor hair of Lisabeta Croce.

Finally Maria sat on a moss-covered block of stone. It was clear that her mother had not returned to the village and that she must search the hermitage and surrounding place. But she was afraid to go at night and alone to such desolate spots. If only her father were around. But she didn't want to be a coward. She had made up her mind and just gotten to her feet when she heard her name being called.

She looked up to see Pepe Falcone walking toward her across the square. As he came closer she noticed that his face looked very pale.

"Maria . . ." He was hesitant, as if groping for the right words.

"What is it?"

"I'm afraid I have terrible news."

Earlier in the day, when Mazzo had finished, he showed no remorse or shame as he calmly adjusted his clothes and took a match to light a cigar and then the fire under the coffeepot. He said nothing to Lisabeta but watched her out of the corner of his eye.

She groaned. She was sitting on the floor, her back propped against the desk that had been the place of his assault. The shoulder wound throbbed where she had been stabbed but the blood had stopped flowing. She felt pain in other places too. Shameful secret places that reminded her of the monstrous ways that he had invaded her body. She fixed her own clothes, at the same time veiling her hatred, biding her time.

The man stuck the knife back into his belt. "You saved your husband's hide, my dear," he said. "I promise to go easy on him."

Was he keeping up a pretense that she had submitted to him voluntarily? She didn't contradict him.

"Ask anybody," he added. "Lorenzo Mazzo is a man of his word."

Lisabeta grabbed the top of the desk and pulled herself up. She straightened her disheveled hair, averting her eyes. He spoke about honor, of keeping his word . . . what about *her* honor . . . In a few short minutes he had destroyed it. How could she ever face her husband again? Or her daughter? Or the gossiping villagers? Or the saints on the altar? Her life was over.

He had sat down behind the desk again. With the trace of a smile he said, "Tell the truth now—that wasn't so bad, was it?"

Lisabeta's tearstained face showed the effort to control her emotions. But Mazzo couldn't see it. "No," she said in a low voice. "Not so bad." The words had tasted like live worms in her mouth.

The smile on his face broadened. "Maybe you'd like to stay for a while. I have great powers of recovery."

She glanced at the man's pitted face. "All right," she said.

Mazzo's eyes glittered.

Looking around the room, Lisabeta noticed an unusual object on a corner table. "You have a gramophone," she said. "I've never heard one played."

"Would you like to hear some music?"

"Yes. Very much."

He went over to the machine, put on a record and began to wind the hand-drive. "Wait till you hear this. It's a recording of Leoncavallo's *I Pagliacci* performed at La Scala. That's the opera house in Milan. It was made under the direction of the composer himself. Baron Quinto of Naples *donated* the gramophone and the record to The Society." He laughed at his use of the word "donated."

The notes of "Vesti la giubba" emerged loudly from the speaker. "Music and love go hand in hand," he said.

She seemed delighted by the miraculous machine.

He turned and saw that the coffee was ready. "Would you like some coffee now?"

"Yes," she said, and added, "sit down, I will serve you."

Canio's lament filled the room. For now, Lisabeta too wore the motley of a clown.

Mazzo nodded and sat down, leaning back in the chair and puffing on the cigar with the air of a pasha. Like all women of the region Lisabeta had been schooled to play on male vanity like it was an instrument. Never was the skill more necessary than now, as, with a smile, she crossed the room to get the steaming pot of coffee.

When she returned, the smile frozen on her face, she threw the entire contents of the pot into his face. And as the liquid scalded his flesh she grabbed the knife from his belt and buried it in his chest. His scream became a death rattle as he slumped to the floor. From the gramophone came the sound of the tenor's ironic laughter.

She stood over the body; the knife was still planted in his chest. She looked at his disfigured face, then covered it with spit.

She waited, listening. Apparently the music had covered the sounds of violence. She took the moment to savor the vengeance, but the scales were not yet in balance. They could never be. She knew what she had to do next.

The guard in the vestibule outside the door to Mazzo's office smirked at her as she emerged, but he seemed to suspect nothing. She bowed as she passed him on the way out the front door. Soon she was also past the guard at the front gate. When the mansion was out of sight she began to run.

As she rushed down the path she didn't notice a man watching her with a curious expression from the doorway of an inn. He was a resident of Miseno, the small landowner Balbi who Pepe Falcone was building a shed for. He had come to Posillipo to buy farm implements and had used the occasion as an excuse to get drunk. Through the mists of his inebriation he still recognized Lisabeta Croce, whose presence here and odd behavior made him scratch his head.

It took Lisabeta over an hour to reach her destination. By this time she was out of breath and feeling a lot of pain. The wound in her shoulder had reopened. On the way she had passed an unknown priest on a horse. Momentarily she had been tempted to beg for his help and forgiveness but she couldn't make herself do it. She was beyond help, beyond forgiveness.

Several people had seen Lisabeta making her way toward the crater. Most had taken her for a mental defective or maybe a gypsy woman who'd strayed from the caravan. She didn't seem to care what anybody thought.

Sitting on a rock near the mouth of the old fumarole, she inspected her wound. It was livid and suppurating. As she caught her breath she inhaled the rancid fumes of Solfatara. To the south lay the sea. Not too far from this spot earlier in the day, a lifetime earlier, she and the Giordanos had eaten lunch. Lisabeta had not eaten a scrap of food since then, but she wasn't in the least hungry.

Perhaps she now thought about Ottavio and Maria. She might even have recalled the dim figures of her dead parents or Aunt Luisa. It was hard to tell from her stony expression.

The sky was darkening as the crater bubbled with mud and spat steam from the bowels of the earth. The musk of the man she had killed was still on her, reminding her . . . What had she done wrong to earn from God such chastisement? It was vain to wonder about this, to try to fathom the whys and wherefores of one small person's existence. The divine blueprint was far beyond the ken of a poor worthless woman like Lisabeta Croce. She was a flyspeck on the plan, wasn't she?

And yet her mind had a life of its own, reaching out for some enlightenment. Maybe since she was born in such unfortunate circumstances she had to end up this way. If you were born under a certain star you couldn't escape your destiny. And nobody really knew why, not even the sorcerers and prophets who plied their trade in this place. Maybe it was different in places like America or Russia, where she had heard that they have no volcano and no king. She had made a fatal mistake for a woman of her station . . . she had made the trip to Posillipo under the delusion that she could change the course of things, and this mistake, this spasm of false pride, had led to her downfall.

She raised her head. Her black curly hair looked as wild as the Medusa's. Suddenly all thoughts drained out of her mind, and just as her daughter Maria was hailing down the cart of the returning Giordanos to ask them where her mother was, Lisabeta got up from the rock, looked down at the black entrance to Hades, and jumped.

Maria sobbed against her friend Pepe's shoulder. There was no doubting his word of Lisabeta's death. After Balbi had notified him, he had gone in person to police headquarters at Pozzuoli, where he identified the body. But the officials also required a family member to sign the death certificate.

They waited all night at the port for Ottavio to return from the fishing trip. Maria's reaction ranged from paralysis to rage. Her eyes were swollen and red. As she looked out to sea she also was terrified about telling her father. Now and then she looked at Pepe. The man was a saint. If it hadn't been for him she might have followed her mother.

Shrieking gulls announced the break of day. The prows of the boats could be seen under a colorless sky heading toward shore.

Soon the men were beaching the boats, chanting as they worked. Later Ottavio appeared along with Romeo Pignataro, carrying a basket of live eels. But when the fisherman saw the look on his daughter's face he dropped the bushel, leaving the eels to writhe in the sand.

Gaetano Pantoleone, the village hunter, had spent the previous evening at the tavern drinking wine, eating salty dried fava beans and playing seven-and-a-half with his fellows. Which explained why in the morning he failed to hear the rooster crow in Donna Carmela's yard and overslept. Of course he was grumpy as he went through his morning routine. After breakfasting on a few slices of cured quail and drinking coffee followed by a liter of water to slake his great thirst, he went as usual to his gun rack in the small storeroom at the rear of the house. Moments later he was muttering to himself in anger and surprise. The rear door was ajar and his double-barrel twelve-gauge shotgun was missing. . . .

Meanwhile Ignazio Martin, the farrier who also kept a livery stable just off the main square, was in a similar state of anger and bewilderment after discovering that one of his best saddle horses, Austriano, had disappeared from his stall. The farrier, going outside to investigate, had an animated conversation with a carter hauling flour from the mill at Baia. The peasant told Martin that he had just seen Ottavio Croce riding the horse to a lather over the road to Posillipo.

A shotgun had been strapped to Croce's back, the carter added.

Don Virgilio was in a foul mood when he arrived at the cafe to have his usual chocolate nougat and coffee. He had already received a full report on the Mazzo affair and had arranged to consult with a few of the elders on ways to uphold discipline and honorable behavior in The Society. He sat down at his favorite table and consulted his vest-pocket watch, glanced over at the two bodyguards who sat at another table a short distance away.

As the waiter put the coffee and pastry in front of him Don Virgilio asked himself what the organization was coming to. First the fiasco with the fisherman Ottavio Croce. Now the farce with Mazzo. Why did these puppies behave like animals? In the old days *cammoristi* lieutenants had nobility, restraint, discretion. Today they seemed like a bunch of savage Berbers with oil smeared over their hair and lust and greed in their hearts. Well, that clown Mazzo paid a high price for his few minutes of stupid pleasure.

Don Virgilio shook his head in admiration. The woman had guts. These peasants, they were like the cactus plant, tough and thorny, needing little to survive. Still they had a code of honor that often resulted in self-destruction. The *commendatore* himself came from a bourgeois background, a class that had learned to compromise some with nature and society.

Don Virgilio's finger traced the gold-leaf rim of the coffee cup. Now that Mazzo had gotten himself killed he had to choose a new second-in-command. He was inclined this time to pick from among the older members who had learned self-control although some perhaps lacked the fighting spirit and hard-edged cruelty of the younger candidates.

As he thought on these matters he was approached by villagers, some who wanted favors, others just to pay respects. Each got a cold once-over from the bodyguards. Most often Don Virgilio dismissed the petitioner with a wave of his hand. He had a rule these louts were obviously ignorant of . . . no interviews at the cafe. He used this place for meetings and for serious thinking. Sometimes he read the gazettes or leafed through albums of picture postcards that they sold to the tourists. Today he merely sat under the parasol in his white suit, thinking, drinking coffee and waiting for his consultants to arrive.

He looked at his watch again. The councillors were due in six minutes. Shielding his eyes from the sun with his hand, Don Virgilio squinted at the road to Marechiaro, the direction they were expected to come from by motor car. How to deal with the fisherman Ottavio Croce would also be a subject of discussion. Maybe it would be the first order of business.

The chief's face looked sad, even sympathetic. Yes, he was hard, he had to be, but he still had some twinges of compassion, even vestiges of idealism. Or so he told himself. In his youth he had been a Republican, idolizing such as Garibaldi, Mazzini, Alberto Mario.

A youngster who wasn't an idealist could only be a swine. But the years tended to sour a man, turning the wine of youthful idealism into the vinegar of pragmatism.

Looking up, he saw a peasant woman selling red carnations and started to call her over.

Just then hoofbeats pounded the flagstones of the square and Don Virgilio looked around to see who it was. But before his bodyguards could even draw their weapons, Ottavio had shouldered the shotgun and taken aim. Austriano's forelegs pawed the air.

Don Virgilio was half-standing, half-sitting as the deadly buckshot pulled his body here and there like a rag puppet. Blood came from his mouth.

The flower peddler took cover by hitting the ground.

And later Ottavio fell from the horse in a hail of bullets. Austriano galloped toward the sea. The bodyguards hurried across the cafe and bent over the boss's body. A flower of red blossomed over Don Virgilio's chest pocket where the carnation would have been pinned.

The bodies of Ottavio and Lisabeta were consigned by the authorities to Don Guglielmo, the pastor of Bagnoli, a cousin of Don Virgilio who also had connections to the Archbishop, a former schoolmate. Don Guglielmo refused to say prayers for the souls of Maria's parents or give them a Christian funeral. He had decided to bury the couple in the potter's field on the outskirts of the Dead Sea.

"Holy Mother Church doesn't allow suicides and assassins to rest in consecrated ground," he argued to Maria, Pepe and Don Gabriele, who had traveled to Bagnoli to request permission to bring the bodies back for the burial in the Miseno churchyard. He looked pointedly at Don Gabriele. "You, Father, at least should know better."

The interview was held in the garden behind the walls of the pastor's tumbledown villa. The balconies needed paint and some of the shutters hung loosely from the hinges. They sat shielded from the noon sun under a grapevine-covered wooden trellis. The aroma of geraniums mingled with the odors coming from the nearby chicken coop. By the weed-grown south wall a young boy booted around a leather soccer ball. All the villagers knew that the boy was the pastor's son by one of his housemaids. Don Guglielmo was worse than a Saracen: he kept not only a wife, but a harem.

Maria's eyes stabbed the pastor, whose stomach girth made his cassock buttons nearly pop. Hypocrites like him were laid to rest in cathedrals with pomp and ceremony while the spirits of her good parents would be granted no peace. Was God really so unjust?

The younger priest looked sheepishly at the ground.

Pepe Falcone's face had turned red with anger. But he knew it was useless to argue with such a man. He kept silent.

Maria gave Don Gabriele a worried glance. She needed him to plead her case for her with as much eloquence as he discoursed on Dante.

The young priest seemed to notice her expression, and, after hemming and hawing a little, mustered up the courage to challenge the older, more powerful clergyman. "With all due respect, Don Guglielmo," he began, "may I be allowed to raise a few pertinent theological points?"

The pastor nodded.

Don Gabriele cleared his throat. "First let's consider the case of Lisabeta Croce . . ."

"Indeed," said Don Guglielmo, interrupting, "the law in this instance is crystal clear. Burial with ecclesiastical rites and in consecrated ground is strictly denied to deliberate suicides." He laced his hands over his big stomach.

"Unless before death some sign of repentance is shown," Don Gabriele said.

"There was no such sign," the pastor said.

"How do we know? If you please, Reverend Father, she might have made an act of perfect contrition."

"And the moon might be fruitcake," said Don Guglielmo. "She jumped into the crater. She had no time for sincere repentance."

"Contrition sometimes comes in the wink of an eye," said Maria's advocate.

"Imperfect contrition, perhaps," said the pastor. "The kind motivated by fear of death or fear of Hell. But sorrow for sin because of a supernatural motive such as love of God? Hardly."

"With all due respect, Don Guglielmo, only God can say," Don Gabriele said.

"You flirt with heresy, young man. We men of the cloth are His surrogates on earth and it is our sacred duty to enforce His teachings."

As they spoke a bell jangled. A kid had strolled over to nibble on weeds in the vicinity. The animal looked obliquely at the debaters under the trellis.

"It would be a scandal to grant the woman a Christian burial," the pastor added.

"And what about my father?" said Maria, unable to restrain herself any longer. "He was no suicide."

Don Guglielmo didn't deign to look at her. "Ottavio Croce," he said in a cold tone, "falls into the same category as a public sinner or a duelist. He died instantly after committing a mortal sin." The pastor wheezed as he struggled to rise from the chair, signaling that the interview was over. "And now if you will forgive me . . ."

Tears streamed down Maria's cheeks. "I beg you, Father . . ."

Don Guglielmo had put on a broad-brimmed hat to protect his bald scalp from the sun. "My hands are tied, young lady. Doctrine is doctrine. The case of your mother is hopeless. As for your father, perhaps you could appeal to a church court."

"Never," she said through clenched teeth. "If they go into unmarked graves, at least they go together. Side by side!"

The pastor shrugged. "As you wish."

Pepe stuck a hand in his pocket where he kept a few bank notes. "All right then, could we buy indulgences?" he asked.

"They are already dead," drawled Don Guglielmo. "Besides, sir, indulgences are not for sale." He looked pointedly at Don Gabriele. "Father, I strongly suggest that you prevail upon this man to confess himself. Good day." He walked off, the skirt of his cassock billowing.

The three stood silently under the trellis. Her cheeks stained with tears, Maria did not make a sound. Her body was rigid and her eyes were fixed on the pastor's stable that contained many animals and a loft for straw and wheat. Beyond the stable was a grove of almond trees. Don Guglielmo apparently was not a close reader of holy scripture, he had laid up for himself a few treasures upon earth. Maria had learned another lesson about power, about those who had it and those who did not.

That night Don Guglielmo's stable mysteriously caught fire. The village volunteer brigade put out the flames but not before five bushels of threshed wheat were consumed, two buffaloes died and the structure was badly damaged. The authorities speculated that the fire had started when an animal kicked over an oil lamp that was found in the ashes. But who had lit the lamp? Busybodies said that a housemaid had been rutting with the cowherd, but nobody could prove anything.

In the morning Maria left the inn at Bagnoli where she'd been able to stay overnight because Pepe had lent her the money. She planned to walk all the way to potter's field to witness her parents' burial. Before leaving the village she heard the gossips in the main square jabbering about the fire, and allowed a smile that didn't fade until she got to the main road.

Don Gabriele had volunteered to go with her and say some prayers over the graves but Maria refused. She didn't want him to get into trouble with the church authorities, and the young priest had seemed relieved. She started walking rapidly up a hill, carrying a straw bag that contained provisions and a shawl to protect her head from the sun when it climbed higher. Not wanting to lose time, she breakfasted on mozzarella and grapes as she walked. The satisfaction over Don Guglielmo's "misfortune" soon gave way to thoughts about her bleak future and her grief over her parents. What was her future except misery and unhappiness? Where would she live, how would she survive? Would she go to a convent and become a nun or to the city and become a prostitute? Yes, she worried about these things, but unlike many of her compatriots she didn't view her misfortunes as a punishment for some evil she might have done. On the contrary, she saw her troubles as dragons to be fought and conquered. She had not learned the old lessons of passivity. The pastor's still-smoldering stable was testimony to this.

Soon after she started out Maria managed to hitch a ride on a cart heading east and reached the graveyard just in time. The diggers were about to lower the pine crates that contained her parents' mortal shells into two small holes that had been dug side by side. The lake that the ancients had compared to the River Styx shimmered in the background. One of the workmen was whistling a tune. The graveyard was a barren place, without headstones, crosses or flowers. A few hawthorns and cypresses bent over the black earth.

Maria approached the gravediggers. Listening to her, the diggers looked around warily. They were afraid of getting into hot water with the provincial officials who paid their wages. Still their dry terracotta faces showed sympathy for what she said. When she had finished talking the two men glanced at each other, then the older one nodded at her and they waited, leaning on the handles of their shovels.

Maria wasted no time. Taking a lever from the straw bag, she pried open the lids of the crates, steadied herself and inspected the contents. When she was certain which corpse occupied which box she reached around to remove the coral horn and pewter crucifix from her neck. She placed the horn in her father's crate, the crucifix in her mother's, thereby marking them. Using the back of the lever as a hammer, she pounded the nails of the coffin lids. When they were sealed shut again she interlaced her hands and mumbled prayers for her dead parents, then got up and paced the distance from the graves to the nearest tree, a cypress eighteen steps to the south. She nodded to the gravediggers and watched as they lowered the boxes and covered the crates with volcanic earth. Finally she crossed herself, thanked the diggers and headed back to the road that led to Miseno.

One day, she vowed, she would be back.

Giacometta was sent to live in the Convent of Santa Chiara after Maria was forced to give up the house. The sisters offered Maria a place there too but she refused. She shuddered at the very idea of taking the veil. Of course Pepe renewed his offer of marriage and taking her to America and she again turned him down. She was indebted to him, but marrying him under such circumstances would not be right.

Next the Pignataro brothers bought the *Santa Lucia* from her for much less than it was worth, because they had little capital and no assets to speak of. Romeo Pignataro, a hard worker, was heartbroken at Ottavio's death, and Maria told Pepe that she believed her father would have wanted him to have the boat. The deal was concluded without a written contract (the fishermen couldn't read) and without using the notary public, who would have exacted a fee for his trouble. Romeo Pignataro made a vague promise to pay Maria more money in the future but Maria shrugged it off. The future was a poor guarantor of the Phlegrian Fields.

The nest egg from the sale of the boat would not last long. When Donna Carmela offered Maria a position as a maid in the priest's house she jumped at the chance. At least she would have food and shelter, and the hard work would keep her mind off her grief.

One morning while Maria was milking a buffalo in the stable Don Gabriele approached her to ask if she wanted to resume her reading and writing lessons.

She had been straddling the stool with her knees spread apart as she squeezed the cow's udders. As she considered the question she tugged her skirts downward to cover her ankles. The day was warm and her cheeks were pink with exertion. She nodded.

The young priest seemed pleased. "And now that you live here," he said, "we don't have to wait for Sunday evenings. You'll progress more quickly; we can start tonight, if you like."

She nodded again.

He gave her an ambiguous smile, then added, "Fine, then, let's see . . ." He stroked his chin. "I'm celebrating the Stations of the Cross tonight at eight. Why don't you meet me in the sacristy after your chores? It's stocked with books and writing material."

He was about to add something when they heard footsteps at the entrance. Don Gabriele's mother, standing in the sunlit doorway of the stable, cast a shadow over the priest and the girl, and at the sight of her Don Gabriele broke off whatever more he had to say.

"Well, then," he said quickly to Maria, "I'll see you later."

Donna Carmela silently watched him go off toward the church, then turned to Maria. "We need the milk before Christmas, girl."

Maria worked hard all day, cleaning out the fireplace, harvesting tomatoes, baking bread, knitting garments, but there was still room in her thoughts for Don Gabriele. For some, bereavement deadened physical appetites. How could one think of bread, wine or sex after having just faced the loss of one's parents? But sometimes a person reacted in just the opposite manner, using things of the flesh as antidotes to grief. At supper Maria took a second helping of Donna Carmela's excellent macaroni soup, then ate a plate of grilled sausage with sage. As she cleaned up after the meal she heard the church bell signaling the end of the Stations of the Cross.

"May I please be excused?" she asked Donna Carmela, who sat on a bench in the doorway hanging strands of macaroni on a stick to dry.

Donna Carmela seemed to know where Maria was going. "Reading corrupts a girl's morals," she said.

Maria had too much sauce in her not to answer back. "Reading opens doors."

"Pah! The doors to cheap romances and love letters?"

"My dear lady, a girl can also read the books of devotion, the missal and Holy Scripture."

"Don't make me laugh," the woman said, drawing more strands of macaroni from the iron press, but her tone had not been angry and she didn't seem inclined to stand in Maria's way. Her son's contentment was more important to her than morality. Donna Carmela nodded toward the kitchen. "Bring him some mare's milk cheese and marsala, he likes a snack after services."

"Yes, Donna Carmela."

Moments later Donna Carmela looked up from her task to follow the girl heading over the cobblestones toward the sacristy, and as she cranked the macaroni press she had to wonder what lessons besides the arts of reading and writing Maria Croce might learn in the sacristy from her son Don Gabriele, a servant of God who, his mother knew, was also a weak-willed young man with dangerous desires.

*   *   *

The streets of Miseno were still deserted when Maria took the bed linens to the public fountain to wash them. She had gotten up before the rooster crowed so that no one would see her and she could start before dawn finished bleaching the eastern sky.

The lion heads spouted spring water into the trough under the trailing ivy as she quickly soaked the linen in the cold water, then sat down and allowed herself tears that she had held back. Virginity was a Neapolitan peasant girl's prize possession, so even one night of love could reduce her to nothing in the eyes of her compatriots. Like an insect or an animal she was marked by the scent of the male and devalued for life. What, Maria asked herself, would become of her high aspirations now? She saw no answers, and the red stains on the linen dissolved in the spring water.

She had to work quickly, first removing the linen from the fountain and placing it in a large earthen vessel, then spreading over the top a fragment of tough linen cloth that she then covered with wood ashes. She fetched from the house boiling water that she poured over the ashes, letting it seep through the top linen into the vessel, then repeated this three or four times and left the material to cool. Later she would rub the linen with soap and press it against the stones of the reservoir until it was washed, and still later she would force out the water by twisting the material with both hands and hanging it on a line to dry in the air and sun. If only, she thought, she could use the same procedures to cleanse her immortal soul . . .

During the next few days Maria noted a drastic change come over the priest, who seemed to go out of his way to avoid her. He never even mentioned resuming the reading and writing lessons. Whenever they by chance passed each other in the house he would avoid her eyes and mumble vague phrases. He didn't seem so much angry as sad, preoccupied. By contrast she looked straight at him and seemed to derive strength from his weakness. She might still love him but respected him a good deal less.

But deprived of normal contact with him, Maria felt her spirits wilt—until once in the middle of the night he came by her bed in the pantry. No, she decided, and sent him away, then cried herself to sleep.

Days later she asked Donna Carmela, well known in these parts as a healer, wise woman and herbalist, to tutor her in the crafts of the *strega*, the arts of poisoning and healing, the antidotes to envy, the enchantments that tapped subterranean forces. Donna Carmela looked her up and down, then nodded. "You have all the markings," the older woman said. "Listen, girl, and you will learn things far more valuable than marks on paper."

Was Donna Carmela gaining a grudging respect for her? Maria wondered.

It was odd to think that while her son practiced the rituals of the Christian church Donna Carmela mastered the rules and ceremonies of a far more ancient religion. He might be a priest of Rome, but she was a priestess of the cult of old Brutium that had survived from the days before the Romans and even the Greeks left their marks and messages. She taught Maria the uses, bad and good, of snakes, wasps, scorpions, spiders and jellyfish, of plants, potions and powders that could cure or kill. She taught her the formulas to chant and the talismans to wave to ward off evil, cast spells of love, cause fevers in rivals, enhance fertility or foster infertility, help breed male offspring—in short, ways to regulate the pulsebeat of life and death.

And Maria was a quick and eager learner. She also seemed to understand that the effectiveness of the technique often depended on the credence of those on whom one practiced.

A month passed, then two. The feasts days of Saint Raphael, patron of lovers, and of Saint Clement, patron of marble workers, had come and gone. Meanwhile Maria's time of the month had come around twice and nothing happened. By the feast of Saint Nicholas, patron of brewers, she knew she was out of cycle with the moon. And she knew this could mean only one thing.

That evening, chopping onions for a fish soup disguised the reason for Maria's tears. Through the window she could see the lengthening shadows of the fruit trees and beyond them Donna Carmela pruning the grapevine in preparation for winter. The church bells rang for benediction. Flies surrounded the shuddering muzzle of a dog sleeping in the yard. The rhythms of nature and men pulsed around and within her. God help her, she loved him still.

She cut and cleaned squid and shucked clams, discarding the shells, and thought that maybe after the death of her parents this spark of new life could be a blessing instead of a curse. The child of a priest was still a child of God, maybe more so. Why was this kind of thing considered so shameful for a peasant girl when the daughters of the gentry got off scot-free? Hadn't she read in a book lent to her by Don Gabriele that Lucrezia Borgia was the daughter of a pope? The seed contained life, and life was precious and mysterious, whatever the source. As she got around to cleaning the red mullet and lighting the carbon she began to feel better. Optimism flared, giving her the courage to consider telling the news to Donna Carmela.

Maria waited till morning to approach the old woman, who was sitting at a wood table in the backyard pounding chestnuts into a flour for *polenta di castagne*. It was a beautiful sunny day. Water gurgled from the mouth of the moss-encrusted face of a satyr carved into the household fountain. Bees droned around the rose bushes. The thump of the marble pestle wielded by Donna Carmela echoed in the air.

Maria put the sack of corn she was carrying on the ground and said, "I beg your pardon, madame, but I'd like a word with you, please."

Donna Carmela barely looked up. "What is it now, girl?"

"May I sit down?"

The woman nodded.

Maria sat on a bench across the table from Donna Carmela, her hands under the table twisting the hem of her apron. Finally she said, "It's a very fair day for December."

"Get to the point," Donna Carmela snapped.

Maria did. "I've missed my period. Twice."

Donna Carmela closed her eyes. Her purple-veined eyelids twitched. "I'm not surprised," she said, opening her eyes and looking past the fence at the narrow cobbled street that led to the church. Here and there you could see a villager going about his business. "Let's go inside," she said abruptly, and covered the chestnut mash with a cloth.

On the way to the house they passed the green-bronze statue of a deity that presided over a basin of the fountain. To Maria the statue resembled Don Gabriele.

"Wait here," Donna Carmela said after she'd led Maria to a chair by the hearth. "I'll be right back." Maria stared at the checkerwork of tiles on the floor . . . Donna Carmela's tone had been neutral, she'd showed no emotion at all. Soon she returned with a bottle of Centerbe, a green liqueur made from wild thyme, and two small glasses. It seemed that the woman seemed to be treating the occasion as a cause for celebration. Or was she?

After pouring, Donna Carmela handed a glass to Maria and asked, "Who's the father?"

Maria frowned at the question. "I'm sure you know."

Donna Carmela sat down opposite her. "It's the carpenter, right? Or aren't you sure?"

The words angered Maria. "Let's put it this way, madame . . . you are the grandmother."

The woman shook her head slowly, then said, "Why don't you drink?"

Maria drank, more to calm her nerves than to celebrate.

"Nobody will believe you, girl. It's all over town. Mrs. Barbalunga saw you go into the olive grove with Falcone."

"That was an innocent matter—"

Donna Carmela laughed.

Maria put her glass down on a side table. "Do you truly believe it was Pepe?"

Donna Carmela shrugged. "What's the difference?"

"I was a virgin when your sainted son took me."

"I believe you're a liar. A girl who would sleep with a man of the cloth can't be trusted."

"And what about a man of the cloth who would sleep with a girl?"

Donna Carmela's prickly pear of a face showed decades of cynicism. "Men are weaklings, whatever cloth they wear. It is up to us women to say no."

"So you admit your son slept with me."

"I admit nothing. Especially not in public. But listen, girl, if he took you, he took used goods, that's for sure."

Maria's eyes filled with tears, but her face was like granite. "That's not true. I love him and I'm going to tell him about it. I should have gone to him first."

Donna Carmela looked at her sharply. "You get that notion out of your head, girl. I'll have you run out of town, by God."

Maria hesitated. She believed in Donna Carmela's power and influence in the village and beyond.

Donna Carmela went on: "Do you think I sacrificed so much over so many years to have a priest in the family just so he could be ruined by scandal? Not on your life."

"He would not be the first priest from around here to father children—"

"Yes, but I want my son to advance in the Church, not to get stuck in the mud in this one-horse village. I have relations on my mother's side to the bishop. Pretty soon they will need a new canon in the Cathedral. Pardon me, but I will not allow a cheap little affair like this to stink up my son's name and destroy his career."

"Even popes had children," Maria pressed on, ignoring the insult.

"In times antique, maybe," the priest's mother said, "but this is the twentieth century. We are very moral these days." She didn't smile when she said it.

Maria could stand no more and she broke down, sobbing into her hands.

"Cut that out," the woman snapped. "You should have thought about all this before you spread your pretty legs."

"God, how can you be so cruel? Didn't you ever make a mistake? Weren't you ever in love?"

"Don't talk to me about love," the woman said. "Or cruelty. Life is cruel, as you should know." She got up and smoothed down the front of her apron. "I do feel pity for you because you lost your parents. So I'm going to help you." She went over to fetch the bottle and poured two more drinks.

Maria accepted the refill. "Help me? How, madame?"

The woman sat down again, leaning closer. "I know a formula. It's made from a solution of seaweed."

What did she mean? Then suddenly Maria understood. She hugged herself protectively. "*No.*"

"You won't feel any pain," Donna Carmela said.

"But it's a sin—"

"Fornication is a sin too. Did you ever think of that? And lying with a priest!" The woman's eyes turned up to the heavens.

Maria drank the green liqueur. "How can you suggest such a thing? Your own grandchild."

"A child of sin. Anyway, at this point it's like killing a fish."

Maria looked doubtful. Of course, it would solve her immediate problem . . . she didn't know what to do . . .

Donna Carmela finished her drink and got up. "I'll give you two weeks to think about it. If you decide to have the child you're on your own, you hear? You'll have to find another place to live." She added with a smirk, "There are lots of girls in your position walking the streets of Naples, which are filled with sailors from all over the world. With your looks you won't starve, that's for sure."

Maria turned away from Donna Carmela to hide her flare of hatred.

"In the meantime stay away from my son." Her words held a threat as well as an order.

For several days Maria wrestled with her decision. Don Gabriele avoided her and she was afraid to tell him about it. She knew that provoking his mother's anger would probably be disastrous for her. Still, Maria sensed that the priest knew something was going on. Every time she passed him he would blush and bury his head in his breviary.

Finally, as the deadline set by Donna Carmela approached, Maria decided to seek help from a higher authority and asked Donna Carmela for a day off to make a pilgrimage to the hermitage of Capua to pray for guidance. Taking money from her nest egg, she hired a donkey from Ignazio Martin to make the journey of some thirty kilometers to the hermitage. She left at dawn and arrived in the middle of the day and was met at the arched entrance by a

Benedictine monk holding a bowl with the image of a dove painted on it.

He mumbled a few pieties in greeting, eyes shaded by a broad-brimmed straw hat. Then in the monotone of a jaded cicerone he recited a short history of the miracles inspired by devotions at the hermitage founded especially to rescue souls from purgatory. On the stone wall beside them was painted a scene depicting cherubs extending their hands to lift from the flames naked bodies repre-senting souls of the recently deceased. Under the painting were hung an almsbox and holy water font. The picture instantly made Maria think about her parents. Weren't they still in purgatory after the way they died? She put a few precious coppers in the box and crossed herself.

The monk told her that the dove on the cup symbolized the soul of Saint Scholastica, the sister of Saint Benedict, who founded the order of monks about 529 A.D. at Monte Cassino. The dove, he said, appeared to Benedict at his sister's death. Maria kissed the bowl and dropped a few more coppers into it. She looked worried, had she brought enough money? These hermits were seasoned extortionists.

She entered the hermitage. The interior was dark and cool and the stone floor was covered with old women on their knees praying aloud like Arabs, clasping their hands and reaching out in supplica-tion toward the holy images. Maria too fell to her knees and with outstretched arms slid along the stone slabs toward the chapel of the blessed mother. She stopped in front of a fresco of madonna and child surrounded by hovering angels. The mother wore the crown of a queen. Maria whispered her prayers.

A while later she left the hermitage, not wiser but poorer than when she entered it.

At every crossroad on the road back to Miseno, Maria saw the display of a crib containing an effigy of the infant Jesus. The dis-plays, she knew, signified the upcoming feast of the Epiphany cele-brating the visit of the Magi to the stable where Christ was born. The westering sun beat down on her kerchiefed head, she felt the warm flesh of the jostling donkey between her legs, and a vision swam before her eyes of bald-headed babies, figures representing the spirits of the unborn floating through the centuries, water babies tumbling like miniature buddhas in an endless stream from the dawn of time to the end of the world . . . was this apparition brought on by the sun or did it somehow come from her prayers? Shaking herself, Maria gripped the reins of the beast's halter and clucked to coax the animal to move more quickly.

By the time she saw in the distance the belfry of San Rocco she knew that she had made up her mind, and the next morning she told Donna Carmela her decision.

The priest's mother imperiously placed her hands on her plump hips and told her, "Pack your things, girl. I want you out of here by tonight." Her face, powdered with flour, had a clownish look. She had been kneading the dough for bread.

"I have nowhere to go—"

"That's not my affair."

Maria was in no mood to surrender without a fight. She was tired of having fate toss her around. "Well, madame, I'll make it your affair. I'll denounce Don Gabriele to the bishop."

"Who's going to believe you? Who's going to believe a girl who goes into the olive groves with men? Who's going to believe the daughter of a suicide and a killer?"

Maria was shouting now, "You leave my parents out of this, may they rest in peace. A witch like you isn't fit to utter their names."

Donna Carmela's pinched face reddened. "You have the gall to call me a witch, you slut," she said, and gave the girl a ringing slap in the face.

Maria took a moment to recover from the shock of the blow, then slapped the woman back.

Surprised, she gingerly touched her cheek, then grabbed Maria by the arms and threw her to the ground near the fireplace.

Looking around, Maria saw an iron hook that was used to balance pots over the brazier. She picked it up and scrambled to her feet. The murderous look in her eyes made the woman flinch and stumble backward as Maria advanced on her.

Just then Don Gabriele appeared in the kitchen archway. "My God in heaven, what's going on here?"

Maria froze.

"This evil girl is trying to kill me," Donna Carmela said.

Don Gabriele turned to look at Maria, who, stunned by her own actions, let the hook fall with a clatter to the tiles. Truly his sudden appearance had saved his mother's life, Maria realized, getting a glimmer, however shocking, of her own toughness, of the iron in her will and capacity to retaliate if pushed hard enough.

The priest continued to look at Maria, as though to ask *why*.

Finally she did look him in the face, which still caused her to catch her breath. "I'm sorry," she mumbled, "I lost my temper."

"But what is this all about?"

His mother said quickly, "Never mind, son. I'll handle her."

"I'm going to have a baby," Maria said evenly. "*Your* baby."

"She's mad," said Donna Carmela. "Pay no attention to her."

"I'm telling the truth and you know it," Maria said.

The priest couldn't look her in the face. He reached out to steady himself on the ledge of the fireplace. "I'm sure I don't know what you're talking about . . ."

Maria stood there motionless, narrowing her eyes at Don Gabriele as if seeing him for the first time.

"I told you she's insane," Donna Carmela said. "She's gotten herself pregnant by the carpenter and now she wants to feather her nest by pinning it on you. Hah, she won't get away with it. Not in a million years."

Maria wasn't listening to the woman, she was studying the priest's face . . . that face she had once thought so sensitive and beautiful . . . as one would inspect an unknown species of animal met up with by chance in the woods—with wonder, curiosity and finally detachment. It was really her own feelings that she was examining with some surprise, because she didn't blame him for the denial. He was a priest who had stumbled, and she quoted Dante to him—" 'Love, which lies smoldering in each gentle heart, Inflamed for him the beauty that was mine.' " She was pleasantly surprised that she could recall the lines. She doubted, though, that at this point he was glad he had taught her such things.

Donna Carmela gave her a look, but her son appeared worn down. He said, "Leave us, Mamma."

"Not on your life. Who knows what the bitch has up her sleeve?"

"Please, Mamma, a few minutes."

Grudgingly, his mother finally shuffled out of the room.

When she had left Don Gabriele sat slumped on a stool and buried his face in his hands. "Forgive me . . ."

"I'm not your confessor," Maria said. "I don't have the power to grant absolution."

"I shouldn't have denied it. It was a moment of weakness."

"You seem to specialize in those," she observed.

He propped his palms on his knees. "Yes. I do, don't I?"

She sighed. "You're only human."

"I'm glad you finally see that."

"Me too." She looked down at the wild blond curls growing above his sad eyes. "Your mother wanted to give me a potion to get rid of the child."

He made a sour face.

"Do you want me to do that?"

"Of course not. I can't condone such a sin."

Ten years older than she, he appeared to her now like a helpless boy. She couldn't help feeling sorry for him. "What now?" she asked him.

"There's only one solution. I will have to make a public admission and take my medicine."

"Take your medicine? Is that how you see a connection to me?"

"I didn't mean it that way."

Did she dare hope? "Would you have to leave the priesthood?"

He shook his head. "Once a priest, always a priest. But I would have to give up the parish post and administering the sacraments. I know many of my colleagues live lives of sin and perform business as usual. I can't."

"Your mother says that you have a promising career ahead of you in the Church. What about that?"

He only shook his head.

"What would we do to earn our bread?" she asked him.

"Well, we could go to Naples, or even Rome. I could probably find work as a schoolteacher."

The idea had a certain appeal for her. But it was tarnished by his dispirited tone of voice. "Do you love me?"

The question seemed to embarrass him. Finally he admitted, "I don't know. I have great affection for you but my feelings are all mixed up now . . ."

"I love *you*," she said. "But I don't want to ruin your career. And I don't want a man to stay with me from a sense of *duty*." She fought back tears. There would be no time or place for tears on the road that stretched ahead. It was time to get rid of tears.

The priest seemed relieved. "What will you do?"

"I don't know."

"How will you manage?"

"I'll manage."

"Will you . . . will you have the baby?"

"If it's the last thing I do I will have the baby."

A haunted look crossed his face. It would, after all, be his child too.

"Good-by," she said.

"*Addio.*"

They looked at each other, without words. Enough. She turned and left the room.

In the pantry, where she had slept for the past three months, she gathered up her few possessions and packed them in a straw satchel. Through the window she could see the buffalo horns mounted over the farrier's stable. She scorned the idea of the evil eye, of chastisements from above. The strong shaped their own destinies, she had already learned.

She finished packing and sat down on the bed of straw. What now? She took a moment to puzzle over the options. All her bridges had been burned. Except one.

Pepe Falcone, opening the door to his cottage, was taken aback when he saw Maria standing there, satchel in hand.

"May I come in?"

"By all means," he said, as he looked around nervously to see if anybody was watching. It was scandalous for an unchaperoned girl to enter a bachelor's residence. No one was in sight. He closed the door behind them. "Please, make yourself comfortable," he said, bustling about the room picking up crockery and clothing.

Maria looked around her. Pepe lived in a one-room tile-roofed stone hovel that stood on the outskirts of the beehive of houses that formed Miseno. Behind the house was a wooden shed that was his workshop. He also cultivated a tomato patch and kept a few free-roaming chickens whose odor wafted through the shutters.

"Sit here," Pepe said, leading her to a wooden rocker that he had made. "Would you like a glass of marsala?"

"Have you anything stronger?"

"Grappa?"

She nodded.

After a few sips of the strong drink she shivered.

Pepe noticed this and said, "Wait, I'll light the urn." He dragged over a ceramic vessel containing charcoal and set it between their chairs.

"I'll get straight to the point," Maria said. "Donna Carmela has thrown me out."

Pepe was seated on a low bench, his stubby arms dangling between his knees. "I'm sorry," he said, his tone betraying hopefulness. "Why?" He didn't really care.

She looked directly at him. "I'm pregnant."

He was silent and openmouthed. She held her hands over the urn to warm them, then answered the question he wasn't able to ask: "It's Don Gabriele's child." She watched his reaction.

"The cowardly hypocrite," he said.

"Don't blame him," she said.

"What do you mean? He took advantage of you."

"I was willing," she said, making him wince. She hesitated, then added, "That old busybody Barbalunga saw you and me go into the olive grove together that day. The villagers will say you're the father."

"*Good*," he said. "Let them say it."

She gave him a look.

Pepe began to laugh. "Why not? I would be proud to say so, Maria."

"I can't let you do that."

"But think of the child. Do you want him or her to be born without a name, to be an outcast in this godforsaken place? The streets of Naples are littered with such children."

"No," she said. "I don't want that."

He reached out to stroke her hair. "Oh, dear girl, marry me. We'll go to America and start with a clean slate. I'll love the child like it was my own. You must know how I feel about you."

"But . . . I don't love you. It wouldn't be right just because I'm in trouble."

He continued to stroke her hair, then her cheek. "It doesn't matter, I have no pride when it comes to you. And we must think of the baby."

After some moments of silence filled only by the buzzing of flies she said, "All right, Pepe. I'll marry you. And I'll do my best to make you happy." And she meant it.

To avoid having Don Gabriele perform the ceremony Maria Croce and Pepe Falcone arranged to be married in a small church in the Old Quarter of Naples called Spacca. The rite was performed by a drowsy curate who stank of beer and onions. Romeo and Italo Pignataro stood as witnesses. Also attending were Enzo Balbi, the landowner for whom Pepe did carpentry, his wife, a skinny woman with crepey skin and hands like chicken bones, and Mr. and Mrs. Stefano Falcone of Pozzuoli, distant cousins of the bridegroom.

Pepe was in a new suit of blue wool, and Maria wore the silk dress that she had made from her lottery earnings. During the ceremony, held at a side altar of the church, Maria couldn't help feeling an emotional void in spite of her efforts to lose herself in the spirit of the occasion. As the curate droned the formulas of fidelity and obedience she studied a stained-glass window depicting Saint Joseph holding a flowering staff.

Blessedly, the ceremony was short.

Afterward they celebrated by dining at a trattoria in the Vicaria Vecchia, a modest place with wax-paper table coverings and cracked stone floors. But the home-cooked food was good. The wedding feast started with cannelloni, followed by turkey breast with mozzarella and tomatoes, boiled octopus, stuffed artichokes and honey sweets. They drank a white Capri and Falerno. The mood, though, was gray rather than gay. No one played the tambourine or guitar, no one danced the tarantella. Balbi, a red-nosed man with a brush mustache and jug ears, toasted the couple with a glass of Falerno, wishing them a hundred years of life and male offspring. As a wedding gift he paid the bill. On the way out Maria stooped to kiss the small son of the owner, a toddler dressed like a prince in a velvet dress and striped leggings.

Pepe hired a hackney coach to take them back to Miseno. The driver of the horse-drawn *calessino* gave the reins to Pepe and, standing on a platform behind the passengers, reached across them to use the whip on the beast's flanks. The animal broke into a canter, making the bells on the harness jangle and the flags strapped to the horse's back flutter. As they rode Maria huddled into the fringed silk shawl that Pepe had given her as a wedding present.

Pepe took her hand, looking at the small gold band on her finger. "Someday I'll buy you a real diamond ring," he said.

"I don't need diamonds," she said.

"But you deserve them."

She let it go at that.

As the horses hooves clopped on the cobbled road Maria looked with a mix of longing and distaste at the faded pink palaces of the rich on the waterfront of Naples, at the moldering kelp-covered sea walls lapped by foamy waves, at the baroque porches and court-yards with fancy surreys and even motor cars and other signs of wealth in this decrepit outpost of Old Spain. She wanted to shake her fist at these things. Instead, she rested her head in the cradle of Pepe's shoulder, which made him beam with pleasure.

The couple was spending the wedding night in Pepe's stone house on the border of the village. The sun had set by the time they arrived. Pepe paid the driver, then helped his bride climb down from the coach. When she reached the ground their bodies were close. "You smell of a hundred flowers," he told her, and meant it.

His gallantry pleased her, but unfortunately didn't stir her to appropriate desire.

Inside the house Pepe coughed, trying to cover his shyness. This was the first time they had been alone since Maria had accepted his proposal of marriage. She had spent the few days before the wedding in the Balbi household, watched like a hawk by the land-owner's wife, one of those public rosary-mumblers who made no effort to disguise her disapproval of Maria and the fix she was in. No wonder Balbi was famous for his visits to the village prostitute.

Maria looked around. Pepe's house was neat as a pin. He had swept out all the wood shavings and chicken droppings and had polished the wood floor. Cut flowers in wine bottles decorated the ledges, sills and mantels. On the plank table in the kitchen he had set a bottle of sparkling wine and a chestnut cake with cream on top.

In spite of her vow to dispense with tears forever, Maria's eyes did fill up.

Pepe was mortified. "Don't cry, Maria, I know it's a poor place to live but it's only for two weeks, then we go to America where they say there are neither palaces nor hovels."

She smiled at him. "No, that's not it, silly man. You've made it so beautiful."

Pepe grinned, delighted, then led her to the table, and the wine. As she drank Pepe just gazed at her.

After a while Maria yawned. "It's getting late."

Pepe was excited and embarrassed. He still couldn't quite believe his good luck. "Are you tired?" he said, looking at the curtain he had set up to partition off the area where the bed was.

"Yes," she said, "I guess it's the wine."

He got up from the chair and led her to the curtain and drew it back. Behind it was the small wooden bunk that he usually slept in. He had built it himself, modeling it after a bunk in a ship's cabin. "You sleep here," he told her.

"And you?"

"It's not large enough for two. I'll sleep in the workshop."

"But it gets cold at night."

"I have lots of blankets."

"Are you sure, Pepe?" she said, blushing because her sense of relief was so palpable.

"I'm sure . . . think of your condition."

Maria looked down at her slightly swelling belly and nodded.

"Listen, Maria," he said, "I desire you, but I will wait until you're ready." He kissed her on the cheek. "Good night."

As she undressed, Maria was grateful to Pepe for his kindness. She thought how different he was from his compatriots, who saw women as property, like animals. Crawling into bed, she wondered what she could do about it . . . she was truly sorry she didn't reciprocate her new husband's obvious feelings. But you needed a spark to light the fire to bake bread. And the spark simply wasn't there.

Two weeks passed and the newlyweds were ready to embark for America. Balbi had offered to take them to the Naples wharf in his donkey cart. Maria liked the gruff landowner who, though a man of property, didn't go around with his nose in the air trying to lord it over the peasants. His boots were muddy like the rest of the villagers and he gave charity where he could. The only thing that set him apart from the *cafoni* was his habit of smoking cigarettes from Turin rather than cheroots or a pipe.

"Give me that," he said to Maria when she tried to lift a cloth sack into the cart. Meanwhile Romeo Pignataro was helping Pepe lift a heavy trunk into the cart while Italo as usual supervised the operation.

When the cart was loaded and ready to go, all the worldly possessions of Pepe and Maria Falcone, including the carpenter's tools, fit into one large trunk and three cloth sacks. Maria and Pepe took turns embracing the Pignataro brothers as the busybodies watched in the main square. "Lucky you," Romeo Pignataro said, "you leave the entrance of Hell for the land of milk and honey."

"We'll see about that," Maria said.

"God bless you," Romeo Pignataro shouted after them as they went off.

"May God fill your nets," Maria called back.

"And fill your beds with a fat wife apiece," Pepe said with a wink. He was sitting up front next to Balbi.

As the cart rumbled past the church Maria turned quickly to look in the other direction, not wanting to look at Donna Carmela and Don Gabriele who were standing in the courtyard of the adjoining house. As the cart climbed the hill she looked out at the slate-colored sky and the sea. Her throat was clogged. She would probably never see him again. Why couldn't she drive him from her mind, purge him from her heart? She realized since she carried his child in her womb it would be impossible to erase the priest completely from mind and memory, but she hoped someday to see him in a cooler light. Meanwhile, she had to fight this feeling for him with all her strength. Well, she was a fighter, wasn't she?

The donkey struggled up an incline, following the same road Maria's parents had taken to their disgrace and doom. Maria asked Balbi to make a short detour to the potter's field, where she picked wild flowers and, counting out the paces from the landmark cypress, placed them on the unmarked graves of her parents.

They continued on toward Naples, passing the magic pool of Bacoli and Solfatara where Lisabeta had plunged to her death. The road then passed Pozzuoli and just north of Bagnoli, where Maria couldn't hold back a satisfied smile when she saw the charred timbers of Don Guglielmo's stable. The road bypassed Marechiaro and the Camorra stronghold of Posillipo. Maria was thankful for this, touched her belly and crossed herself. This morning Pepe had told her about a dream he had had during the night in which a man in luminous white appeared warning him that Don Virgilio's successor had learned about Maria's pregnancy and ordered his lieutenants to kill any male descendant of Ottavio Croce who might avenge his grandfather by spilling Camorra blood. People took such dreams seriously. Maria tried not to.

The cart came to the top of a bluff, where finally they could look on the beautiful Bay of Naples, its splendor somewhat diminished by the cloudiness of the day, muting the usual radiant merger of sea and sky. But the port was visible from this distance and Maria's keen eyes picked out the red star on the smokestack of the steamship *Leonardo* on which they had booked passage to their deliverance.

Balbi tightened his grip on the reins, making the donkey stop, and the three persons in the cart surveyed the panorama, lost with his and her own thoughts. Would this be the last time, Maria asked herself, that she and her husband would view Naples from such a vantage? Maria for one devoutly hoped so as Balbi clucked again and the animal started on the downward path.

The dock was swarming with emigrants carrying trunks, battered valises, cloth bags, wood crates, folding chairs, mattresses, bed linen, screaming children, babies at the breast and hopes, hopes,

hopes. Wails of farewell echoed from pillar to post like the keening at a Syrian funeral. Adding to the pandemonium were the shouts of porters, sailors and hawkers of ices and watermelon slices, pizzas and mulled wine. Little boys in sailor suits tightly held the hands of petticoated peasant women. Brown-faced men with black mustaches sat on wooden crates staring as quarrels erupted all round them. Neighing draft animals and droves of frightened sheep were led up the gangplank.

Still sitting in the cart, Maria surveyed the scene, then gave her hand to Pepe, who helped her climb down from the cart.

"Have you got the documents?" he asked.

She nodded and patted her bodice.

Maria, Pepe and Balbi weaved their way through the crowd, heading toward a shed at the south end of the wharf that served as a customshouse. Suddenly, though, their progress became easier as the people shrank back from an approaching figure—Geremio, a one-eyed old beggar who haunted the port and was thought to possess the evil eye. Balbi whispered to Maria and Pepe, advising them to give the man a wide berth.

But Maria shook her head. She was fed up with the old superstitions that the ruling class used to keep the peasants in a state of ignorance and bondage.

As Geremio came near she stood her ground, putting her hands on her hips, pushing out her swollen belly and staring him straight in the scrambled egg that was his right eye.

Geremio stopped and frowned. He wore a battered felt hat with a Tyrolean feather stuck into the band and baggy cotton clothes. He looked at her stomach.

"Your son will be a servant who suffers," he said.

"Get out of my way," Maria said. She would fight tooth and nail to make sure that her son would be a servant to no man. And as far as suffering went, wasn't everybody born to suffer?

Geremio's good eye burned into her back like a glowing coal.

Before boarding they had to stop at the customshouse and file past a procession of pompous officials in gold braid and sparkling boots who barked questions and demanded documents from the intimidated passengers. After running a gauntlet of passport, customs, excise and maritime officials, each of whose palms Balbi greased, they climbed the gangplank. Balbi paid a porter to carry the luggage aboard.

On deck they queued up in front of the commissary table to receive food rations. As they waited Maria said to Balbi, "We can never thank you enough."

"Don't mention it," he said. "After all, you deserve a few good turns of the wheel."

She clasped his hand and pressed it to her cheek while Pepe craned his neck to see how quickly the line was moving, and watched the officer with the built-in suspicion of every southerner for a man with a registry and pen.

When they had finally finished their business a sailor was circling the deck blowing a whistle and shouting, "All ashore that's going ashore!"

Balbi rolled his cigarette to the side of his mouth and said, "Well, good voyage, eh?" He embraced Pepe, then Maria. "I have a going-away present for you," he told her.

"You shouldn't, you've done more than enough for us already."

He handed her an envelope. With Pepe peering over her shoulder, Maria opened it. It contained separate sepia photos of her parents at a very young age.

Maria gave Balbi a puzzled look.

"They were taken when they applied for a marriage license," Balbi, a village councilman, told her. "I pinched them from the Records Bureau at Town Hall."

Maria was deeply moved. They were the only photographs of her parents that she knew existed. She looked at their youthful, optimistic faces for a long time, then said to Balbi, "I will never forget you for this," and stood on tiptoes to kiss him on the cheek.

Balbi puffed furiously on the cigarette.

"I wish you were coming with us," Pepe said, clapping his friend on the shoulder.

"Bah. An old fig tree like me would wither and die on foreign soil."

The sailor blew the whistle again. The landowner said, "Better go or they'll arrest me as a stowaway." He laughed. "Wonder what the old lady would say to that."

And then he was gone. The gangway was hauled ashore, the dock ropes cast off, the foghorn groaned. The steamer, nearly imperceptibly, began to glide away from the pier.

Men and women were separated. Maria descended a steep ladder to her tiny berth between-decks, lucky to be situated near a porthole where she could somewhat escape the reek of humanity around her and watch the city lights appear in the distance like a diamond bracelet around the bay.

Determined to turn her face toward the new world, Maria Croce Falcone still could not resist one last lingering look at the place that had spawned her. From this vantage the land rising from the sprawling bay, winking with lights in the descending dusk, resembled more a magical utopia than the cursed place she knew it to be, a country of malaria, brigandage, earthquake, endless tyrannies of nature and man. Look, the old firegod Vesuvius reared in the east, a sleeping monster who could awake in a snap and without warning rain fiery death on the people below. To live in his shadow served as a craggy reminder of the precariousness of life here.

From a cloth packet strapped next to her left breast, where she also kept the few lire that she possessed, Maria removed the daguerreotypes of her parents and looked at them again.

No tears. Then why was it so hard to leave? Maybe because it had been the land of her people since the days before Julius Caesar invented the calendar that today read January 25, 1920.

Maria sighed, put her head down and tried to sleep on the rocking cradle of the sea that would carry her to the promised land.

GODMOTHER

America, named for an Italian. As the *Leonardo* steamed into New York Harbor, Maria Falcone stood sour-faced and shivering on the foredeck. Was this windy greenless place the promised land? It was a gray glowering day and since winter never really laid his icy hand on the Bay of Naples she was unprepared for the leafless landscape that met her as she gripped the railing and huddled close to her husband.

"What a strange-looking country," she said to Pepe. He made no reply, silently agreeing.

Maria gazed wonderingly at the landmarks of Lower New York Bay. Instead of a volcano she saw a Ferris wheel on the shore of Brooklyn. Instead of baroque pink stone palaces she saw big wooden mansions on the hills of Staten Island. Sailing through the Narrows she saw the spidery steel of the Brooklyn Bridge, the green ghost of Lady Liberty, a female Colossus, and the tall buildings of lower Manhattan dominated by the spires of the Woolworth Building piercing the misty sky. America seemed a colorless, sunless place.

Soon a smaller boat took them to Ellis Island, where they were herded into a great drafty hall and instructed to sit with their belongings on long wooden benches to wait for processing by quarantine, customs and immigration officers. Wire fences and armed guards were all about, making Maria feel more like a prisoner than a pilgrim. She looked up and saw suspended from a mezzanine railing a large banner bearing stars and stripes. No more the tricolor; this would be her flag from now on.

The collective voice of the crowd was a roar. Officials barked commands. The wailing of babies echoed. In spite of two potbellied coal stoves the place was very cold and Maria wrapped herself in the thin silk scarf. It was clear their clothes weren't warm enough for this harsh climate.

* * *

Hours later they finally had run the gamut of registrars, clerks and bureaucrats, the last of whom asked them their destination.

"Bethlehem, *Ben Silvania*," announced Pepe Falcone.

The tender then took them through waters scalloped by heavy wind to the Battery, where they disembarked. Maria's teeth chattered from the cold. Men with the Italian language on their tongues but ice in their hearts hustled the crowd, exchanging foreign currency at unfavorable rates, peddling rail tickets at exorbitant prices, steering immigrants to the Labor Exchange, where the *padroni* would arrange for the newcomers to find jobs that amounted to an indentureship.

But Pepe Falcone told all the jokers in stiff collars and Stetson hats to get lost. His brother Claudio had forewarned him about these sons of Machiavelli. Pepe already had train tickets and paper dollars pinned to the inside of his jacket. Following Claudio's written instructions, the carpenter and his wife hopped a trolley to Pennsylvania Station, where they boarded a train that in another miracle of engineering tunneled under the Hudson River and steamed through New Jersey, beginning the eighty-mile journey.

Maria looked forlornly out of the smudged window at the snow-covered landscape and skeletal trees flying backward. America had plenty of gold but little sun. In the compartment the Falcones ate bread and salami and drank soda pop while fellow passengers seemed to look right through them. They spoke to no one, and no one had the courtesy even to say good day. Even the train conductor collected their tickets without a word of greeting or pleasantry of any sort. Were the Americans a race of barbarians? Maria marveled at the babble of guttural sounds the people made. How, she wondered, could one sing in such a dissonant tongue.

The train passed hamlets, farms, swamps, creeks, rivers and pine woods. So many houses made of wood instead of stone. And front porches where ordinary people with no apparent official connection to the government flew the national flag. Wooden churches with no statues and little ornamentation. They made Christ a peasant rather than a king. She saw many motor cars and telegraph poles stretching for mile after mile. There was a lot to get used to.

Throughout the journey Pepe had sat stiff as a board, as though expecting at any moment to be attacked by red Indians or robbed by train bandits. Now, though, he became animated as the train crossed a wide river called the Delaware, which formed the border of New Jersey and Pennsylvania. He knew this meant that their destination was near. Soon they saw the smokestacks of concrete factories, steel mills and other industries, belching fumes in a way that reminded them of the volcanic earth they had just left behind. Then they crossed another river, the Lehigh, and Pepe heard the words that Claudio had coached him to listen for—"Next stop, Bethlehem." Pepe and Maria exchanged looks of relief.

With a hiss of steam the train crept to a stop. Maria carried the sacks while Pepe struggled to get the big trunk down on the platform. As other passengers, many dressed warmly in fur-lined coats, moved briskly and confidently around the station the immigrants in wrinkled clothing stood fearful and hesitant, squinting in the gathering dusk.

Suddenly Pepe let out a shout. "Claudio!"

Maria looked around.

He came out of the shadows, approaching from the north end of the station. He was a head taller than his older brother and as dark as Pepe was fair. He wore a wool overcoat and scarf but no hat. His head was covered with a thatch of chestnut-colored curls dusted with snow. With gloved hands he was pushing a wheelbarrow. As he came nearer Maria studied his face, bright with a smile of welcome. She caught her breath. Claudio was surprisingly handsome.

Whistles blew, a conductor shouted and the train crawled out of the station as the brothers embraced. Finally Pepe clasped her hand. "This is Maria," he said. And after a pause: "My wife."

Claudio gave her a hug. His physical strength was apparent even though he wore a heavy wool coat. He gave Pepe a sidelong look, as if to say, sly dog! He was courtly toward her and aware of her delicate condition. "I am very pleased to meet you," he said. "And for charity, put down those sacks!"

Claudio helped Pepe load the baggage in the wheelbarrow, then trundled it up a hilly street. As she followed, Maria fingered the garlic amulet she wore around her neck and eyed the strange sights. She had disavowed the old country superstitions, but ingrained habits were hard to break. Snowflakes danced in the shafts of light thrown by the gas lamps that lined the street. The city was built on hills rising from both banks of the river. As they walked Maria caught glimpses of the black humps of mountains looming in the north. Steel mills and other factories stood on the south bank.

Finally they came to a cluster of drab wooden structures huddled on a hillside overlooking one of the mills. Putting down his burden, Claudio didn't even seem winded after the long climb. "This is it," he said with a somewhat apologetic tone.

The "hotel" where he and the other single men lived was a large cheerless crackerbox of wood and tar paper. He told his brother and sister-in-law that he had arranged for them to stay in a shed behind the house, where the proprietor kept a few animals.

"It's really not too bad," he added. "It has a wood stove and I bought straw from the company store for you to sleep on."

Maria looked grim. They had crossed the seas and traveled thousands of miles to the land of opportunity to sleep in a stable? "It's only temporary," he said quickly, "we'll find something better when you get on your feet."

As the brothers renewed acquaintance, swapping stories about Miseno and America, Maria, beneath the many skirts and petticoats feeling the movements of the life inside her, lay her head down with a sigh. She might have fled the afflicted land of her birth, but she was still sleeping on straw.

When spring finally came to the Lehigh Valley, Maria and Pepe still lived in their "temporary" lodgings. The river swelled with the melting snows of the Blue Mountains, and Maria's stomach swelled in synchrony. Certainly life was hard here too, Maria thought. Were people like her forever doomed to a hard life? Pepe couldn't find work as a carpenter, so Claudio had to apply through the local job contractor to get his brother a place hauling pig iron at the mill. The contractor, a burly German whose cousin was a foreman employed by the steel company, reminded Maria of the stewards who worked for the landlords back in Campania. He did no work, took a big fee for his trouble and carried a side arm in case anyone objected.

Muscular Claudio had a job shoveling coke into the blast furnace, an infernal machine that turned iron ore into a molten material that reminded Maria of the lava of Vesuvius. It was as if the weavers of fate were reproducing the evils of the old country in slightly different form on the reverse side of the cloth.

Maria herself earned a dollar or two a week as a day laborer doing odd jobs on a farm across the Delaware in New Jersey, where she and other Italian women were transported each day by horse cart. These days Miseno seemed a misty memory after three months in America. But Maria had little time for nostalgia. Sometimes she missed the reading lessons with Don Gabriele—time and distance had somehow made him seem almost innocent. She had told herself he was a victim of her seductiveness, not a weakling and a rogue. It made her feel better about him. She thought about her parents, but mostly she tried not to look back.

America was an odd place, full of curiosities and paradoxes. Although farms dotted the landscape, people in towns and cities drank milk delivered to the doorstep by a horse and wagon. How clever and inventive the people were, with their electric lights and telephones and movie theaters showing Douglas Fairbanks, Mary Pickford and Charlie Chaplin. How skillfully they quarried rock from the surrounding hills and turned it into cement and steel to make useful things like bridges and buildings.

At the same time, she noted, they were wasteful and careless and full of contradictions. The trees and skies swarmed with squirrels and plump birds that nobody bothered to shoot and eat. In front of their houses people cultivated useless lawns instead of growing tomatoes. Politicians stood in the village squares making speeches about democracy and equality while Negroes shined their shoes for a penny. At least in Italy the big shots weren't hypocrites. A peasant was a peasant and a baron was a baron and nobody pretended different.

The women also made Maria shake her head. In appearance they went from one extreme to the other. Either they dressed like harlots with paint on their faces and skirts worn above the knees or they dressed like Nordic nuns covered from head to toe in Mother Hubbards and sunbonnets in the manner of the people they called Pennsylvania Dutch. They had a topsy-turvy relationship with men too. In public, men bowed and scraped before women, treating them like queens. But at home it seemed the women had little or no real power. In Italy it was just the opposite. In the village square the women deferred to the men, who preened like peacocks. But at home the women ruled the roost.

What an *odd* place. Maria had heard that the politicians in Washington, incredible as it sounded, recently passed a bill outlawing wine and other alcoholic drinks. Yet she saw public drunkards on every corner. How could a society survive that *outlawed* wine? It was like telling the sun not to shine.

Maria decided she and her family would be successful if they could learn how to be clever and inventive like the Americans and at the same time preserve the resourcefulness and tenacity of the Italians. They needed, somehow, to eliminate the follies of each race. She nodded, pleased with herself, resisting the temptation to kiss the garlic amulet around her neck . . .

The horse cart reached an embankment where the Lehigh River came into view, a roll of silver reflecting the rising moon. The women were singing "Il Mazzolin' di Fiori," an old folk tune. On the outskirts of the city a motor car puttered by, which made the horse buck. By the time things had settled down the women had stopped singing and the rare spell of serenity was broken.

In the yard behind the hotel four men were taking advantage of the mild weather to escape the fetid air of their berths by playing a game of *briscola* on a plank table by the light of an oil lamp. One of them was Claudio, who looked up from his cards as Maria approached.

"Salutation, Maria," he said. "How do you feel?"

Maria shrugged as she climbed the steep path, lacing her fingers in front of her to support her bloated stomach. She stopped, resting against the trunk of an old elm tree. "Not too bad, by the grace of God," she replied. She glanced toward the shed. "Is Pepe home?"

Claudio, grimacing at his hand of cards, shook his head. "Overtime."

Maria sighed. "I'd better start dinner."

Claudio threw in his hand. "Wait," he said. "I'll help you."

The other men exchanged sly looks. "What about the game?" one said.

"Who cares a rap?" said Claudio. "Look here, the girl's eight months heavy."

"Thanks, but I can handle it—"

"No, wait, I'm coming," he said, leaving the trio of his cronies grumbling, and speculating.

Inside the shed the air was filled with the smells of damp hay and animal urine. Still, it had been made fairly comfortable, thanks to Pepe's wizardry with scrap wood. He had made rude furniture and a food locker where Maria kept cured meats and fish and preserved edibles as well as fresh fruit, vegetables, grains and nuts. The pantry was fitted with a lock to keep out the animals, four-footed and otherwise, who might sniff out its existence. Maria fished amid her skirts for the key.

"What can I do to help?" Claudio asked.

"Go to the pump and fill the kettle," Maria said, taking cured fish and preserved tomatoes from the locker. By the time he returned she had already lit the fire. She took the heavy kettle from him and placed it over the wood stove.

"Now what?" he asked.

"Sit down and keep me company," she said in a mock-imperious voice as she sliced an onion into the kettle.

He sat on a pile of hay and lit a cheroot.

"Watch you don't start a fire."

He nodded, puffing away with a thoughtful air. "You hear what happened in Massachusetts? They arrested two Italian anarchists for murder. I read it in the Philadelphia newspaper." Claudio was proud of his ability to read "American," a skill he had picked up from a Milanese schoolmaster named Rinaldo whom he had met at the Society of Victor Emmanuel III. Rinaldo, a man of ambiguous sexual leanings, had taken a shine to the handsome well-built laborer.

"And who do they say they murdered?" Maria asked, feeling uneasy.

"Two payroll guards. The names were Nicola Sacco and Bartolomeo Vanzetti."

"The guards, they were Italian too?"

"No, this was the names of the anarchists." Claudio blew smoke through his nose like a dragon. "People say it's a frame-up. Prejudice. That's my way of thinking too."

"Prejudice about what?"

"Well, partly politics. These men were radicals. Americans don't like radicals."

"What's a radical?"

"You've got a lot to learn, girl."

"Teach me."

"A radical is . . . someone who's a revolutionary, wants to change the way things are . . ."

Maria frowned at the parsley she was mincing. She remembered Don Gabriele having her read a book that compared Garibaldi and America's George Washington. "I thought this country was started by radicals."

Claudio threw back his head and laughed. "That was a long time ago."

Maria, gesturing with the knife, waggled her head. "Sure, it's the same in Italy. When you sleep in the hut, you're a radical. You sleep in the palace, you're against radicals."

Claudio nodded vigorously. Maria was a smart one. What, he wondered, was she doing with his brother . . .

"What other kind of prejudice?" she was saying.

Claudio slammed a fist into the palm of his hand. "Many Americans think Italians are an inferior people."

Maria seemed truly puzzled. She understood class prejudice, but this was alien to her. "Then these people here know nothing about who we are."

"That's a fact," Claudio said, puffing like a chimney.

"Did they never hear of Julius Caesar?"

"Or Michelangelo?"

"Or Bonaparte?"

As she stirred the stew Maria looked determined. She'd show these Americans who was *inferior*. She was glad for this exchange with her brother-in-law.

As she waddled over to set the table Claudio clasped her wrist. "Here, let me do that," he said.

She thanked him and went back to the kettle. "What will they do to these anarchists?" she asked him.

Claudio shrugged as he put the plates on the table. "Probably put them in the electric chair."

Maria frowned over the bubbling fish stew. "What's that, for God's sake?"

"It's a killing thing invented by the Americans."

Maria shook her head. In this country the machine was like a god. It made things that gave life and took it away. The land of opportunity could be a dangerous place.

Pepe came home then, weary and in low spirits. Maria handed him a glass of bootleg wine, tousled his hair and shook her head. Poor Pepe, the life of a laborer was doubly hard for him. He was a craftsman made into a jackass.

"You stay for supper?" Pepe asked Claudio.

"If you invite me."

"Favor us," said Pepe formally.

"I'll cut the bread," Claudio said.

Maria smiled as she put the food on the table. She lit a candle, making the shed seem more festive. She might pretend that they were in a fine house. But the illusion was quickly gone when the lamb that shared their quarters padded over to chaw hay from the trough.

That night, after sleeping for a while in her straw bed, Maria suddenly was wide awake. She had no idea what time it was or why her eyes had abruptly opened. She found herself staring through the window at a moon that looked like a gold coin bearing the weathered outlines of an emperor's face. Lying still for a while, she soon heard the intermittent sound of water rushing. It wasn't raining. What could the sound be? She got out of bed to investigate.

The sky was black and minted with stars. Somewhere in the distance a rooster crowed, dawn was near. Maria's keen eyes took in the yard.

She saw a man standing by the pump throwing buckets of water over his head and washing himself. She recognized Claudio. And he was naked.

Maria quickly turned away from the window and leaned her back against the wall of the shed. Her mouth went dry as sawdust. In the moonlight his body had looked like a marble statue of Ares that she'd once seen in the National Museum at Naples, except that his muscles had rippled with life in the act of washing, and his genitals, as he soaped them, had dangled like a . . . a cluster of ripe fruit on a bower. She felt her cheeks burn in the darkness.

She bit her lower lip, then went back to the window for another look. His back was turned now. His balustrading shoulders surmounted a finely carved back, tapering waist and squarish, muscular, deeply cleft buttocks. He was washing his underarms.

After a few seconds she turned away again and stole back to the mattress of straw that she shared with Pepe Falcone. She still had not seen her husband naked. In fact he had not yet even touched her in a man-woman way. She supposed it was because of her condition. Claudio's body was very different from the priest's, as different as granite from limestone.

Maria tossed and turned. Under any circumstances her condition made it difficult to find a comfortable position for sleep. Now it was nearly impossible. She lay there, eyes wide open, and listened to the pulse of two heartbeats in one body.

Maria had had to stop working on the farm; it was early June and her time was near. So now she took in sewing and washing to earn money. The nest egg grew. One thing about America, there was plenty of work for people willing to bend their backs, callous their hands and, to a certain extent, kowtow to the bosses, all activities that were second nature to most southern Italian peasants. Maria was not afraid of hard work but she refused to bootlick. She realized her attitude might have lost her jobs cooking for some of the local German women, but she had her dignity. They were doing fine so far without bowing and scraping to anyone. They had plenty to eat and were able to save money each week. They even had a little for pleasure. One evening Pepe took her to a movie theater where they saw John Barrymore in a film called *The Test of Honor*. The girl from Miseno had been mesmerized by the images on the screen. On Saturday nights Claudio sometimes would brilliantine his hair, put on a boiled shirt and go dancing at the parish hall of the Moravian church. Seeing him all dandied up and looking like a film star did give her an unwelcome pang of jealousy. She would silently scold herself: such feelings were unbecoming in an expectant mother and faithful wife. Except she knew that while she was faithful she was also something less than a wife.

Claudio had even less patience than Maria for the arrogance of certain Americans, and he had a very short fuse. Once he came back from a church dance with his jacket torn and a livid bruise under his left eye. He had got into a scrape with a couple of local boys who vented their jealousy over his evident popularity with the girls by insulting Italians and questioning his masculinity.

"I got the best of them," Claudio said as Maria applied a cold compress to the shiner. "You betcha, they were spitting teeth all over the dance floor."

"That temper of yours will get you in deep trouble someday," she predicted.

"Am I supposed to take such insults lying down? Am I the sweet fennel they said I was?"

"No, but a real man knows the smart way to get even. You avenge yourself in secret, not in public." Maria must have been thinking of Don Guglielmo's stable.

Claudio grumbled as she continued to treat the wound, was not happy at being rebuked by a woman. Meanwhile Pepe sat smoking his pipe in the background, saying nothing.

The next day, as she sat in a chair, fingers laced over her stomach and carrying low, Maria sensed that the baby boy would come any day now, if not at any hour. Why was she so sure that it would be a boy? She was very tired, and soon she dozed off, dreaming of John Barrymore.

She was wakened by the sound of loud voices coming from the backyard. It was dusk and the men had returned from the steel mill. Among the booming voices she recognized Claudio's; among the quieter ones she made out Pepe's. As far as she could tell, the argument had something to do with working conditions at the mill and also the foreman, a man called Beinbrecher. She didn't pay close attention because she was flustered at having fallen asleep.

Pepe would be starved and she hadn't even started preparing supper.

"I'm sorry, Pepe, I fell asleep," Maria told him when he came inside. "Supper will be ready in a jiffy."

"That's okay," said her husband, sitting down and grunting as he pulled off his boots. "Girl in your condition shouldn't have to work so hard anyhow." He looked at his grimy hands. "I better wash up."

"You're going out to the pump in your stocking feet?"

He shrugged and went out. When he came back he said, "Wish I could hire servants for you like the fine ladies on the other side of the river. You're just as good as them. Better." He sat down and lit his pipe.

Maria was jostling bits of garlic spluttering in a frying pan. "Sure," she said. "Then I'd sit around all day eating caramels."

"Why not?"

Maria nodded toward the yard. "What was the commotion all about?"

"Oh, the boys were arguing about whether we should join a labor union. A fellow came around today, said he was from the American Federation of Labor. Beinbrecher tossed him out on his ear."

"Why? Was he one of those troublemakers? A Communist."

Pepe shrugged. "Nah, Beinbrecher's a lackey of the bosses. Claudio says the mine workers belong to a union and last year they went on strike and got a twenty-seven percent wage increase. Claudio was so mad I thought he was going to box the foreman's ears."

Maria crammed spaghetti into the boiling water. "I keep telling him to control his hot temper."

"Well, he did this time. But he told all the fellows he would like to have heard what the organizer had to say. He kept yelling about free speech and all that. Said that in the old country even jackasses didn't work a twelve-hour day."

"No, but the peasants worked fifteen hours," Maria said.

Pepe laughed. "That's the truth. Anyhow, the steel bosses have us by the balls, pardon the expression. We strike and they hire a bunch of new immigrants to take our place."

"Unless . . ."

"Unless what?"

"You appeal to the loyalty of the new immigrants."

"An empty belly has no loyalty," Pepe said.

"Then you show them it's good for them. You make them see the light."

Pepe smiled at this pregnant girl's idea of how to play American games of power. Still, he listened respectfully. Maria was smart. "And how do you make them see the light?"

Wiping her hands on her apron, she faced him, then opened the grid of the wood stove. "You lead them to the fire," she said solemnly.

Pepe bit the stem of the pipe. Maria and her talk was making him uneasy.

After supper and two glasses of wine Pepe fell asleep, leaving Maria thoughtful and alert. The unusual late afternoon nap made it impossible for her to turn in now. She sat by the window and gazed at the night sky. The hotel was dark and quiet. A breeze sighed through the leafy trees and the river water murmured below.

She was startled by a shooting star that streaked across the sky and fizzled out in the east. It was the first one she'd seen in America. Not long afterward she felt the first contraction. She would not sleep at all that night.

She went over and woke up Pepe.

The baby boy was born before daybreak. The hotel keeper's sister, a Calabrian, had served as midwife. After suckling for a long time the infant was swaddled in a linen blanket and laid in one of the troughs to sleep. As Maria also slept Pepe sat near the baby, stealing glances at the puckered, rosy face of the son of the priest Don Gabriele.

Later Maria smiled down at the tiny face after the infant had fed a second time.

"He looks like an angel," said Pepe.

Maria nodded vigorously as the baby's soft hand curled around her forefinger.

"He's not missing anything," Pepe added. "I counted all his parts."

Maria smiled at her husband. Her face was shiny but her eyes were tired. Wasn't she fortunate to have such a man by her side?

"I always wanted a son," Pepe said, caressing her hair and cheeks. "Thank you, Maria, for giving me one."

She took his rough hand and kissed it.

"What will you name him?" Pepe asked.

She glanced at the baby's face again, puzzling over his question.

"Ottavio?" Pepe suggested.

Maria thought about it, then shook her head. "No, this is a new country." No looking back.

"I got it—Woodrow Wilson," he said half-jokingly.

Maria made a tart face. "I can't even pronounce it," she said.

Pepe laughed. "What then? Come, we must name him something. After all, we don't want him to be a *niente nomen*."

Maria thought some time before her face lit up. "I know—*Angelo*! We will baptize him Angelo."

"Angelo Falcone," Pepe said, testing the name on his tongue. "Sounds fine. Very fine."

Maria looked at the baby again and repeated the name. "Angelo."

Pepe got ready to go to the mill. He would have liked to take the day off, but he was afraid the bosses would find a permanent replacement for him. The Falcones would need even more money now, but he brought extra cigars to hand out to the boys around the blast furnace.

Maria stayed by herself with the baby, constantly examining him. Every once in a while the Calabrian woman would look in to see if they were all right. The woman, Francesca Carletti, was a widow who had had her full share of heartache. Her first husband had died in the Great War, she said, and her second husband had died in a coal mine collapse. She had had three miscarriages and lost two children to childhood diseases in Reggio. So as midwife and mother she often had stood with the souls of children at the portals of life and death. She was regarded by her neighbors as a wise woman, of sorts.

"Did you see the shooting star last night?" she asked Maria on one of her visits.

The new mother's mouth fell open. "Why, yes . . ." she said.

Francesca Carletti nodded. "I saw it too. Believe me, it means your son is marked for great things."

Maria had heard this kind of mumbo-jumbo before and was determined to make these omens and amulets things of the past. Still, deep down, she wanted to believe this prediction. Maybe she even did . . .

Suddenly the woman dug into her pocket. "I have a gift for the baby," she said, handing over to Maria a set of rosary beads that seemed to be gold-plated.

Maria shook her head. "Signora, I can't accept this."

"Do you wish to offend me?"

Maria shook her head again, slowly.

"*Beh*," Francesca Carletti said, folding her arms in a gesture of satisfaction.

Later, when the woman had gone, Maria sat by the makeshift crib studying the sleeping baby's features. Could she see on his face the stamp of her once beloved priest? Although the baby, who had dark fuzz on his head, reminded her mainly of her own father, his grandfather, she saw a certain something in the chemistry of the newborn's face that she thought reflected his physical link to Don Gabriele. She took the gold-plated beads and wrapped them around his tiny hand. She gazed at him for a long long time . . .

Claudio, hair slicked back and center-parted, stood as godfather at the baptismal font. In his rare spare hours Pepe carved models of trains and cars and animals for the baby. And Maria soon went back to work harvesting green beans on the New Jersey farm. Pooling resources, Pepe, Maria and Claudio rented a small but airy apartment in a private house nearby, on the south bank of the Lehigh. Finally, they would live like human beings instead of animals.

The Falcones were improving—with, for Maria, one exception. The baby was already three months old and Pepe Falcone *still* had not touched her. Was something wrong with her? Was something wrong with him?

In Miseno there was a man the villagers would whisper about behind their hands. He dressed in colorful clothing and walked in a funny mincing way. But the carpenter didn't behave like that. Still, who could tell about such things?

Worse, maybe she was at fault. One day after she had bathed, Maria stood in front of a full-length mirror and took stock of herself. She could tell from the way the men in town looked at her that she had the kind of body that sparked their desire. Her breasts were large but not ponderous. They stood high and firm on her body. Her waist had already shrunk to its normal form. Her hips billowed in a round womanly way. Her legs, though not very long, were sturdy and shapely, her complexion, as always, near-flawless. Her eyes and hair shone with health. The sliced fig of her sex puckered prettily. She was not ashamed to think it.

She whirled, posed, bent slightly at the waist, studied her image from various angles and in various attitudes. No, nothing wrong with her. Nothing at all.

She sat down heavily on the bed. She and the baby slept in a real bed now, not on straw or pebbles. But Pepe slept on a campaign cot over by the bay window. With old-country modesty they dressed and undressed behind a screen. But often, as now, she had wanted to display her body to him. To *someone*!

Maria had not been to confession since she gave herself to Don Gabriele . . . she could not picture herself telling her sins to the pink-cheeked American curate who had baptized Angelo. Well, she would just have to suffer from a bad conscience.

Living in the same apartment with Claudio didn't help matters. Although his behavior had always been proper, Maria was a woman, and she could sense the desire that flowed between him and her. But wife and brother, both would rather cut off their hands than betray Pepe.

Finally, though, Maria reached the end of her rope and decided to take the bull by the horns, so to speak. It was a night when the baby was fast asleep and Pepe was already dressed in his nightshirt, sitting on the cot and whittling a toy. The oil lamp on the night table was turned low; a half-moon festooning the sky shimmered in the river below. Maria stood naked behind the screen, about to tug a nightgown over her head. Instead she let it drop to the floor.

She stepped out from behind the screen. Her erect nipples rose and fell in the moonlight as she breathed heavily. For a girl of her background to parade herself like this, even before her lawful husband, was unusual. Even her encounter with the priest had been quick and covert rather than bold. She stood there now motionless and silent in front of Pepe, waiting for him to react.

The hands that held the knife and wood carving suddenly hung limply at his side. He said nothing, showed no sign of passion or reproach.

Maria broke the silence. "Don't you like what you see, Pepe?"

"Yes . . ."

"Don't you want to touch me?" she said, taking two steps closer to the cot.

"Yes . . ."

She sat down beside him. "Why don't you share my bed tonight, Pepe? My body is back to normal now."

Pepe's answer was to bury his face in his hands. His shoulders shook.

Which upset and baffled Maria. She wanted to put her arms around him to try to comfort him, but somehow her nakedness made her reluctant to do that.

"Listen, Pepe, you must tell me what the matter is. As your wife I have the right to know."

Slowly he raised his head. His cheeks were blotchy, his eyes red-rimmed. "I should have told you," he said. "It was very wrong of me not to but I was afraid."

"Told me *what*? Tell me now."

And finally Pepe told her what had happened to him crossing the Piave facing Austrian guns in the campaign of Vittorio Veneto.

Maria's face was white marble in the moonlight, cold, immobile. Also speechless as she got up and put on the nightgown.

Pepe buried his face in his hands again. "Words can't say how sorry I am, Maria. I won't blame you if you decide to leave me. You could go to the Church and have the marriage annulled."

Her face softened at that. She sat down beside him again and took his hand. "Look here, Pepe, I won't leave you. You saved my life. You brought me to this country. You gave my child a name. I owe you everything . . . but I don't understand why you wanted me. I mean, under these circumstances our marriage is . . ." She didn't need to finish. Their marriage was not a marriage.

"I love you, Maria. I lost my manhood but my heart is whole. A man needs a woman for more than just *that*."

"But such an arrangement must be torture for you."

"The thought of living without you—that is the torture."

He sensed what she was thinking. "But what about you, what you suffer, eh? You're a normal healthy girl with normal desires. I don't expect you to live like a nun."

"That's not important," she said, knowing it was a lie as she said it.

"I won't blame you if you want to take lovers. I only ask you to do it . . . discreetly."

"I wouldn't think of doing that." What else could she say?

"We'll see," he said, dropping the subject. He hesitated, then: "Promise me you won't be embarrassed if I say something else."

"Embarrassed? After all, I'm a farm girl."

His voice became a whisper. "Look here, there are different ways a man can give pleasure to a woman."

And finally the farm girl blushed.

"Let me do it for you," he said.

"Please, Pepe, such things, they're unnatural."

"No act is unnatural when performed out of love. Please let me."

"I . . . I can't."

"Please. It would make me very happy, to help you . . ."

She was silent, not able to say yes, not wanting to say no.

He took her signal, gently raising the hem of her nightgown. She did not stop him.

Although Maria's breasts brimmed with milk, baby Angelo seemed pale and listless. Francesca Carletti, whom Maria came to view as a sort of good version of Donna Carmela, prescribed beer and old-world potions. Maria wanted to take the baby to the doctor but she hesitated because of the cost, and when the child's condition improved the matter was dropped.

Baby Angelo was sweet-natured and intelligent. He seemed to enjoy lying on the lawn in front of the house and gurgling at the birds. He was always smiling at strangers when his mother took him for walks in the carriage. Indeed, Maria started calling him Saint Francis of Assisi.

In October Maria got harvesting jobs and often left the baby in Francesca Carletti's care. Meanwhile, she was swiftly becoming Americanized. She had her hair bobbed and began wearing traces of lipstick. She learned "American" words and phrases like "jim-dandy," "kiddo," "speakeasy" and "the Kaiser's *geburtstsag*," which was what the workers at the steel mill called payday. Her spirits were high, and even the onset of cooler weather and the prospect of facing the winter couldn't dampen them. The apartment was furnished now with both a wood fireplace and oil stove. The Falcones had enough money to eat well, drink bootleg wine with dinner, even go to the movies once a month. In short, the Falcones were tasting the sweet plum of previously unknown prosperity.

Claudio, however, was often in a black mood. Pepe would clap his brother on the shoulder and say, "Chin up, kid. I know what you need, a nice girl, marriage."

Claudio would scoff at this. "That's the last thing I need, a halter around my neck. Besides, these American women are too bossy."

"So?" Pepe replied one day. "Find yourself a nice Italian woman."

Maria, who was ironing clothes and pretending not to listen, was all ears.

"Bah," Claudio said, "the ones around here are more American than the Americans. Someday I'll make a trip to Italy to pick a wife."

"Well, you better hurry," his brother told him. "After all, you're pushing thirty."

"I got plenty of time," Claudio said. "Besides, why should I buy the nanny goat when I get the milk and cheese for free?"

Did he really say that? Maria's cheeks burned. The serpent had entered the garden. Although who could say it was not invited . . . ?

Claudio's immediate problem came from trouble at the plant. Beinbrecher, envious of his popularity with the men, had been giving him a hard time, docking his pay when he showed up two minutes late, assigning him the dirtiest most back-breaking jobs at every opportunity. Claudio often felt like breaking the swine's neck and might have, except Beinbrecher carried a Colt .45 and his henchmen carried Winchesters. Claudio could only grumble and wait, shoveling coke and hatred into the mouth of the blast furnace.

Maria, who had heard secondhand the stories of Claudio's troubles, worried that he would explode and do something foolish. He was a firebrand, a hothead. Yet she also admired him. At least he didn't have the passivity that for so long had condemned his ancestors to lives of servitude.

Pepe, on the other hand, though not exactly passive (how could you call someone passive who was always making something— bread, wine, tables, chairs?), was docile as a lamb. It was hard for Maria to believe that they had sprung from the same womb.

Often her glance would pass back and forth between them: Pepe nibbling his tongue as he sanded a wooden cabriole chair leg; Claudio glowering over a page of newspaper as he chewed a cigar butt.

She had not forgotten what Pepe had told her, that if she wanted to take a lover he would look the other way.

It came as no surprise to Maria when the hostility festering between Claudio and the foreman finally erupted.

A Lutheran minister, the Reverend Klaus Mittag, was a champion of workers' rights in the local steel mills. A member of the Interchurch World Movement, the clergyman often thundered from the pulpit against the steel directors, branding them "unscrupulous and unchristian pharisees who put profit before piety, steel production before the salvation of souls." He criticized the twelve-hour day, which, he contended, impaired workers' health and destroyed family life, "the cornerstone of Christian vitality." He distributed to parishioners who worked in the mills copies of an Interchurch report condemning the steel industry.

One copy found its way into Claudio's hands. As he tried to decipher the big words one day at lunch, Beinbrecher walked by.

"I didn't know wops could read," the foreman said. "Thought you only looked at dirty pictures."

Claudio looked up. Beinbrecher stood there with his hands on his hips, his rosy toper's nose redder than usual.

Claudio tried to ignore the comment and went on reading.

"Give it here," demanded Beinbrecher, extending his hand.

Claudio looked up again. "It belongs to me. Let me eat my lunch in peace."

"Listen, dago, I'm not gonna ask yuh twice."

Blood flooded Claudio's face, but he handed over the document.

The foreman scanned the report. "What the hell are you, Falcone, some kind of bolshie?"

"It's a free country, I can read what I want."

The foreman rolled the document into a tube and patted it against his open hand. "I been looking for an excuse to get you canned. This is just the ticket. I'm showing this to the boss."

Claudio got to his feet, fists balled. "I don't want trouble with you, Beinbrecher—"

The foreman laughed. "I'll bet you don't."

"Just give the papers back to me," Claudio said in an even tone.

"I told yuh, I'm showing them to the boss."

"Hey, it's no crime to read something. It's a free country, no?" he repeated.

"Yeah, and it'll stay free if we get rid of all you goddamn dago anarchists."

"Is Sam Gompers an anarchist?"

"He's a Jew, ain't he? I rest my case."

As Beinbrecher turned to go Claudio grabbed him by the arm.

"Get your paws offa me," Beinbrecher said, attracting the attention of other men in the yard. The foreman's palm rested on the butt of the revolver in the holster at his hip.

Claudio let him go but his eyes were hard. "Be a good fellow, eh? Give back the papers."

"You gonna make me?"

"Yes."

"That's a hot one. A daffodil like you?"

Claudio seemed puzzled. "Daffodil? What's that?"

"Don't play dumb, Falcone. Everybody knows about you and Rinaldo, that queer teacher at the Italian club—"

Before the portly Beinbrecher could get the pistol halfway out of the holster the blow had fallen, landing with the force of a hammer on the foreman's cheek, severing flesh and crushing bone. Staggering and cursing, he pointed the weapon.

Claudio lunged and after a struggle managed to get the pistol from Beinbrecher.

The foreman sat on the concrete floor, blood streaming down his face.

"Come on," said Claudio after catching his breath, holding the pistol limply at his side. "I'll take you to the infirmary."

Beinbrecher reacted by picking up a near-by shovel and rushing at Claudio with a roar.

Claudio fired. The fat foreman folded to the floor. The shot had resounded on both banks of the Lehigh River. And for the Falcones way beyond.

Maria Falcone had never laid eyes on the foreman Beinbrecher but she knew him. Oh, yes, she knew him. He was Il Spagnuolo and the rapist Lorenzo Mazzo. He was Don Virgilio and Don Guglielmo. He was every rotten tyrant and crawling tarantula put on earth to sting and torment the miserable creatures of Campania wherever they went. He was the hydra who haunted their existences. As soon as you cut off his head he grew back another.

"Get the baby ready, Maria," Pepe said solemnly. "We must get out of here. I'll pack up everything we'll need. *Quickly*, girl."

Maria began to do as she was told.

"Where's Claudio?" Maria asked, rummaging in a dresser drawer.

"Hiding in the Catholic Church. We meet him there at nightfall. It's arranged."

The baby squalled as Maria picked him up from the crib and said, "Why does Claudio have to run? He shot in self-defense, there were witnesses . . ."

"Yes, but the whole thing started when he socked Beinbrecher. They'll say Claudio started it."

"He was . . . was provoked!"

Pepe shook his head. "It's no use, Maria. Beinbrecher was a

German just like all the big shots around here. What chance does Claudio have? The men in those cutaway coats will measure a rope for him for sure."

"Excuse me, but why do *we* run away too?"

"He's my brother. We must stay together as a family."

Maria nodded, knowing the answer before she heard it, unbuttoning her blouse to suckle the baby and keep him quiet. Family was all important. It was the same everywhere. Especially for immigrants. Also, she told herself, she didn't want to say good-by to Claudio. She looked around at the tidy apartment, the first place she'd lived that didn't smell of animal waste and cooking oil.

Pepe embraced her. "Don't worry, dear girl. We'll come through this too." He looked down lovingly at the priest's son clamped to his mother's breast.

A gust of wind coming off the river blew through the open window, ruffling Maria's unpinned hair. Abruptly she tore the garlic amulet from her neck and threw it out the window. The hell with it. You made your own life or you died.

The teacher Rinaldo had arranged for the Falcones to ride in the canvas-covered van of a surplus army truck hauling apples to New York City, where they would try to lose themselves among the masses of immigrants in lower Manhattan. The teacher also had given them a letter of introduction to a Signor Malatesta, a *paesano* from Campania who would see to their needs, for a fee. He was, of course, a *padrone*, the kind of broker in human flesh that up to now they had managed to avoid. Peering through an opening in the canvas top, Maria gazed at the star-sprinkled night sky passing over her as the truck went toward the church to pick up Claudio.

The driver stopped the truck in front of the Catholic Church, a building of craggy stone and splintered wood. The silencing of the motor's cough made Maria's pulse race. She heard nothing but her own and Pepe's shallow breathing; the very stillness upset them. But soon Claudio had climbed into the van and was embracing his brother and sister-in-law. The driver, a fat man with kind eyes, put his forefinger to his lips before clambering into the cab.

As the truck turned onto the surfaced road that led from Allentown to Phillipsburg, Maria figured that if all went well they soon would be safely across the state line in New Jersey.

Not so soon.

Before crossing the bridge the driver had to stop for gas at one of the few Standard Oil Company filling stations on the route to New York City. When Maria peeked out of the van she saw signs nailed to trees advertising Coca-Cola, ice cream, hot dogs and coffee. She saw the driver lumbering over to the shed to rouse the sleeping attendant—then she heard a sound that froze her . . . the puttering of a motorcycle.

A state policeman had stopped his vehicle right in front of the gas pump. He hopped off and stood with his hands on his hips, looking around. He wore a high-necked military uniform and a brush mustache. The star pinned to the flap of his breast pocket gleamed in the twilight. A pistol was holstered at his hip.

Maria reached out and took hold of her husband's clammy hand. Claudio's face was taut as a drumskin.

The policeman caught sight of the driver and walked over to him. For a while the two talked in tones too low for the trio in the van to overhear, and as they spoke the policeman and the driver inched closer to the truck.

Claudio reached for a tire iron in the corner of the van.

Suddenly the driver laughed and clapped the policeman on the back. They talked for a long while before the policeman touched the brim of his cap, climbed back on the motorcycle and drove off.

The driver's moon face appeared smiling at the back of the van. "Looking for rumrunners," he said. "Wanted to search the van."

"How did you convince him to leave?" Pepe asked.

The driver chuckled, glancing at the sky. "You folks must be travelin' under a lucky star. We got to talkin', turns out his mother's my second cousin."

Family again. It counted for more than all her amulets. More than anything.

It was midnight by the time the truck hit the cobblestones of the Washington Market area of Manhattan and Pepe paid off the driver, who directed them to a cheap hotel on Chambers Street. In the morning they would seek out Malatesta in the Italian district, a short walk away, the hotel clerk said.

Next morning they went to pay their respects to Antonio Malatesta, also known as *Il Colonnello* because of some vague military background. Following the directions of the hotel clerk, they walked east on Chambers Street to Lafayette Street, where they turned north toward Grand Street, the heart of the Italian ghetto. As they walked, the fugitives . . . that's what they were, but they had tried not to think about it . . . gaped at such sights as the Woolworth Building soaring sixty stories above Broadway and at the streams of office workers disgorged from a hole in the ground that served as the subway terminal at City Hall Park. Down the wide street puttered more motor cars than Maria had thought existed in the whole world. Cradling the baby Angelo in her arms, trying to protect him against a stinging wind that came off the river, Maria turned her head first in one direction, then another. What a place! What a contrast to Bethlehem and Miseno! Such a city seemed to smell of danger, and great possibilities.

On the way the Falcones passed several policemen, reminding them of what they were, but the officers ignored them.

Malatesta's office was above a bank on the second floor of a building on the corner of Grand and Mulberry. To Maria's surprise he was a good-looking man with a kindly face, curly red hair and green eyes. He greeted them warmly, chucked the baby under the chin and showed Maria to a comfortable chair. Before getting down to business he served the newcomers cups of espresso and exchanged pleasantries with them, reminiscing about the old country and expressing concern about the drift of politics in Italy. He told them that he was born in Naples proper and implied without saying it outright that his father and grandfather had been honored members of The Society.

Maria's body became tense in the chair. Any reference, veiled or direct, to the Camorra was not likely to produce confidence or ease in her. Still, she was inclined to give this man the benefit of the doubt. Besides, they had no choice. With his fair hair, boiled shirt and cutaway coat Malatesta resembled more than anything an American banker or businessman. He might turn out to be an exception to the rule. Involuntarily Maria's hand went to her throat, reaching for the garlic amulet that she had thrown away. She quickly put her hand in her lap, irritated with herself.

The padrone made no direct mention of the trouble that had brought the Falcones to his doorstep. "Good people, blood is thicker than water. We paesani must stick together if we want to survive in the forests of America where we are like lambs among wolves. One hand washes the other, etcetera, etcetera."

Maria noted that the man spouted clichés like the lion's head spouted water in the village square. She noted too that he kept sending glances in her direction, although he pretended to be mainly addressing the menfolk. She also thought she detected a certain heat behind the glances. Maybe she was imagining things. Maybe.

When Angelo began to fuss and kick, Maria began to undo her blouse, then seeing Malatesta's look, she got up and stood in a corner of the room breast-feeding her baby with her back to the men. The walls, she noted, were adorned with portraits of various members of the House of Savoy.

"They need men to work on the BMT, the subway," the *padrone* was saying as he offered Pepe and Claudio cheroots to smoke with coffee. "I got good connections with the supervisor of the work gangs. Believe me, you came to the right place." He added that Pepe's carpentry skills qualified him as a timberman and that Claudio's obvious physical strength at least assured him a spot as a laborer.

Maria, looking down at the baby at her breast, liked what she was hearing. Soon Angelo would need solid food and fruit juices. Coal and oil had to be purchased for the stove and lamps, and warm clothes were required for the harsh winter. The jobs would help provide these things. A future bishop needed a good start in life, and Maria too was willing to sweat blood to see that he got it.

Pepe blew out a gust of cigar smoke. "How much money we make?" he asked.

"Eighteen dollars a week," Malatesta said.

"That's all?" from Claudio.

"Listen, times are bad. Haven't you heard about the recession?"

"What's that?" said Claudio.

"The business slowdown," said Malatesta, clucking his tongue.

"It's been very bad since the end of the war. But now the country just elected a new president—Mr. Warren Harding. He's a Republican. He'll fix things up just like that." He snapped his fingers.

"What will he do?" asked Pepe. "Start another war?"

"I thought America was already a republic," said Claudio, scratching his head.

"You're good fellows," the padrone said with a condescending flourish of his hand, "but such matters are above your heads. Count yourselves lucky to find work, eh?"

Pepe didn't seem to be offended, but Claudio's frown showed he took offense. He bit his tongue, though. His temper had gotten them in enough trouble.

Maria had been eavesdropping. Twice eighteen made thirty-six dollars a week. She was confident she could contribute to the household strongbox by washing and sewing. Of course, she had little or no idea of how expensive it might be to live in New York City as compared to Bethlehem. But she was happy at their prospects—

Until Malatesta's next remark. "Of course, you will have to pay me a certain tribute. I have to oil the palms of a lot of people along the line." His pleasant mouth wasn't so pleasant now. "And I have to live too."

"How much?" said Claudio.

"Consider it a tax," Malatesta said, still smiling. "All citizens must pay taxes. You know what they say about death and taxes. But maybe you haven't heard this American expression."

Maria turned to face the padrone. Had the hydra grown another head already? Wherever they went the tentacles curled, grasping *tangenti*. Were they sharecroppers again, digging subways instead of tomatoes and corn?

"How much?" repeated Claudio.

The man's smile dissolved. "I'm not sure I like your tone."

Pepe jabbed his brother with an elbow, and Claudio looked down at the pine floor. "Forgive me, Colonel, I meant no disrespect." The son-of-a-bitch.

"We'll say no more about it," the *padrone* told him, sniffing a carnation in his lapel. "I take twenty-five percent. You won't have to worry about paying me. It comes out of your envelope automat-

ically. There, you see? That's not so bad, is it? All things considered?"

Maria resisted telling what she thought. She was good at figures.
That came to almost ten dollars. And he thought that was not bad?
Well, they had no choice. They would just have to tighten their
belts.

Malatesta went on: "Of course, in return you receive my full
protection. And the police will not come around asking questions
or poking their noses into your documents." He rubbed his thumb
over his fingers, indicating that the police were on his payroll.
"Why, you're getting a real bargain."

He had a point, Maria thought. At least they wouldn't have to
live as fugitives, afraid of their own shadows. That was worth something, wasn't it?

Maria buttoned her blouse and rejoined the men. "Please, sir,"
she asked, "where will we live, with all due respect?"

Malatesta looked at her fondly. "Ah, the mother partridge, always thinking of the nest. Right you are, right you are."

Maria said nothing, continuing to look directly into his eyes.

He patted her hand. "Don't you bother your pretty head, eh? I
will provide an apartment for you too. At a modest rent."

"Where?" asked Maria, withdrawing her hand.

"Right here in the neighborhood, of course. On Mulberry
Street where our fellow Neapolitans have settled. You will feel right
at home."

Maria made a face. She felt no special affection for her compatriots and their ways, but she supposed it would be helpful to speak
the familiar language and set the table with familiar food and drink.
And maybe she could gain an advantage for the family by using
Malatesta's obvious interest in her. "Please, sir," she said, "what
rent will you charge?"

"A modest rent. We'll discuss the particulars once you are settled."

"How many rooms?"

"Three big rooms. And the hallways have electric wiring."

"Colonel Malatesta, with respect," she said, "could you give us
some notion of the sum? I must manage the household expenses."
She looked down at the baby.

"Well," he said, "for this kind of apartment the usual rent is ten dollars a month."

Maria looked horrified. As the man put more of his cards on the table their potential income was shrinking.

Malatesta added quickly in a sugary tone, "Don't look so downhearted, little lady. The colonel has a soft spot for you people. I will give you a discount. Ah, someday this bleeding heart of mine will bring me to ruin."

Give him some soft soap, Maria told herself. "They say that generosity is the mark of a noble spirit. God bless you, Colonel."

"If I may ask," said Pepe, "how much rent will we pay?"

But Malatesta still dodged the question. "We'll see, we'll see."

No longer able to control himself, Claudio began to grumble, and got a sharp look from the padrone. "Young man," he said, "you could learn some lessons from your wife here."

A moment of silence before Pepe said, "Excuse me, Colonel, but Maria is *my* wife."

Malatesta could not have received more welcome news.

They called it Mulberry Street, but where Maria came from the *mora del gelso* had a sweet smell, not a foul one like this. Truly the place sparked memories of the sunless alleys of Naples, though the buildings were made of brick and wood instead of stone and tufa, and the horse carts here were outnumbered by motor vehicles with horns like bassoons out of tune. Still, the flags of hanging laundry fluttered in the wind and the shoeshine boys gesticulated like orating senators in the piebald street.

This neighborhood would be their world for God knew how long. Maria took in the sight of the buildings webbed with iron fire escapes, the pushcarts thronging the cobbled streets, women still wearing layers of peasant clothing and balancing outsized cartons on their heads like worker ants, front stoops crowded with people even in November, chestnut peddlers and ragmen huckstering and trading, *cafoni* idling in front of taverns and candy stores, delivery wagons weaving through traffic, a crazyquilt of people and things merging the spirit of the old country with the new.

The apartment was located in the rear of the top floor of a four-story brick tenement, its three rooms arranged "railroad" style, one following the other. The front door opened to a kitchen with a porcelain bathtub with claw feet, coal stove, sink with cold running water and a window leading to an air shaft. The first two rooms were dark but the back room, which Maria immediately saw as a bedroom for herself, Pepe and the baby, had three windows facing west and overlooking a sunny back alley. Maria was very pleased that the apartment included a real toilet in the hallway, shared by the other top-floor tenants. The wood floors were bare and creaky and the paint on the walls and ceilings was blotched and blistered. But elbow grease would take care of that, Maria thought. The long climb up to the apartment was compensated by having use of the tar-paper roof, where Maria planned to exercise her green thumb, grow tomatoes, herbs and maybe even a grapevine. It was no palace, but it would do for now. Malatesta had also arranged for Maria to get piecework, sewing garments and making lace at home and avoiding joining the union.

"Malatesta says you can buy an icebox on the Bowery, just a couple of blocks from here," Maria told her husband.

Claudio smirked at his brother. "Look how you let her boss you around."

Pepe laughed. "A wise man once said, 'From the moment a woman becomes your equal, she becomes your master.'"

Maria laughed too but her eyes were not laughing. The realization was dawning that she probably had more intelligence and guts than both of them. If they were to prosper, and more important, if her son were to thrive in America, she would have to be the one to do it.

But it was rough going. Malatesta got payment for "services" in advance. He had reduced the rent to eight dollars a month but it was still hard to make ends meet; the cost of coal, ice, oil and food were very high in the city. The waking hours of all three Falcones were consumed by labor. Pepe built furniture for the apartment in a workshop he created by converting part of the main room that already served as a kitchen and living area. In spite of his bravado, Claudio pitched in to help with the shopping and housework. Maria, of course, did all the cooking and most of the cleaning and washing as well as taking care of the baby and sewing piecework until her fingers ached and her eyes were strained. They celebrated their first Christmas together in America with a modest dinner of chestnut ravioli and muscatel.

But the baby again seemed unwell, vacillating between crankiness and listlessness, and was slow to begin crawling. In the new year Maria took Angelo to a Sicilian doctor on Spring Street who diagnosed anemia and prescribed doses of medicine and liver that put a major strain on the family finances.

Meanwhile Malatesta, his red hair brilliantined and his buttonhole everlastingly adorned with a fresh carnation, would come around once a month to collect the rent and more often would make unannounced visits to Maria on some pretext or another when the men weren't around.

Did he take her for the village idiot? Maria knew what he was sniffing around for.

"I'm sorry to hear that the child is sick," Malatesta said on one of his unwelcome visits. He looked at her bosom. "Are you still breast-feeding?"

Maria, stirring a pot on the stove, looked down her nose at the man as he sat toying with his demitasse. "With all due respect, Colonel, why do you want to know?"

He kissed his fingers. "Ah, the lucky little fellow!"

Maria hesitated to slap his face and show him the door as decorum dictated. She was a realist . . . he had too much power over them. Look what had happened to her parents for going against the rules of power in the name of dignity and honor. Those qualities now rotted with them in unmarked graves. No, Maria had learned a lesson consummated in the ashes of Don Guglielmo's stable. She would bide her time, play by the rules in the new world.

But she still couldn't help stinging the pomaded padrone with her tart tongue. "Thanks for the compliment, Colonel. The next time I see your wife in church I'll tell her what a cavalier you are."

The coffee cup clattered as he mumbled something, then, recovering his composure, said, "Sharp as a tack, you are. To me intelligence makes a woman even more desirable."

Maria continued stirring the pot. "So go chase the schoolteacher. She lives just down the street."

Malatesta laughed and finished his coffee.

When he was gone Maria sat at the kitchen table and took stock. Surely the neighbors had noticed Malatesta's unchaperoned visits. What would she do when the tongues started wagging? And how long could she hold him off with verbal barbs?

In late March, when she thought that no more frosts would come, Maria started work on her rooftop garden. Since the roof got plenty of sunlight she planned to grow tomatoes, sage, parsley, basil, cucumbers, radishes, beans, squash and maybe even spinach and peas. She would also experiment with growing Concord and Seneca grapes, which would take a few years to bear fruit.

The seeds, sun, water and working in the earth sparked memories of her homeland . . . and the priest. Her girlhood had ended the day she realized that she was pregnant some eighteen months earlier. It felt like a century had passed. She frowned as she planted seedlings of radishes. She didn't like to live in the past. But her work in the present, with the earth, seemed to bring her womanly desires to the surface. Malatesta's overtures, unwelcome as they were, stimulated her too. And Pepe's way of giving her pleasure just did not satisfy. She was only human, she told herself. Living in such close quarters with her brother-in-law added to the explosive mix.

Claudio slept on a cot in the room between the bedroom and the kitchen and, since the men worked nights and slept days, Maria often had to pass through Claudio's room while he was sleeping.

One morning that spring on her way to the kitchen she allowed herself to look at him and saw that he had kicked off the sheets, exposing the lower half of his body. He was dead asleep, but his penis was wide awake. Maria tried to shrug off the incident, but it had its long-term effect.

She was a normal woman, that was all. But she wondered about these Americans. America was puritan, they said, but sex was everywhere. The magazine and billboard advertisements for hosiery actually showed women in their undergarments. Occasionally Maria would splurge and spend five cents for a copy of *La Domenica Illustrata*, and often couldn't believe her eyes. What they *showed*, even in a magazine for Italian immigrants. And the movies, they were full of men and women kissing, naked slave girls, half-dressed men. Women *smoked* in public, powdered their knees and danced to music called jazz. At the bakery on Grand Street she overheard married women make naughty comments about an Italian movie actor named Rudolph Valentino who was very popular after appearing in a film called *The Four Horsemen of the Apocalypse.*

Meanwhile, the perfumed padrone continued to show up without being invited and make his verbal advances. The day would come, she suspected, when he would try physical ones.

It happened on a mild night in early May. The men had gone to work, the baby was asleep and Maria was washing dishes in the sink.

A series of knocks came at the door. She wiped her hands on her apron. Of course, she knew who it was. He always gave three short taps followed by another one, as if they were illicit lovers and had some prearranged signal. Besides, she could smell his cologne three blocks away. She frowned at the paint-blistered door—the man had some gall!

"Who is it?"

"Antonio."

"What do you want, Colonel?" What excuse would he have this time?

"I have to read the gas meter."

"You read it last week."

"I have to read it again. For charity, Mrs. Falcone, open the door."

She turned the knob.

He smiled in an attempt to look winning. It came out lecherous. "Let me add, my dear girl, you make the best coffee of all my tenants."

Soon he was sipping espresso as she tried to make it plain that he was unwelcome, turning her back to him and continuing to wash dishes. Not put off, he chattered on and on.

Finally: "Have you forgotten the gas meter?"

He waved his hand. "Plenty of time for that. As they say in American, I want to rest my dogs."

Maria cursed under her breath. Soon she had dried the dishes, and as she was bending over to stack them in the cupboard under the sink Malatesta reached out and squeezed her bottom. "Who could resist?" he said in all innocence.

Maria smacked him in the face so hard her hand stung.

A glint of menace came into his eyes, but then he shrugged and said, "You pack a wallop, girl."

"Keep your hands to yourself and on your wife," she said.

"Ah, if my wife only had an ass like yours—"

"How dare you speak to me that way?" She pointed to the door. "You leave."

Malatesta lounged in the chair. "I haven't finished my coffee."

"I said leave," she insisted.

"Don't play-act with me, girl."

"What do you mean, play-act?"

"The pure young wife . . ." He took a sip of coffee. "Who keeps a harem of two brothers."

"And what are you saying?"

"*La sultana!*" He looked around at the furniture that Pepe had built. "The old man is pretty handy, eh? Tell me, what about the younger brother? What's his special talent?"

She tried to slap him again but he grabbed her by the wrist, pulled her against him and pressed his lips to her mouth. She broke free and spit on the floor.

Malatesta stood still for a moment, then picked up his straw boater. "Well then, I'll be going," he said.

"So soon?" she said, sarcasm dripping.

He smiled. "I'll be back, dear girl."

"Don't hurry, eh? My compliments to the *missus.*"

He stopped at the door and turned to face her. "Listen, I'm not greedy. I want only a small piece of the goods."

"When mules fly," she said, resisting the impulse to add, over my dead body. Her mother's fate had cured her of the notion of using extreme measures to preserve her honor.

He put on his hat, tilting it at what he considered a rakish angle. "My dear, I'm not a subtle man so I'll give it to you straight. Let me remind you that one word from me and the Falcones are unemployed and out on the street. So you better try to be nice to me."

"Have you no pride?" was the best she could do.

"Absolutely none, in this."

"We can find work. And a place to live."

"Yes? Well, don't forget to leave a forwarding address so the Pennsylvania officials will know where to bring the extradition warrant."

He tipped his hat and left.

Maria leaned against the door and took shallow breaths. She had no doubt he would carry out the threat. Claudio might go to jail or even to the gallows. They would be in the street. From the bedroom came the sound of baby Angelo crying . . .

What could she do? Die like her mother? Sacrifice the health of her son to her honor? Destroy her husband's only brother to preserve a virtue she had already lost to a sinful priest?

Soon after that night in early May, Colonel Malatesta's straw hat was pegged to the clothes tree in Maria Falcone's bedroom.

Afterward Maria took a long bath in the kitchen to wash away his musk from her body. Later as she sewed pillow lace she felt contorted by a mix of emotions. She hated him. Did she hate herself too? To make matters worse, he was not repulsive and was a good lover. The water snake was a complicated evil thing. The heads he grew were not always so loathsome on the surface.

Hour after hour, day after day she spent tatting floral patterns and trying to think of a way out of her predicament. She would not, she told herself, be indefinitely made a victim by Malatesta or anybody else.

Meanwhile, he came to her bed about once a week.

Pepe did not suspect the truth but he sensed something was wrong. "You look like a hen about to hatch an egg," he told her one afternoon in the kitchen, drinking coffee while Maria was sewing. "What are you thinking about?"

"How hot it is today," she said, mopping her brow with a lace handkerchief.

"You think it's hot here? You should feel what it's like in the subway tunnel we're digging. I tell you, it's the ninth circle of inferno."

Angelo, also feeling the heat, toddled into the room and rested his face on Pepe's knee. In Miseno the sea breezes almost always had offset the temperatures, and the months in Pennsylvania had not prepared them for the heat of New York City in the summer.

"Why don't we go to Coney Island on Sunday?" Pepe suggested, popping salted fava beans into the little boy's mouth.

"Sure, we'll spend our hard-earned coins on roller coaster rides."

"Why not? And we'll take Angelo on the merry-go-round. Maria, you gotta have some fun in this life."

Maria sighed. She was not yet eighteen but felt twice as old. She had no time for frivolous pleasures. Pepe loved her dearly, but sometimes she reminded him of a first sergeant he had served under at Pederobba.

If life was not all roses in the Falcone household, it was even less so in the Italian ghetto. The starched shirts in Washington had passed a law restricting immigration from southern, central and eastern Europe. And, of course, Malatesta was especially put out since the law slowed the flow of souls he could happily exploit.

"The United States Congress is a nest of pickpockets," he complained to Maria one evening as he buckled his belt.

She was silent. But she too detested the Immigration Act of 1921 that branded her ancient race as inferior to the polyglot people who might have preceded the Italians to these shores but were still clubbing each other with crude stone axes when Maria's ancestors among the Greeks, Romans and even the Brutii already had produced great philosophers and built great cities. Even supposedly educated Americans like those in Congress were mostly ignoramuses. Once again they lived under barbarian rule!

Malatesta doffed his hat and smiled his smile before leaving. She too lived under barbarian rule. For how long?

Sometimes the *padrone* would leave gifts, a bag of oranges, a sausage, a trinket or two. Maria would add the food to the larder but throw the costume jewelry down the air shaft. Who did he think they were, Romeo and Juliet?

One day . . . it had to happen, she knew . . . Pepe found the stub of Malatesta's cheroot in a coffee cup in the bedroom. Claudio also smoked Di Nobilis. Miserable, he confronted Maria. "What's this doing here?"

Maria sat herself down on the bed with a sigh of relief. At last things were in the open. "Listen, Pepe . . . I don't know how to tell you this . . ."

Pepe, to her annoyance, looked more sad than angry. "I know I said you could take lovers . . . but not my own brother . . ."

At first Maria was surprised, then gave a sour laugh. "Don't be a jackass, Falcone. I'm not sleeping with Claudio."

"No?"

"God as my judge."

He actually seemed relieved as he squinted at the cigar butt. "Then who . . . ?"

"*Malatesta*, the pig has been blackmailing me, all of us. He threatens to have us fired from our jobs and says he will report Claudio to the police if I refuse."

Pepe sat down beside her and tried to take her into his arms, but she squirmed out of his embrace and quickly stood up. She didn't want to be comforted, she wanted him to show some backbone.

"We've got to *do* something," she said. "I'm tired of being used by the Malatestas of this world."

"You're right, you're right . . . but what can we do against him, his power . . . ?"

She looked at him. Truly he had lost his manhood on the Austrian front. Claudio wouldn't show such a weak liver but she couldn't ask him to help. He was in enough trouble already.

It was up to her. "Never mind, Pepe. I'll take care of this."

When Pepe went off to sleep, Maria took Angelo by the hand and led him past the sleeping Claudio to the kitchen. She fed the boy farina and studied his sallow and dimpled face. Did she see in his curly hair and almond eyes shadows of his grandmother, Donna Carmela? How would the resourceful witch of Miseno get out of the fix that Maria found herself in? Then and there, Maria resolved to take a leaf from the old hag's book.

Meanwhile, to help the family finances, Maria had started making small amounts of bootleg wine and grappa in a pot-still in the kitchen. The grappa, distilled from the stems, pips, skin and pulp of the grapes—the *vinaccia*—was especially popular with the residents of Mulberry Street, who praised its rustic flavor and hearty kick in such glowing terms that the drink's reputation soon spread even beyond Bleecker Street. The special quality was mostly the mint Maria added to the brew.

The brandy's reputation soon reached Malatesta's ears and the padrone instantly sniffed an opportunity for profit. He offered to go into partnership with Maria, bankrolling the enterprise so she could produce larger quantities of the grappa and distribute it to a wider area.

"You also need to grease the cops," he said. "Otherwise you'll get arrested."

Maria looked sidelong at the man's talcumed face. Was this a threat that he would inform on her if she didn't agree to the partnership? Everybody knew that the police in New York, where the politicians were lukewarm or opposed to Prohibition, tended to look the other way, especially when it came to small-time bootleg operations. Becoming his partner as well as his mistress would entangle her even more in Malatesta's web. But how could she say no?

"What's the deal?" she asked.

"Twenty-five percent of the profits?"

"That's all you want?"

He threw back his head and laughed. "You got it all wrong," he said. "Twenty-five percent's your share. After all, I take most of the risks. I bankroll the operation. I provide the protection. On second thought, maybe I'm giving you too big a piece just for making the rotgut." He placed his hand over his heart. "But I have a soft spot for you, Maria." Then his hand went lower. "And a hard spot too."

Maria bit her tongue. Someday he would laugh from the other side of his filthy mouth.

"Well, what do you say? Are we partners?"

"Give me time to think about it—"

"Sure. Take a minute or two."

In fact, she didn't need any time for the decision. Even if he didn't have her over a barrel, she realized, she probably would have agreed to the proposition. It was at least a start for her as a woman of enterprise. More, it seemed a way out of the cul-de-sac of poverty and passivity that had always afflicted her kind.

"Colonel, it's a deal."

They shook hands over the kitchen table.

The Godmother was born.

She quit the job sewing piecework, making the grappa took up too much of her time. She used different kinds of grapes for the brandy that wasn't aged in barrels but drunk *giovane*—young. The Colonel kept his part of the bargain, supplying the fruit, bottles, equipment and Carlo Vacca, a young deliveryman who brought the grappa to customers in a milk van. Malatesta collected the money and gave Maria her cut. Of course she could never be certain he was giving her a square deal. But the money, even her short end, was good and she didn't question him.

Besides, she was hatching a permanent solution to the Malatesta problem, as she had come to think of it.

Maria frowned as she blended pomace in a big pot. The red-haired snake had extorted more than a handshake to seal the deal that day. Though she was his business partner she was still in bondage to him. For now. Her experience as a gardener and lessons she had learned from Donna Carmela would, she hoped, help change all that.

When Angelo woke from his nap she dressed him and took him with her to the hardware store on Canal Street, where she bought weed killer. On the way back she looked at the child toddling beside her. "My son, your grandma was a bitch but she was quite a clever bitch."

In response, Angelo clasped his mother's hand and looked up at her with soft brown eyes.

Back in the apartment she gave him a jack-in-the-box that Pepe had made, then she went to work.

The beetles she had harvested from the flowerpots were drying on the windowsill in the bedroom. In a mortar she ground them up till they were as fine as face powder. Then she extracted arsenic from the weed killer and mixed it with the cantharides formed by the insects. Finally she dissolved the mixture in a vial of clear water.

Aquetta di Napoli, Donna Carmela had called the formula. The Little Water of Naples. What a sweet-sounding name. Four to six drops of it would cause a painless death in mere hours. Her only regret was that it would be painless. Standing on a stool, she hid the vial on the top shelf of the kitchen cupboard and wiped her hands on her pretty flowered apron.

She would have to wait for just the right time. Well, it would be worth waiting for.

Meanwhile, with extra money coming into the household, the Falcones were able to enjoy more luxuries. They went to the movies and band concerts more often and ate *prosciutto di Parma*. One Sunday Pepe surprised them by bringing home a Victor Talking Machine and a batch of opera records featuring Enrico Caruso, the Neapolitan tenor who sang at the Metropolitan Opera. The popularity of Caruso and Valentino reinforced Maria's ethnic pride. She and Pepe would spend hours listening to the opera singer's spine-tingling voice emerge from the magic machine. Only Claudio sometimes grumbled that the Falcone family was "putting on airs."

But Claudio was pleased with their new prosperity and impressed by how easy it was to make money bootlegging.

"I'm tired of breaking my back in a hole in the ground twelve hours a day," he once appealed to Maria. "Maybe you could ask Malatesta to find a position for me in the booze business, eh?"

"No," Maria said. "You gotta lay low."

Claudio shot an incredulous look at his brother. "Listen to the way this little girl talks," he said. He turned again to his sister-in-law. "Listen here, I'm wasting my talents digging subway tunnels. I'm not a jackass. I'm strong, smart and good-looking. I could be very useful to the operation. I'm sure they already forgot about me in Pennsylvania. What do you say, Maria?"

"I say be patient."

Claudio waved her away. *"Bah-fahn-gool,"* he said.

Pepe shrugged and put an aria from *La Bohème* on the talking machine.

Maria did envision an eventual role for Claudio in the grappa business and whatever branches it might grow. She appreciated his obvious talents. But the time was not ripe. First she would have to erase Malatesta from the picture. Then she would have to accumulate enough payoff money to make Claudio safe from the threat of extradition. Then she would bring him into the business.

She smiled to herself, feeling a rush of vitality as she schemed and planned. She felt *alive*.

When the men left for work she fed Angelo and put him to bed and schemed and dreamed all night long. But she woke up the next day in a more sober mood. She fed Angelo toast and milk for breakfast and began having second thoughts about her plans, especially the most drastic one. Malatesta was a tough customer in spite of his dandified appearance and airs. He had connections and confederates from East Harlem to City Hall and a reputation for brutality and ruthlessness, some of which she knew firsthand. Did she really have the stomach for this, a girl whose worst sins so far were sleeping with a wayward priest and torching a stable?

As she gazed at the child calmly eating his breakfast she shook her head, as though to exorcise the doubts. For his sake as well as her own she was determined to find the courage from somewhere. Besides, who else would launch the Falcone family on the right road? Pepe was a jellyfish, and Claudio a hothead. Who but she in the family had the daring and craftiness to see things through?

Later that night when she was alone again and the baby slept she took time as usual to improve her English by reading True Story magazine. As she flipped through the pages she came across an advertisement for "cures for female ills." At first she was puzzled. She was still so naïve in such matters. But then a glint of understanding came into her dark eyes. Maybe the ad had to do with preventing pregnancy. She had read in the *Daily News* about a woman who was arrested for conducting a birth control clinic in Brooklyn. Women were so bold in public in this country and so meek in private.

The subject made her frown. After every encounter with Malatesta she had purged herself with a solution of vinegar and water, a formula learned from the old wives of Miseno. The douche also helped ease the revulsion she felt. But did it really do the trick?

Maybe it only worked in the air of Campania. She had never felt so uneasy about it until this moment.

She clipped the mail-order form from the magazine, got a five-dollar bill from a coffee can where she squirreled money and sent away for the advertised "cure." Better safe than sorry—unless it was already too late.

Maria slept badly that night.

On Friday she went to the fish market on Prince Street and bought squid for dinner. In the shops and on the streets residents of Little Italy were beginning to treat her with deference. The word had gotten around that the pretty young mother was in partnership with Malatesta. Besides, in the fish store she commanded special respect because of her expertise at buying, cleaning and cooking fish.

Annibale Lorella, the owner, usually gave her extra weight in her purchases. "How you gonna cook it, Signora Falcone?" he asked as usual, squinting at the scale.

"I'll stew it with fresh vegetables," she said.

"Use plenty garlic, eh? Want me to cut off the ink sac?"

"I'll do it, thanks."

Lorella wrapped the squid in wax paper. "Let it marinate at least four hours."

"Absolutely."

"And don't forget to throw in a little white wine."

She darted him a look of mock horror. "But that's against the law!"

At which they both laughed heartily.

On the way home she bought lemons for the calamari; all the rest that she needed for the stew was already in the pantry or growing on the roof. Later, as she skinned and cleaned the squid, she hummed a chantey that her father used to sing. But soon she stopped humming, stared at the tentacles and sepia staining the granite cutting surface. She stared at the jagged blade in her hand. How long could she stand Malatesta's coiling arms around her and the taint of his seed?

In that instant her doubts and misgivings dissolved.

*   *   *

Maria was just replacing the "Little Water" on the top shelf of the cupboard when she heard his footsteps on the stairs. She quickly got up from the stool and wiped her hands. I'm not nervous, she told herself. Everything is ready.

She opened the door.

He mopped his brow with a handkerchief. It was a hot September night and he was sweating from the climb. "I think I'll evict the Capalinos and give you their apartment on the first floor," he said.

She let him in. "No thanks," she said. "I like having the roof garden."

Malatesta removed his white linen jacket and draped it over the back of the chair. The Mauser pistol fit snugly in a shoulder holster. "Got anything cold to drink?"

"Sure," she said, leading him to the kitchen table with a bottle and two glasses of chilled grappa.

Malatesta sat down heavily. "I'd rather have ice coffee."

"I ran out."

"Cold water, then."

Maria looked around. Now she *was* nervous, things weren't going according to plan.

A minute or two later she brought him a glass of ice water and sat next to him. He drank it down in two quick gulps, nodded with satisfaction, and without further ado reached over and began to fondle her breasts. "I haven't much time," he said. "I have an important meeting later."

She removed his hand. "Patience," she said. "I want you to try this grappa. I'm experimenting with the recipe. I added rue."

Malatesta frowned. "Your grappa is famous all over the neighborhood. Why change a successful formula?"

"People are fickle," she said. "A good businessman has to keep offering his customers something new."

He raised his manicured hands in a negative gesture. "I don't want to risk losing our regular clients."

"Look, Colonel, we could offer people a choice between grappa with mint and grappa with rue. We could say that one went better after a meal of fish and the other after a meal of meat. With all respect, I've been reading the advertisements in magazines. They

know how to make people want things they don't need and this
builds up the business. See what I mean?"

He rubbed his chin. "I don't know . . ."

She shoved the glass toward him. "Taste it. What's the harm in
trying?"

He shook his head. "I trust your judgment. This stuff has a kick
and I got to keep a clear head for the meeting later. Couple big
shots from the West Side. If I'm not sharp they'll put one over on
me."

She tried flattery. "That'll be the day!"

He looked at her. Up to now she'd given in but was cool to him.
Was his skill at lovemaking thawing her out? Was she finally warming up to him? He reached for her again.

She disentangled herself and got up. "Wait," she said. "I want to
put a record on the talking machine."

He seemed pleased. "Good. I like the jazz."

"No. I have no jazz discs. But I have Caruso singing Verdi."

He shrugged, satisfied by her apparent attempts to please him.

After putting on a record she came over and, to his surprise, sat
on his lap. "I'm in a good mood," she said. "I want to celebrate
with you."

"Celebrate what?"

"Our partnership."

"Okay. Let's go to the bedroom."

"Please. Let's have a drink together first." She ran her fingers
through his greasy hair.

He seemed beside himself with pleasure. "Will you be extra-nice
to me, girl?"

"Of course," she said.

"All right, then."

Maria's heart beat faster as she reached over, picked up the two
glasses and handed him one.

They clinked glasses.

"*Salute*," she said. "Your health."

"*Salute.*"

They both drank the liquid down in a gulp.

He frowned. "Tastes a little bitter."

"It's the rue. It's supposed to taste bitter." She picked up the bottle. "Try another glass."

He shook his tousled head, then buried it between her breasts as Maria smiled at the blistered wall.

It was three hours later when Antonio Malatesta took his last earthly breath. On the talking machine Enrico Caruso was singing "La donna e mobile."

Maria Croce Falcone kissed the photos of her parents. She had decapitated the hydra. She held her hands out in front of her: steady as a rock, she was pleased to see. Now she would carry out the rest of her plan, convinced that the key to its success was its boldness.

She removed Angelo from his crib in the bedroom and put the sleeping child in Claudio's bed, then sat down and waited for the men to come home from work.

They arrived as usual before daybreak. She said nothing but the seriousness in her face told them something unusual was going on. She put her fingers to her lips and led them to the bedroom, where Malatesta's body lay.

She gave them no more than a couple of minutes to get over their initial shock, then proceeded, calmly and clearly, to give them instructions, which they were too dumbfounded and scared to object to or question her about. From the roof garden Pepe got the wheelbarrow, a spade and a burlap sack. Claudio took off Malatesta's clothes and burned them in the stove.

"What about this?" he asked, forcing himself to hold up the leather holster. "It won't burn."

"Leave it on him."

"And this?" He held up the Mauser.

"Give it to me."

Claudio shook his head, meaning both surprise and admiration as he handed over the weapon. She put it in the cupboard next to the potion.

Now Malatesta's body, naked except for the holster, lay on the bed, limbs helter-skelter like a discarded puppet. The three of them stared down at him.

"What now?" Pepe asked.

"You put him in the sack and bury him," she said.

"Where?"

"Where else? In the graveyard."

She had thought it through. They would have to work fast to be finished before dawn. They could put him in an old burial plot in the graveyard of San Gennaro's. Nobody would bat an eye at the sight of immigrants pushing a wheelbarrow through the streets, even at this hour. With luck they could get him underground before anyone was the wiser. She knew that the pastor was an old drunk who slept like a deaf man himself, and the sacristan was a half-wit and a deaf-mute to boot. In September the churchyard was still heavily foliated, providing lots of cover. A cemetery, Maria said, was the last place the police would look for a corpse.

Pepe shook his head. "But what if we're caught?"

Maria shrugged. "Then we're caught. Look here, we lose nothing. With Malatesta alive we were in prison already."

Claudio was watching them with a curious expression. "Hey, what was going on between you and Malatesta?" he asked.

Maria and Pepe glanced uneasily at each other, then Maria turned to her brother-in-law and said, "No matter, it's over now. But I'll tell you one thing . . . Maria Falcone is through being trampled by the snakes of this world. From now on I do the trampling."

"You little wife has grown fangs," Claudio told Pepe.

Pepe, in admiration, said, "I think she always had them. They've just grown a little longer and sharper."

"Well, we better hurry," Claudio said.

Maria, who had heard but ignored their exchange, said, "One second," and hurried into the kitchen. When she came back she had the paring knife that she used to clean fish.

"I want a trophy," she said. "You can turn your faces, if you want."

And with the dexterity of a seasoned fishmonger she severed the late padrone's genitalia.

*   *   *

Claudio steered the wheelbarrow that was Antonio Malatesta's secret hearse over the ruts and cobblestones of Mulberry Street. Maria and Pepe walked by his side. They attracted no attention and encountered no problems until crossing Prince Street, when Maria jabbed her husband in the side with her elbow and nodded in the direction of the lamp post.

Standing under the arc of electric light was a cop.

Maria caught Claudio's eye, whose return glance told her that he had noticed the cop too. In a few seconds the policeman was beginning to walk toward them, tapping his nightstick on his palm.

Now he stood directly in Claudio's path, squinting suspiciously. They stopped. Pepe tipped his hat.

"Now, what're you guineas haulin' this time o' night?" The cop was a thin man with a snub nose and buckteeth.

"*Non capisco*," said Claudio in a sullen tone.

Maria gave her brother-in-law a disapproving look. This was no time for discourtesy. "Potatoes," she said, pronouncing the English word as well as she could.

The cop edged closer, still tapping the stick in his hand. "Potatoes, eh? Sure it ain't *vino*?"

"No *vino*, potatoes," repeated Maria.

"Now how come I don't exactly believe you, pretty lady? Think I'll just see for myself, eh?"

The cop's hand extended toward the opening of the burlap sack. Color flooded Claudio's face and his fists clenched.

Maria, who had prepared for this, quickly moved in. "Let me shake your hand, officer," she said, pumping his hand.

The cop glanced with satisfaction at the twenty-dollar bill she had placed there. He shrugged. "I suppose if you've seen one potato you've seen them all," he said. Then he tipped his cap. "Good night to you, then."

As they watched him walk off toward Broadway, Pepe took out a handkerchief and mopped his brow. Claudio spat in the gutter. Maria nudged him. "Let's hurry," she said.

The dark graveyard seemed filled with the sounds of nature's fiddlers and flutists. Pepe took the spade from the wheelbarrow, spat on his palms and began digging. When he got tired Claudio took over. Meanwhile Maria stood watch. Glancing at the sweating men, she had to smile at herself. That's what they were good for, bending their backs. Had either of them thought of bringing bribe money? Where would they be without her? She flinched at the notion. What was the American expression? Up shit's creek.

She turned her head and saw something that made her catch her breath. Her eyes narrowed. A light had been turned on in a room on the second floor of the rectory. Quickly she gestured to the men to be silent.

Claudio stopped shoveling. Pepe stood rigid. Maria lost her smile. Did the American courts send women to the electric chair too?

A figure appeared at the lighted window and opened it with a clatter. The person—was it the old pastor or the dim-witted sacristan?—cast a goblinesque shadow on the ground near the feet of the three persons cowering in the graveyard hoping not to be seen. The figure at the window coughed, spat into the air, and the window again was shut and the light was out.

Maria's rigid face softened. After waiting a few minutes to make sure it was safe, she nodded to Claudio, who resumed shoveling the earth that would soon cover the perfumed carcass of Antonio Malatesta.

Maria's trophy ended up in a pickle jar in the pantry next to the preserved meats, salted fish and stewed tomatoes. The plan had gone without a hitch and Maria was free from her bondage.

Moreover, she was proprietor of a thriving bootleg business. Carlo Vacca, driver of the milk van, was no problem once he became convinced that Malatesta was gone for good. Actually he was glad to work for Maria instead of the padrone who had treated him with disrespect. Vacca had a harelip, and Malatesta had thought it good sport to make fun of it. Maria cemented her relationship with the driver by giving him a big raise. She was surprised to discover that the operation yielded almost twice as much money as she would have guessed when Vacca handed over the collection sheets. She had found a notebook with a grease sheet in Malatesta's pocket so she knew whom to pay off. Now all she had to do was make the grappa and wine and rake in the profits.

The police never connected the padrone's disappearance to the Falcones. Malatesta had kept his visits to Maria discreet. Detectives suspected that he was bumped off by the West Siders he was scheduled to meet with the night he disappeared. But they weren't inclined to exert themselves investigating the disappearance of some wop gangster in a milieu where blood feuds were as common as spaghetti sauce. They preferred to look the other way unless the mayhem spilled over into the lives of "respectable Americans." That was the attitude of the honest cops. Cops on the take didn't care who croaked whom as long as the palm oil kept flowing.

Maria, a fast learner, caught on fast. The persecutions of her early years had taught her the realities of power politics. She also understood that before she could become a really successful *business-woman* she still had a lot to overcome . . . mostly her sex and youth.

But her intuitive smarts told her that the art of diplomacy, especially for a young woman, required her to wear a velvet glove over an iron fist. So when she had enough money she gave a nice sum to Malatesta's widow. She did this not only to keep her quiet but also because she felt sorry for her, a childless woman of middle age whom the wagging tongues of the neighborhood portrayed as simple-minded and long-suffering, with dim prospects for the future. Besides, she deserved a reward for living with Malatesta all these years. The widow promptly took the money and booked passage for her birthplace in Calabria.

Maria also made a down payment on the milk van that Vacca had leased from a garage on the East Side and had a telephone installed in the apartment to conduct business. And business was multiplying; customers liked dealing with a fair-minded supplier like Maria rather than a two-faced crook like Malatesta who always had looked for ways to jack up prices or dilute the product. And soon her grappa and wine were bought by local speakeasies that catered to an Italian clientele. Maria also started making some whiskey as the business expanded.

The rosy picture, though, was marred by one unforeseen problem. Buried in the churchyard of San Gennaro's was the father of Maria's second son.

Maria noticed the signs of her pregnancy just two weeks after

Malatesta's death. She had missed her period and her breasts were sore. Now there was no doubt in her mind that the old-country formulas had failed to perform their magic against the higher wizardry of nature.

Pepe reacted to the news in his usual stoic fashion. "What do you want to do about it?" he asked Maria, puffing on his pipe as they sat in the kitchen. Maria was making pomace for the grappa.

"I'm asking your advice," she said.

"I'm sure you know how to get rid of it."

"Yes."

Pepe glanced over at Angelo, who was in the kitchen bathtub playing with a balsa-wood duck. "I like having kids around," he said. "But it's up to you."

Maria's eyes seemed transfixed by the smoke from the pipe curling in the air. "I don't know . . . the child of that red-haired pig," she said.

"A child is a child . . ."

Her mouth was tight as she strained the grape residue, shaking her head. "Never liked the idea of abortion," she said. "Each is a child of God, they say. What right have we got to just barge in and cut the line?"

Pepe cleared his throat. "Excuse me, but wasn't Malatesta also a child of God?" He braced for a stormy reaction.

But she answered without anger: "Malatesta was a child of the Devil, Pepe."

In the end Maria decided to have the baby, which created another problem for her with her efforts to win respect from business associates in spite of her sex and youth. Her increasingly obvious state of pregnancy tended to make her appear more a vulnerable female. It was decided that Pepe would quit the subway job to care for the household, the garden and young Angelo, freeing Maria to devote herself more to the growing bootleg operation. Naturally Claudio wanted to quit the subway job too but Maria said no.

"We still need the extra money you bring in," she told him.

"Don't make me laugh," Claudio said. "What I make doesn't buy chick-peas. You know I could help you and Vacca in lots of ways. Business is growing so much he drives ten hours a day now. I could take a second shift."

Maria thought on it. He was right about that. She could use a man of his guts and strength. But she was also afraid he might do something to get himself in trouble with the law, which would put two and two together and send him in handcuffs back to Pennsylvania.

"No, Claudio," she said. "We can't take the chance."

Claudio fumed and cursed all the saints in heaven but he did as he was told.

Soon, though, the decision to employ Claudio in the business was made for Maria. One snowy night just before New Year's Eve a big shipment of Falcone grappa was hijacked and Vacca was beaten to a pulp.

"It was those West Siders," Vacca managed to say through swollen lips and missing teeth when Maria visited him in the hospital. "The Marino gang."

She patted the hand that stuck out from the plaster cast covering his broken right arm. "Don't worry about a thing, Carlo. You just get better. We'll take care of everything."

Her first big test had come.

"They been just itching to hit you, Maria," Claudio said over espresso that evening. "They only been waiting to make sure Malatesta was really out of the picture. They think you're a pushover."

Maria said nothing. Her smooth young face, its angles softened by the advancing pregnancy, was thoughtful.

"We gotta teach them a lesson," added Claudio, pounding his fist on the table. "If we don't strike fast and hard, well, you better go back to sewing piecework."

Maria finally gave a small nod. "You're right," she said. "It's what I've been thinking too. Listen here, this is what we have to do."

Claudio moved his chair closer to the table.

Maria's plan was simple but bold. They would set a trap for the Marinos, using another big shipment of booze as bait. Only this time the Falcones would be waiting for them. During the day Maria had tapped neighborhood sources provided by Vacca to learn whatever she could about the Marino gang, which came from the neighborhood called Hell's Kitchen near the railroad yards on the West Side of Manhattan. The first thing she learned before planning a counterstroke was that they were not allied in any way to Rico Longo, a Neapolitan boss who headed up a loose confederation of Manhattan gangs operating from midtown to the Battery. Longo, the local version of a Camorra chief, was too strong for a newcomer like herself to lock horns with. She was glad to learn that the Marino gang was composed of young free-lancers, peacock *cafoni* who had bravado and brutality but little real muscle. Three tough guys, including one of the four Marino brothers, had attacked Vacca at a stop signal at night, using rubber hoses and chains to work him over. Maria was pretty sure that they had no heavy hardware or, if they did, it was probably a small arsenal that they reserved for emergencies.

Hoodlums of the day were still reluctant to use firearms, afraid of a public outcry that would force the authorities to crack down. Prohibition was still in its infancy, the gangsterism of chattering tommy guns and complex webs of alliances was in the future.

Maria spread the word along the neighborhood grapevine that she was delivering a big supply of booze to a speakeasy on Bleecker Street for a New Year's Eve party. Then she instructed Claudio to recruit a trustworthy driver "with balls and brains" to help them in the venture. He picked George Bonaventura, a fellow laborer with shoulders like steel beams and a crafty mind that contrasted with his neolithic appearance. Like Claudio, Bonaventura often grumbled about working in the subway and had jumped at the chance to join the Falcones.

Maria's plan was based on the assumption that the Marinos would be confident enough to attack again without firepower. It was a calculated risk.

"How we gonna handle them?" Claudio asked as they sat around the kitchen table with Bonaventura mapping strategy. It was two nights before New Year's Eve and one night before the booze delivery was scheduled.

Maria didn't reply with words. Instead she went to the cupboard and came back with Malatesta's loaded pistol. She laid it on the table.

Bonaventura, stubby fingers laced together, raised his bushy eyebrows.

Claudio reached out to grab the weapon but Maria stopped him. "It's not for you."

Claudio looked puzzled. "Who, then? George will be driving. He might not have time to draw a gun."

She jabbed a finger into her own chest. "Me," she said in an even tone of voice.

Claudio gave her an incredulous look, then threw back his head and laughed. She was eighteen years old and four months pregnant.

Maria didn't see the humor as she leaned closer to the table and crooked her finger at the men. "Listen here," she began, "this is the way it's going to happen."

The plan was launched the night before New Year's Eve. Bonaventura loaded the truck with cases of grape juice and water. Claudio, armed with a blackjack, and Maria, toting the Mauser, hid themselves among the cases in the rear of the van. Rain mixed with sleet fell from the black sky.

When Bonaventura stopped the truck at the corner of Lafayette and Kenmare streets four men hopped on the running boards and ordered him to pull over. Bonaventura did as he was told.

The vainglorious Vacca had been beaten up because he resisted the hijacking. Maria had instructed the brutish-looking driver to behave as meek as a lamb. The four gangsters took one look at the mountainous Bonaventura and seemed just as glad not to have to resort to force.

Bonaventura had hopped out of the driver's seat and was standing on the cobblestones. "I want no trouble," he told the hijackers, who circled him. Two carried chains, one a baseball bat, and another wore brass knuckles. "Take every last bottle."

Then, looking sheepish, he edged around to the back doors of the van. "But listen, fellows," he added, "I got a piece of tenderloin back here. You know how it is, I don't want the old lady to find out." He opened the doors, revealing Maria's pretty face, smiling invitingly.

Bonaventura continued talking, shielding his mouth with the back of his hand. "She's just a tart I picked up on Canal Street.

Hey, maybe she'll give you all a taste, one at a time. Or even all at once. I'm sure she won't mind. I'll tell yuh, fellows, she's got a real hot tongue."

The hijackers, hardly more than boys, looked at each other. It took about a second for them to make up their minds and climb into the rear of the van.

Four flies in the web.

Bonaventura slammed the doors behind them and jammed the lock. Simultaneously Claudio had jumped from his hiding place, swinging the blackjack.

Meanwhile, Maria pointed the pistol at the surprised hijackers. It was over, one, two, three. Not a shot had been fired. No fuss, no cops, just as Maria had planned and predicted.

They drove back to the deserted garage where they had gotten the van and herded the captives into the back room. The gangsters looked stunned at being corralled by a gun-toting expectant mother. They were ordered to sit on their hands in a circle on the concrete floor. The hanging electric light cast shadows on their pale, perspiring faces. Two bled from the head where Claudio's blackjack had landed.

Bonaventura stood over them, smacking the baseball bat against his palm. Claudio sat on a carton.

Maria pointed the pistol at the ceiling and promenaded around the captives. "Who goes by the name of Marino?"

Silence.

"I don't ask the same question twice."

A dark-eyed fellow in a soft cap raised his sullen face. "Me."

"Anybody else?"

"No," said the one who had identified himself as a Marino. He wore a brush mustache and looked two or three years older than the others.

"Stand up," Maria commanded.

He shuffled to his feet.

Maria took the kerchief from her head and wrapped it around the muzzle of the weapon. Then she pointed it directly at his groin.

The man's knees began to sag. His breathing was shallow. But he did not beg.

Maria lowered the weapon and squeezed off a round, hitting him in the right kneecap. Marino groaned and fell to the floor.

"Maria Falcone," Maria said in a calm Sunday school voice. "Remember that name and repeat it to your brothers. *Maria Falcone.*"

Marino hugged his shattered knee, a bag of smashed strawberries. "Maria Falcone . . ."

Gesturing with the Mauser, she added, "That's all. Now get out of here."

The three men scrambled to their feet and helped their wounded up a small flight of stairs and out the back door of the garage.

1922 was a banner year for the Falcone clan.

The business prospered and expanded beyond bootlegging. Maria used her skills as a herbalist to make patent medicines based on cocaine, an outlawed drug. She also bought a piece of a local bookmaking operation, mainly sticking to enterprises, such as liquor and gambling, that the public and, by extension, the police didn't strongly disapprove of. Once in a while she would give in to Claudio and agree to let the gang knock over a warehouse containing shipments of sardines and other canned goods that she would then fence to the wholesalers. But as a rule she disliked robberies, afraid that some innocent night watchman might be killed.

The profits grew and the size of the gang grew with them. Besides Vacca—whose cleft palate was worsened by the beating and who had a cocker-spaniel devotion to Maria after she paid all his hospital bills—Bonaventura and Claudio, she hired three other men after carefully screening them for character and qualifications. One candidate even came from the trio of Marino gang members who had been there when she shot Cooky Marino in the knee. His name was Joey Irish, very clever with figures, so Maria employed him to help keep the accounts.

The Marino brothers never bothered her again.

Maria ruled the operation with a firm hand and the enterprises thrived, helped greatly by her superior organizational skills. Unlike the men, she never planned a job or took a step without thinking things through. She tried never to act on impulse or to prove something to the world like most men did.

The name Maria Falcone that she had "advised" Cooky Marino to repeat after shooting him was taking on the aura of a legend in Little Italy and even beyond. But with it she had a biological date to keep.

Cesare Falcone was born in the middle of May.

The baby had reddish hair and, of course, everybody including Claudio assumed that Pepe was the father. And a doting parent he was, to both Cesare and Angelo.

Maria, on the other hand, could never warm up to Cesare, much as she tried. The reason was obvious: he reminded her too much of his hated natural father. Anyway, her activities occupied more and more of her time, leaving little room for the domestic rites of maternity.

In November, Maria paid cash for a large brick townhouse on Sullivan Street. It had sixteen rooms, four fireplaces, a large wine cellar and a big sunny backyard where Pepe could grow fruit trees, flowers, vines, plants and vegetables to his heart's content. There was also enough room in the cellar for a woodworking shop.

Claudio finally got a place of his own, renting an apartment on Horatio Street. He bought fancy clothes, a yellow Pierce-Arrow runabout and started squiring show girls to the speaks, jazz clubs and movie palaces. He ran through women like a kid with bon-bons; none lasted very long.

Maria was surprised that her brother-in-law's skirt-chasing upset her. But there it was, and luckily she could push aside her sexual attraction to Claudio . . . where else were her natural feelings supposed to go? . . . by putting all her energy into building up the business. Or at least so she hoped.

Meanwhile her relationship with her husband was cooling even more. They had never been lovers, except in an unconventional way, but at least they had always been friends. Now that seemed to be going. Pepe could tell how his wife had lost respect for him when he failed to do anything about Malatesta's abuse of her. And she was right, he was less than half a man. He could accept his odd role in her life, so long as he could find a way to keep their friendship. But Maria was becoming a different person from the village girl of Miseno whom he had married almost three years earlier. She was on the way to becoming *La Cumare*—the Godmother.

Maria and Joey Irish were sitting in her office on the second floor of the townhouse going over the ledger when a discreet knock came at the door. Maria impatiently tapped the fourteen-carat gold-and-platinum nib of her fountain pen on the desk. "See who it is, Joey."

Joey nodded and got up. At eighteen he was the only gang member younger than the boss. His given name was Giuseppe Soldo but they called him Joey Irish because his mother was Irish.

He opened the door now to Bonaventura's simian-shelved face.

"There's a lady downstairs wants to see you," Bonaventura said to Maria. "Says she's your *cumare*."

"My cumar'?" repeated Maria. Among southern Italians the bonds of godmotherhood and godfatherhood were mutual connections based more on social and familial alliances than on religious ceremonies. And claims of such kinship were often made on the slenderest thread, especially if the object of the claim was a person of prominence. So Maria's voice had a skeptical tone when she asked, "What's her name?"

"Camilla Balbi," said Bonaventura, whose role in the gang had evolved into gatekeeper and personal bodyguard for Maria.

Her heart jumped at the surname of their old friend of Miseno who had paid for the wedding feast of Maria and Pepe and done so many kindnesses for them when they were in trouble. "Tell her to go into the parlor. I'll be right down."

Camilla Balbi was sitting on the brocade couch when Maria entered the room. She didn't rise, rather looked at Maria questioningly.

"Miss Balbi?" Maria said, also showing a curious manner toward the woman who appeared to be about twenty-five-years-old.

"No," she replied shyly. "I'm Mrs. Petri, really."

Maria frowned. "I'm confused. I'm Maria Falcone. What can I do for you?"

The woman sprang up from her couch. "For charity, I beg your pardon. I never dreamed you could be so young."

Maria laughed. "I hope you won't hold it against me." She motioned toward the couch. "Sit down, won't you?"

Still flustered, the woman sat down again. She had auburn hair and strikingly large brown eyes, but her creamy complexion was violated by a purple bruise under her right eye. "Of course I was told that you were young, but it still comes as a shock. And you're so pretty too."

"I hope you don't hold that against me either."

"Oh, not at all! Forgive me, Godmother, for being so awkward."

Maria had taken an instant liking to the woman, but she was still puzzled and guarded. "I'm still confused," Maria said. "I was told your name was Camilla Balbi."

"I gave the man my maiden name so you would recognize it."

"I see." Maria sat in an armchair opposite the woman. "Now then. How are you related to my old friend, Balbi?"

"He's my father."

Maria raised an eyebrow. As far as she knew, Enzo Balbi and his dry hag of a wife were childless. Over coffee and Easter rolls recently baked by Pepe, the visitor told Maria the whole story.

Camilla was the illegitimate daughter of the landowner by a piano teacher of Naples with whom he had a long relationship. It was, the daughter related, a lovematch while his marriage had been an arrangement based on dowry and family connections, like most liaisons of the middle class in Campania. In the face of convention, Balbi insisted that the daughter bear his own name rather than the mother's. And he always gave her financial support and lavished love on her as a child. Of course, divorce was impossible in Italy so he never left his legal wife. Although Camilla's mother had died two years earlier, the father never lost track of the daughter and continued to treat her like an affectionate parent. And over his wife's objections he had even walked her down the aisle in a public display of paternity that many thought scandalous when Camilla married Livio Petri in the Church of San Domenico in Naples the previous year.

And Livio Petri was the cause of her present visit to her god-mother.

In spite of laws restricting immigration the newlyweds had managed, with Balbi's skill at greasing palms, to get the necessary documents to come to America six months earlier. Camilla's husband Livio, who fancied himself a stage actor, planned to find work in one of the Italian theaters that had sprung up on the Lower East Side. For a while he pounded the pavements and banged on the doors of casting agents and directors, but after one or two impresarios had slammed the door in his chiseled face he started drifting north to the dance halls and wine cellars of Union Square, where he rehearsed the role of Bacchus with every Venus or Ariadne he could manage to charm. He would come home drunk and broke and reeking of cheap perfume and expect his wife to wait on him hand and foot. At first Camilla put up with his behavior in silence, alibiing to herself for him . . . he was young and handsome and confused in this new world where the women threw themselves at him . . . his manly pride was hurt by his failure to find work and his having to rely on the salary his wife earned working at a paper-box factory on Varick Street.

But she ran out of excuses for him the third time that he hit her.

Maria reached across the marble coffee table and gently touched the bruise under Camilla's eye. "That python," she said.

Camilla looked down at the fidgeting hands in her lap. "I wouldn't mind so much if it was only me," she said. "But now if he flies off the handle I'm afraid for the baby."

"Eh?"

"I'm two months pregnant."

Maria sipped coffee. "Why do you come to me?"

Camilla raised her eyes to Maria's and gave a small smile. "My father always spoke of you with great affection and admiration. He didn't know you were in New York and when I heard your name mentioned so often in the neighborhood I never thought it possible you were the same girl from Miseno. But then when somebody said you were married to a carpenter named Pepe Falcone, I figured it had to be you."

"So, people talk about me, eh?"

"All the time, Godmother. But always with respect and esteem."

"Hmmph." Maria tried to cover her embarrassment. But wasn't it also mixed with some pleasure? "In any case, Camilla, what do you want me to do about that *vigliacco* of a husband of yours?"

Camilla shrugged, looking miserable.

"Do you still love him?"

"Yes, I think so. Anyway, I don't want him hurt . . . I don't know, I just had the feeling that you would know how to handle him . . ."

Maria thought for a moment, then said, "Okay, leave it to me. Another Easter roll?"

Pepe Falcone found a good spot to plant his fig tree on the south side of the house where she would be sheltered from the north wind and absorb all the sun's rays. Before winter came and after the family had feasted on the juicy purple fruit, he would prune her, wrap her in wooden fencing, fill the protected area with leaves and cover the top with roofing paper until spring. He figured he would harvest his first crop in July.

The prospect made his mouth water now as he sat on the wrought-iron bench in the yard. He hadn't tasted a proper fig since leaving Italy three years ago. As his homeland receded in actual time, memories of it became more and more rosy. Still, he had refused Maria's offer to go with her on her scheduled visit to Italy in the summer.

Why didn't he want to go with her? His motives were fuzzy. Maybe he just didn't want to horn in on Maria's private quest to vindicate her parents by having them disinterred and buried in consecrated ground. More likely, he decided, it was because he didn't want to leave the children for as long as six weeks. Angelo was almost three, and though still somewhat frail, made as much mischief as most three-year-old boys. But Pepe worried most about Cesare, whose first birthday was approaching. Though he barely walked he already showed signs of having a red-hot temper and a chip on his shoulder. He threw his baby bottle around as if it were a bowling pin.

Pepe took out a red handkerchief and mopped his face. He was sure that Cesare somehow resented Maria's coolness toward him.

For the first few months of his life the boy suckled a wet nurse, and Pepe had tried hard to fill the other gaps in his upbringing. But the child needed his mother—that was clear. More than once Pepe had wanted to raise the subject with Maria but each time he'd lost his nerve.

He put down the spade and squinted at the hole he'd made. Plenty big enough. He walked over to the wheelbarrow with the plant, roots wrapped in burlap, and rolled it toward the hole, then planted the fig tree, and under his breath cursed a certain day in October 1918 when they threw the pontoon bridges across the Piave. At least this tree would bear fruit.

To make sure that he came without question, Maria had sent Bonaventura to fetch the fancy-pants actor Livio Petri. Even so, he showed up in Maria's parlor with a wise-guy expression on his clean-shaven, too-pretty face. He also kept looking at his pocket watch, as though he was impatient with this intrusion on his valuable time.

Maria didn't offer him refreshments and made him sit on a hard straight-backed chair. He gave her curious glances, surprised as almost everyone was by her youth and good looks.

"So you're an actor, eh?" Maria said.

"Yes."

"Then why don't you start acting like a good husband?"

"What business is that of yours?"

"Your wife and I are *cumari*."

He made a motion in the chair as if to say so what? But he kept silent.

Maria leaned across the marble table. "What kind of Mameluke are you to sneer at such a relationship? Do you come from Napoli or the Barbary Coast?"

"I come from Castellammare," he said.

Maria stared at him, surprised to hear it. The seaside resort of his birth was famous for its strutting gigolos. She decided to try first to reason with him. "Look here, Petri, your wife is pregnant. She's carrying your own child. Surely you don't want to injure your own flesh and blood."

"She provokes me," he said. "Besides, I hit her only in the face."

"What if she falls down?"

He muttered under his breath. "Hey, I don't have to justify my actions to you. Where I come from a man is over his wife."

Maria leaned back on the couch, looking steadily at him. This popinjay would not listen to reason. That was now clear. She said, "You will never lay a hand on her again."

"Now you ask too much," he said with a sly smile.

"You know what I mean."

He again consulted his pocket watch. "Is that all, young lady? I have an appointment . . ." He started to get up.

"Keep your seat, Petri."

With an indulgent smile he sat down again. "I will humor you," he said, "for a few minutes more."

"You beat her again, you'll pay for it. Dearly."

"Is that so?"

"Yes."

"Come now, Mrs. Falcone. You know what they say . . . a wife is like an egg. You have to beat her once in a while if you want to eat cake."

Enough. Maria got up and said, "Come with me."

He hesitated, but a mixture of curiosity and the beginning of apprehension finally compelled him to follow her. She led him down a flight of stairs to the pantry adjoining the wine cellar. Gathering up the hem of her long skirt with one hand, she stood on tiptoes and reached up to a high shelf to fetch a jar from among many jars of preserves.

She handed it to Petri. "Here, take a look at this."

He peered at the object swimming in liquid preservatives in the mason jar. The light was dim and for several moments he couldn't make out what it was. But then the shock of recognition literally made his eyes bug out and his face go pale.

"This belonged to the last man who behaved badly to me," she said quietly. "He also liked to abuse women."

The hand holding the jar shook visibly. Petri's throat was clogged.

She took the jar from his unsteady hands before he dropped it and put it back on the shelf, then turned to him with a smile. "Promise to behave yourself?"

He nodded like a marionette.

Livio Petri kept his promise. He even became a fairly dutiful husband after Maria exerted her influence to get him some acting jobs in the local Italian theaters where he managed to receive good notices in the Italian-language newspapers. Maria also would stand at the baptismal font as true godmother to Maria Petri after her birth some months later. And with all this the young *cumare*'s reputation for wisdom, fairness, compassion and strength of character spread far and wide in the neighborhood.

Maria had one other matter to straighten out before leaving for Italy. One day she asked Claudio to come in for a chat.

"What's up?" he asked, removing the spoon from his mouth. They were sitting in the kitchen eating strawberry ices.

She studied his chalky face. He had been laid up with an illness for a couple of weeks. "How do you feel? Are you over this flu?"

"I'm on the mend," he said. He had had a dose of the clap, but of course he didn't tell her that.

"Good." She shoved aside the metal cup. "Feel fit enough to travel?"

"Where am I going?"

"To Bethlehem, Pennsylvania."

He managed to restrain his surprise. "To do what?"

"To stand trial for killing Beinbrecher."

"What's the joke, Maria?"

She reached across the table to touch his wrist. "It's no joke, Claudio."

And then she outlined her idea. Since he was guilty of nothing but self-defense, Claudio should have the cloud of being a fugitive from justice removed forever. The business had generated enough money by now for her to hire a top lawyer to defend him in the murder case. She had already employed an investigator who visited Bethlehem and rounded up witnesses who were willing to testify that the foreman had tried to shoot Claudio and had been rushing at him with a shovel when Claudio pulled the trigger.

"*Se defendendo,* the lawyer called it," said Maria. "Justifiable homicide."

"You already talked to a lawyer? It's my ass, Maria. You should have asked me first." Claudio's cheeks were now tinged with red.

"Only to feel him out. I went to see this fellow Spivak on Broadway. Frankie Yale recommends him."

As she rose in reputation La Cumare had met many of the men who were making names for themselves in bootlegging and related industries. Mostly they were Sicilians and Neapolitans: Charlie Lucania, Joe Adonis, Frank Costello, Willie Moretti and Frankie Yale. At first they had had misgivings about her. But word soon got around that she was a "stand-up guy" and they treated her with respect.

"Maria, I still say you should've asked me before you saw a lawyer."

She shrugged. "What's the harm?"

Claudio grumbled, but swallowed his objection. Did he have a choice? Then he said, "But I ran—that won't look so good."

"Don't worry. Spivak said that even if they charge you with what he called evading the course of justice, they'll probably just give you a suspended sentence."

"*If* I beat the murder rap."

"The charge is manslaughter," she said, serving him another portion of strawberry ice. "Look here, Claudio, I won't pretend to believe there's *no* risk, but I think you have a *very* good chance of being acquitted. Spivak says you might not even have to stand trial. He could get the charges dismissed. Anyway, the decision is up to you."

"Thanks a lot." His face, pale from the illness, was etched with lines of indecision. Finally he sighed and said, "Okay, Maria. I suppose you know best."

"You're sure?"

"Who's sure?" he said, then shook his head. "Everybody knows you're the brain in this outfit. If I go to jail will you bake me a *torta pasqualina* with a file in it?"

"You won't go to jail," she said. "I scheduled a meeting for you with Spivak on Thursday at three. He'll go with you when you give yourself up."

Claudio had finished the second helping of ice. He lit a cigar. "You must've been pretty sure I'd say yes."

"A meeting can always be canceled."

He squinted at his sister-in-law. "You'll guarantee I won't go to jail?"

"If you go to jail, I'll kill Spivak."

He laughed but it had a hollow sound. And then: "You know, I believe you would."

She looked at him, then down at her hands fidgeting on the table top. Her cheeks felt on fire when she said, "You are right."

Maria sailed for Naples on the *Giulio Cesare*, this time in a first-class cabin, not the third-class dormitory.

As the steamship plowed through the bay she stood on deck and gazed out at the pastel horizon of the open sea. The children had cried at the pier. She eased her guilty conscience with the thought that Pepe would take good care of them. He always did. She told herself that one day she'd spend more time with her children. Maybe when Claudio came back from Pennsylvania she would delegate more authority to him and become a proper housewife and mother.

A spray of salt water hit her in the face but she didn't flinch. It had felt refreshing. Who was she kidding? Who else could run the operation as efficiently as she did? Who else commanded the kind of respect she did? And how could she give up the deep-down satisfaction she derived from her life and status as La Cumare? Giving orders, wielding power, even handling the minor details of the betting and bootleg operations made her blood run hot like some Renaissance duchess.

She was destined for this kind of life. She had to believe it.

What about little Angelo? He was frail and needed the loving attention of his mother. And Cesare? Maria frowned at the foaming water below. It was not his fault that Malatesta was his father. How could she continue to treat her own flesh-and-blood son as an unwanted foundling? She swore to reform, she was only twenty, she had plenty of time to mend her ways . . .

The steamer reached the three-mile limit, where a veritable armada of rumrunners could be seen circling the heaving seas. And the sight rekindled an old idea in Maria: why bother to still make bathtub wine and booze when it would be much more profitable to go big-time and get uncut Scotch and Canadian whiskeys right off the boat? Soon her mind hummed with plans, and her well-intentioned thoughts of the children had faded.

Enzo Balbi wrapped Maria in a bear hug, then held her at arms-length and nodded approvingly. She looked very prosperous and very pretty in her cloche hat, white silk dress reaching just below the knee and silk stockings.

"What a picture you make!" he said. "The American flapper girl."

"You look pretty good yourself," she lied. He looked heavier, grayer and unhealthy. They were standing in the Piazza Plebescito, a fashionable section of Naples near the hotel where she was staying. He suggested that they walk to the cafe for lemon ices, and on the way they chatted and reminisced. "I hear you have two boys, God bless," he said.

She nodded, peering sidelong into the windows of the stylish shops along the Via Roma.

"How's Pepe, the old war horse?"

"Just fine."

Balbi wheezed as they walked and talked. "Why didn't he come with you?"

"He's taking care of the children."

He gestured with a sweep of his arm. "You should have brought them along. Naples is full of kids."

Maria shook her head. What if the local Camorra bosses got wind of the visit of two grandsons of Ottavio Croce? "I hope they never set foot on this soil," she said.

Balbi understood.

They sat down at an outdoor cafe table and ordered ices. On the wall nearby was pasted a Fascist poster saying "Whoever does not vote is ill. Whoever is ill needs castor oil." Maria looked at the poster, puzzling over it.

"I want to thank you for what you did for my daughter," Balbi said.

She turned to face him. He was mopping his forehead with a handkerchief on this hot October day. "You sly old goat," she said, "you should have told us you had a daughter."

He shrugged.

"Nobody blames you," she said, recalling his wife. "I'm sorry about her mother."

He shrugged again. "Thanks."

Boisterous laughter from a nearby table distracted their attention. Maria turned to look. Four men in uniforms and black shirts appeared to be comparing notes on the anatomy of the waitress who had just walked away from their table.

Maria turned questioningly to Balbi, who was glowering at the quartet of blackshirts. "Buffoons," he muttered.

Maria had taken quick stock of them too. They reminded her of bullies and blowhards she had known. Cocky in groups or with a weapon at the hip, but catch them alone and unarmed when the chips were down and they would double-cross their own mothers.

Balbi spoke just above a whisper. "This country is going to hell."

"Why do you say that?"

"We bow down before a dictator with a lantern jaw."

"Well, he showed the Greeks where to get off, didn't he? And I read that King George of England made him a knight."

Balbi looked from side to side, then leaned closer. "He's a fraud, Maria. A clown. Mark my words."

She spooned the ice, looking serious. "I trust your judgment."

"I should have gone to America with you, like you said."

"Come now."

"Too late. The politicians in Washington have shut the gate."

"You managed to get Camilla the papers."

"Yes, and I used up all my markers to do it. Besides, I'm too old and sick. I'm grateful that my daughter and granddaughter live in America."

"Sick? What's wrong?"

He tapped his chest. "The pump is breaking down."

"Have you gone to a heart doctor?"

He glanced at the blackshirts, then hunched his shoulders, the gesture and his general attitude signifying to Maria his lack of will to live. He was probably pining for Camilla's late mother. "I would like to see my granddaughter once before I go," he said.

"Don't talk like that. Why don't you get a tourist visa and buy a boat ticket?"

"My wife would kill me."

"To hell with her."

Balbi chuckled. "She's too mean for Hell. Not even Satan could put up with her." His terra-cotta face turned serious. "Funny, though, I have affection for her."

Maria shook her head, then changed the subject. "How are things in the old town?" Actually she knew that nothing had really changed in Miseno since the days of the Greeks. People died, people were born; the seasons ran their cycles; tyrants came and went but nothing really changed. She also had no intention of visiting the village and seeing for herself. She intended to keep a low profile, shielding herself from old envies and the Camorra. Naples was large, sprawling and anonymous.

He made the sign of the cross. "Donna Carmela passed away six months ago," he said.

Maria was not about to utter any bogus pieties.

Balbi sensed the tacit question in the silence that followed. "Did you hear?" he added, trying to sound casual. "Don Gabriele quit the priesthood."

Maria was clearly stunned. "When?"

"Six weeks after the old lady kicked the bucket."

She coughed. Her throat felt tight, made of sawdust. "Where is he?"

"They say he's working as a schoolteacher in Rome."

"Is he . . . does he have a woman?"

"I don't know." Balbi leaned on the cane he had been using since his heart started to sputter and clank and fixed her with a heavy-lidded gaze. "Don't, Maria," he said.

She met his glance. "Don't worry," she said. "I have no intention of going to him." As she spoke the words the truth of them took shape. She couldn't even picture his face at that moment. Each time she tried, the image fused with Claudio's, the bronze bust outshining the marble. Besides, she had crossed the bridge to another place. No man ruled her heart or her mind. Her girlhood was over.

"Well, let's get down to business," she finally said.

"I've arranged everything," said Balbi. "They will be buried in the Holy Field of Torre del Greco." He reached into the breast pocket of his jacket. "The Monsignor sent this note thanking you for your very generous gift." He handed her the envelope.

Maria glanced at the note and nodded. "Thank you. And the stone?"

"Just as you requested, Maria. I inspected it myself yesterday. The finest pink marble, inscribed with the quotation from Dante. It's beautiful."

Maria leaned back, then reached across the table to clasp her friend's rough hand. "It seems I'm always thanking you for some kindness."

"And I you," he replied. "It's a good arrangement, don't you think?"

The ceremony took place in the coastal village two days later. The tombstones and cypresses under brooding Vesuvius were gilded by the setting sun. Monsignor Franchi intoned the prayers for the dead. In addition to Maria, only Balbi, the Pignataro brothers and the chattering birds were mortal witnesses to the interment of her parents Ottavio and Lisabeta in ground consecrated by both the legates of God and the lava streams of centuries. Music was provided by the vespering birds and the drum brush of the surf below.

Maria Falcone stood tall and proud in her black silk dress on the knoll of volcanic earth where her parents now were laid to rest. Her face showed the joy of vindication. Over and over she read the words chiseled in marble: "*e quindi uscimmo a riveder le stelle.*" *And then we emerged to see again the stars.*

Yes.

She had kept her vow to free her parents from the purgatory of their disgrace. Now their spirits could merge with those very stars.

*   *   *

In the years to come Maria Falcone, the Godmother of Sullivan Street, had other moments of great satisfaction as she followed the winding destiny predicted by the midwife when the volcano made the earth shake at the hour of her birth. She found fulfillment piloting the family enterprises toward power and prosperity. She was pleased to have accomplished her ends without resorting any more than necessary to the vial of acid and stick of dynamite, to the goon squads, arsonists and button men, to the tools of intimidation that all rulers of nations and heads of clans from times antique have had to use to keep their enemies at bay. She relied on the arts of diplomacy and compromise more than the cruder craft of mayhem to achieve her goals. Violence she regarded as a necessary evil, though she did not flinch at using it when all other options failed.

The Falcone family never got too big, deflecting the focus of rival mobs and the law. And the Godmother kept the grease sheet small and tried to stay in her own territory. The Falcone enterprises were also aided by a few strokes of luck. Since they were not yet truly big-time, the Falcone clan was able to avoid the scrutiny of the Seabury crackdown in the early 1930s. When the so-called Noble Experiment of Prohibition ended just before Christmas 1933, La Cumare was poised to make a smooth transition, pouring most of the family's resources into neighborhood gambling operations—policy games, slot machines, candy-store punchboards.

In running the show Maria could count on the help of her loyal lieutenant Claudio, who, as his sister-in-law had predicted, beat the rap in Pennsylvania and came back with a renewed respect for her brainpower. And in spite of the whispers about them, Maria and Claudio never consummated their sexual hunger for each other. Soon Claudio kept his word by going to Italy to fetch a bride, a docile and pretty country girl named Marta Volo who bore him one son, Johnny. In fact, Maria's only lovers were the quicksilver priest and the despised padrone. Since the one experience was so ghostly, and the other so ghastly, Maria would always consider herself a kind of spiritual virgin.

So she poured her energies into her work and community activities. She became a regular churchgoer and large contributor to local charities. People came from here, there and everywhere to seek her counsel, formulas and help. As a Neapolitan she formed an alliance with the Camorra satrap Rico Longo and managed to remain outside the much more powerful (and intrusive) Unione Siciliana, giving the clan enviable flexibility and independence. When Longo soon died of colon cancer, the Falcones had a clear field.

The moments of satisfaction, of course, were tempered by disappointments and sorrows.

The next news she had of Balbi came in the form of a requiem-mass notice from the crow who called herself his wife.

Maria, as she'd promised, did make attempts to give love and attention to Cesare, but the damage seemed already to have been done. She saw him grow up weak and resentful, and though she tried to groom him to take a leadership role in the organization he lacked the iron that would enable him to meet her expectations. His escape was the bottle.

Maria was officially widowed in 1927 when Pepe also had a sudden heart attack, and she grieved for him as she would have for a beloved brother. How unlike his fig trees and grapevines he was, dying in the shade of his young and spirited wife.

But at age thirty-five Maria too became sick and a year later doctors removed her right breast. The better to draw the bow-string, the Godmother liked to say.

In August 1944 word reached her that Don Gabriele had been killed by a stray bomb during an Allied air raid in the Alban hills outside Anzio. She didn't know what the defrocked priest had been doing there. And she was surprised at how little emotion she felt at the news.

Yet all these satisfactions and sorrows paled before the exultation she felt under a canopy of stars that evening in the ceremony of Torre del Greco when they threw sacred earth over the mortal remains of her parents.

The only experience to surpass it was the joy she felt now as she gazed on the crucifix in Saint Patrick's Cathedral while witnessing the ordination of her son Angelo.

MINISTRY

†

The celebration was held at Puccio's restaurant, where the newly minted priest handed out cigars to all the male guests, relatives and friends, who in return gave him big kisses on the face and gifts, mostly envelopes stuffed with cash. Father Falcone, turning beet-red, didn't want to accept the money, but they pressed it on him, reminding him that most priests got paid in Hail Marys. He shrugged, anticipating that he would come across plenty of charity cases when he began his ministry.

Puccio's was a big family-style Neapolitan restaurant on Prince Street, where the bill of fare, while not fancy, was cornucopian. The owner, Stanislao Puccio, was beside himself with pleasure at having been chosen over all his local rivals for the singular honor of hosting this reception. Needless to say, he would present the family with no bill. To do so would be unthinkably bad form, offensive to both God and man. Of course La Cumare would make a show of insisting on paying. But Signor Puccio would not be fool enough to accept. Hey, don't worry. He knew how to present a handsome figure. Twirling his outdated waxed mustachio, he rocked on the soles of his feet, surveying the room with eagerness and pleasure. Why, even Congressman Vito Marcantonio was there. It was truly a red-letter day.

Father Falcone stood by the nude cherub of a gurgling bronze fountain in the center of the banquet hall greeting well-wishers and doling out cigars. He was a handsome enough fellow, tall and thin with a mane of thick dark curly hair. His very pale complexion made him appear somewhat ascetic, which considering his calling might have been appropriate but was not, in fact, the case. He was an earthy man of robust appetites.

Father Falcone embraced his younger brother Cesare.

"Glad you could make it," he said, tongue-in-cheek.

Cesare wore his reddish hair in a crew cut and sported Ivy League clothes. His hazel eyes and stocky build made him resemble the late Pepe Falcone more closely. "Level with me, Ange'," he said, squinting sarcastically. "Did you take this job because you get to wear a lot of dresses?"

The priest looked from side to side in a vein of mock intrigue. "Don't tell anybody."

"And did yuh read the fine print on those vows you took?"

"Yeah. Have a cigar."

Cesare declined, instead lighting a cigarette with his Zippo. He shook his crew-cut head. "I can't get used to the idea of calling my brother *father*, you know what I mean?"

Father Angelo smilingly brushed his fingernails on his lapel. "Just call me Your Excellency, okay?"

Cesare laughed, then glanced over at their mother seated at the main banquet table, where she nursed a whiskey sour and extended her hand to a flattered guest. Her brother-in-law Claudio sat beside her, devouring a plate of antipasto. Behind them hovered Bonaventura, the bodyguard, a sphinx in wash-and-wear poplin, mountainous, wary-eyed.

Cesare looked back at his brother. "You're married to the Church now, right?"

"Something like that."

"Make sure you don't cheat on her," he drawled.

"That's not my style," he replied, momentarily annoyed. Then his expression softened. "Gimme a kiss."

As the brothers hugged again, Angelo smelled a strong odor of tobacco and alcohol. He frowned at Cesare. "Starting early?"

Cesare sniffed the air, looking offended. He had a thin, finely carved nose. "So?" he said. "It's a celebration."

"Yes." The new priest decided not to press the issue. He glanced around the room. "Seen Johnny?" he asked.

Cesare shook his head.

"He wasn't at the cathedral," Father Falcone observed. "I'm worried."

"Hey, he's probably shacked up somewhere . . ." Cesare covered his mouth with his hand. "Oops!"

Father Angelo was not convinced. They both knew that Cousin Johnny, Claudio's son, was no skirt-chaser, quite the opposite.In fact he had an almost monkish flair for self-denial and a seeming disdain for worldly pleasures. Some people said that Johnny should have been the priest instead of Angelo. His traits of austerity and self-control marked him for a future high place in "the family business," except that he was considered a bit of an oddball.

But he was always on time.

What, Father Angelo couldn't help wondering, if Johnny's absence was in some way connected to the feud between his mother's organization and the rival group headed by Koenig? Father Angelo took pains to stay as ignorant as possible of such family affairs, but sometimes he couldn't help reading things in the newspapers and hearing things on radio and television. Especially now with the Kefauver hearings going on in Washington. He glanced at his wristwatch, worried.

Father Angelo lit a cigar and glanced around. The room was getting crowded and noisy as people shouted greetings and cracked jokes with typical Neapolitan brio. The young priest reflected on how much he loved these folk even if he didn't always approve of their way of life. Yes, he was a priest now, but not a judge, and the olive oil of Holy Orders did not automatically confer moral clarity. Maybe these are my publicans and sinners, he thought.

"You look terrible in black," said a familiar voice. "Brings out your chalky skin color."

Father Angelo turned and shook hands with his old pal Junior Scario. "But congratulations anyhow, if that's what we're supposed to say on this occasion."

The big mole on Junior's walnut-colored cheek was buried in the wreaths of a quick smile that came and vanished like a conjurer's trick. He wore a pin-striped suit, too heavy for the season, and his perpetual look of uneasiness. The priest had great affection for Junior, ever since the days when they did everything together, from pitching pennies on the sidewalk to showering under fire hydrants to playing stickball in the street. They received their first Holy Communion on the same day. They even used to dress alike, as little *carabinieri* for the feast day processions. They hopped turnstiles together for jaunts to Coney Island. They went on their first double-date together. They were like that—Chang and Eng, Italian-style.

Father Angelo now jostled Junior's shoulder. "Glad you could make it, kid. I missed you in church."

"Ah, church is for old ladies. And priests. Sorry."

"That's okay. Have a cigar."

"Yeh, sure, thanks."

As he lit the Havana for him Father Angelo studied his boyhood friend's face. He had always seemed possessed of demons of some sort. Of course that was understandable, given his background. No doubt they had been hatched in the desperate poverty and ostracism that the Scario family suffered after the old man was bumped off in 1929. Father Angelo was sketchy on the details, but Junior's father was rumored to have been a stool pigeon, a species that, any amateur ornithologist could tell you, didn't live long in this habitat. No wonder Junior Scario always seemed to go for the quick buck.

Father Angelo, watching Junior as he made his way over to the bar, thought about how he now was supposed to have the power to cast out devils. He wished he could help Junior.

He glanced toward the banquet table and saw his Uncle Claudio whisper something in his mother's ear. A sudden heat filled the son's face and he felt . . . what? Something he couldn't name. Or wouldn't name. He frowned, resisting the impulse to cross himself.

He noted that Uncle Claudio didn't seem troubled by his son Johnny's absence. Maybe he had sent him on an errand, but he wondered what might have been so urgent that it couldn't have waited until after the celebration . . . and suddenly there flashed in Father Angelo's mind the image of his father's copper-lined wooden coffin being lowered into the grave . . .

His mother caught his eye and called him over.

She nestled his hand in both of hers. "This is one of the happiest days of my life," she told him. "Father Angelo Falcone," savoring the words like wild strawberries.

On the table in front of her was a platter of sliced figs and prosciutto. Her dark wavy hair was streaked with gray, but she had the pale and delicate features of an ivory cameo. Right now she seemed troubled. "You're happy, Angelo, no?"

"Yes, Mamma." And it was the truth. He believed that he had a genuine vocation to serve the Lord as a priest. He wanted to help people and this was the best way he knew how. The years of indecision, of getting his Ph.D. and sowing wild oats, he now viewed as the typical Augustinian struggle between flesh and spirit. Like the sainted Bishop of Hippo, he had said, in effect, "Give me chastity, but not yet!"

She patted his head. "Good. Good. You'll be a bishop someday. A cardinal."

"Why not Pope?"

"Why *not*?"

He shook his head. "I just want to be a parish priest, Mamma."

"We'll see," she said, patting his hand again. "Sit now." She turned to Claudio. "Eh, tell Puccio we're ready to begin the dinner."

Claudio, gnawing a stalk of celery, quickly obeyed, crooking his finger at a flunky who hustled over.

Father Angelo gave the blessing before the meal, his first public prayer as a priest. And what a meal followed! Fried mozzarella, pork and vegetable soup *alla Napolitana, lasagna di carnevale,* fried squid, boiled octopus, roasted squab, garnishes of bitter green olives, sweet red and yellow peppers, onions in marsala, stuffed artichokes, *zeppole* pastry rings, sweet ricotta turnovers, bowers of fresh fruit, great wheels of aromatic cheese, white and whole wheat bread, sparkling wines, muscatels, brandies, liqueurs. Father Angelo also gave the blessing after the meal.

Strolling musicians appeared and some guests began dancing and singing. Maria took her elder son aside and handed him a small gift-wrapped box. "I hope you like them," she said.

Mumbling thanks, he unwrapped the present—diamond-studded gold cuff links in the form of angels.

"*Bello,* no?"

"Exquisite," he said, thinking how expensive they must be and of all the causes the money might have helped.

"Listen, I know what you're thinking," she said. "But promise me you won't sell them and put the money in the poor box."

"I promise, Mamma. Thank you."

"It's no sin to be rich, you know. Not all saints wore sackcloth. And who's got more money than the Vatican?"

Father Angelo might have said something about the difficulty of a camel passing through the eye of a needle but held back. He was her son and the last thing he wanted to do was hurt his mother's feelings. Especially today. So he said nothing and kissed her. Besides, she had a point. Priests took no vow of poverty, only of chastity and obedience. As she left his side to go over and chat with some guests he thought about her reasons for so badly wanting him to become a priest. It was no surprise that a woman of peasant stock from southern Italy would see the Church as a favored way to importance and respectability. Still, his mother had started so early talking about it, and treated the subject as though it were somehow a *personal* matter with her . . .

He picked up a paring knife and began to peel an orange at the banquet table. Of course, he saw his vocation differently. He believed he had been called to help his fellow man, and that his mother had been acting as God's agent. Staring at the helix of the orange rind, he realized that she had never indicated she was aware of that. No, with her it was something he must be . . . for her.

Meanwhile Signor Puccio, in his old-fashioned morning coat, approached the table bearing a large gift-wrapped box. His obsequious smile was ornamented by two gold teeth. "*Padre reverendo,*" he said with too much deference for Angelo's taste, "*mi scuza,* but this just came by Western Union. Special delivery," he added, making the words sound like the high notes of an aria.

Everybody gathered round to see what was in such a big box and watch Father Angelo remove the wrapping and open the box. He looked inside, blanched and vomited the orange pulp, dropping the box to the floor. Out rolled the severed head of Johnny Falcone.

"*Requiescat in pace,*" Father Angelo intoned from the altar.

So it was that among the very first acts of his young priesthood was to celebrate the bloodless sacrifice of a requiem mass for the immortal soul of his cousin Johnny Falcone. It was a less than auspicious way to launch his ministry.

The wake and funeral were closed-coffin affairs that took place many days after the killing when the medical examiner had completed the autopsy and the authorities finally had released the body to the family. Johnny's torso had been found under a causeway on

Broad Channel in Jamaica Bay on the day after the ordination party. Birds had banqueted on his entrails.

The police went through the motions of investigating the beheading but everyone knew they would be less than zealous. To some extent their hands were tied since even the victim's family and associates would not cooperate with the investigation. So the detectives shrugged and said to themselves, as long as innocent people don't get hurt, why not let the bad guys kill each other off? Sometimes, though, it got out of hand.

But not this time. Not if the Unione Siciliana had anything to say about it. Immediately after the news of Johnny's rub-out got around, the wheels were set in motion to quash the feud between Koenig the Jew and the Falcone clan. The last thing the Syndicate needed was a headline-making bloodbath in the streets, especially as a junior senator from Tennessee named Estes Kefauver was turning up the heat by holding committee hearings on organized crime. This kind of publicity was bad for business, and the bosses were bottom-line men at heart.

Both Koenig as a Jew and the Falcones as Neapolitans were, strictly speaking, outsiders. But both organizations were loosely allied to the Syndicate at a time when the underworld was in transition, trying to shed the old image of the Mustache Petes with their blood feuds and old-world codes of honor, and to enter the modern age, the second half of the twentieth century when business would be conducted in a more coolly rational American way.

The Falcone family, heirs of the Neapolitan Camorra rather than the Sicilian Mafia, did not have enough muscle to buck the trend. Moreover, La Cumare was a sharp practical businesswoman and sympathetic to the notion of running their affairs in a more legitimate and respectable manner. It fit with her vision of the family as atavus of a great dynasty of future leaders and power brokers. Claudio, of course, lusted after vengeance, quick and hot. But Maria would handle him. She could always handle him.

Shortly after Johnny's killing, La Cumare and Claudio attended a sitdown where the matter would be adjudicated. Koenig and his second-in-command, a Barese named Albano, also were invited.

Johnny had been killed in retaliation for trying to muscle in on the gambling turf of a Koenig underboss in East Harlem, a man

also connected to Francesco Castiglia, known to the gossip columnists as Frank Costello. This was a provocative act, but the Koenig
gang had killed without getting prior approval, committing an
even greater violation of the code of conduct.

And Claudio Falcone, a respected lieutenant in the small but
prosperous family run by Maria Croce Falcone, had lost his only
son, an injury for which there was really no suitable reparation.

However, the Council of Elders imposed what they considered a
diplomatic solution. Koenig was ordered to pay an indemnity of
$500,000 to the Falcones and cede them territory for gambling
operations downtown east of the Bowery, a section with a heavy
influx of Chinese and Puerto Rican clients. In return the Falcones
had to vow not to start competing businesses on a rival's turf without first applying to the Commission for a license. Koenig, swallowing hard, accepted the terms, he had little choice. But Claudio,
sitting beetle-browed at Maria's right hand, expressed dissatisfac-
tion with the conditions, demanding to know the name of the
button man. To him, vengeance was a dish best eaten hot, not
cold. He was a man of action, and this quality made him valuable to
La Cumare, as it had over the years. But he was also a man of
unbridled passions, which, as before, could make him a millstone
around her neck.

She took him aside and set him straight.

When she came back to the table she sealed the pact with a firm
nod of the head. Somebody brought out anisette and cookies and
the matter was not mentioned again. In spite of her sex, and in a
way even because of it, Maria Falcone commanded special respect
among these men, products of a crypto-matriarchal culture. She
had earned her bones many years earlier and many times over. She
was *una donna honorata*—a woman of honor. Yes, her flesh was
soft but she was renowned for having a mind and will of tempered
steel. She had her historic antecedents, after all, in such as Lucrezia
Borgia and Catherine de Medici, and the comparisons would have
pleased La Cumare. Maria Falcone was not, and had not been, the
ordinary ruthless and acquisitive crime boss. Thanks to a simple
parish priest so many years ago, she was a reader, a thinker and a
dreamer who was able to take the long view of her and her family's
role in life. She had had to scrape, connive and sacrifice for so many

years, but she had never lost sight of her family and what she believed in. Yes, there was cruelty in her profession, but ideals too. Founder of what one day would be called the House of Falcone, that was her life and what she worked for.

After all, wasn't Salvestro de Medici himself an outlaw, a wool-carder who led the revolt of the Ciompi? And who was Cosimo the First but a Renaissance gangster whose rise to power was as brutal as any Mafia chief's? How many generations did it take that great family to go from carders to cardinals? Just three or four, as she recalled. It was the way of the world. Today's outlaw was tomorrow's ambassador. Today's gangster was tomorrow's pope. Maria Falcone aspired to far more than riches. And how did such families make the climb to greatness?

One way, she thought, was to give sons to the Church. Father Angelo Falcone was the beginning.

Father Angelo soon got his first assignment, curate at San Gennaro's Parish on Spring Street. People might have remarked that it was unusual for the Archdiocese to assign a newly ordained priest to a post in his home neighborhood. They might have speculated about it, observing that the Falcones often made handsome contributions to Catholic Charities. They might have drawn certain conclusions. But never aloud. Such thoughts did not enter the young priest's mind. Angelo was content to work among people he knew, eager to begin his ministry.

San Gennaro's was a large church built in 1885 by immigrant Neapolitan stonemasons and bricklayers with trowels and mortar and sweat and love. It was done in a mixture of architectural styles, with touches of Greek Revival, Gothic and Romanesque. It was surrounded by a high brick wall that enclosed a garden and small graveyard as well as the two-story brick rectory. It was an oasis of greenery, fruit trees and flowers amid the cement and asphalt of downtown Manhattan. Father Angelo anticipated spending pleasant hours in the garden, smoking Camels, composing sermons and gardening.

Finding the time, however, turned out to be difficult with his very busy schedule. The pastor, Father Martin Meara, was getting old and found it harder and harder to keep up with his duties. The cranky Irishman had a kidney ailment, bad eyesight and lack of sympathy for the pyrotechnical brand of religion practiced by his flock, a race of people that had produced the flying monk of Pomigliano and the annual liquification of San Gennaro's blood, among other beliefs and practices spawned by a history of earth-quakes, foreign subjugation and poverty. And if he lacked under-standing of the ways of Neapolitans, the pastor was even more out of tune with the newer immigrants from Puerto Rico, who increas-ingly filled the pews of his church as the Italians began an exodus to the outer boroughs and suburbs.

Over the summer, as Americans fought on a crab-claw of land called Korea, Father Angelo Falcone immersed himself in priestly work, saying mass and benediction, presiding at baptisms, wed-dings and funerals, hearing confession, dispensing communion to bedridden parishioners, giving last rites to the deathly ill, refereeing basketball games, counseling newlyweds on the evils of using rub-bers, serving as moderator of the Holy Name Society, the Don Bosco Club, the Dominic Savio Club and the Youth Group, and organizing bingo games, church bazaars and other fund-raising activities. In his very little spare time he pruned the flower beds.

With all his activities he became a very familiar and popular fig-ure in the neighborhood, this chain-smoking curate with the grav-elly voice who wore dark glasses wherever he went and could crack an off-color joke with the best of them. Unlike the pastor, he had the common touch and his conduct reminded people of the differ-ence between sanctity and sanctimony. Housewives were always giving him tins of freshly baked *taralle*, fruit peddlers presented him with bunches of grapes and baskets of figs. Not surprisingly, he soon gained weight.

He also became known for possessing a silver tongue, and his sermons got rave reviews from the pundits of Spring Street. Father Meara, too tired and jaded to be jealous, was relieved to have so many pastoral burdens lifted from his stooped shoulders and gave his assistant a free hand. As a result Father Angelo was overworked but diverted from his troubles.

He still, though, got the night sweats over Johnny's death. A rolling head with carmine lips haunted his dreams. Family associates hinted that the murder was the handiwork of a husband who wore the horns. Father Angelo didn't buy it. His mother said nothing by way of explanation. She wouldn't lie; that wasn't her style. At such times, she knew the art of silence.

Of course he was also troubled by the whispers about his family, but he was not good at stone-casting. A priest was schooled in forgiveness and understanding. In any case he would never renounce his own flesh and blood. He loved his mother dearly and that was that. He knew that the Falcones had interests in real estate, vending machines, garbage disposal, restaurants, food products, produce, waterfront operations, and other so-called legitimate enterprises. He knew too that the organization was somehow connected to illegal gambling. So? Didn't he run bingo games and wheels of chance at church functions? He took with a grain of salt the stories about the Falcones circulated by the pharisees of the press and the police. He dismissed them as mostly the fabrications of ambitious persons who were out to make names for themselves or who had overactive imaginations. He viewed his mother as a great and, yes, powerful woman whose position naturally inspired envy and slander. Were her ways so different from those of, say, the chairman of United States Steel or the Speaker of the House of Representatives? No, he could not and would not judge her.

He kept a ferrotype photo of her as a young woman on the dresser in his room in the rectory. It was right next to the reproduction of Raphael's *The Alba Madonna* that he had found in an antique shop near Cathedral College. They were the first two images that he saw each morning as the alarm rang, summoning him to seven o'clock mass.

This particular September morning he stumbled out of bed and groped toward the bathroom for a glass of water, the only food or drink that could pass his lips before consuming the body and blood of Christ at mass. Then, still bleary-eyed in the darkness before daybreak, he ran the shower, adjusting the temperature. As the warm water ran over his body he said his morning prayers. He did have a quicksilver scruple: was it sacrilegious to soap his genitals while reciting "Jesus deliver us from the snares of the Devil, from the spirit of fornication, from everlasting death . . . "?

In the sacristy he thumbed through the church calendar. It was

Friday, September 1, first Friday of the month, Month of the Queen of Martyrs in the season of Pentecost, feast day of Saint Giles, confessor, abbot. Vestments would be white.

He was already struggling into the chasuble when Billy Fauci, out of breath from running, finally appeared to serve as altar boy. The other kid whose name appeared on the roster sheet never showed up. The ten-year-old Billy hurriedly put on his cassock and surplice, Father Angelo winked to signal that he was ready, and making tents of their hands, they filed out the side door and climbed the altar steps.

Once during mass Father Angelo was distracted by the sight of a spider stilting along the altar rail but forced himself to keep his mind on the sacred reenactment of Christ's passion and death. The mass was theater, requiring concentration.

Mostly, a few old ladies were scattered around the church. Early masses on weekdays attracted only the devout, the insomniac, the very old. Except . . .

Another sight distracted Father Angelo, a young woman in the front pew. A light raincoat was draped loosely over her tan shoulders, revealing the billowing tops of her full breasts over a low-neck blouse. The old women kept sending disapproving sidelong glances at her.

She was, no question, quite a sight, with her bright ginger hair, dark eyes and painted face. On her head sat a small white cotton handkerchief. A lady of the night, the priest concluded. Still, in spite of her vulgarity she had an appealing quality, he thought. Not innocence, of course . . . but what? Honesty. She looked like an honest person. Perhaps a whore, but not a hypocrite.

Father Angelo bowed down and struck his breast three times, chanting, "*Agnus Dei, qui tollis peccata mundi, miserere nobis* . . ." Have mercy on us.

After mass he gave Billy Fauci a crisp dollar bill.

"Gee, thanks, Father!"

The priest made a habit of this, and word soon got around, which meant he rarely lacked volunteer altar boys at his masses.

* * *

One evening the young priest was "churching" the mother of a newborn baby—a ceremony in which he sprinkled holy water on the mother as a sign of thanksgiving for the healthy birth. He had just settled into an armchair in the rectory dayroom and switched on the round-screen television set when he remembered that he'd forgotten to lock up the church.

With a sigh he rose to his feet.

The votive candles winked and danced in red glasses as he was about to lock the front door from the inside, intending to go out the side door. Suddenly he noticed a worshipper kneeling in the shadows before one of the side altars. His hand froze on the key. He surely didn't want to disturb a person at prayer. He had to wait. Church, after all, wasn't a movie theater where one could shoo out the patrons when the show was over. The Lord's welcome mat was always out. Or was supposed to be.

Quietly he slid into a pew and waited. As his eyes grew accustomed to the darkness, Father Angelo saw that the worshipper was a husky man who seemed unaware of his presence. Father Angelo glanced impatiently at his wristwatch. He was tired and wanted to close shop and kick off his shoes.

Abruptly the man's shoulders slumped, his hands cradled his face as he started to cry. The priest fidgeted in the pew, an embarrassed witness to private grief, a spiritual peeping tom. The man took a handkerchief from his pocket and wiped his eyes. He turned his face to profile—and Father Angelo suddenly recognized him. It was his uncle Claudio.

Father Angelo had long had mixed feelings about his uncle Claudio, who apparently had come to church to try to cope with his grief over his son Johnny's awful death. Since boyhood, Angelo had had misgivings about the relationship between his uncle and his mother. As he knelt now before the holy tabernacle containing the sacred vessels he couldn't lie to himself . . . he had suspected them of the sin John the Baptist had rebuked Herod and Herodias for. The suspicion itself was sinful, because he had no proof that Maria and Claudio had made Pepe "wear the horns," as they said in the old country. Though he had confessed this evil thought time and again in the Sacrament of Penance, he still couldn't wipe it from his mind.

Finally Claudio got up from the pew and went to the altar rail, where he lit two candles. Then he left the church by a side door.

That night Father Angelo went to bed with a head-hammering migraine.

He was heading down the Bowery, having walked in the apple-crisp autumn air all the way from Columbus Hospital, when he saw her again. She was some ten paces away at the curbside, hugging a brown bag of groceries and looking both ways at traffic before crossing the street. He had spotted her by the unusual rust color of her hair.

She turned and noticed him watching her and she smiled, teeth sparkling in the gathering dusk.

Father Angelo nodded, then looked straight ahead, resisting the temptation to watch her hip-swivel across the street. Turning on to Spring Street, he sighed. A priest didn't stop being a man. Did he heed the scriptural warning: "Whosoever looketh on a woman to lust after her hath committed adultery with her already in his mind"? He allowed an ironic smile. He didn't want to pluck out his offending right eye. And then he thought of a girl named Veronica so many years ago and the ironic mood disappeared.

Arriving at the rectory, he went to his office and riffled through the mail, then checked his appointment book: he was scheduled that evening to hear confession, serve Benediction and referee a CYO basketball game. But his thoughts kept drifting to Veronica. Had he been in love with her? How could he be sure, especially now that his emotions were so confused by remorse? They had been so young, what did they know about love? They knew sexual desire . . . and pain. One thing was sure—what had happened to Veronica had more than a little to do with his decision to enter the seminary, not slighting his mother's long-standing persistent influence. They said the Lord worked in mysterious ways. Sometimes, Father Angelo thought, His ways were not so much mysterious as devious.

He put his head in his arms on the walnut desktop, feeling drained.

After a minute or two he raised his head. What made him feel so hollow? The trip to the hospital didn't help. It was always depressing, dispensing Communion to the half-alive, performing the rite of Extreme Unction. His nostrils still were filled with the mingled odors of medicine, ether, holy oil and death. The worst part was visiting the pediatric ward. Sick kids, even dying kids. They got to him the most. Oh, he knew that ministering to the sick was supposed to be a spiritually uplifting experience for a priest. But he just wasn't that far advanced on the priestly path.

He glanced at the oil portrait of Mother Cabrini hanging on the wall and wondered if saints also had any qualms like his. Of course, he decided. What made them saints was the successful struggle to *overcome* human weakness, not the lack of it.

The idea gave him little comfort.

Father Angelo inflated his cheeks and blew the referee's whistle. On a drive to the basket Joey Morales had been fouled hard by a visiting player from Our Lady of the Assumption. Joey retaliated by giving the kid a wicked punch in the nose.

The priest rushed over and separated the two windmilling youngsters, but the presence of a priest did not inhibit the stream of obscenities from their mouths. Blood still geysered from the nose of the visitor, who was being restrained by his coach.

"Leggo me, Brother Basil," he growled. "I'll kill the Spic bastard."

"Calm down, Kevin," said the coach, an Irish Christian brother in civvies. "And watch your mouth or, b'Jesus, I'll slug yuh too."

Joey Morales just stood there glowering, arms hanging at his side.

Brother Basil said to the priest, "Can't you do something to control this here delinquent, Father Angelo?" He meant Joey.

Joey darted the man a venomous look. "The jerk-off clotheslined me. Nobody gets away with that."

"Shut up, Joey," Father Angelo said. "Take a shower, you're out of the game. But wait for me. I want to talk to you later."

Muttering, Joey shuffled off to the locker room.

The game resumed and, mostly due to Joey's absence, San Gennaro's lost, 28–21 . . .

The priest found him fully dressed and smoking a cigarette in the locker room.

"Put it out."

The boy flipped the butt into the wet shower stall, where it sizzled and died.

Father Angelo glared at the wet cigarette but stifled the impulse to tell him to pick it up. He wasn't sure how to handle the boy. He was surprised even to have found him still waiting for him. Actually he had expected him to take a powder. Yes, Joey was a hard case—suspicious, quick-tempered, pugnacious, always getting into scrapes with his own teammates, not to mention opposing players. He had all the signs of a kid from a troubled household.

"We lost, huh?" Joey said.

The priest nodded.

Joey gave an eloquent snort. Father Angelo knew what he meant. With him on the court the home team would have wiped the floor with the visitors. The way Joey could shoot and dribble reminded the priest of the All-American from Holy Cross, Bob Cousy. Trouble was, Joey also punched like the heavyweight champion Ezzard Charles.

"Sit down, Joey."

The boy sat on the low wooden bench between the rows of lockers and waited, deadpan and silent, for what the priest had to say. Father Angelo sat down too, closely looking at the boy's seemingly untroubled features. He had dark eyes, prominent cheekbones, a stubby straight nose and a nice mouth marred by yellow teeth. "You're right, Joey. The team would've won with you in the game."

"No kidding."

"You've got to learn not to fly off the handle like that. Why do you do it?"

Joey shrugged. "Hey, he clotheslined me. What else could I do? A guy's gotta defend himself."

"You broke his nose."

"Looks better that way, the ugly Mick."

"You could be arrested for assault."

Joey shrugged again, as if he expected nothing less in life than a few stretches in stir.

"How old are you, Joey?"

"Fourteen."

Father Angelo was still getting to know many of the parishioners, especially the ones who lived east of the Bowery and north of Spring Street, mostly Puerto Rican. He didn't know Joey's background, and in spite of the chip on the boy's shoulder, liked him and wanted to know him better.

"Why don't you play for your high school team? You're good enough."

"I got no time for that."

"Where do you go? Cardinal Hayes? Power Memorial?"

"Nah, I go to public school," Joey said, avoiding eye contact.

A truant, the priest thought, without hinting that he thought so. He had decided to make a special project of Joey Morales, a candidate for his circle of publicans and sinners. You didn't need to be Sigmund Freud to figure out that the boy's attitude covered up a huge lack of self-esteem.

"How'd you learn to play basketball so good?"

"I dunno. Comes natural, I guess."

"Your father teach you?"

"What father? I got no father, *Father*."

Father Angelo shut his mouth for a moment. Born in sin, he thought. That was the mindless popular expression for Joey's bastard state. We'll all born in sin, aren't we? Except for the Immaculate Conception.

"You mean your old man's dead?"

"Who gives a shit? Pardon my French, Father. I mean I never knew him."

Was there something in Joey's eyes that betrayed sadness, regret?

"My mother, she's dead," the boy said.

"I'm sorry. What happened?"

"Bum ticker."

"I see." No wonder the kid was so troubled. "Who do you live with? Who supports you?"

"My sister. She's twenty-two." The boy had seemed to be warming a little to the priest's interest in him. But now a guarded look came into his eyes.

"How come she doesn't come to the games?"

"She works nights. Can I go now?"

"Look, Joey, I run the sodality and the Don Bosco Club. Why don't you join?"

"Nah, forget about it. Those clubs are for fairies."

"Fairies like me?"

"Nah, you're a priest."

"At least think about it, Joey. We go to Radio City. We go on camping trips. We do lots of stuff."

"Okay, I'll think about it, but I ain't promising nothin'."

"That's good enough for me."

Joey got up and shuffled his sneakers. "Can I cut out now?"

The priest nodded.

Before reaching the door, Joey glanced back. "By the way, Father, thanks."

"For what?"

"Well, I thought you was gonna belt me. Or at least bawl me out real bad. Thanks for not doing it, for treating me—"

"Don't mention it. But hey, if you thought I was going to hit you, why did you hang around? Why didn't you just beat it?"

The boy gave him an incredulous look. "You're kidding, right?"

"No. I was surprised to find you waiting for me."

Joey laughed. "Nobody'd be dumb enough to disobey you, Father."

"Why, because I'm a priest?"

"Nah. Because your name's Falcone."

Joey Morales left Father Angelo sitting in the locker room, sadly enlightened.

Winter came, and Father Angelo's reputation as a compassionate and effective shepherd of his flock grew. Every Sunday after mass little children clustered around him, tugging at his cassock. The line outside his confession box on Saturday mornings grew longer and longer. Young men who received draft notices to fight in Korea came for his blessing. Female parishioners, magnetized by his gruff charm, flocked to his Benediction services and the Stations of the Cross. Attendance at Sunday masses doubled. To the pastor's pleasure, proceeds from the collection plate also grew, even though the parishioners were mostly a needy group of people.

One day an altar boy rehearsing a wedding ceremony fainted and the priest discovered that he hadn't eaten in almost twenty-four hours. The father was jobless, both parents spoke no English and didn't know the first thing about applying for so-called Home Relief. It was a common story, Father Angelo soon learned. Many of his parishioners often went to bed hungry, and city and private welfare agencies were too snarled in red tape and too short of funds to provide sufficient help. The parents had no skills, no work, no education. Many of them drank cheap wine to fog their troubles. The families lived in drafty cold-water walk-ups in condemned tenements where the kids had roaches and rats instead of spaniels and Siamese cats for pets.

The curate rolled up his sleeves, called in a few neighborhood markers and proceeded to try to become a one-man Welfare Department. He made the rounds of local bakeries, fish markets and grocery stores, soliciting regular donations to a new parish food program that he had started. When not one merchant said no he remembered Joey's comment about the name Falcone. Amen, he thought. It was all in a good cause.

In the most severe cases he even enlisted the direct help of his mother. One man, a member of the Holy Name Society, was going blind with chronic glaucoma and needed an expensive new drug treatment. In less than a day La Cumare came up with an unnamed benefactor to pay for the treatment. The raging polio epidemic took so many young victims in the neighborhood. Again using the good offices of La Cumare, Angelo raised enough money to buy five wheelchairs. He had no qualms of conscience about where the money might be coming from. The result was what counted.

Soon Father Angelo was revered by his flock as a kind of miracle-worker. But he was far from content. The problems of the neighborhood were too deep to be solved by one priest, no matter how dedicated and well-connected. He had his failures as well as his successes. One day he had to give Extreme Unction to a six-year-old boy who had died of bulbar polio that had attacked the nerve cells in his brain. This incurable disease was a plague on children. Father Angelo had read that polio had afflicted some seventy thousand American kids over the last two years. The disease had struck the Lower East Side with the force of a biblical retribution. He personally knew about a dozen kids who had the illness, with varying degrees of disability. Why, he wondered, had the Lord decreed the suffering and death of so many children?

Back at the rectory he tried to get his mind off the question by watching the Jimmy Durante Show on television. And slowly the dream formed: he would build a Childrens Hospital and Research Center on the Lower East Side. He didn't know how, he didn't know when. He just knew that he would do it.

In the spring he planted two fig trees and an olive tree in a section of the churchyard sheltered by the south wall of the stone church. He would cover them with tar paper in the winter to keep them alive year after year, a technique of simulating the climate of the old country he had learned from Pepe, who died when Angelo was only seven.

Although twenty-three years had passed since the old man went to his reward Father Angelo still had vivid memories of Pepino Falcone, and he conjured them now as his hands were deep in soil. The old man had had a kind of nobility. A carpenter with nothing to build, he put his crafty hands to other useful and life-giving enterprises, planting trees, flowers and tomatoes in their sunny urban backyard, kneading dough for pasta and bread, pressing grapes for bootleg wine and touching his children affectionately. Angelo could still feel those rough warm hands on his face. Pepe was a sunny man, bright with the spark of life, who finally withered and died in the shadow of his wife.

Father Angelo had loved him as much as he still loved his mother. But he loved them in different ways. He had loved the man he had been raised to think was his father in the way he automatically loved God's gentler creatures. There was nothing automatic, though, about the love he felt for his mother, whom no one could portray as a docile creature. It was a much stormier and more complicated emotion. Angelo had always sensed a rift in the relationship between Pepe and Maria, broken cords in the conjugal knot.

Father Angelo made a hasty sign of the cross, then went over to turn on the hose spigot and water the trees. The notion of becoming a priest had dawned slowly, he remembered, in the weeks and months after Pepe died. And it surprised him that when he first told his mother of his intention she seemed delighted. But, of course, it was she who had planted the seeds of his vocation by cultivating in him habits and tastes for things if not necessarily spiritual surely ecclesiastical. She made certain he became an altar boy, studied catechism, attended regular Friday and Saturday devotions as well as on Sunday and holy days of obligation, sang in the boys' choir. She had carefully groomed him for the role.

Of course, when the hormonal storms of puberty struck he rebelled, dropping out of Cathedral High School and landing in the clutches of the Jesuits of Fordham Prep who steered him toward the study of philosophy. His mother bit her tongue as he took a nearly ten-year detour, earning his doctorate at Columbia, haunting the coffee houses of Greenwich Village in black beret and turtleneck, smoking a pipe and squiring various young women around. She might have bossed a lot of tough and dangerous men, but her instincts seemed to tell her that strong-arm methods would not avail in the case of her son.

So she bided her time.

And her patience paid off.

He retraced his steps and entered the seminary. After what happened with Veronica . . . La Cumare never knew Veronica, the priest reflected, and it was just as well. However it came about, he believed today that he had chosen the right path. He would atone through good works—

His thoughts were interrupted by an unfamiliar voice: "Excuse me, Father . . ."

The voice, deep and slightly reedy, belonged to a middle-aged man with a barrel chest and rosy cheeks fringed by a brown beard salted with gray. He stuck out a meaty hand and introduced himself.

"Simon Fisher. I guess you've heard of me."

Father Angelo turned off the hose and shook the slightly moist hand. He grimaced, searching his memory. "Can't say that I have."

"Forgive me. Didn't mean to sound egotistical. I run the Benedetto Croce Democratic Club down the street. You know, the reform club?"

"Oh sure. Glad to meet you."

Simon Fisher put his hands over his ample hips and surveyed the budding garden. "So you've got a green thumb, eh? On top of everything else."

"God willing," said the priest.

"Well, I'm afraid you won't have much time for gardening anymore."

Father Angelo squinted quizzically. "Beg pardon?"

"I got a proposition for you."

"Oh? Well, can I offer you some tea or lemonade?"

Fisher made a tart face. "No thanks." He jerked his thumb toward the tavern corner. "I got a better idea. Lemme buy you a beer."

Father Angelo began to remove his apron. The hard work of gardening had left him parched. "Lead the way," he said.

They sat on bar stools and ordered two bottles of Rheingold. They made small talk, touching on various subjects from fallout shelters to Ingrid Bergman's affair with Roberto Rossellini.

Finally Fisher got to the point. "Ever think of going into politics?"

Father Angelo savored the tangy brew, put down the glass and said, "I've already got a job."

Fisher nodded briskly. "Yes, and you're doing good work, too. You've made quite a name for yourself already. That's why I'm here."

"I'm not sure I get the picture, Mr. Fisher."

"Look, the primary's coming up and I need a candidate for the City Council."

Without hesitating the priest shook his head. "Not interested."

"Don't dismiss it out of hand, Father Angelo. You wanna help these people? Sure you do. Well, you can do a helluva lot more for them with political clout than you can without it. And you can win, too. You got all the qualifications. You're young, attractive, energetic, popular. Think about it, please."

"Even if I were interested, I'm just too busy. Father Meara's getting on in years and the parish needs a full-time curate, and—"

"No sweat, Father. The Archdiocese intends to assign a third priest to San Gennaro's anyhow. His name's Father Trapani. Comes from Tarrytown."

"How did you know that?"

"I got a rabbi in the Chancery."

Father Angelo laughed. "You're a smart one, Mr. Fisher."

"Call me Simon."

"Okay, you call me Angelo."

"I'd rather call you Councilman. What d'yuh say?"

This time Angelo hesitated. "I don't know, I'd have to get permission from Cardinal Spellman."

"Not exactly a stranger to politics," Simon drawled.

"Not exactly a liberal Democrat either," said Father Angelo.

"That's for sure. But somehow I believe you can swing it."

"Yes, maybe. As long as he doesn't think I'm a pinko." The priest smiled and fell silent, sipping thoughtfully. The people needed public housing, civil-service jobs, legal services, alcohol treatment centers, health clinics. And what about the children's hospital he dreamed of building? Was Simon right? Did he have a better chance of realizing these plans as a political insider who also happened to be a parish priest? Could he serve God and give tribute to Caesar? All these were considerations, but he had to admit that the proposition was already beginning to intrigue him.

Fisher sensed that he was wavering and artfully lightened up on the throttle. "You don't have to give me an answer right away," he said. "Just promise to consider it carefully. I'll get back to you in a couple of weeks."

Father Angelo was staring at the beer glass in front of him. He turned to face Fisher. "Who's the opposition?"

Fisher smiled. This one went right to the heart of the matter. A natural. "Syd Riccio. A real hack that the regulars are propping up. I know him well, we attend the same temple."

"A guy named Riccio goes to temple?"

"Yeah, his folks come from the Roman ghetto. As a politician he can work both sides of the street like LaGuardia. In an Italian crowd he tells scherzos and plays the mandolin. In a Jewish crowd he wears his yarmulke and introduces himself as Syd. He'll be tough to beat but you can do it if anybody can. Once you get past him in the primary the Republicans will be pushovers. Especially in this neighborhood."

"Why don't you run?"

"Me?" Fisher said, poking his barrel chest with his thumb. "Nah, I'm strictly a behind-the-scenes type of guy." He stroked his beard. "But you're different. You'd make a very appealing candidate, really. You could deliver the Catholic vote, the Italian vote, the Puerto Rican vote *and* the women's vote. I'd get some of the Jews to back you. You're not a lock, but you'd have a good shot. Another beer?"

"No thanks."

Simon Fisher swiveled the bar stool to face the picture window looking out on Spring Street. It was Saturday morning and shoppers and strollers thronged the pavements and cobblestones. "They're good people out there," Fisher said. "They need a man like you to represent them. Somebody with guts and brains and heart. You know what I mean?"

Father Angelo also looked out the window. In the alleyways between the tenements and warehouses he saw the fluttering laundry hanging from clotheslines, the motley flag of Naples. He couldn't decide what to do about Simon's offer, but he had time to think it over. Meanwhile, he would pray for guidance.

The priest stuck out his hand and Fisher clasped it.

"I'll give it some thought," Father Angelo promised.

"That's all I ask, my friend. That's all I ask."

Over the next few days Father Angelo prayed to Our Lady of Good Counsel for help in making his decision. But to cover his bets he also decided to ask the advice of his earthly mother.

He picked a Sunday evening when he went to the town house for supper. They had spaghetti with shrimp and a little white wine. After the meal he sipped an espresso and lit up a Di Nobili.

"Can you do this as a priest? Run for political office?" his mother asked.

"It's been done before," he told her. "I've done some research. I just have to get permission."

"Who from? The Pope?"

The son chuckled. "Not that high, Mamma. Just the Cardinal." He blew out a gust of smoke.

The dining room, situated in the rear of the house, had a picture window overlooking the garden where red-and-white geraniums now bloomed in profusion under electric lights. Carmela, the Somalian maid, cleared the dishes from the table. Bonaventura, the palace guard, sat in the parlor playing solitaire. Out front was parked a long black car and two men leaned against the sparkling grill.

"But the Cardinal's a Republican, right? So is Mayor Impellitteri. If you have to run for office, why don't you run as a Republican?"

"For one thing, a Republican would have a hell of a hard time trying to get elected on the Lower East Side."

She looked at him. "Eh, I could make sure you got elected. And don't say bad words. Some priest, you are."

"Sorry, Mamma. But no thanks. I don't want to win that way. And I'm not the Republican type."

Carmela set a bowl of fresh fruit on the table. "Anyhow, I don't like the idea," she said. "You know the Bible says you can't serve two masters."

"I serve the Lord alone. But there are many ways to do it."

"Listen to me, *figlio mio*," she said, pointing with the dessert knife, "if you want to get ahead you got to play politics *inside* the Church, not outside. And you should vote Republican."

"I don't want to get ahead, not in the way you mean."

Looking reflective, she sliced a pear. She was not accustomed to contradiction, even from her son the priest. In her domain she was an absolute monarch, but the queen had a soft spot for her first-born son.

"I still don't like it," she said.

"But this way I can help the people better."

"The family comes first, the family *always* comes first."

"Yes, Mamma. The human family." He smiled at her. Winningly, he hoped.

She sighed. Her eyes had a faraway look. "Where do you get such ideas?"

"Mamma, I'm a priest!"

She grunted. "You think most priests want to help people?"

"I don't care what most priests are like. I have to live with myself."

Chewing a slice of pear, she narrowed her eyes. "Why do you come to me? You sound like you already made up your mind."

"I came for your advice."

"You don't listen to it." She hunched her shoulders.

"And I guess I came for your blessing."

She laughed. "Priests give the blessings, not women."

"Please, Mamma . . . "

She mocked him with the sign of the cross. "*Pax vobiscum.* Still, I think you make a mistake. A big mistake. What about your connection to me?"

"What about it?"

"Doesn't it hurt your chances?"

"This man Simon Fisher says no. Not in this neighborhood."

She nodded proudly. She liked to hear that. "Probably it helps," she said. "Sounds like a smart man, this Fisher. *Furbo. Beh.* Who ever knew a Jew who wasn't smart?"

"I like him," said Father Angelo. "He strikes me as a good man."

She shrugged. "You really want to do this, okay, I help you."

He tried to concoct a diplomatic way of telling her to butt out, but before he could do so the bodyguard came into the room to tell La Cumare that she was wanted on the phone. Long-distance.

Father Angelo could not help overhearing bits and pieces of her conversation. It was Uncle Claudio in St. Petersburg. He had gone to Florida to negotiate a loan from none other than Johnny Torrio to embark on some kind of real-estate deal. The former king of the Chicago rackets, having ended his exile in Naples, was back in the Land of Opportunity acting as a sort of financier for certain enterprises, mostly on the New York scene. Father Angelo concluded from his mother's obvious pleasure that the negotiations had gone well.

The priest finished his coffee and squashed out the stinker in an ash tray. He ate a banana as he waited for La Cumare to return to the table. He was eager to leave soon, he served six o'clock mass on Mondays.

"More coffee?" she asked when she returned. Carmela, with her impassive butterscotch face, stood ready to pour.

He made the sign of the cross and rose from the chair. "No thanks, Mamma. Gotta run."

On the way out he met his brother Cesare, who was just returning home from somewhere. They embraced. Cesare looked around the entranceway in a conspiratorial fashion. "The old lady at home?"

"Sure. I'll tell her you're here."

Cesare put his forefinger to his lips. "I'm trying to steer clear of her."

Angelo was aware of the ongoing friction between his mother and brother, whom she had marked as future boss of the family business, a role he appeared to have no talent for or interest in. Alcohol and amours were more up his alley. "Come on, Chip," he urged, "she's in the dining room. Have a cup of coffee with her?"

"Why don't you go peddle your indulgences," Cesare snapped, brushing past his brother and heading up the ornately carved circular staircase to his room on the second floor.

The priest's eyes followed him until he vanished from sight, then he put on his black fedora and dark glasses and left the house. The two men leaning against the car nodded deferentially as he passed.

Walking back to the rectory in the cool spring air, Father Angelo reflected on his mother's reaction to the idea of his running for the City Council. He had guessed that she probably wouldn't like it, so why had he asked for her advice? Because he wanted her approval, her imprimatur on his plans. And she had, grudgingly, given it. Of course it was now clear, he thought as he crossed Houston Street, that he had decided to say yes to Simon Fisher. Somehow, he felt, there was a rightness to the decision. He had no idea why, but he seemed destined to serve God and his flock in a public way, using his gift for oratory and his popularity beyond the pulpit where they could do the most good. The Blessed Mother had answered his prayers for guidance, not in a Pauline flash of lightning but in a more gradual dawning of illumination. He would phone Fisher after mass tomorrow.

As he turned east on Spring Street he saw the boy and the woman walking a few paces ahead. He peered at them through the dark glasses as they passed under a pool of light cast by the over-hanging street lamp. Yes, it was Joey Morales and the red-haired streetwalker whom he had first noticed in church. He hadn't seen Joey for a while—not since basketball season ended in early March. The boy had not responded to his invitation to join the Don Bosco Club. What were they doing together? Surely she wasn't soliciting a fourteen-year-old boy? As he followed them the truth suddenly occurred to him. Something in the familiar way they walked to-gether, some chemistry in their gestures betrayed the relationship . . . *she* was the sister who worked nights to support him!

Father Angelo fumbled for his Zippo and lit another cheroot. He swallowed hard. She wore a tight short dress of light blue that displayed the roundness of her buttocks and the curves of her legs. He couldn't deny what he felt, the long-suppressed sexual longing. Oh Lord, why didn't You make it possible for a man to check his libido at the door when he entered the priesthood? Why in Your wisdom didn't You make eunuchs of Your servants? At least about one event there was no question: his regular confessor's ear would turn beet-red tomorrow.

He tried to make light of it, but it was a serious matter and he knew it. He badly wanted to obey his vows, to be a good priest, to atone for the errors of his past. Oh yes, he wanted . . .

Father Angelo went home, took a cold shower, recited the divine office and went to bed. But he had a restless night. Migraines again. At three in the morning he got out of bed and went across the hall to the bathroom to take three aspirin tablets.

In the morning he felt better. A new day. Life should be lived day-by-day. Later he had to do marketing since the housekeeper, Mrs. Morelli, had taken the day off to celebrate her sixty-third birthday. In the evening her grandsons were taking her to see *South Pacific* on Broadway, which she had been crowing about for two weeks running.

Shopping gave Father Angelo the chance to stroll the neighbor-hood under a clarion sun, to sample the tastes and odors of Little

Italy and *chiacchierare* with his neighbors. Today it would be especially good for what ailed him.

Everyone saluted the priest in a friendly familiar way as he walked past the fruit stands and pushcarts, the butcher shops and bakeries, the fish markets and salami stores, the restaurants and cafes. Old crows in the black clothes of perpetual mourning gave him toothless smiles. Fat men in greasy aprons boomed greetings that contained an odd mixture of deference and irony. Matrons in flowered house dresses with bambini slung round their hem-plump hips said good day to the handsome Father as their cheeks reddened. Young men even asked him to bless their new Buicks and Packards.

The market stands overflowed with colorful fruits and vegetables. The store windows showcased wagon wheels of cheese, garlands of sausage, lurid shanks of smoked ham, and slaughtered rabbits still oozing blood. Big round loaves of crusty bread sent savory smells wafting out into the street. It was enough to make anyone feel happy to be alive, especially Angelo Falcone's people, villagers at heart.

At each stop he had to haggle with the merchants in reverse, insisting on paying full price or even just paying. He didn't want the Roman collar to give him an edge on poor, generous and often superstitious people who would buy God's blessing with a hunk of *baccalà*.

He was soon loaded with shopping bags that included the pastor's favorite chianti and provolone—Father Meara was always saying how much he loved "guinea food."

On Mulberry Street he stopped for an espresso at Monte Vesuvio Pasticceria, sitting at a round cafe table under an oil portrait of Benito Mussolini. The place was a gallery of local icons that ran the gamut of history, celebrity and sanctity from Mother Cabrini to Giuseppe Garibaldi. As he waited for his coffee Angelo surveyed the autographed photos that covered the wall—Joe DiMaggio, Fiorello LaGuardia, Rocky Marciano, Mario Lanza, Guy Lombardo, Vic Damone, Jimmy Durante, Louie Prima, Frank Sinatra.

He was lighting up a Di Nobili when his old boyhood friend Junior Scario walked in, came over to the table and kissed him on both cheeks.

"What's up, Your Holiness?" Junior said as he sat down. "Hey, don't you know smoking stunts your growth?"

"Sure, runt, what's your excuse?"

Junior smiled. He stood about five-six in his penny loafers.

"Let me buy you a coffee," Father Angelo said, motioning to the waiter, who came over with two coffees that he spiked with anisette at the table. They chatted for a while, speculating on whether Willie Mays would win Rookie of the Year, and whether the Yankees would repeat as World Series champs. Angelo noted that the normally closemouthed Junior seemed more talkative than usual. Actually, he had some tension and awkwardness with Junior ever since what happened with Veronica. It wasn't Junior's fault, he told himself. He had acted as a friend in need. But recalling the role he had played in that whole ugly business . . . the abortion . . . simply kindled painful memories and remorse. Though he valued the relationship and wanted it to survive, he found himself starting to regard their friendship as somehow tainted, like a wine gone sour.

Junior put down his coffee cup and peered at his boyhood friend. "Between you and me, Angie, you really swear off broads?"

Angelo shook his head and smiled. As adolescents they used to spend hours talking about sex. In this regard, at least, Holy Orders didn't change a thing. "Yeah, Junior, and guys too."

"Come *off* it. You wasn't no swish." Junior scratched the mole on his cheek. "I don't know how you do it. Me, I couldn't live without pussy. I'd go bananas, pardon the lingo."

Father Angelo half-smiled. "It's part of the deal. You know me —I'm not a welsher. At least I try not to be."

"Yeah, but don't you think you took this penance business a little too far? Why didn't you just say ten Our Fathers, ten Hail Marys and ten Glory Be's?"

The priest became silent.

This was a subject he felt he couldn't discuss with Junior. "I don't want to talk about it," he said. With Junior around, the priest felt the Devil nipping at his heels.

"How's La Cumar'?" Junior said, changing the subject.

"Fine. I saw her last night."

"Was your uncle there?"

"No. He's out of town."

"I've been trying to talk to him about a little business deal but he keeps avoiding me. I'd like a sitdown. Could you put in a good word for me?"

"I've got no influence with him. But I'll try talking to my mother, if you want."

"Thanks . . . Where did Claudio go?" he asked casually.

"St. Petersburg."

Junior massaged his chin. "Johnny Torrio's down there now, right?"

"Yes, they're doing some real-estate deal. I really don't know anything about it."

"Big bucks, I'll bet."

Father Angelo shrugged over his coffee. He was uncomfortable discussing the family business.

Junior sensed this and dropped the subject.

"Why don't you come to church some Sunday?" Father Angelo suggested as his friend prepared to leave.

"Sure, I'll be there," said Junior, rolling his shoulders like a boxer waiting for the gong. "When they carry me in in a casket."

"By then it'll be too late."

Junior joined four fingers to thumb and gestured. "Look, Angie, if I went to church the roof'd cave in. *Bah-dah-boom.*"

"No, Junior, the Lord welcomes gluttons and winebibbers, publicans and sinners. He'd welcome a *gavone* like you too."

Junior waved him away. "Yeah, well, I'll take a rain check."

After Junior left the cafe, the curate brooded over just what sort of business deal Junior wanted to propose to his uncle Claudio. He knew that the young soldier was dissatisfied with his low position in the Falcone organization and his slow progress up the ladder. Junior was proud, petulant and hotheaded. Angelo hoped he would do nothing rash. The priest was reluctant to talk to his mother about it, as he had promised, because he made it a policy not to mix in the business and because he knew La Cumare had doubts about Junior's worth and abilities. His lineage, for one thing, was a black mark against him. The sons of stoolies usually didn't have bright futures in the business. Italians took to heart the sins of the fathers . . . Only through his friendship with Angelo Falcone had Junior managed to get into the organization at all.

Father Angelo went back to the rectory, unloaded the provisions in the fridge and pantry and dialed the number of the Benedetto Croce Democratic Club. As expected, Simon Fisher was overjoyed at the priest's decision. Father Angelo muttered a prayer of petition that it was the right one.

Meanwhile, four blocks away, Junior Scario was also dialing a call, from the pay-phone booth of Grasso's candy store. As he waited for the connection he took out a handkerchief and dabbed his upper lip. Nearby two teenage boys were thumbing through girlie magazines. Junior shut the door of the phone booth.

"Is Tony there?" Junior murmured into the mouthpiece.

"Who wants to know?" replied Tony "the Squid" Albano, Koenig's underboss.

"Junior Scario." Junior had recognized the voice by now but kept a respectful silence.

"Okay, what gives?" said Albano.

"I've got some information. Might be useful."

"I'm listening."

"Claudio Falcone is in St. Pete's for a parley with Terrible John about a loan. Probably some real-estate deal but I'm not sure."

The Squid was called "The Squid" (not to his face, of course) because of his blob-like appearance, fleshy features and veiny complexion. This could be very useful intelligence. If Falcone was jawing with the Fox, that meant they were branching out again. And in any kind of a squabble Torrio might provide muscle to protect his investment. Whatever, this alliance was bad news for the Koenig firm, but it was better to know about it sooner than later. Scario had provided a service here.

"Thanks, kid," Albano said.

"You'll remember me on payday?"

"Sure. Pick up the envelope at the usual place. And, hey, there'll be something special in *la busta* for yuh."

"Yeah, what?"

"A round-trip ticket to the Windy City and two ringsides for the Ezzard Charles-Joey Maxim fight."

"Hey, thanks," said Junior.

"Sure, sure, don't mention it. *Una mano lava l'atra*, right? You take care of us, we take care of you."

Junior replaced the telephone with a sense of satisfaction. If the Falcones didn't appreciate him at least somebody did. As he left the candy store he was already thinking about who to lay bets with on the fight. He favored Maxim over the *mool-en-yom* but Charles was the better bet. He would study the odds right away, he decided, as he headed down Houston Street whistling "From This Moment On."

He wore the turncoat with a natural ease, like a snake wears its skin.

Father Richard Trapani, the new assistant pastor, assumed his duties at San Gennaro's in the nick of time as Father Angelo's campaign activities were intensifying. Father Angelo liked Father Trapani on sight—a bald, middle-aged man, pious without being pietistic, who seemed a hard worker. Father Angelo liked the way he plunged right into parish activities on the first day, offering to take over much of the younger priest's confession and benediction roster and to lead the Holy Name Society. He seemed not at all ambitious, just eager to help. He had a cherubic simplicity that was very appealing. Maybe his light bulb flickered now and then, but he had the grace to know his limitations, exemplified by his declining the pastor's suggestion that he help balance the parish books. He was, it seemed, fashioned in the mold of the kindly but slow-witted village sacristan from whom God had withheld certain intellectual gifts but for whom He had reserved a special place in heaven among the shepherds who had stood watch at the manger.

So parish affairs ran smoothly.

Meanwhile Father Angelo took to the campaign trail with the skill and gusto of a seasoned hand-wringer and baby-kisser. Dealing with large groups of people came naturally to him.

At the Fiesta in onore di S. Antonio di Padova in late May, for example, he was picking up at least three thousand votes a day, according to Simon Fisher and the other advisors. Ah, the brass band leading the *processione* was a host of trumpeting angels to his ears! The streets named Mott, Hester and Grand were transformed in his mind's eye into a winding village of tufa on the bluffs of southern Italy. The bowers of multicolored lights arcading the streets were electric vines of grape and flower and prickly pear. The banners stretching between the tenements, bearing the insignia of religious and cultural societies, were the streamers of popes and foreign kings. The garbage cans and lamp posts were painted the green, white and red of the Italian tricolor. It was *il paese* resurrected.

And the people, a sight to behold! The kids in peasant costume, the teenage boys wearing white tee shirts with short sleeves rolled up to show off tattoos and sculpted biceps, the trios of girls holding hands and tittering, the grown men hurling firecrackers while wives shook scolding fingers and, of course, the ancients, stooped men and women with canes and crafty eyes full of rheum and remembrance.

And the food! It was a spread fit for Bacchus: sausages and peppers sizzling on the grill, squabs and chickens turning on the spit, fritters bubbling in oil, pizza baking in brick ovens, watermelons sitting on beds of ice, scoops of ice cream brimming in sugar cones.

Meanwhile the horns of brass made sounds of gold as the bouncing effigy of the monk of Padua, pinned profanely with bouquets of paper money, was carried through the streets on the balustrading shoulders of sanitation men and construction workers. The plaster statue gazed at the plaster baby Jesus in his arms.

Father Angelo and his aides were swept along on the rapids of humanity that coursed down Mulberry Street. At each wooden stand he was handed something to eat and given a hand to shake or a cheek to kiss.

"Weh, Father Angelo, have a *zeppole*, you too skinny," said one burly vendor.

They motioned to him to take a chance, spin the wheel, pick a card, knock over the milk bottle, hit the balloon with the dart, ring the bell, test his strength and shoot the clay pigeon. He tried them all.

"I'm gonna vote for you, you bet," shouted Bobo Cippolino, who hadn't registered to vote in twenty years.

"Me too," said Carlo Fiore, who didn't even have his citizenship papers, much less a voting card.

"I'm voting for you twice," promised Teddy Carbone.

And so he got lots of pledges and even more free advice.

"Just keep saying rent control and tax cuts," suggested Mike Danilo, cupping his mouth with his hand, "you'll get elected."

"Kick the crooks outta City Hall," yelled Katie Mancuso, who ran the *salumeria*.

"We could use some religion in government," said her sister Lucy, crossing herself and curtsying to the priest.

The constituents that night touched on every civic subject from sanitation to boccie courts to off-track betting. Simon Fisher was pleased with Father Angelo's performance. "You've got them in the palm of your hand, Father."

The priest looked a bit sheepish. "I didn't make any promises I don't intend to keep," he said.

"Of course not," Simon said. They were alone for once, standing on Grand Street near a large parking lot that had been converted for the occasion into a mini-amusement park, containing a merry-go-round, a whip ride and a small Ferris wheel. The squeals of excited youngsters filled the air.

"They're good people, they deserve a fair shake," Father Angelo said.

"You bet."

Suddenly the two men heard a commotion coming from the area around the Ferris wheel. They rushed over to investigate. Gales of sobbing came from a woman in a polka-dot dress who was being restrained by two men. On the ground lay a girl of about twelve. Another man had his ear to her chest. He straightened up and shook his head. "She's not breathing." He clucked his tongue. "I think she's dead."

"What happened?" asked Simon Fisher.

"She got dizzy from the ride or something," a bystander said. "Fainted dead."

The mother in the polka-dot dress wailed, "She got asthma. I told her not to go . . ."

"Somebody get an ambulance, quick," said Simon.

"Get the undertaker," said the bystander, under his breath.

Meanwhile Father Angelo had shoved his way through the crowd and was on his knees by the stricken girl's side. "Move back, give her air."

The man who had checked her breathing frowned and shook his head. "It's too late, Father."

Father Angelo wasted no more time. He placed his right hand under the girl's neck and lifted it. Then, with his left hand supporting the back of her head, he pushed her chin gently with his right hand, tilting her head back. Next he gave her artificial respiration by bending down and breathing into her mouth and nose.

He exhaled again and again, praying to the Holy Spirit. He was surprised that he remembered the technique so well from first-aid training all those years ago in CYO day camp. Suddenly he felt a trace of her breath on his cheek, and by the time the ambulance arrived she was breathing regularly.

Before climbing into the rear of the ambulance with her daughter the mother ran over and kissed the priest's hand. "*Bacio le mani*," she said. "You bring my child back to life."

Afterward he stood shamefaced amid a circle of bystanders who buzzed with wonder and admiration. Some applauded, others reached out to touch his clothing. He nudged Simon, pleading that he was tired and wanted to go home. The political leader fairly beamed.

In the days that followed word spread through the neighborhood that Father Angelo Falcone had performed a miracle by bringing a girl back to life. The report did not hurt his reputation or chances for election. And many wondered, friend and enemy alike, just what kind of man was this?

One night after taking the stump all day from synagogue to bingo parlor to Chinese restaurant Father Angelo returned exhausted to the rectory. He removed his clothes and got ready for bed, then remembered that he hadn't yet fulfilled the daily obligation of reading the divine office. With a sigh he went downstairs to the library to get his breviary.

The phone rang. It was nearly midnight and Father Meara and Father Trapani were already asleep. He picked up the receiver.

"San Gennaro's," he said quietly.

"Father Falcone, please." A man's voice.

Father Angelo supposed it was a sick call. "Speaking."

"Sorry to disturb you at such a late hour, Father. My name is Sergeant Albany, Fifth Precinct."

"That's okay, Sergeant, I don't punch a time clock. What can I do for you?"

"We have a Spanish boy in custody, he gave us your name."

"Who is he?" He believed he knew the answer.

"Joey Morales. At least that's what the punk said his name was. He carried no identification."

"I know the boy, Sergeant. What did he do?"

"He stole a chicken."

"He stole a *chicken?*" the priest echoed incredulously.

"Yeah, a live one from the Chink market on Broome Street. The old man who owns the place nearly used his hatchet on the kid. Officer Gilroy stopped him just in time."

"Thank the Lord for that."

"We gave him a few whacks with the belt and read him the riot act. The kid hasn't been in trouble with us before and we checked and found out that he has no JD sheet. So I'd rather not hand him over to those bleeding hearts at the Youth Board. But I have to release him to a parent or guardian or somebody. He says he's an orphan. That true?"

Father Angelo dodged a lie by saying, "I'll be over as soon as I can get dressed."

Sergeant Albany was shaking his finger at Joey Morales. "I don't want to see your face around here again unless it's to join the PAL."

They were standing under the green light on the station house steps. Joey said nothing. Father Angelo put his hand on the boy's shoulder. "I'll see to it that he stays out of hot water, Sergeant," wondering if it was a vain promise.

Joey murmured something; the priest gave him a stern look,

nudging him along the sidewalk. They walked north on Elizabeth Street in the phosphorescent glow of the city in the dead of night. Trucks rumbled over the stones of Canal Street ahead.

"Where to?" Angelo said.

Joey shrugged.

"I'll take you home."

Silence.

"Were you hungry?"

"Nah. I just did it for kicks."

Angelo resisted the impulse to lecture him. That kind of thing, he recalled from his own youth, did nothing but rub salt into adolescent wounds. They strolled in the general direction of the neighborhood where he supposed the boy lived.

"What's your address?"

"One-ten Forsyth."

"Anybody home?"

Joey shrugged, rubbed his behind. "The flatfeet beat my ass. They had no right to do that."

"Would you rather go to reform school?"

"For stealing a lousy chicken? Don't make me laugh."

The offense had been minor enough but Angelo had the feeling that the boy probably was committing other perhaps more serious crimes. Crossing the Bowery, he asked, "What made you think of calling me?"

"Aw, I don't know, my sister was out working. You're the only one I could think of. Besides . . ."

"Besides what?"

"You're a pretty okay guy."

Father Angelo tried not to show his pleasure. He knew how hard it was for Joey to go that far. "Thanks," he said.

Finally they stopped in front of a five-story brick rat-trap tenement. "Here we are," Joey said, "home sweet home. Hey, can you come up with me?"

"Sure."

They entered the aromatic vestibule and climbed the slate stairs to the second-floor rear. Joey took a key out of his sneakers and slowly opened the door.

He had hardly crossed the threshold when he got a ringing slap in the face.

"Where you been, you goddamn juvenile delinquent?"

She stood there, panting, her black calligraphic kimono open down the front. Finally she noticed that somebody was standing behind her brother in the shadowed hallway. She clutched the material at the neck of her gown, pulling it closed. "Hey, who's that?"

"Excuse me," Father Angelo said, stepping into view.

"Oh, *madre de Dios*," she said, hand flying to her mouth. "Forgive me, Father."

Angelo dismissed it with a wave. "I just wanted to make sure Joey got home okay, Miss Morales. I'll be going now."

"No, Father, please come in. I want to know what happened."

Angelo kneaded the brim of his hat in his hands and moved into the apartment.

Joey kept giving his sister black looks.

A calico cat nuzzled the priest's ankles. The place smelled of cat litter and cheap perfume. Joey's sister scooped up clothing and magazines, clearing a place on the couch. "Please sit down, Father."

"This is my sister," Joey said, like an apology, or a complaint, it was hard to say.

"I'm sure he figured that out," she said. "You go to your room."

Angelo sat down, leaning forward like he was about to leave, elbows on knees, hands revolving the hat brim.

Joey left them.

Father Angelo looked around. The apartment was better than the building. It needed a fresh coat of paint but the furniture looked new and tasteful. The kitchen had new appliances and a television set with a rectangular screen sat on the deep-pile living room rug.

He held out his hand. "I'm Father Angelo."

She took it, a little shyly, but on the whole her voice and manner were without diffidence. "I know you, Father Angelo. Everybody knows you. I attend your early masses very often. You preach beautiful sermons. I'm Lena Morales."

"Thanks for the compliment."

"That's pronounced *Lay*-nah," she added. A smile played on her lips. "You have a way with words, a silver tongue. I must tell you, your sermons sometimes make me shiver. Sometimes they make me cry. You talk with such . . . such feeling."

He mumbled another thank you, embarrassed, feeling awkward, yet somehow magnetized by the woman, by her lively manner, her abundant red hair, her . . .

She scrutinized the ghostly pallor of his face. "You look tired, Father. Would you care for something? A cup of tea?"

"Don't go to any trouble."

"No trouble at all," she said, getting up. "Let me take your hat." As she removed the hat from his lap her fingertips brushed his leg.

She went into the kitchen, talking to him over her shoulder, asking about Joey. He explained about the silly theft of the chicken and the call from the station house. On the end table he noticed a copy of Confidential magazine with a picture of Ava Gardner and Frank Sinatra on the cover.

Soon she returned to the couch, placing the tea tray on the table. As she leaned over, the dressing gown fell open, showing her breasts. What was he doing here? Was he performing his Christian duty or putting himself in an occasion of sin? Both, he decided.

"Joey is really a good boy at heart," she was saying. "But he needs a man to guide him. I guess it's too late now. He's almost grown up." She sat down next to him. "Milk and sugar?"

"Please. It's never too late, Miss Morales . . ."

"Call me Lena."

"Jesus Christ will guide him." And what about yourself? he added silently.

Lena didn't look convinced. She grabbed a pack of cigarettes from the end table and offered him one. "Please understand, Father Angelo, I don't want to make light of religion, I'm a religious person, you know." She looked at him. "Do you believe me?"

"Yes." He sipped his tea, which tasted good.

"Do you know what I do to make money?" she asked.

"Yes."

"I know it's sinful, Father." With a rustle of silk she shifted her position on the couch.

"I'm not hearing your confession, Lena. I don't judge you." She crossed her legs and the dressing gown parted at the knee. He looked down, studying the tea leaves.

"I believe in Christ," she went on. "But Joey needs more than Christ. I need more than Christ."

"I sympathize with what you're saying. People require material things too. Christ understood this. That's why he fed the multitudes with loaves and fishes."

She blew out a gust of cigarette smoke and smiled at him. "There you go, making sermons."

Her remark prompted him to think of how late it was and how suddenly tired he was. He was scheduled to celebrate eight o'clock mass in the morning, followed by a full slate of political activities. He drained his teacup. "I really have to go, Lena."

"Of course," she said. "I'll get your hat."

As she got up from the couch he noticed how the flesh was dimpled just above her knee.

At the doorway they shook hands. She seemed reluctant to let him go. It was still early for her; she slept in the daytime. And, he had to admit to himself, he wasn't all that eager to leave her. He liked her and, of course, she invoked memories of his wild oats season and the happy times with Veronica—get thee behind me . . .

"Thank you, Father, for helping Joey."

"I'm only doing my job," he said lightly.

"Your Father's business, eh?"

"That's right." He was fiddling with his hat again.

"And thanks for helping me."

He looked puzzled. "How did I help you?"

"By not judging me. Pray for me," she said.

"I will." And for yourself, while you're at it, he added silently. He squared the hat on his head and turned to leave.

"And, Father?"

He turned to face her again.

"Pray for Joey too."

"Of course."

"And don't let him play basketball any more."

He looked mystified. "Why not?"

"Didn't you know? He has heart trouble."

"No, I didn't know."

She nodded her head. "Something he inherited from *Mami*. He has a murmur. I'm not too clear on it. A doctor once tried to explain it to me in medical terms. Let's see, I think he called it a congenital malformation. And a septal defect—something like that. It means the wall that divides the chambers of Joey's heart isn't all there, so the blood flows back and forth."

Angelo looked stunned. "Is he getting good care?"

"The best, when I twist his arm to make him go. I hired a specialist on Park Avenue."

Now he thought he really understood why Lena sold herself. What about Saint Maria Goretti, whom the Pope had canonized last year . . . the Italian peasant girl who died in 1903 was made a saint for being stabbed to death rather than yield her chastity to a rapist. But wasn't Lena's behavior virtuous too, in its own way? She sacrificed herself for a greater good. Morality was a mixed-up thing, sometimes holiness could look like sin. He also thought that if his dream of building a children's hospital in the neighborhood came true, maybe Lena wouldn't have to walk the streets. He promised her that he would make sure that Joey didn't play basketball anymore and that he would try to help them both any way he could.

He went home to the rectory and sank into a deep sleep. The next day he performed his priestly and political activities with all the energy and animation of a zombie. He was bone-tired from his back-breaking schedule. And he kept thinking of Joey, and of Lena, and kept picturing that dimple above her knee.

And he daydreamed of her beautiful autumn-leaf hair.

The primary election was held on Tuesday, September 4, 1951. To the surprise and chagrin of the regulars in Father Angelo's election district, the reform candidate had fused the support of various ethnic and religious groups to win by a narrow margin. Just as Simon Fisher had predicted.

The priest became the toast of Little Italy. They threw a party for him at Chang Dow on Bayard Street. The mayor sent a congratulatory telegram. Auxiliary Bishop Fulton J. Sheen phoned to give his blessing. And the next morning the district leader invited him to dinner at Mare Chiaro "to talk things over."

After the party Father Angelo stopped by the church to say a prayer of thanksgiving. He also prayed for strength not to let all the adulation go to his head, not to allow political compromise to divert him from championing social justice in the neighborhood, the only reason he had gone into politics in the first place. He could see now how easy it might be to forget this.

He was relieved that the primary campaign was over. It had been a grueling ordeal, especially during the last few days when the campaign had coincided with celebrations of the Feast of San Gennaro. He could relax now, even take a couple of days off, Simon Fisher had said. The general election campaign would be a cakewalk, requiring him to make only a few token ceremonial appearances. The real tough work would take place behind the scenes, mending fences with the regulars and extracting political promises from them. He would have to make a dinner date with a district leader. Otherwise, Simon promised to do most of the dirty work.

Angelo next got permission from the pastor to take a week's holiday and made a reservation at a hotel in the Catskills where he intended to play some golf and loaf by the swimming pool.

He returned tan, rested and raring to get back to work. On the first night back he put on the gold angel cuff links that his mother had given him as an ordination present. He rarely wore them, mainly because most of his shirts had buttons but also because he considered them too flashy and expensive-looking. But tonight was a special occasion: he was escorting his mother to the wedding of a *paesano*'s daughter in the Bronx.

He stood in front of the dresser mirror in a collarless white shirt, boxer shorts and black socks. His best suit, a navy blue serge that appeared black in most kinds of lighting, was laid out on the bed. He pomaded his sable-colored hair and combed it straight back, regarding his image with some satisfaction. Deep down, most Italian men, even priests, considered themselves God's gift to women because their mothers always told them so. Angelo Falcone, though pledged to celibacy, was no exception. In his case, too, there was some truth to the notion. He had a fine hawkish nose, strong mouth, pale skin, a clear gaze and a thick mane of hair. Women found him attractive. In fact, at the Catskills resort from which he had just returned, where he went around in mufti most of the time, he had had to deflect the overtures of various females on the prowl. Soon there were whispers poolside that he must be queer. Then he pointedly appeared at dinner one evening in his clerical garb, creating quite a stir. The news that he was a priest created even more interest among some women, but he managed to escape with his priestly chastity intact.

One day at a time.

He finished dressing and picked up his breviary, intending to read it as he waited for his mother and the driver to pick him up in her Cadillac. But he couldn't concentrate on the prayers. He was gazing into a mental crystal ball, looking beyond the general election and trying to envision the next four years as a city councilman. He wondered what committees and subcommittees he would serve on, what accommodations he would be prepared to make, how he would merge his vision of helping people with the hard, practical realities of politics. Was he entering into a Faustian pact? He had to be careful, the snares were everywhere.

One good thing, he trusted his chief advisor Simon Fisher. He seemed adept at bridging the gap between altruism and pragmatism, of distinguishing between workable idealism and pure quixotry. He also thought that when the chips were down Simon's heart would rule his head, and that was good too. He could see from the way Simon dealt with ordinary people in the neighborhood that he genuinely liked them and that his motives were good. He lived simply, didn't seem to be in politics for a quick buck. He was a *mensch*, as Simon's people would say, and Father Angelo was pleased to be in such good kosher hands. He had promised to call Simon the next day and continue his low-key campaign schedule the day after that.

The housekeeper was rapping on his door to tell him that his mother and Bonaventura were downstairs in the car waiting for him.

*   *   *

The wedding was held in the Sons of Italy hall on Kingsbridge Road. Father Angelo and La Cumare were treated like visiting royalty by the mother and father of the bride, whose connection to the Falcones and Croces derived from their common roots in Miseno. The father, a stocky red-faced man with blue eyes and calloused hands, wore an ill-fitting suit and an air of servility, conditioned by centuries of sharecropping and bowing to barons with oiled mustaches. His wife, dark-eyed and thin as linguine, had the darting glance and pursed lips of a social climber. The young newlyweds sat behind stacks of macaroons, almond cookies and confetti candy. Sheep being prodded toward the doors of the abattoir was the image that came to mind.

The father, a day laborer, kept mopping the sweat from his forehead, the pained expression on his face seeming to reflect the cost of every sandwich and glass of beer or wine consumed.

The Falcones were seated in a place of prominence at the main table. Angelo, after all, was not only a priest but a famous politician. And La Cumare was La Cumare.

It was a humble affair. The tables were covered with oilcloths and artificial flowers. The fare consisted of plates of ziti and lasagna cooked by the mothers of the newlyweds, cold cuts in hard rolls wrapped in wax paper, salads and condiments provided by the caterer, bottled soda and kegs of beer and wine. Paper bunting of red, white and green was wrapped around the posts and porticoes. A strolling musician, who happened to be the bridegroom's uncle, sang and played Neapolitan airs on the mandolin.

Father Angelo, refreshed from the vacation, felt in a good mood. He drank a glass of beer while his mother drank wine. The mandolin player was joined by a violinist, guitarist and accordionist, all recruited from among the guests. They began to play "Torna A Surriento." Angelo and his mother promptly got up to dance a waltz.

Vide, 'o mare quant'e bello,
Spira tantu sentimiento,

Comme tu a chi tiene mente,
Ca scetato 'o faie sunna.

Mother and son glided in graceful circles around the room. Maria looked beautiful in a blue silk gown custom-made for her in Torre Annunziata.

"Wasn't *Zio* Claudio invited?" Angelo asked.

She simply shook her head.

Guarda, gua' chistu giardino
Siente, sie' sti sciure arance:
Nu profumo accusi fino
Dinto 'o core se ne va . . .

"And Chip?" he added, using the family nickname for his brother Cesare.

She looked exasperated and he got the message: Chip was off somewhere on a bender again.

E tu dice: "I' parto, addio!"
T'alluntane da stu core . . .
Da sta terra de l'ammore . . .
Tiene 'o core e nun torna?

The ardor of the music was getting to Angelo, but his mother seemed unaffected as she moved with him around the dance floor.

Ma nun me lassa,
Nun darme stu turmiento!
Torna a Surriento,
Famme campa!

The song ended to enthusiastic applause, and many eyes followed them as they made their way back to the table. Soon, as Angelo listened with a fixed smile to an old woman describing in excruciating detail a recent religious retreat she had made, he noticed out of the corner of his eye a look of concern on his mother's face. Her attention was on the bride's parents, who seemed to be arguing. She got up and went over to talk to them.

In a few moments she returned, and saved her son from the woman's droning voice. "Would you excuse us, *signora?*"

"*Certo, certo,*" said the woman apologetically, and went back to her table.

"What's up?" Angelo said.

Maria motioned in the direction of the bride's parents. "They're running out of wine and the old man, he has no money to buy more."

"Do they have enough beer?"

"Angelo, you must do something."

He hunched his shoulders. "Me? What do you want me to do about it?"

She said nothing but let her severe expression talk for her.

Finally, he excused himself from the table and went to the car to talk to Bonaventura. He took out his billfold and thought for a moment. He still had money left over from the gifts he had received at his ordination over a year ago, and since adolescence he had been accustomed to carrying around a wad of money. Figuring that there were about fifty guests inside, he peeled off three twenties and handed them to the bodyguard. It should be enough to buy at least sixty bottles of good though not vintage table wine. After hesitating, he peeled off another twenty and told Cheech to get some champagne too. It was for a good cause, wasn't it?

He returned to the banquet hall and whispered in La Cumare's ear. She looked pleased.

As the wine and champagne continued to flow, the party picked up steam and the bride's father kept refilling the priest's glass. Soon he was feeling very mellow. The musicians played *O Paese d' 'o Sole*, a song about a native's sentimental return to Naples, prompting Angelo to think about how so many of the songs that tugged the southern Italian's heartstrings were paeans to a place rather than a person. And he wondered why his mother rarely became nostalgic over the Old Country or told tales about her girlhood like the other women did. Come to think of it, she was pretty close-mouthed about her origins, and Angelo didn't even know what kind of wedding his parents had had. He only knew that they were married in Italy just before emigrating.

La Cumare noticed his solemn expression. "We are here to have fun, Angelo. Why do you think so hard?"

He looked at her. "I was just wondering, Mamma. All these songs about Napoli and Sorrento, do they make you miss Italy? Do you sometimes long for the sun and the sea, for the old days?"

Her face became stone. "Never."

"But you surely miss some things about Italy. It's a beautiful country, isn't it?"

She looked around the hall, obviously uncomfortable, then looked at her son. "Who misses *la miseria*?" she said. "Who misses the empty belly and the cruel landlord on his high horse, eh? Is work without end beautiful? Is hopelessness?" She thumped her chest with her thumb. "No, I'll take this country. America the beautiful!"

"Sure," he said, voice tinged with sarcasm. "Where the streets are paved with gold."

"No, the streets are paved with garbage. But the gold is there, for those who know how to get it. For those with the stomach for it." And she pounded her tummy.

Well, Angelo thought, if his mother had anything she had intestinal fortitude, literally and figuratively. He was surprised, though, by the vehemence of her reaction and for some reason wanted to pursue the subject. He'd been wanting to for a long time. He knew many immigrants who had suffered hardship in the Old Country but still had a soft spot for the homeland. Why was she so bitter?

"Anyhow," she added, "it's not gold that I want. And it wasn't wanting riches alone that made us pull up roots."

"What then?"

She opened her mouth, then closed it again and shook her head. "*E una longa storia*," she said. "Too long."

He should have known better than to try to coax her out of the shell when she was determined to keep it shut. It would be easier to uncurl an armadillo or get the Sphinx to reveal the riddle. He was always troubled by his ignorance of the family background and his mother's early life both in the United States and in Italy. Oh, he knew the broad strokes of her history but not many of the concrete details that formed the true picture of her life. He wanted to know so many things. What, for example, were his grandparents like? Did she marry Pepe Falcone for love or some other reason? Was the trip to America in steerage horrible? Did she actually take care of animals when she was a girl in Miseno? Or did she pick fruit? Did she grub in the ground or spin lace on the wheel? He knew that she was never convicted of a crime but was she ever arrested? And what about the rumors that she was a suspect in the disappearance and presumed killing of an important man in the neighborhood many years ago? Even though he was a favored son he never had the courage to ask her such questions. She could be an imperious and forbidding woman, especially when she wanted to be, not easily wheedled into revealing matters that she preferred to keep unknown. Still, he couldn't help trying, and fortified himself further with several gulps of champagne for courage.

"Tell me, Mamma . . ."

"Tell you what, *figlio mio*?"

"What was your wedding like?"

"It was a poor affair."

He looked around. "Poorer than this?"

She chuckled. "Compared to my wedding this is a royal celebration."

He was encouraged . . . her replies had been laconic but at least she wasn't shutting the door. Someone brought over coffee and liqueurs and he poured for his mother, adding plenty of anisette to the demitasse. She too was drinking more than usual.

"Did you love my father?" he blurted out.

"*Yes.*"

The answer, or the force of it, surprised him. He sipped more champagne, and had the odd feeling that he had crossed some forbidden portal and was following a path where there was no turning back, which could lead to . . . what? All around them the wedding guests were singing, dancing, kicking up their heels, but they might as well have been tin figures twirling on a music box for all the notice Father Angelo and La Cumare took of them.

"Lying is a mortal sin," he said, amazed at himself.

"I *never* lie. It is beneath me to lie."

She spoke the truth, he thought. As a code of behavior silence was superior to deceit. And her life had been filled with Sahara-like stretches of silence.

"It's time you knew," she said suddenly.

He held his breath, trying to concentrate on his mother's face through blurred vision. "Knew what?"

"The truth." She folded her hands on the table. "I loved your father. I loved your father with all my heart and soul. But Giuseppe Falcone was not your father."

Blood seemed to pound in Angelo's ears, the room shifted before his eyes. He got up from the chair, and steadying himself on the edge of the table, toppled the champagne glass.

Heads turned and hands covered whispering mouths.

"Sit down, Angelo," she said quietly.

But he did not sit down. Instead he staggered out of the Sons of Italy hall and hailed a cab on Kingsbridge Road.

The next morning, the seventeenth Sunday after Pentecost on the calendar of moveable feasts, Father Angelo Falcone celebrated two masses with a bell-clanging hangover. He read the gospel according to Saint Matthew, Chapter XXI, verses 35–46, narrating Jesus's verbal duels with the Pharisees over issues of law and lineage. To the lawyer's challenge concerning the great commandment, Jesus talked of loving God and loving they neighbor, then He parried the scholars' questions with a riddle of the Messiah's lineage: "What think you of Christ? Whose Son is He? They say to Him: David's. He saith to them: How, then, doth David in spirit call Him Lord, saying: The Lord saith to my Lord: Sit on my right hand, until I make Thy enemies Thy footstool? If David, then, call Him Lord, how is He His Son? And no man was able to answer him a word . . ."

Father Angelo recited this story of paradox and bloodlines with a dour expression. He spotted Lena sitting in the rear of the church, and she noted his expression.

Afterward he spent the afternoon in the garden, reading prayers, browsing through the newspaper, eating right from the tree the last figs of the season, hearing the squeals of children coming from a nearby park. Summer was on its death march and maple leaves danced in the breeze. Through the open window of the rectory library the radio crackled with news of a place in Korea called Heartbreak Ridge.

Who *was* his father? If it wasn't gentle Giuseppe Falcone could it have been his brother Claudio, whom Angelo had suspected for a long time of having slept with his mother? Why did it matter so much? Was this just vanity? His status as a priest, as a child of God hadn't changed. Why couldn't he just leave it at that?

Thumbing through the prayer book, he came on the Litany of Saint Joseph and scanned the words: "Saint Joseph, Illustrious Scion of David, Light of Patriarchs, Spouse of the Mother of God, Chaste Guardian of the Virgin, Foster-Father of the Son of God, Watchful Defender of Christ, Head of the Holy Family." He shook his head, a flat taste in his mouth. He read on: "Joseph most just, Joseph most chaste, Joseph most faithful, Mirror of patience, Lover of poverty, Model of workmen . . ."

No more. He buried his face in his hands and let the tears come.

As evening shadows gathered he went up to his room and dressed in civvies: khaki windbreaker, blue slacks, golfing cap. He had an unaccountable urge to prowl the streets unrecognized, and even put on dark glasses.

He strolled south on Lafayette Street smoking a Camel, Marco Polo exploring old Cathay. The store signs were in Chinese calligraphy. Weathered faces from the plateaus of Mongolia and the valleys of Manchuria were on every square of pavement. The people looked right through him. He passed a storefront where the activity inside caught his eye. It was a Buddhist temple. Three monks in saffron robes were sitting on their knees and bowing their shaved heads in the direction of a stone effigy of a seated bodhisattva. He stopped to watch.

As a priest he had more sympathy with the secular clergy than the mystics, but two years ago while he was still in the seminary he read *The Seven Storey Mountain* by the Trappist monk, Thomas Merton, and so he at least had a sketchy idea of the uses of meditation for resolving matters of life and death. Without thinking he shoved his hand into his pocket and fingered his rosary. As he watched the monks recite the mantras on the path to divesting the ego, he felt more serene than he had all day. Why was he so much of the world? he wondered. Why couldn't he enter their trance of bliss too?

Looking at the bodhisattva, he thought he had received an answer. Where Saint Matthew had fallen short and Saint Joseph had failed, the attendant of Buddha, the minor deity of an alien faith, had supplied the key. He, Father Angelo Falcone, was destined in this incarnation of pale flesh and unknown blood to serve and suffer, to wear the musty fleece of time, death and sacrifice.

After what some might have considered some very gloomy thoughts indeed, he went home feeling much better. But not for long. He was, after all, a man. And before he could do his duty totally, without compromise, he wanted to know where he came from.

A stiff breeze trifled with the candles on the altar as Father Angelo celebrated a funeral mass. Death, he reflected as he intoned the *requiescat in pace*, was part of his stock in trade. The priest wore black every day.

He sprinkled the coffin with holy water. Inside the box of hard wood and lead lay the husk of a man who had lived eighty-four years before expelling his spirit to mingle with the breezes that now whipped the flames of the candles in church. Eighty-four years by the senseless measure of time. Why did people, including priests, have such a clownish attachment to time and the things of the earth? Surely it was unholy to fear death, wasn't it?

Over the gaping grave in the cemetery in Queens he read from the black book: "I am the resurrection and the life, saith the Lord: he that believeth in me, though he were dead, yet shall he live: and whosoever liveth and believeth in me shall never die."

He looked at the faces of the mourners who gathered round, then looked back at the book, hiked up the lace sleeve of his surplice and chanted the Latin texts. He knew that he was not praying for the soul of the old parishioner alone, since even in ordinary circumstances the subject of death could never cover merely one person. He was also praying for Joey Morales and for his cousin Johnny. He was praying for strangers dying right this instant all over the world. He was praying for the man who he used to believe was his father, Giuseppe Falcone. And maybe most of all, he was praying for himself.

The old man over whom he now prayed stood before a portal. Wasn't it the mirror image of the gate that his and Veronica's offspring had been barred from entering by their sinful action a few years ago? Was the birth canal a kind of river Lethe? Had this mistake exiled him from true grace?

He finished the prayers, and the mourners, many keening and staggering, tossed single roses on the coffin. Then the grave diggers began to shovel dirt into the mouth of the grave. Flinching, the priest turned away from the sight.

The church bells knelled nine times as he left the dinner table and headed upstairs to his room. She was waiting for him, sitting under the crucifix by his bedside. He started, said nothing.

"The housekeeper let me in," La Cumare told him.

He crossed the room and sat down on the bed. He had not seen or spoken to his mother since the wedding.

She looked well, dressed in a finely tailored gray suit that somehow managed not to dim her femininity. The tight curls of her dark hair indicated a recent visit to the beautician. He lit a cigarette and waited to hear the reason for her unusual visit.

His mother frowned. She disapproved of smoking. Although she took an occasional glass of wine, her habits were otherwise abstemious. She knew she had to be disciplined to survive in her world. She had known that since she was a teenage girl.

Suddenly the rain began to flail the windowpanes. Late September having a tantrum. Father Angelo smoked quietly.

"You have the right to know," she said.

"To know what?"

"Everything."

The hand holding the cigarette between two fingers trembled slightly. Did he really *want* to know everything? Absolute knowledge could be a definition of hell. The wind whined against the glass panes.

She shook her head slowly. "I know you have the wrong idea," she said in a rueful voice. "It's my fault for speaking without thinking that day at the wedding in the Bronx."

He allowed a slight smile. "That's not like you."

"I know. Too much wine."

"Yes," he said, "me too." He noted that a shedded yellow leaf was matted to the outside of the window. He looked directly at her. "Who is my father?"

"I'll tell you, but I have to start from the beginning. You see, I don't want you to judge me too harshly."

He waited.

"You have to know how everything was," she began, looking down at her pink manicured hands.

He made a show of consulting his wristwatch. "I have plenty of time, Mamma."

So, sitting under the carved oak effigy of Christ crucified, Maria told her son the story of her girlhood in Miseno and her struggles when she came to America. She told him the story of her life. And of his. He couldn't know then, but one day the knowledge of his history would at least help fortify him for the troubles to come.

PASSION

✝

To celebrate Father Angelo's thirty-third birthday La Cumare threw a big party at the Glen Island Manor in Pelham, New York, a grand old nightclub overlooking the waters of Long Island Sound. She spared no expense, hiring a high-society dance band, ordering vintage champagne and providing a banquet for more than one hundred guests.

The event drew news photographers and reporters who were posted outside the wrought-iron gate, popping flashbulbs and hurling unanswered questions at the sedans, limos and taxis that crunched over the pebbled driveway.

At a safe distance from these activities Father Angelo stood inside the manor nursing a glass of Louvois brut and greeting well-wishers. The expression on his face suggested that he considered such functions ordeals to be endured for the sake of his constituents and his mother's feelings. At his side stood Simon Fisher, tugging at his gray-brown beard and taking in the crowd with the opportunistic gaze of a seasoned political adjutant.

Fisher seemed pleased. Halfway into his second year on the City Council, his protégé had accomplished as much as one could as a member of that toothless debating society. He had fashioned an image as a compassionate champion of the poor, a Robin Hood in Roman collar whose mottled family background gave an air of romance to his political career. Meanwhile, he had made real if modest progress toward helping the poor people of the parish. His status as priest-turned-politician had attracted press attention, providing a built-in forum for him to demand better housing, cleaner streets and more city services for the neighborhood. But his biggest achievement, accomplished with La Cumare's discreet help, was cutting through the red tape and getting the financial backing to fulfill his dream of building a local children's hospital. The blueprints were on his desk and the ground-breaking was scheduled for the spring. He had also managed to avoid making too many political enemies and to keep his reputation spick-and-span. All of which had spurred Simon Fisher a week earlier to advise Father Angelo to throw his black hat in the ring in the upcoming race for a seat in the U.S. Congress.

And Angelo was thinking hard about the proposal.

As his hand was wrung and his back slapped, he surveyed the room and saw Junior Scario standing by the proverbial potted palm, sipping Scotch and inspecting his fingernails. Nearby, Uncle Claudio, in an eggshell dinner jacket gored at the lapel by a red carnation, huddled with the banquet director. Continuing to scan the room, Angelo saw Father Meara and Father Trapani exchanging greetings with the rectory housekeeper, Mrs. Morelli, and her young daughter. By the bandstand, Chip was flirting with the girl singer, who wore a slinky dress and had buttery brown skin. His dallying brought a brief frown from La Cumare, standing about ten paces away near the huge french doors that led to the terrace. Behind her, looking clownish in a plaid dinner jacket, was the hulking Bonaventura, eyes darting here and there.

"More champagne?" asked a waiter floating by with a tray of crystal.

Father Angelo shook his head.

"I'll have one," said a velvety female voice.

Father Angelo turned around. The voice belonged to Lena Morales, who scooped the glass from the bobbing tray.

"Hi," she said.

The priest's ears pinked. "Hello," he said.

"Surprised to see me?" She was dressed in a peach-colored ball gown, long and ruffly. The neckline headed south.

"Yes. I mean, no. Glad to see you."

"I came as Joey's date."

"Sure, terrific," he said. "Where's your brother?"

She smiled. Her hair was a bright conflagration of curls. "He went to the bathroom." She raised her glass to let the bubbles tickle the tip of her upturned nose. "Bottoms up," she said.

"Aren't you gonna introduce me?" said Simon.

"Of course," Father Angelo said, placing his right hand on her elbow. "This is Miss Morales. Joey's sister. Simon Fisher."

She held out her hand. "Lena."

"Well, well, Lena," Simon Fisher said, "delighted to make your acquaintance."

"Likewise." She sipped and fluffed the edges of her hair."So what do you fish for, Simon?"

He laughed. "I'm a fisher of men."

"No kidding. So am I."

He laughed louder.

"He's my Machiavelli," Father Angelo said.

"Yeah? He doesn't look Italian."

She turned to the priest. "You forgot my first name."

"No I didn't."

She waved her forefinger. "Don't be naughty, Father. It's a sin to tell a lie."

He said he was sorry. What else could he risk saying?

As they continued to chat Simon Fisher dissolved into the background. He'd better keep an eye on this situation, he decided.

Joey Morales joined them now, tugging at the starched collar of his dress shirt.

"You look great in that tux," Father Angelo said.

"Thanks, how come you're not wearing one?"

Father Angelo gave a mock sigh. "Only bishops and cardinals and popes get to wear fancy duds."

"You'll be there someday, Father."

"God forbid!"

The boy laughed. He did look handsome. His hair was cropped and gleaming with Vitalis. His complexion was clear and his brown eyes sparkled. Under Father Angelo's patronage he had bloomed. At seventeen he was about to graduate from Loyola High School with a partial scholarship to Iona College. As he helped Joey straighten out, Father Angelo also was trying to do something about the septal defect in the chambers of the boy's heart. With the help of the Falcone family doctor, Angelo had located a surgeon who had a reputation for performing medical miracles with an operation he had invented to correct heart deformities like Joey's. The boy was placed on the surgeon's waiting list. Meanwhile, Angelo was trying to raise the money to pay for it.

The waiter returned and Joey reached for a glass of champagne. Lena slapped his hand. "Ginger ale for you, kid," she said, grabbing another glass for herself. Then to Father Angelo: "Point out your mother for me."

He looked about, finally spotting her conferring with the band leader. "There," he said, pointing toward the bandstand. "The lady in the grape-colored silk."

"You bet," Lena said. "Now there's a woman who doesn't fool around, eh? You can tell just by looking at her." She turned to face him again. "You can also tell where you got your good looks."

Simon Fisher cleared his throat.

Father Angelo glanced at his mother. At fifty-three she was getting plump, but she was still a beautiful woman.

The orchestra started playing "Begin the Beguine."

Lena cocked her head at Father Angelo. "How about it?"

"Eh?"

She made a circle with her forefinger. "Dance with me?"

He laughed. "I'd better not."

"Think of me as your sister, Father."

"I don't have a sister."

Simon Fisher quickly stepped in. "May I have the honor, Miss Morales?"

Lena shrugged and gave Fisher her hand.

As he watched them walk off, Father Angelo let out a sigh of relief.

Joey shook his head. "Sorry about that, Father."

"About what?"

"My sister. Sometimes she doesn't know when to put a lid on it. She's a good Joe, no kidding."

"Joey, she didn't do anything wrong. Don't give it another thought."

Joey tugged again at the collar, then said, "Anyhow, I want you to know that she's giving up the life."

"That's wonderful."

"Yeah. By day she's going to secretarial school. Soon as she finishes she's gonna get a straight job. Anyways, that's what she says."

"You sound like you don't believe her."

"I guess I believe her. Lena's always kept her word, that's one thing about her."

But Joey still sounded doubtful. "Okay then, what's the problem, Joey?"

Joey watched her in Simon Fisher's arms. "Sometimes I think tricking's in her blood."

Father Angelo looked at the dance floor. The Cole Porter tune was still playing. It was a marathon song. "I doubt that, Joey. Anybody can change. Hey, look at you."

Finally the orchestra stopped playing and Simon and Lena came back. Dinner was about to be served, and Joey and Lena went to their table, leaving the priest and his advisor alone. Simon smoothed his beard as he watched them go off. "She's a chili pepper, that one."

"Now, now, Simon. You're having impure thoughts."

Simon Fisher turned his round face toward the priest. "That's okay, I'm allowed. I'm Jewish. And I don't wear my collar backwards."

"What's that supposed to mean?"

"Like the lady said a few minutes ago," Simon said, wagging his forefinger, "don't be naughty."

Father Angelo stammered something to the effect that the man was talking nonsense, but his crimson face said otherwise.

The party was almost over and most of the guests were leaving when Father Angelo finally got a chance to chat with his brother Chip. He had been watching as his brother cupped his mouth and whispered something in the girl singer's ear, then saw Chip take a pen and scribble something on his starched shirt cuff, presumably her phone number. Chip teetered a little on his feet as he did so and his eyes were glassy.

When the girl had gone, Angelo walked over, clapped his brother on the back. "Hail, Cesare," he said, invoking an old joke about his given name. "Did you have a good time?"

"I always have a good time," he said, spacing his words carefully. He squinted toward the bar. "Let's have a nightcap."

Father Angelo was reluctant to preach the obvious. Chip weaved a little as they made their way to the bar.

"What're yuh drinking?" Chip said.

"I'm ready for a bromo."

"Come on, it's your goddamn birthday. Loosen up a little."

Angelo smiled at the poker-faced bartender. "Cognac," he said, holding up his forefinger and thumb. "Make it a short one."

"Straight bourbon," said Chip. "And make it a long one. Happy birthday, brother. I mean, Father. Or Your Holiness, whatever."

Ever since he had learned from his mother Chip's true lineage he wondered how to handle it. How to handle *him*. Sometimes he thought that he should tell him that his true father was moldering in an unmarked grave in the churchyard of San Gennaro, that the truth, however hard, would be healing, maybe even cathartic. But his mother had made him promise not to tell. She thought it would only add to Chip's problems and make them worse. Father Angelo felt that at least it would explain things some. But La Cumare refused to release him from the vow of secrecy. And that was where the matter stood. She herself gave an oath to show more consideration and warmth to her younger son, and she had kept her word. But it was impossible to manufacture true feelings out of thin air, and Father Angelo suspected that Chip saw through the pantomime of emotion.

"I had a birthday a little while ago too," Chip said, ordering another drink.

His brother sipped cognac. He well knew what his brother meant: *his* birthday had passed without fanfare, almost without notice. He alibied now: "She's busy, it must have slipped her mind, Chip . . ."

"Sure, I notice your birthday doesn't *slip her mind*."

"Well, this bash wasn't really for me. It's a political thing. A fund-raiser, sort of. The idea is to keep on the good side of people we invited so that we can persuade them to contribute to the children's hospital and my campaign fund. It's public relations, Chip. And it's all for a good cause."

Chip turned to his brother. "So you're a good cause and I'm bad news."

"I'm *not* saying that."

"No, but I am."

Angelo put a hand on Chip's forearm. Chip looked down and saw the gold angel cuff link reflecting the light of the overhead chandelier. Then he swigged the rest of his drink.

*   *   *

All through the party the stool pigeon's son with the mole on his cheek had kept to himself, sipping bubbly and nursing grievances. The high-and-mighty Falcones. La Cumare treated him like a leper and Claudio wouldn't give him the time of day. Even his old pal Angelo, the big-shot politician who wore a dress on Sundays, hardly said two words to him. Who did they think they were, high-hat society types, bluebloods and bishops? Nah, they were guinea gangsters just like him.

Junior Scario scowled into his champagne glass. Twice in the last three years that scumbag Claudio had given bookie joints to new-comers while leaving him out in the cold. And whenever an impor-tant job came up some other goombah got the nod while Junior Scario got crumbs. They treated him like an errand boy. Well . . . every dog had his day and Junior Scario would have his.

He looked at his friend the priest boozing it up with his brother Chip and wondered why he had been invited to this shindig at all, the way everybody was ignoring him. He could buy his own cham-pagne and prime ribs. He didn't need their goddamn charity, he thought, patting the billfold in his breast pocket that contained a wad big enough to choke a Neapolitan buffalo. He was flush in spite of the Falcones and their dumb rules against dealing this and dealing that. The family was behind the times major league. How was a guy supposed to make any real dough when he couldn't deal junk or broads? Hey, La Cumare better wise up . . . this was the rackets, not a Sunday school picnic. So, sure, he'd been doing some free-lancing selling smack. What the old lady and her clan didn't know wouldn't hurt them. Or him.

Junior went over to the bar on the terrace and got another glass of champagne before they closed the joint. As he drank he looked out over the inky waters of Long Island Sound. The moon was like a silver coin in the summer sky. A money moon. He liked that thought. Koenig and Albano, now they didn't let any grass grow under their feet. Word had passed over the grapevine that they'd been ferrying junk over from Turkey ever since World War II. They dealt coke, horse, reefer, everything. How could you blame them? They were good businessmen, going with the law of supply and demand. Good capitalists. He'd like a piece of their action. He was tired of dealing small-time. He'd jump ship in a finger snap but so far he hadn't been asked, probably because he was more valuable to them in the rival camp. He had to figure a way to get a passport out of no-man's land and into the fields of clover where everybody else seemed to be. Junior Scario brooded above the lapping water, scummy on the rocks below.

"Penny for your thoughts, Junior."

Surprised, Scario turned around. It was the guest of honor.

Junior smiled. "Better up the ante," he said. "I got no use for copper." And the turncoat gazed out again at the silver moon.

In early September the neighborhood bustled with preparations for the Feast of San Gennaro. The streets were arcaded with multi-colored lights, and signs were posted in every storefront window. Workers were hammering up wooden stalls from which to sell food and games to the hordes who descended on the neighborhood each year for a dose of heartburn and local color before returning to the gothic provinces of Gramercy Park and Teaneck, New Jersey.

Father Angelo frowned at all this hurly-burly as he rushed home to the rectory from a sick call on Baxter Street, carrying a warm loaf of bread under his arm like a football. Father Trapani had come down with the flu and he had been dragooned to perform more sacerdotal duties than usual since he had launched his political career. He had given last rites twice in the last three days, which put him in a foul mood. Tonight was first Friday of the month and he was scheduled to serve Benediction. At least he felt like a priest again.

As he turned right onto Hester Street he came face-to-face with his own image on a poster plastered to a lamppost. Simon Fisher had finally convinced him to run for Congress. Even Vito Marcan-tonio, who had had his ups and downs in politics, had urged him to make the race, promising him the backing of the American Labor Party, of which he was state chairman. That could be Angelo's ace-in-the-hole if the Democratic bosses should deny him the nomination. He would never consider running as a Republican, especially now that Fiorello LaGuardia had gone to his heavenly reward.

Soon he reached the steps of San Gennaro, where he looked up toward the sound of a commotion coming from behind the doors of the church vestibule.

Inside he quickly surveyed the scene. The doors of the narthex were thrown open to reveal the center aisle leading to the altar on which sat the gold-plated monstrance containing the Blessed Sacrament. Before the eye of this holy object a picture of disorder and blasphemy reigned. The commotion that he had heard outside was the haggling between a vendor and customer over the cost of a gilded relic of the charlatan-saint Januarius. More hubbub came from the other vendors of statues, scapulars, medals, beads and candles who occupied the vestibule and rear section of the house of prayer.

Father Angelo saw red. He swept the articles off the noisy vendor's table. The vendor, a thin man with a shiny bald head and bowing paunch, gaped at the priest.

"What's the idea, Father?"

"This is the house of God, not a department store."

The man looked distinctly pained. "But we always give a cut to the church—"

"Mister, get out of my sight."

Slowly, the vendor packed up his things. What, he wondered, had gotten into the priest, usually a regular guy.

Angelo was wondering something of the same himself. Too much the politician, too little the priest?

Herbert Koenig, face red and round as a beefsteak tomato, pulled out his pocket watch and frowned at the diamond-studded dials. The guinea bastard was late again.

The delicatessen he sat cooling his heels in was famous for its devil-may-care, wisecracking waiters. But in boss Koenig's presence the same characters turned into toads.

"Another glass of celery tonic, sir?" a particularly obsequious one was inquiring of the gangster.

"Get lost," said Koenig, and the waiter withdrew in a hurry.

Five minutes later Tony the Squid finally arrived and parked his equally fat posterior on a bentwood chair across the table from his boss.

"What kept yuh?" Koenig barked at Albano.

Albano kept a straight face. "I had to visit my mother," he said, picking up the menu. "How's the corned beef today?"

"Your mother, in a pig's ass," said Koenig. "You was visiting that sixteen-year-old quail on Union Square or my dick ain't kosher."

Albano, still pretending to study the bill of fare, said, "I swear to God, Herb, I had to drop in on the old lady. She's got liver trouble or something."

Koenig narrowed his eyes. "Don't lie to me, you pussy-mad wop son-of-a-bitch or I'll fix it so's you never get a boner again."

The pleasantries over, the two proceeded to the business of stowing away their food, keeping the waiters hopping for over two hours. Then came two fat Havanas, and finally they were ready to discuss serious business.

Koenig leaned back in the chair and opened his coat. His waistline bulged where he carried iron under his vest. "Let's bump the old lady off," Koenig said. "The rest of the clan will fall like a house of cards."

Albano was working on an incisor with a toothpick. He shook his head. "You know better than that, Herb. We try that kind of stuff the tribunal will vote to cut our balls off."

Koenig knew the Squid was right. Their hands were tied. The whole Lower East Side flanking the Bowery was ripe for the picking, a junkman's paradise. But the path to all those potential profits was blocked by a guinea mamma and the terms dictated three years earlier by the Sicilian board of directors. Veins were popping out on Koenig's forehead as he lit another cigar.

"No," Albano went on, "we gotta figure out another way."

Koenig puffed reflectively. Okay, maybe he'd let his wop lieutenant puzzle this one out. After all, Albano should understand the wop mentality better than he did. He had to admit he wouldn't be in this fix if he hadn't gone nuts and rubbed out Johnny Falcone. That's what happened when a guy thought with his dick instead of his head. Yeah, it was all Rhoda's fault, she had talked him into it.

Rhoda Hellman was Herbert Koenig's mistress. Her daughter Sally was a stripper who had had the hots for Johnny Falcone but he wouldn't give her a tumble. Koenig rubbed his knuckles over his double chin. He was an oddball, that Johnny, especially when it came to dames. Sally's favorite game was strip poker, Johnny's was solitaire. His indifference seemed to arouse her lust, then, when not returned, ignite her anger. At least that was what Koenig got from Rhoda's version of the situation. Lately, though, Koenig had been having his doubts. He had begun to believe that it was his Rhoda, the two-timing slut, and not her daughter who had got the cold shoulder from young Falcone. Anyway, the upshot was that Koenig had let two broads twist him around their nail-polished fingertips and he was still paying for it.

Rhoda had led him to believe that the hit on Johnny Falcone was his own idea and a smart business move. But now Koenig knew better. It was a bonehead play that he had made for the sake of a piece of young tail. No fool like an old fool, Koenig thought, remembering that night.

Rhoda had given him her own daughter like a present tied with a red ribbon. First the girl performed a private striptease for him. That was when he found out that she was a real redhead. Then she took him around the world. Twice. When the mother a little later in the evening made the pitch for Johnny's head, Koenig was in no mood to say no. Falcone was a dead duck.

Koenig glanced at a pinup calendar on the delicatessen wall. He sighed. No use raking over ancient history. He had given Rhoda the heave-ho months ago. And Sally was a junkie with the life expectancy of a moth. They were history, but the Falcones and La Cumare weren't.

A waiter had appeared. "How about some nice strudel or a slice of cheesecake?" he said.

Koenig waved his hand in the air. "Not for me. Just tea."

"I'll have cheesecake and coffee," said Albano.

"Any brainstorms?" Koenig asked Albano after taking a sip of tea.

Albano wiped crumbs from his mouth. "One or two."

"Wanna clue me in?"

The coffee cup clattered slightly in the saucer as Albano put it down. "Well, we can't use muscle, right?"

"Right."

"Then what's left?"

"I hate guessing games. You tell me."

Albano shrugged. "The double-cross."

"I'm not sure I catch your drift."

Albano fiddled with the cloth napkin in his lap. "If we can't put La Cumare out of business, then maybe we can arrange for the police to do it for us."

"That kind of stuff can backfire."

Albano hunched his fleshy shoulders. "I admit it takes a delicate hand."

Koenig fixed his associate with a look of wary interest. "We may have to use some wallop downtown."

"No problem."

"And we have to cover our tracks. We don't want the Syndicate tracing the leaks to us."

"Right."

"And we'll need to catch a canary."

"Right again," said Albano, squinting at his polished fingernails.

They discussed the matter for about ten minutes more. Then Albano had a second helping of cheesecake and coffee while the boss got into his bulletproof Caddy and drove off to Idlewild to meet a business associate who was flying in from Marseilles.

A sideways solution to the dilemma fell into Tony the Squid's lap a couple of months later when he happened to run into Junior Scario at the dog races in Miami.

"What're you doing this far south of the Battery?" asked Albano, his eyes pressed to the binocular lenses fixed on the pack of greyhounds chasing the dummy bunny.

"Business," said Junior Scario.

Albano averted his attention from the oval track and looked at the short dark Scario. What errand could Scario be running for the Mount Vesuvius Import and Export Company or the Saint January Trucking Group or any of the other front organizations headed by

La Cumare? He didn't think on this for very long. The pigeon's son usually wasn't trusted with major deals or any operation requiring smarts or guts.

"That's nice," said Albano, returning his attention to the glaringly bright grass track. They were standing in semi-darkness on the terraced banks below the grandstand. He pumped his fist as the hare made the first circuit with the dogs in pursuit. His money was on number five in the yellow coat in third position. But the animal got slowed down jostling with a rival on a turn and then missed his footing on a hurdle. The race was over in half a minute. Albano's pick finished next to last.

"Crap," the Squid said. "That dog's a real dog." He turned to Junior. "How'd your mutt do?"

"I sat this one out," Junior said.

Albano squinted at him. "Lose your shirt already?"

Junior denied it but Albano knew better. Albano pointed to the tower, where an official controlled the speed of the mechanical bunny. "The trick is to grease the man upstairs," he said. "Then you'll be a winner in every race."

"Why don't you try it?" Junior said.

Albano smiled. "I like sporting chances better than sure things."

"There ain't no sure things," said Junior.

Albano kept smiling. "Wanna bet?"

Junior said nothing. He wasn't that sharp a conversationalist. Singing was his strong suit.

After the last race Albano said, "Have a nightcap with me at my hotel?"

"Where you staying?"

"The Fountain-Blue, naturally."

"Sure, why not?" said Junior.

They sat poolside and ordered daiquiris. Slivers of moonlight danced in the chlorine water. Junior ogled all the fine dames in brief bathing suits.

"Your first trip to Miami?" Albano asked.

Junior sipped the drink, reluctant to admit he wasn't exactly a world traveler. Finally: "Yeah, first time."

Albano looked over the surroundings, lingering on the hula-ing palm trees, moonlit beach, swashing surf and women. "A guy could get attached to all this."

"Hey, you said a mouthful."

"There's plenty of action down here too," Albano said. "Gambling, broads, junk. And politicians with their hands out like plaster saints. There's plenty of scratch to be made."

"Sure, like picking oranges right off the trees."

"You said it." Albano took out a gold cigarette case and offered Junior a smoke.

As Junior talked on, the Squid kept his eyes on him. His expression said loud and clear how discontented he was with his present circumstances in La Cumare's clan. So Albano pushed a few more buttons and pressed a few more levers.

"And look here, Havana's only a hop-skip-and-a-jump away. What a place! Casinos, dope and more whores than Florida got flamingoes."

The flame of the cigarette lighter lit Junior Scario's black eyes.

Albano then said it outright: "Why don't you come to work for me and the King?"

Junior shook his head. "I'd love to, but the old lady'd have my hide."

Which set Albano to thinking. The tribunal certainly would approve a contract on a defector to a rival mob. Especially since La Cumare had a history of not abusing the privilege by overusing strong-arm methods. The word was that she had resorted to hits only two or three times in her career. And she had always played by the rules: before each one she called for a "table." And one of the hits practically earned her the Congressional Medal of Honor. That was the time she put out a contract on that shitheel Ruby Bacco, a Sicilian-American gang boss who in the late thirties tried to win favor with Mussolini by assassinating David Torrone, editor of *La Torcia*, an anti-fascist magazine he printed in a Broome Street basement. La Cumare, a true-blue patriotic American who hated the blackshirt crowd, blew her top. She got the okay from the tribunal to take out Bacco to avenge Torrone's death. Anyhow, so went the word on the street. And he, for one, believed the story. It fit the Godmother. Say what you want about her, she had high principles and balls. A dangerous combination. He shook his head as he smoked the filter-tip. What a woman! He always wondered if she were good in the sack. He'd give good odds that she was . . .

Albano blew smoke and watched it float away into the velvet night. So far La Cumare had led a charmed life in the rackets. She'd avoided the Castellammarese bloodbath and all the skirmishes that followed it. Except for the hit on Johnny, the Falcone clan had had pretty smooth sailing. Too smooth, in Albano's book. Their luck had to change. Maybe now was the time.

The Squid looked at Junior Scario. "We're gonna put La Cumare out of business," Albano said.

"How?"

"One way or another."

Junior was skeptical. "She's got too many friends. Big-time friends."

"We got friends too. Look, Junior, she's standing in the way with her old-fashioned attitudes. We're sitting on a potential gold mine in junk traffic and she's queering the deal."

"Yeah, but what're yuh gonna do? She's always played square. The goombahs on the council will back her up."

"We don't have to take her out. We'll let somebody else put her out of business."

"Like who?"

"Like the DA. Or the feds, maybe."

Junior shook his head. "Squealing ain't healthy either. The board of directors believe it sets a bad example."

"How they gonna find out who spilled the beans?"

"They have ways."

"Junior, you gotta risk a fall if you wanna reach the mountain-top." Albano was proud of that one. He considered himself a very smart fellow.

"Maybe so," Junior said. "But the old lady's real smart, you know that. She covers her tracks real good. What're you gonna pin on her?"

Albano toyed with the swizzle stick. "We thought maybe you could help us out there."

Junior shook his head vigorously. "I got nothing on her."

Albano leaned forward in the chair. "Maybe you could lay your hands on something."

Junior badly wanted to be of service but didn't know how. He was also afraid Claudio Falcone would cut his balls off and serve them to the family for dinner. "I don't have that kind of access to files or nothin' like that. They never showed me much confidence."

"We have confidence in you," Albano said. He knew that Junior Scario was at least in a position to help, even if he wasn't sure how. "Look," he said, "I know how it is, they treat you like an errand boy, right?"

"Right."

"They pay you peanuts and demand loyalty."

"Yeah, you said it. I always got a case of the shorts."

"You help us in this matter, not only will we give you a big hike in salary but a piece of goods that you can count on for the future. This way you won't have to keep coming with the hands out."

Junior leaned forward to make sure he caught every word. "Like what, for instance?"

"Look, kid, I own this silver mine in Hildago, Mexico. I'll deed you, say, thirty shares. You'll have an annuity. However the winds blow, you still get your dough. What do you say?" Junior seemed to be thinking it over. Albano waited. If he read him right, the kid wasn't too bright but he was a good hater. And greedy as hell. Made to order . . .

Finally Junior said, "I got nothing on the old lady, but I think I got something just as good. Maybe better."

Albano studied the glowing end of his cigarette. "Yeah?"

"I got something on her son, the priest. Something big."

"I'm listening," said Albano. Junior reminded him of the dogs chasing the dummy bunny.

On a Friday night in early March, Father Angelo had a fried calamari dinner on Prince Street and then walked over to the church to preside at a Benediction service. He went through the ritual motions preoccupied by details of the political campaign. In the middle of the service rain began pattering on the roof and windows.

Near the end of the ceremony he took the monstrance in his hands and turned to face the congregation, making the sign of the cross with the Blessed Sacrament over the people—and spotted Lena Morales kneeling in a side pew.

He rushed through the Divine Praises that closed the ritual and quickly got out of his vestments and into his street clothes.

She was waiting for him in the church vestibule.

"Good evening, Lena," he said, "is everything okay? How's Joey?"

"Joey's fine, everything's fine," she said.

"That's good," he said, peering out the door at the rain-slick streets gleaming under the lampposts.

"I'm just waiting for the rain to let up," she said, then pointing toward the altar, "I'm making a novena."

"Oh? Any special intention?"

"I'll give you three guesses."

"Of course." Then he added, "Don't worry, Lena. Joey will have that operation."

She nodded. "I trust the Heart of Christ and the twelve promises. I made seven of nine first Fridays already. Two to go." She held up her crossed fingers.

He smiled at the simple nature of her faith. Who was he, a priest, after all, to question the efficacy of devotions to the Sacred Heart? Her method was at least as good as any other way to appeal to the power that guided the hand of the heart surgeon.

She pouted at the slanting rain. "I wish I'd brought an umbrella," she said.

"I'll get one for you from the rectory."

"I don't want to trouble you."

"No trouble at all. I'll be right back." He huddled into his coat collar and went out through a side door, jogging across the alley.

By the time he'd returned with the umbrella the rain had slowed to a drizzle. Lena was lighting a candle to Saint Teresa of Avila, whose emblems included an arrow, a book and a heart. Angelo saw a single-minded consistency in her religious devotions.

He handed her the umbrella. "Here. But you may not need this now."

She took it with a small shrug. "It might start up again . . .
Would you mind walking me home?"

He didn't mind at all, which bothered him. As he looked at his
wristwatch she quickly added, "It won't take long. I bought a
statue of Mother Cabrini on Lafayette Street. I just want you to
bless it for me."

"Well, sure," he finally said.

They walked east on Spring Street through the gauze of mist and
fog. Since they had to share the umbrella she took his arm as he
held the handle. He looked around, grateful for the dark wet
weather.

Crossing Chrystie Street, he stepped into a puddle, sinking both
feet into muddy rain water up to the ankles, and tried to laugh it
off.

Inside her apartment she removed her wet raincoat, gave it a
couple of shakes before hanging it on a hook, then as she helped
him off with his coat she looked down at his muddy feet.

"What a mess," she said, "looks like there was diesel oil or
something in that puddle."

He shrugged. "I'll survive."

"You will, Father, but I just waxed the linoleum. Better take off
your shoes and socks."

With some embarrassment he obeyed, supporting his weight by
holding on to the door frame as he bent to remove his shoes and
socks. As she walked into the kitchen, which was visible from the
hallway, he asked, "Is Joey home?"

"No," she said, taking down a coffeepot from the shelf. "He's
staying with a friend in the West Village. What you need is a nice
hot cup of Latin coffee."

He stood up straight, feeling slightly ridiculous in his black suit,
Roman collar and bare feet. What he really needed, he thought,
was a good stiff belt of whiskey.

He made it over to the couch in the living room, from where he
could see her bustling about in the kitchen. Wearing black slacks, a
white shirt and a red-and-yellow scarf, she was soon putting a tray
down on the coffee table in front of him. "Milk and sugar?"

"Uh . . . no thanks."

She looked up from the tray, sensing the significance of his hesitation. "Maybe you'd like a little something stronger?"

He held his forefinger to his thumb, indicating a short one.

She nodded and walked over to fetch a bottle of dark rum, pouring a dollop into the coffee cup, then did the same for herself.

"Thanks."

"Sure. Takes the chill out."

He watched the pale flesh of her throat ripple in the act of drinking, then stared down at his cup.

"Where's the statue, Lena?" he finally said.

She cocked her head to the right. "In the bedroom," and after a pause added, "I'll go get it."

When she returned and gave him the plaster-of-paris object—a replica of the Italian-American saint Mother Cabrini—he held it in his left hand and sketched a quick blessing with his right, mumbling the Latin phrases.

Handing the statue back to her, he said, "Good choice of patrons, I would say. Mother Cabrini conned a bunch of bankers into putting up the money for Columbus Hospital. Did you know that?"

"Conned?"

"Well, let's say charmed."

Lena's hair had been pinned back by a comb made of bone and shaped like a heart. Suddenly she removed it and the rusty jungle of curls fell over her shoulders. The sight made him catch his breath.

He stood up. "I'd better be going, Lena."

She kept seated and pointed to his grimy feet. "In that condition?"

"I'll clean up back at the rectory."

She placed the heart-shaped comb on the coffee table. "Wait," she said, and left the room.

He sat down again, uneasily. He was tired, feeling lousy, and thankful, for once, to let someone else think for him. His gaze was fixed on the comb . . . sparking jumbled images of valentines and sacred hearts and heart surgeons and cupids. The pump in his chest was beating rapidly.

She returned with a basin of water and knelt at his feet, and with gentle hands and no words she coaxed him into soaking them in the water. He stifled an urge to protest. Why not? What harm could there be in this? Her hands wielding the soapy washcloth felt good. So good.

Smiling, she looked up at him. A roaring silence reigned between them. One word would have destroyed the moment and both seemed to know it.

When his feet were clean she removed them from the water and, without pretense, as though it were the most natural thing in the world, began to dry them with her hair.

And still without a word from either, Father Angelo surrendered himself to the currents.

He tore the leaf marked "March, the Month of Saint Joseph," from the diocesan calendar on his desk, exposing "April, the Month of the Holy Eucharist." Having finished saying mass, he glanced at his appointment book, confirming that for a change it was blank. He glanced out of the window overlooking the garden. It was a sunny Thursday morning, really springlike. Persuaded that no more frosts would come this season, he decided to spend the rest of the morning unwrapping the burlap and tar paper from the fig and olive trees in the churchyard where his brother's father was buried, and doing other work in the garden.

He put on blue jeans, a plaid shirt and his customary sunglasses. As he worked he smoked his first cheroot of the day. When the trees were exposed to the sun he went to the potting shed for a spade and some sand and vermiculite to lighten the soil. As he spaded the earth around the roots of the fig tree he found that he tired quickly.

He sat on the concrete garden bench and gazed at the tree that represented womankind. His face was flushed: he had, after all, savored the forbidden fig. Actually committing a sin of the flesh didn't trouble him so much as having broken his sacred vows, which made him a moral welsher.

He got up from the bench and walked over to the garden hose. As he watered the soil he heard the cooing of pigeons that strutted on the cornices of the church and the twittering of unseen sparrows, rustic sounds reminding him of another time and another place . . .

It was spring then too, the season of promise when he had escorted Veronica Carolino to the Cloisters on the bluffs of upper Manhattan. Veronica, with wheat-colored hair and hazelnut eyes. Angelo Falcone was head over heels. He was twenty-five, she was twenty-eight, the first female to eclipse La Cumare in the transits of his heart.

On that spring day some eight years earlier Angelo and Veronica had fallen under a spell conjured by youth and love and art and the harmony of the natural setting of Fort Tryon Park. The Hudson River furled in a glittering ribbon of water below a pristine stretch of palisade. The chalices, tapestries, paintings and statues in the collection conveyed to their young minds a near-holy sense of beauty, kindling less exalted feelings in the blood.

Veronica was a painter in oil and watercolor. Her canvases showed an innate gift for color and form that matched her appearance in Angelo's eyes, a harmonic merger of sex and esthetics, spirit and flesh. They made love outdoors in the park that surrounded the museum, the sound of Gregorian chants wafting dimly in the background. Holy and profane, some might say.

But in the end there were no contrasting shades.

Veronica became pregnant. She told him about it over capuccino on MacDougal Street. She was wearing a red beret and a serious pout. Angelo almost immediately decided they would get married and have the baby. She shook her head firmly no. She wasn't ready to be tied down. She had seen what happened to her mother, made old before her time by the conventional demands of household and motherhood. It was not for her, not yet anyway. She wanted to paint, travel, experiment, pick orchids on mountain peaks, savor life as she put it. She lit a Gauloise and looked at him with frank brown eyes. He knew a lot of "influential" people, she said, couldn't he help her make arrangements to "take care of it"?

Angelo took a deep breath. The idea was morally repugnant to him. And frightening. He fiddled with his coffee spoon, looking sour and thoughtful.

Responding to his hesitancy, she studied the smoke curling from the tip of her cigarette and said something about how she had known she couldn't depend on him to act in a strong supportive way, that she had always considered him a bon-bon, sweet but soft-centered, and that she really wanted a man made of hickory with some ice in his heart.

At that age and time, her words achieved the intended effect—made him furious and moved him to action.

He promised her he would handle it. He thought things over for a day or two before it occurred to him to ask Junior Scario for help. Junior, who approached sex like a rabbit, would have the "connections," wouldn't he?

Yes, he would. Junior, hardly able to mask his satisfaction that his friend was in a moral fix, told him not to worry about a thing. He would make all the arrangements, take all the risks. But he needed five hundred dollars.

In 1946 that was a small fortune, especially to a jobless graduate student. Where would he get the money? What excuse could he use to ask his mother for it? Who else might lend it to him? Finally he scraped the money together from a combination of sources—he closed his savings account, withdrawing $118; he borrowed $50 from Cousin Johnny and $100 from Chip. The rest he got from pawning or selling personal belongings, including the gold rosary the midwife had given his mother at his birth.

Junior hired the services of a Hong Kong doctor who had hung out his shingle in the basement of a tenement behind Chatham Square. Safe, clean, quick, no questions asked. At least that was how he billed himself. In fact he should have hung in his window the carcasses symbolizing the butcher shop. But how was young Angelo Falcone to know this?

Junior had chosen a cut-rate abortionist, pocketing half the money. There was no way Angelo could have known this either.

He remembered sitting in a dingy foul-smelling anteroom listening to the tick of a monumental dragon clock on the faux marble mantelpiece. Inanely, as the clock ticked away, he kept consulting his own wristwatch. Junior sat next to him smoking and trying to decipher the racing form in the dim light of a rice-paper-shaded floor lamp. Looking at Junior, one would think they were waiting for a bus. The ticking of the clock grew loud as a metronome.

Angelo nervously paced and massaged his moist hands. Veronica had been in the operating room (if that was the right term for the airless dark cubicle she had gone into) with the doctor and a female assistant (his wife?) for what seemed forever. Of course he had no way of knowing how long it was supposed to take. The man performing the curettage was understandably reticent and when he did talk he did so in a halting mangled English. As he waited Angelo couldn't help worrying whether the man was really a regular doctor at all. Looking around, he saw no AMA journals on the table, no beribboned medical diplomas or citations hanging from the blistered-paint walls, no comforting symbols most doctors had on their walls. He glanced over at Junior, who still squinted at the tout sheet.

Finally Veronica stumbled out of the room, looking in pain, her face sheet-white. The assistant, a plump woman with a vaguely Spanish-looking face, supported her by the elbow.

Angelo sprang up from the chair. "Is she okay?" he said.

"She's okay," the woman said. "Now please leave quickly."

Junior cocked his head toward the door. "Come on," he said, stamping on his cigarette butt.

Angelo took hold of Veronica by the shoulders and looked into her face. "Are you sure you're alright?"

She merely groaned in reply.

"It's normal for her to have pain," the woman said. "He couldn't take the chance and give her full anesthesia. Now please get *out* of here."

Junior stood with a hand on the doorknob. Angelo put his arm around Veronica and walked toward the exit. Before leaving he turned to face the woman again. "Is . . . was everything taken care of?"

Shoulders hunched, Veronica stood there hugging her own middle, a dazed look in her eyes.

And the woman that day in 1946 had nodded and quickly shut the door behind them . . .

Even now, as he watered the fruit trees in the garden of San Gennaro, Angelo could picture the woman's expression as she tacitly attested that his seed had been taken from Veronica's womb. It had been an expression of, at best, indifference. Plus contempt? Or was it guilt by hindsight that made him think so? How many times over the last eight years had he mentally autopsied that day and the awful days that followed?

Veronica Carolino had not been okay. The illegal abortionist apparently had plied his trade with all the art of a hatchetman. He had used an unclean curette. Within hours of the procedure Veronica began to hemorrhage badly and run a high fever, indicating that her uterus had been infected. Her roommate, an Indian girl from Bombay who was studying literature at NYU, pleaded to be allowed to take her to the emergency room at St. Vincent's Hospital but Veronica repeatedly refused. With quick medical attention she might have survived. Drugs might have been used to contract the womb, helping to stem the bleeding and expel the afterbirth that probably had been left inside her. Antibiotics might have cured the infection probably caused by a perforated uterus. But Veronica was too afraid of the legal consequences of admitting to hospital authorities that she had had an abortion, and being young, she trusted the curative powers of nature and time.

She had been fatally wrong.

There were tears in Father Angelo's eyes now as he watered the garden in that spring of 1954. He should have admitted his part in it instead of letting it be covered up. Maybe if he had taken his medicine and everything had been out in the open, at least he wouldn't have ended up with such a guilty conscience. But his friends and family had persuaded him that doing so would ruin his life, sabotage whatever career he chose, reflect on his mother. And it wouldn't bring Veronica or the baby back. So family connections, including intervention by the family doctor, made sure Veronica's death was never linked to the Falcone name, and Father Angelo had struggled ever since to expiate for the wrong, whose roots were buried in his past like the radicles of the trees in the churchyard of San Gennaro.

Or so the priest believed.

On Palm Sunday Father Angelo said the ten o'clock mass, blessed the dry fronds and handed them out to the parishioners. Later, as he removed his vestments, he glanced out of the mullioned window of the sacristy and saw that the day was clear and bright. Holy

Week was beginning on an auspicious note under a brassy-trumpet sun. The priest-politician gave a sigh of contentment. Somehow he drew strength from fine weather.

He went to his room in the rectory, where he dressed in street clothes and hurriedly laced up black shoes. He was scheduled to meet Simon Fisher at noon for a rally in Washington Square Park and he didn't want to be late. He brushed some lint from his shoulder pads, put on sunglasses and left.

From the south end of the park he could just see the speakers platform erected for the occasion under the Washington Arch. The monument, designed by Stanford White, reared like a chalk cliff in the sunlight. He headed for it.

The fountain in the center of the park swarmed with folk singers, beatniks, tourists and curiosity-seekers, providing a ready-built crowd for a rally. An old man leading a donkey and carrying a Polaroid Land camera was charging fifty cents a ride and a dollar per snapshot. Murmuring excuse me's, Angelo snaked his way unnoticed through the crowd.

Until he felt a tap on the shoulder.

He turned around to see a short man with a beer-bottle nose and a press card dangling from a chain around his neck. Father Angelo recognized him as a political columnist for the New York *Post*.

"You're Father Falcone, aren't you?" said the columnist.

"That's right. How are you today? If you'll excuse me?" The priest started again to make his way through the throng, but the newspaperman stopped him, held a notebook at the ready and moistened the tip of his lead pencil with his tongue. "How about a quote, Father? Say, what does the Cardinal think of your running for Congress?"

Father Angelo paused and looked at the reporter. It was a question he couldn't dodge. "The Cardinal," he said, "has not done anything to oppose my candidacy."

"So he supports you?"

"I didn't say that. We have had no communication on the subject. In general his policy in such matters is to allow priests a certain degree of leeway as long as we do nothing detrimental to the Archdiocese or harmful to faith and morals. I expect he understands that I'm in this for the purpose of helping people."

The reporter scribbled away, then looked up from the notebook with a smile. "How about your . . . uh, esteemed mother? Does she support you?"

Father Angelo was smiling too. "Wholeheartedly. Why wouldn't she? She's an Italian mamma, remember."

The columnist recorded the quote. A man carrying a camera with a flash attachment appeared at his side.

"Can I get a picture?" the photographer asked.

Father Angelo hesitated, searching the crowd for Simon Fisher. He knew the advisor would be put out if he rejected this chance for favorable publicity and told the man to go ahead. Some people now turned to look at who the celebrity was, and several recognized him and began calling out his name. Others applauded and whistled. People who had just come from church services waved palm branches at him. By the time Angelo got to the speakers platform the applause had crescendoed. Simon Fisher was waiting for him, beaming like the father of triplets.

After his speech he was clapped on the back so often and his hand was pumped so much that he felt he'd need a chiropractor. Meanwhile the overjoyed Simon stood in the background, preening.

"Keep this up you'll take the primary in a landslide," Simon said later as they walked toward Christopher Street. "Those people love you to death."

Somehow those words were more unsettling than reassuring.

"Let's have a beer and a snack at the White Horse," Simon suggested. "We've got a lot to talk over."

"Okay," said Father Angelo, and they turned west toward Hudson Street and a blinding orange sun.

It was almost dark when Father Angelo left Simon at the tavern and headed for the rectory. The day had been exhilarating and exhausting. Now he pictured only the down-filled pillow that awaited his shaggy head.

At first he didn't notice the long black Caddy cruising slowly alongside him. By the time he did, it was too late. Two men had hopped out of the back seat, grabbed him by the crook of the elbows and forced him into the car.

A fat man with veiny skin and amorphous features removed the cigar from his mouth and pointed it at a brown metal folding chair. "Siddown," he ordered the priest.

Father Angelo sat.

They had taken him to the back room of a candy store on 111th Street in East Harlem, the headquarters of Herbert Koenig's uptown book. There were four men, led by the cigar smoker with the fleshy face. Angelo had never seen them before but he was pretty sure that they hadn't been sent to bring him by the Holy Name Society.

The room was full of the desks, filing cabinets, sheets of paper spiked on hooks that made it appear like the typical office of a small manufacturer or businessman. Taking an educated guess at the identity of the fat man, Angelo said, "If you wanted to see me so bad, Mr. Albano, all you had to do was make an appointment."

"Shut your trap, Falcone." A bon mot from Tony the Squid. "That collar you wear don't cut no mustard with me."

"I don't suppose it does," said the priest, patting his pockets. "Got a smoke?"

One of the henchmen first looked at the boss for silent approval, then handed him a cigarette.

"Thanks," Father Angelo said, accepting a light. "What can I do for you gentlemen?"

"Hold your water," said Albano.

Angelo shrugged, sizing them up one by one. However you added it, they were definitely tough customers. Goons, in the vernacular. The man who had given him the cigarette had a certain sleek grace, dark curly hair and a brown complexion. His skin was dry like chestnut meat and his face had a distinct Caribbean cast, maybe Cuban or Dominican. The other two were burly white men who wore glazed expressions and slack sensuous mouths. They resembled each other enough to be brothers.

Father Angelo was puzzled. What could they really want with

him? Trying not to show how honestly scared he was, he chain-smoked two cigarettes before Herbert Koenig arrived.

The mob chief, in a pearl gray fedora and a gray Saville Row suit, tugged at the fingers of doeskin gloves as he removed them.

"Do you know who I am, Father Falcone?"

"I can guess."

Koenig sat down behind a desk and spoke sotto voce to one of the men, who nodded, went out and soon returned with a bottle of whiskey.

Uncapping the bottle, Koenig said, "My private stock of Irish. How about a taste, Father?"

"No thanks."

Koenig squinted. "Surely you're not a teetotaler," he said. "I thought you priests were famous for belting 'em back."

"Beware of stereotypes, Mr. Koenig." Actually he could have used a shot of booze to steady his nerves but didn't want to give Koenig the satisfaction of having him accept the offer.

"Suit yourself," Koenig said, draining the shot glass. He looked at Albano. "Tell him anything yet?"

"Not a word."

Koenig smiled at the priest. "Good. I wanna see his face when he hears about it."

Father Angelo tried to compose his features, appear calm. He succeeded until Koenig's next utterance:

"Ever hear of a quiff named Veronica Carolino?"

Silence.

"Sure yuh have," said Koenig, tilting his large head back and exposing a moving Adam's apple. He produced a small gold box from his pocket from which he took a pinch of something that he sniffed with both nostrils, then poured himself another shot.

"Cat gotcha tongue, Your Holiness?" said Albano from the side-lines.

Koenig grinned. "I thought only Trappist monks took a vow of silence. You're not a Trappist, are yuh? Nah, I didn't think so. Under that black suit you're just another pussy-worshipping wop, aren't yuh? Well, aren't yuh?"

"No."

"No? No? Well, you couldn't prove it by past history. We got the goods on you, Saint Falcone. And it's three yards long."

"I never claimed to be a saint." It was a statement.

Koenig laughed. "A halo doesn't go with prison stripes, *Father*."

"Get to the point." Of course he knew what the point was—blackmail. He just didn't know the particulars. Not yet. But he was beginning to get an idea.

Koenig provided them. He drew a picture of what he knew about Angelo's part in Veronica's abortion and death. He said they had affidavits from witnesses and relatives, including Veronica's roommate, the medical attendants who brought her to St. Vincent's, where she died, and her parents in New Jersey who had been bought off. They had other evidence—a batch of papers and depositions that they would deliver with Easter seals to local prosecutors. *Unless* . . .

Koenig paused, to give it full effect. Then: "Give us something on La Cumare, something we can use to persuade her to retire. You might call it a public service. I assure you we won't use it unless she's unreasonable. Which would be against her own best interests, and yours."

"You mean you want to blackmail my mother as well as me."

Koenig shrugged. "That's a nasty word, Father. I'm surprised at you."

Angelo realized he had to stall them. Shaking his head, he said, "What do you mean by 'something'? You know I have no connection to . . . the family business."

"But you have access," Koenig said quickly.

"I don't understand," Father Angelo said. But, of course, he did.

Koenig, warming to the situation, fluffed the handkerchief in his breast pocket. "You're a smart man, use your imagination. But let me help. Maybe ledgers for a tax rap. Joey Irish always kept real good books." He broke into an expansive grin. "That's it, a tax rap, the same thing that brought down Al Capone and Waxey Gordon, may their souls rest in peace. She'd be in very elite company."

Father Angelo looked him in the eye. "You expect me to betray my own mother?" To pretend to go along too quickly or easily would not be believed. But time . . . he needed time . . .

"Hey, I know it's a tough thing. Believe me, I had a mother too." He leaned across the desk. "But I guarantee she'll never find out where we got it from. Look, like I said, it's doing her a favor. She's behind the times. She's got plenty of dough. All she has to do is retire from the scene and nobody gets hurt."

"And make way for you?"

"That's right, so what? No skin off her chinny or yours. She could join a bridge club, go to museums and concerts. Play with her grandchildren." A big smile again.

"She has no grandchildren."

"Not yet," Koenig said, beaming with amusement. "But I'm sure you'll take care of that soon enough." His tone shifted abruptly. "I don't give a flying fuck what she does, see? Just as long as she steps aside."

Father Angelo got up from the chair, prompting the two soldiers who looked like brothers to lay firm hands on his shoulders.

"Who said you could get up?" Koenig said.

"I assumed the interview was over."

"Don't assume anything. I want an answer."

Angelo could no longer pretend to be cool, to be possibly thinking it over. "Here's your answer," he said, thrusting his left fist into the crook of his right elbow and sticking his right forefinger into the air. "In Italian."

Albano got up and grabbed hold of the priest. "Siddown. You ain't going nowhere."

Koenig, whose face had colored only slightly, studied the sparkling rings on his fingers. "For a smartass, you're pretty dumb," he said.

Angelo, who had been shoved back into the metal chair, stared at the wood-plank floor and said nothing. At the moment he almost agreed with Koenig—it was a dumb thing to say, under the circumstances.

Koenig got up. "I'm going to dinner now," he said, looking at his watch. "I'll be back in, say, a couple of hours. You boys have fun."

With a nod toward Albano, he left the room.

It was deathly silent.

Tony the Squid went over and sat on the leather couch in the corner of the room, propping his feet up on the arm and lacing his hands behind his head. "Strip 'im," he said.

The two brotherly looking soldiers roughly removed Angelo's clothes. Albano then cocked his head at the third soldier. "Julio."

Julio smiled the smile of a student selected to show his stuff. Quickly, he removed the leather belt from the loops of his pants and wrapped the end around his fist. He looked to Albano.

Albano gave the nod.

The scourging lasted several minutes, until Julio was breathless and Father Angelo lay bloodied on the floor.

"Get something to clean him up with," Albano told the soldier standing next to him.

The man returned with a big scarlet bath towel that he threw over Father Angelo's shoulders as he lay sprawled on the floor.

"Hey, look," the man said, "a naked prince of the church."

"Yeah," said his look-alike. "Maybe he should say a few prayers. Maybe God will send down some angels to help him out."

"Shut up," said Albano, laboriously crossing the room and standing over Angelo, who silently began to dab with the towel at the wounds.

"Change your mind?" Albano asked.

Father Angelo shook his head, more sadly than defiantly.

Albano, to show his contempt for such an unreasonable man, spat on him.

Father Angelo used the towel to clean his face.

They waited until Koenig returned. The boss briefly consulted with his lieutenant before he spoke to the shivering naked man on the floor. "Get dressed and get out of my sight," he said. "We'll give you twenty-four hours to let it sink in. You'll come to your senses, I'm sure."

Later, they pushed him out of the car on a lonely road in the North Bronx, from where he walked a mile before he managed to hail a cab.

*　*　*

The next day the priest suffered from throbbing migraines. His whole body ached from the beating. He said mass, skipped breakfast and tried to read a newspaper over coffee in the booth of a luncheonette on Lafayette Street. But it was impossible for him to focus on the text of Ike Eisenhower's latest rambling speech or the newest chapter in the continuing saga of the stormy relations of Frank Sinatra and Ava Gardner. All he could possibly do was agonize over the terrible problem posed by Koenig's threat.

He had a bitter choice: either betray the family of his blood, or betray the family of man, which he had dedicated his life to. Being revealed as a criminal accomplice to a felony and a depraved, weak sinner would not just bring prosecution and disgrace down on his head but, much worse, would destroy all his efforts to help the poor people of the Lower East Side. It would kill the hospital and destroy the chances for Joey's operation. It would wreck his campaign for Congress and eliminate from the scene one of the few spokesmen the people had . . .

But how could he even consider going against his own mother?

He drained the coffee cup, paid the check and walked over to the church, where he knelt at a side altar and prayed before a tableaux of statues depicting the Holy Family—the infant Jesus with Mary and Joseph. Here in painted stone stood the sacred model of kinship. As he stared at the statues tears filled his eyes and sweat appeared on his forehead. Couldn't he just run away from it, go off to a South Seas island or Patagonia? Of course not. He had to face it. It was a bitter cup God had given him, but it was the same cup everyone had to drink, sooner or later.

He left the church and placed a phone call uptown to Herman Koenig's headquarters.

When he was angry, like now, Herbert Koenig's face had the coloration of boiled ham. He put down the phone to ponder his next step, popped a couple of pills and washed them down with a shot of Irish. An objective observer might say that he was riding a chemical seesaw, lowering his blood pressure on the one hand and elevating it on the other. But Herbert Koenig didn't surround himself with objective observers.

So the priest refused to play ball, eh? He might have guessed. A guinea was a guinea no matter what kind of collar he wore. What a bunch they were, worse than the Jews. Well—maybe he just needed another turn of the screw.

Koenig looked over the day's betting slips. Peanuts. Someday he hoped to jettison the whole book. It didn't seem to be worth the time and trouble. The really big money was in the junkyards.

Koenig frowned at the black telephone near his hand. While he was no Sicilian wearing the gag of omerta, he still didn't relish the role of canary. Left a bad taste in the mouth. He shrugged, riffling the betting slips. If he didn't violate the code now and then, he'd soon be out of business. After all, what damn good was it having a long grease sheet and political connections if he never pulled the string?

He got up and walked across the room to a filing cabinet from which he extracted the dossier on Father Angelo Falcone. All the affidavits, hospital records and summaries were contained in a large unsealed brown envelope tucked into a file folder. Koenig didn't have to read the material again; he had it nearly memorized. The most damning testimony came from the girl's roommate who in the intervening years had become an anti-abortion fanatic champing at the bit to punish the baby killers. The abortionist himself had pulled a vanishing act but they had managed to strong-arm a statement from the nurse even though it incriminated herself as well. They had calmed her fears a little by promising to persuade the prosecutors to grant her immunity in exchange for her testimony. She also had been induced to develop amnesia about Junior's role in the matter. Scario had kept his part of the bargain, thanks to the Squid, whose fancy footwork in this dance of treachery belied his ungainly form. Thirty shares in the Mexican silver mine would be a small price to pay if everything worked out the way it was supposed to and he toppled La Cumare, the major obstacle to his becoming drug kingpin of the East Side from the Harlem River to the South Street seaport. El Dorado!

Koenig smiled as he finished thumbing through the papers. The file was complete.

He returned it to the filing cabinet and locked the drawer, then sat down again behind the desk. He laced his hands in front of him.

The next thing to do was make sure the file found its way into the right hands. He thought about this for a while, then picked up the telephone.

The hands that held the file the very next day were beautifully manicured and slightly calloused from years of wielding tennis rackets, polo mallets and ski poles. They belonged to Roman Pyle, the United States Attorney headquartered in Manhattan. He read the material with a frown of interest mixed with distaste.

Soon he put it down on top of a stack of paperwork, drummed his fingertips on the desktop and stared into the distance. The file had come to him not directly from Herbert Koenig but through the usual serpentine channels that linked the underworld to officialdom. The network, though winding, was quick and effective. The federal prosecutor swiveled his chair to face a picture window that gave out on the buildings and bridges of lower Manhattan. He gnawed a fingernail. What a sordid story the file contained! It might prove very useful to him. But he would have to apply a delicate hand.

Roman Pyle got up and paced the wood-paneled office. His strides were long—like his pedigree and legs, the latter clothed in stiff blue gabardine from Brooks Brothers. He paced under the benevolent-looking portraits of President Dwight D. Eisenhower and Governor Thomas E. Dewey and the framed parchments attesting to the degrees Pyle had earned from Dartmouth College and Yale Law School. He was dressed in vest and shirtsleeves, with cuffs rolled up to the forearms. Although it was late in the work day, the striped rep tie was still firmly knotted at the corded neck, the pale blue eyes still clear, the sandy thinning hair still neatly combed.

He paused before the purse-mouth portrait of Dewey. Pyle too sometimes mused about winning glory as a racket-buster to catapult himself into the political stratosphere. Maybe the chance now had been left like a beautiful foundling on his doorstep. He was not really interested in some stale shabby story of a priest's implication in an illegal abortion that went awry, at least not for its own sake. First of all, the crimes of accessory to involuntary manslaughter and accessory to criminal miscarriage did not come under his jurisdiction but the local district attorney's (a Democrat, by the way). And secondly, any action by him against a popular priest who was also a prominent figure in the rival political party might be disparaged by many observers and portrayed as politically inspired backbiting. What to do?

He studied the airbrushed icons on the walnut-paneled wall, then sat down behind the desk and toyed with the intercom buttons. Of course he might use the information as a friendly persuader, so to speak. A blackjack wrapped in silk. The dossier on the priest had been accompanied by the strong suggestion that it might be used to pry evidence from him that might incriminate Maria Falcone in a tax-evasion or tax-fraud case, both federal raps. Ah, to put the handcuffs on the ivory wrists of La Cumare. Wouldn't it be a feather in his homburg?

He pressed the intercom button.

"Mrs. Schultz, please bring me the file on one Maria Falcone, alias La Cumare, aka Godmother. Right away, if you will."

The secretary's voice crackled, "La Coo-who?"

Pyle spelled it for her before breaking the connection.

Soon he was thumbing through the collection of news clippings and confidential memos on Maria Falcone and her organization. The file contained "soft" evidence of the gang's activities, information that was trustworthy but would not stand up in a court of law. During the war La Cumare had prospered from selling black-market ration stamps and food, among other activities. The statute of limitations now applied to any prosecution for these offenses. Moreover, they were balanced by certain unnamed "services" she was known to have performed for the War Department in efforts to undermine Mussolini's fascist political machine. While the feds at the time might not exactly have been ready to pin a medal on her, those secret actions at least served to take the heat off her.

Pyle wet his thumb and turned the page. More recently La Cumare had been raking in profits from gambling and the trucking business, dealing in black-market goods and bootlegging cigarettes and booze that were sold without tax stamps. The report also indicated that the Falcone clan got contract kickbacks from trade unions. He jotted a note on a pad. Hard evidence of many of these activities or failure to pay taxes on the profits might provide the basis for federal prosecution. What he needed was documentary evidence, copies of the dummy bank accounts and dummy corporation papers all the goombahs used to conceal their incomes. With those in hand, he could lay the foundation of a case, using the documents to flush out potential witnesses from among bank executives and accountants who did business with the Mount Vesuvius Import and Export Company, Saint January Trucking Group and other front companies. Soon, following the usual pattern of past tax prosecutions, turncoat associates and disgruntled employees would likely come out of the woodwork ready to parade in front of a grand jury and a federal judge. He might even persuade a black-robe to authorize wiretaps of the old gal's house and headquarters. Armed with the threat of contempt citations for Fifth Amendment pleaders who would be granted immunity from prosecution, the prosecutor figured at least one or two high-level puppets of La Cumare might sing on the stand and help him put Maria Falcone in a denim dress.

He closed the file and swiveled to face the cityscape. As he had suspected, La Cumare was too smart not to have filed income tax returns for 1950–1952. The fates of Capone and others had taught her a lesson. But Pyle would bet his desert boots that she had under-reported by hundreds of thousands of dollars in each year. The ledgers and documents undoubtedly would prove it. He was counting on it.

Pyle reached for the briar pipe on the desk and filled it with Dunhill tobacco, then pressed the intercom button and instructed his private secretary to place a phone call to the rectory of San Gennaro's Roman Catholic Church in lower Manhattan. For a moment his eyes rested on the graceful manicured hand that held the bole of the pipe. Then he leaned back in the chair, lit the tobacco and watched the smoke rise upward, slowly and surely.

Vapors from the incense burner being held by Father Angelo floated up to the wood rafters of San Gennaro, symbolizing the ascent of prayer to God. As he celebrated mass the priest's face appeared sad and drawn. His own prayers seemed to have risen to a deaf God.

Spasms of coughing echoed here and there in the congregation.

The chain of the swaying censer tinkled against the metal vessel. He conducted a dreary, dispirited service that matched his mood. As it was Holy Week no bells were allowed to be rung.

After mass he took a nap, trying to regain his strength. He woke up, went over to the closet and chose a black suit to dress for his afternoon appointment with Roman Pyle, the federal prosecutor.

As he buttoned the shirt and attached the collar Father Angelo wore a frown of disgust. Why didn't he just flatly refuse to appear for the interview with Pyle? He was not under subpoena. Why make it easier for the circling sharks to reach the prey by diving into their warm seas? The answer was simple. His conscience wouldn't let him dodge the law and its figureheads. He was still a priest *and* a public official.

He shrugged his arms into the suit jacket and stood in front of the mirror. The jacket fit loosely on his scarecrow shoulders. It came as no surprise he had lost a lot of weight since he last wore it. He turned away from his reflection in the mirror and lit a cigarette.

He sat on the bed and smoked. Would all his plans and good intentions soon go up in smoke and be reduced to ashes like the cigarette he held? The idea of it was bitter and gnawing to him. But so was the notion of betraying La Cumare, his mother.

He combed his hair and put on the fedora, cocked at an angle, affixed dark glasses and began the walk downtown to the federal building.

Soon he found himself locked in a handshake with Roman Pyle, whose gesture of greeting managed to convey both firmness and sympathy. The man had oddly memorable hands, hands that somehow hinted of both power and artistry. They were long, graceful and expressive—hands that in another age might have held the scepter and in the priest's own milieu . . . the crozier.

Pyle pulled up a chair next to his desk and the priest sank into it. He held out a platinum cigarette case.

Father Angelo shook his head, crossed his legs and waited.

Pyle replaced the case in his coat pocket and sized up the visitor. Finally he said, "I've heard lots of good things about you in the smoke-filled rooms, Father."

"Uh-oh," said Father Angelo in a dry mocking tone.

"No, really," insisted Pyle. "Very good things. You have what the news magazines like to call 'a sterling reputation.' "

Father Angelo returned an icy smile. "I'd rather be brass in the reform clubs than sterling in the Republican board rooms. Thanks all the same."

Pyle inclined his head in ironic acknowledgment.

Now the priest measured his interviewer, a large man with an angular, patrician head and friendly blue eyes. Also a trifle foppish, sporting a bright foulard handkerchief in the breast pocket of a gray dacron jacket.

Pyle went on: "While most of us are politicians, you're the real article—a public servant."

"Thanks, but let's dispense with the big buildup before the letdown, eh?"

Pyle leaned his rear against the front of the desk and folded his arms. "Then you know why I asked you here."

Father Angelo nodded. He noted on the desk the gold-framed photo of a pretty dark-haired woman he supposed was the prosecutor's wife. He winced when he saw . . . or thought he saw . . . that she bore a certain resemblance to Veronica.

"Let me make it clear that this is, well, an informal chat, not an official interrogation," Pyle said.

The priest nodded again. He knew that he didn't have to say a word and that he had a right to have an attorney present. But he wanted to hear what Pyle had to say.

The prosecutor reached across the desk and picked up a file of documents that he tapped against his palm. "I have here photostats of documents outlining some serious allegations against you. You don't have to say anything unless you want to."

Father Angelo shook his head and said nothing.

Pyle walked around the desk and sat down, looking for a moment at the color photo of his wife, remembering that she had told him at the breakfast table that she'd had a disturbing dream about a priest. Well, Cynthia had a rather mystical bent. He had shrugged it off this morning, but now he had to wonder about it. "Look here, Father Angelo, maybe we can make some kind of deal. A deal you could live with . . . I admire your work, I don't want to see your career destroyed. I want to prosecute criminals not priests."

"Then why don't you prosecute the criminals who gave you those documents?"

"I work with what I have, and I have no angle on them right now. I do have an angle on the Falcones." He stroked his chin with a bloodless hand. "You have to face it, Father Angelo. Sooner or later you have to face it."

The priest looked up. "God judges my family, not me. God judges you and yours too."

"Well, if you can't bring yourself to help us with your mother, perhaps you'll have less trouble with Claudio Falcone. And in the process save yourself."

Father Angelo took a deep breath and got up from the chair. "You're wasting your time, Mr. Pyle," he said, revolving his hat by the brim.

Roman Pyle smiled a nearly benevolent smile. "I figured it would be useless," he said with a shrug of his tailored shoulders. "No harm trying, though." He extended his manicured hand to be shook.

The priest ignored it, put on his hat and turned away. . . .

When the priest had gone Pyle allowed himself a private philosophic smile. He didn't relish persecuting an essentially blameless man, but he had no choice now that the dice had been thrown on the felt. And he had to cultivate men like Koenig for the sake of future deals. The prosecutor again used the squawk box to ask his secretary to contact the Manhattan DA's chief assistant, a man with whom he had attended law school. After speaking to him for some ten minutes Pyle hung up and went to the lavatory adjoining the office, where he washed his pink and perfect hands.

On Maundy Thursday Father Angelo looked stoic as a wooden Indian as he said the nine o'clock mass. But under the white brocade vestments his trip-hammer heart pounded hard. Only one mass was celebrated in each church on this day that marked the institution of the Holy Eucharist by Christ at the Last Supper, a supposedly joyous occasion. The priest's mood was sepulchral.

Standing at the foot of the altar, he joined hands and recited the Confiteor, a ritual confession to God, the Virgin and a host of angels and saints. The Latin phrases seemed to echo reproachfully, amplified by marble and stone.

Finishing the prayer, he raised his head and saw La Cumare kneeling in a pew. Oddly, her presence startled him, but he should have known she would attend mass on Holy Thursday. Seeing her reminded him that he could no longer postpone the decision.

After the gospel the priest recited the Nicene Creed and when he came to the narration of how Jesus was made flesh by the Holy Ghost of the Virgin Mary (". . . *incarnatus est de Spiritu Sanctu ex Maria Virgine*: *ET HOMO FACTUS EST*") the congregation knelt to ponder the mystery. Above them might have hovered the spirits of a country priest and a peasant girl.

At the consecration of the bread and wine Father Angelo lifted his eyes and outstretched his hands, imitating the Nazarene, who presided at a seder some two thousand years earlier. "For this is my body," he said, kneeling, rising and elevating the host.

Soon he was holding the chalice of wine and chanting, "For this is the chalice of my blood of the new and eternal testament, the mystery of the faith: which shall be shed for you and for many, to the remission of sins."

He glanced at his mother, stood and elevated the chalice. When he sipped wine from the chalice he tried not to show his distaste. It was sour. He gave a stern look to one of the altar boys. Somebody had neglected to tighten the cap of the wine bottle the last time it was stored in the sacristy pantry. It tasted like vinegar and gall.

Father Angelo walked toward La Cumare's town house, wearing a crown of pain from the migraines. He glanced at the rectangular face of an old copper clock that was attached to the side of a building. He would be a few minutes late for the dinner party that his mother was throwing for him.

The house scintillated with crystal, candlelight and cheerful talk. The living room was filled with familiar faces wearing festive smiles and mouthing greetings to La Cumare's son, the priest, who could manage nothing better than wooden gestures and artificial phrases.

His political disciples who had been invited mingled easily with family members and friends, including his brother Chip, Uncle Claudio, Camilla and Livio Petri (the reformed philanderer and actor) and their daughter Maria, La Cumare's namesake and god-daughter, who had grown into a beautiful young woman with a chiming laugh and spectacular hazel eyes. And of course Bonaventura hovered in alpine stillness in the background.

Father Angelo was kissed by his scented mother, who was too busy being a hostess to notice his pallor and subdued mood. She then steered him to an armchair, where he sank down and accepted a cocktail from Carmela, the Somalian maid.

Simon Fisher, who arrived late, came over and clapped him on the back. "How you doing, Congressman?" he said brightly.

The priest looked up at his advisor. "Shouldn't count your congressmen before they're hatched."

Fisher waved it away. "You'll win in a walk," he said, pulling up a chair and sitting down. "I could use a drink." He crooked his finger at the maid, who promptly brought him one.

After a few sips of good Scotch, Fisher squinted at his candidate. "You all right?"

"Sure."

"You look kinda tired."

"Well, Holy Week and all that. Keeps a priest hopping." Father Angelo sipped the drink. "You're a little late."

"I went to an early seder at my aunt's on the Grand Concourse."

"Oh, sure, I forgot. It's Passover."

Fisher patted his stomach with a frown. "Yup. The feast of the unleavened bread."

Father Angelo nodded toward the kitchen. "My mother has a big spread laid on, that's for sure. She'll be insulted if you don't eat."

Fisher raised his bristling beard. "Who won't eat? Hey, my Aunt Flo's gefilte fish would make your hair curl and her brisket tastes like burnt rubber." He patted his big stomach again. "I'm dying for a good Italian meal."

Father Angelo, only half-listening, thought of Passover and Holy Thursday and how the blood of the yearling surely had been sprinkled on the lintels and sideposts of his mother's house, but would

the Angel of Death pass over it? He glanced over at his brother
Chip, who was chatting animatedly with Maria Petri, and the
thought occurred to him that as the firstborn of La Cumare, maybe
it was up to him to reap the early harvest of atonement for the
family's bloody rise. Was he beginning, he wondered, to glimpse
some meaning in the recent twists and turns of his life?

Simon Fisher's voice broke into his train of thought.

"What?"

"I said, what's on the menu?"

Father Angelo had no idea.

Roast lamb, it turned out. And a cornucopia of other dishes. La
Cumare had baked her own bread and the wine flowed. Father
Angelo, who gave the blessing, sat at the head of the table surrounded by associates, friends and family. Soon he had had a little
too much to drink and the bread and wine sparked images of hunger and blood and suffering. The place and people around him, the
ideas swarming in his head had a kaleidoscopic quality in which
internal and external realities were jumbled together in bursts of
color and sound. The migraine, softened by alcohol, still was at his
temples. The bruises on his body were tingling reminders of his
tormentors in East Harlem. But all these afflictions melted before
visions of hollow-eyed children without bread, of old men wres-
tling with demons of disease, of ragged beggars. They marched in
the jumbled procession of his imagination . . . and above them
hovered an embryo crucified on a curette.

He shook his head, trying to drive out the images.

Over Asti and walnut pie Simon Fisher rose to give a toast. "To
the Godmother of us all," he said, and everybody applauded. Then
he added, pointing the fluted glass at her firstborn son, "And to
the next congressman from the Seventeenth District . . ." More
and even more enthusiastic applause.

An unexpected guest appeared at the door. Junior Scario. La
Cumare's face betrayed her annoyance but she offered him a glass
of sparkling wine and instructed Carmela to bring another chair to
the table.

Junior walked over to Father Angelo and kissed him on the
cheek.

Something made the priest recoil, some dry, intangible quality that conveyed falseness. He had been wondering how his mother's enemies had found out about Veronica. Now he thought he knew. It had to have been the turncoat's son, openly bitter at his treatment by the Falcones, hungry for money and respect. He held the key to the closet that contained the skeletons. Father Angelo tried to hate him, but mostly all he could do was look at his former friend with regret and pitying eyes.

Junior, apparently sensing the priest's revulsion, walked off and after a glass of wine quickly left.

When all the guests had gone La Cumare asked her firstborn son to stay and talk. Both the bodyguard and maid had retired to their rooms on the ground floor.

"More coffee?" said his mother.

"Sure." He shoved his cup across the table and she poured. They were sitting in the kitchen that overlooked the backyard and garden where in the long ago past Pepe Falcone had labored with such pleasure.

"You don't look so good," she said, tilting her head.

He smiled. "I think I had a little too much to drink."

And he in turn studied his mother. She had pouches under the eyes and the milky skin sagged slightly at her neck. But the general brightness in her eyes and clarity of her complexion made her, at least to him, still look almost girlish. Could he really even think about betraying her for some greater good? At least "good" as he saw it. The coffee was strong and bitter. He added a spoonful of sugar.

La Cumare seemed distracted. When she spoke her voice resonated with a fervor that came from deep down inside her. "You'll win this election, won't you? Then the sky's the limit."

He made no comment, sipping his coffee.

"Someday you'll run for senator, eh? Then who knows? I'm very proud of you."

The priest looked at her and saw the peasant girl of Miseno balancing jars on her head and dreaming of a golden future for herself. He saw the virginal victim of priest and padrone, the immigrant woman of talent and wit. He saw her in all her incarnations, including leader of a criminal organization.

"Look, Mamma," he said, "I'm not looking for all that. I—"

"A man can't escape his destiny."

She said it like a sentence. A death sentence? He stared into the coffee cup. "I believe that too." He seemed on the brink of telling her all about what had happened to him but held back.

"You were born under a certain star," she said.

He shook his head. "Maybe so, but I assure you I won't be a ruler of men. Not in the way you think."

She made a face. "You have to aspire. Have I taught you nothing?"

"Mamma, you've taught me a great deal."

The traces of freshness and beauty that lingered on her aging face suddenly were shadowed. "Well then," she began in a low voice, "what have I taught you? What good and useful lessons, eh?"

"The best lesson, Mamma. No matter what else, you taught me how to love. How to love deep and hard."

There were no more words necessary as mother and son reached out and embraced each other.

It was only ten o'clock when Father Angelo left the town house and walked home to San Gennaro's. The night was warm, and he went to sit on the carved stone bench in the garden. The olive trees and budding greenery filled the darkness with their fragrances. He fiddled with the cuff links his mother had given him at his ordination. The gold angels, he noted, were tarnished. Funny, he hadn't noticed before.

He heard a crunching of footsteps.

"Who's there?" he called out, peering at a figure coming down the flagstone path.

"It's only me, Father."

He recognized Simon Fisher's voice. The plump manager sat down next to him with a heavy sigh. "Figured you'd be here," he said, dabbing his neck with a handkerchief.

The priest said nothing. He was not pleased at Fisher's unexpected visit; he had wanted to be alone. Needed to be alone.

Fisher talked on: "First I called the rectory and you weren't home, so I checked with La Cumare and she said you'd left. I put two and two together."

"How did you know I wasn't at a girlfriend's?" Father Angelo said it with a straight face.

The hand holding the handkerchief froze under Fisher's chin. "Not even as a joke," he said. "Not good for your image."

"How about being the son of a crime boss? Is that good for my image?"

Fisher shrugged. "That hasn't hurt you. Not yet, anyway. Not with the constituents you've been facing so far. That's one of the things I came to talk to you about."

The priest cocked his head questioningly.

"It might get to be a problem when you shoot for higher office. We should start right away laying the foundation for dealing with it. Got any ideas?"

"Simon, I'm not running for any higher office."

"Don't rule it out, Angelo. You've got a gift, the common touch. Why waste it? Think of all the good you would be able to do."

It was time to enlighten Simon Fisher. "Let's go for a walk, Simon. I have something to tell you. It's very important. And you won't like it."

They walked along the flagstones, going out of the garden and onto the street. As they reached the stone steps that led to the front door of the church Fisher grabbed his companion by the arm. "Come on, Angelo, what's this all-fired deep dark thing you have to tell me?"

Angelo hesitated, then was about to speak when a car rolled up to the curb and two men, dressed in near-identical rumpled raincoats, got out.

"Father Angelo Falcone?" said the taller man.

The priest nodded, understanding in his eyes.

"Come with us, please."

Simon Fisher spoke up. "Who the hell are you?"

Father Angelo patted his associate on the arm. "Take it easy, Simon. They're detectives."

The shorter detective put a rough hand on the priest's arm and produced handcuffs.

"You don't really need those, do you?" Father Angelo said.

The detective frowned down at the cuffs in his hands, then shrugged.

"Let's go," said the taller man, showing a piece of paper. "We have a warrant."

Fisher looked from face to face in confusion. "Will somebody tell me what the hell's going on here?"

"We're from the DA's office," said the tall detective sergeant, a jowly man with pale blue eyes. He advised Fisher, "Better call a lawyer." Consulting his wristwatch, he added, "I'd say we'll be in front of the arraignment judge in about an hour."

"What's the charge?"

"You'll find out in night court," the sergeant said, giving the priest a slight shove in the small of the back. "Now let's go."

Ninety minutes later the defendant stood before Judge William Packer, a wizened man with drowsy eyes, a cynical mouth and the aura of clubhouse politics clinging to his dusty robes.

Fisher looked on from the first pew of the courtroom, a place filled with the drunks, streetwalkers and petty thieves who routinely passed through the blindfolded lady's revolving door after the sun had set. Fisher mopped his forehead with a handkerchief, relieved not to see any reporters covering the arraignment of the well-known priest. Maybe the district attorney, a fellow Democrat, had staged the court appearance at night as an act of mercy to avoid all the popping flashbulbs and bad publicity. If so, he was grateful for small favors, but the story was bound to leak out sooner or later.

Fisher strained to hear but couldn't make out any of the words, they all mumbled so up there. Justice, it seemed, was incoherent as well as blind. He had called a friend, Abe Sachs, to act as Father Angelo's lawyer and obeyed the priest's request not to inform his mother of his arrest. It was probably wise not to employ the services of the usual Falcone family lawyers, not yet anyhow.

Soon the presence of a roman-collared defendant in the dock had prompted a buzz of curiosity in the courtroom. A woman sitting next to Fisher said, "Isn't that Father Angelo, the councilman? I saw him at the rally last Sunday."

Simon shrugged, not wanting to talk to strangers.

The women looked hard at Fisher, then added, "You look familiar too. I remember the beard. Aren't you the guy who was with him on the speakers' platform?"

"No," said Fisher, placing his forefinger on his lips.

"Sure you are," she said. "I never forget a face."

"Lady, I don't know what you're talking about," Fisher said and got up to change his seat.

Father Angelo was arraigned on the two felony counts and, since the assistant district attorney didn't object, the judge released him without bail pending a hearing.

In the lobby of the Criminal Courts building Father Angelo put both hands on Simon's shoulders. "You got to promise me something, Simon. Whatever happens, I want you to carry on my work."

Fisher shifted his weight on the tiled floor. "I'm a behind-the-scenes kind of man, Angelo. You know that."

Father Angelo frowned and tightened his grip on Simon's shoulders. "Look here, Simon, you have got to be a rock, for the sake of the people that you and I have been working for."

Fisher nodded, said nothing.

"Come hell or high water, Simon."

"Ah, you'll beat this," protested Fisher, shoving his hands into his pockets and staring at the tiled floor.

The priest shook the head that was thorned by migraines, clasped his friend's hand and left.

Fisher stood in the drafty high-ceilinged lobby, still frowning at the floor. He was not feeling happy with himself. In fact, he was ashamed . . . he had been disloyal with the woman who had asked him about his association with Father Angelo. Could he be entrusted with helping the poor people who looked to their priest as their champion? He told himself he'd better try . . . a promise was a promise, especially one made to Angelo Falcone. As he shambled out of the courthouse, Simon Fisher heard a cock crow twice in the live chicken market of Chinatown.

Now came Good Friday, name steeped in irony, especially for Father Angelo, now clad in purple, who celebrated the Mass of the Presanctified. He had not shaved, his face was bathed in sweat. This was the Day of Atonement. He read lessons from scripture and chanted passion prayers. He led the parishioners through the Stations of the Cross. The congregation sang, "At the cross her station keeping, stood the mournful mother weeping, close to Jesus to the last."

He stood before the first of fourteen mosaic tile tablets on the church wall depicting the passion and death of Jesus, and as he began to lead the people down the Sorrowful Way the pain at his temples became so great that for a moment he slipped through the nets of space and time to the cobblestones of old Urusalim to the Savior bleeding from the soldier's lash, his head platted with the mock-laurel brambles, soldiers and jeering citizens, the captive's mother who kisses him before being shoved aside by the soldiers, the prisoner nailed to the cross and raised between two crucified thieves on the gibbet, the body wrapped in linen carried to a garden with a new tomb carved out of the rock, the body laid to rest, a big stone rolled up to cover the opening . . .

He was brought back to the present as the congregation of San Gennaro sang, "Thus Christ's dying may I carry, With Him in his passion tarry, And His wounds in memory keep."

The Stations of the Cross finished, Father Angelo stood frozen before the last mosaic, then sleepwalked through the rest of the service, stripping the altar cloths as the Good Friday ritual dictated and receiving the presanctified host.

"*Deo gratias*," the altar boys finally chanted. The mass was ended.

He quickly dressed in street clothes, borrowed the pastor's old blue Ford and drove to a church on West Twenty-third Street where he entered the confession box of an unfamiliar priest named Father Lyons.

Returning much later to the rectory, he went to his room and wrote a letter and sealed it in an envelope that he addressed to his mother and his brother Chip. He wrote a second letter to Simon Fisher.

Angelo wept.

He put on a jacket, went outside and walked around the neighborhood. He passed a group of men playing dice in front of a plumbing supply store on Spring Street. South on Lafayette Street, he lingered in front of the storefront Buddhist temple. Would Dharma, the lord of duty, be ousted by the god of fear? Viewed from the vantage of the Bodhisattva, the crucifixion was a rapture, a joyful participation in the suffering of the world, a compassionate sacrifice for the sake of others. And death was an atonement as well as a fulfillment.

He walked back toward the rectory. A grizzled dog slept in a warehouse doorway. The sky above the checkered streets bristled with electricity. A storm threatened.

As he turned the corner at Kenmare Street images of his own and his mother's past seemed to unroll helter-skelter before him . . . the sulphur springs of Miseno and severed head of Johnny Falcone . . . the defrocked priest who gave him life lying in the rubble of Anzio . . . the flaring nostrils of the horse that carried Ottavio Croce to the slaughter . . . the blob of flesh named Albano and the rapist of his grandmother . . . the abortionist whose glinting scoop infected Veronica's womb and cut the lifeline . . . the foreman Beinbrecher and Camorrista Il Spagnuolo . . . all the griffins and gargoyles carved in the masonry of his imagination . . .

He arrived at the church and went into the garden, glancing about at the flowers, trees and plants silhouetted by the gathering dusk. They needed weeding and pruning, he noted. He sat down on the bench and looked up at the knotted boughs of the olive tree.

He got up and walked over to the potting shed, where he knew he would find the sturdy and flexible green rubber garden hose, coiled serpentine in the corner by the bags of peat moss.

*   *   *

On Holy Saturday Father Thaddeus Lyons got up at the crack of dawn, mumbled the matins and made his draggle-tail way to the all-night newsstand on Twenty-third Street and Seventh Avenue, where he bought copies of the *News* and *Mirror*. Then he went back to his room and thumbed through the papers, drowsy eyes flickering anxiously from article to article.

Finally Father Lyons put down the newspapers. He craved a cup of coffee but had to wait until after mass. To the indignities of old age were added the piddling prohibitions of priesthood. Well, nobody had twisted his arm to take Holy Orders some fifty years earlier. And he had known the terms of the contract, even down to the fine print. Still, the plow was hard to pull, especially in the vesper hour of his life.

The newspapers did not contain the item he had been searching for. It was probably too soon to make the papers even if the young priest had carried out the plan he had told to him in the confessional. Father Lyons even had a glimmer of hope that he might have changed his mind or lost his nerve. But he never doubted the penitent's sincerity. Not for a moment. He had stated the case with too much clarity and conviction.

Father Lyons looked down at his hands, branched with bulging blue capillaries. Useless things they were, tied by the confessional vow. There was nothing he could do to stop the young fool. Could he, after all, jeopardize his immortal soul by breaking the confessional's sacred gag order? Of course not. Especially not when he was this close to the throne of judgment. Yet his worldly instincts spurred him to interfere, to break the silence imposed by church authority and save a life. He stared gloomily at the photo of Pope Pius XII on the wall. He had tried praying to discover what God wanted him to do. No answer came.

He leaned across the desk now and switched on the radio. Maybe he could find a news program amid the caterwauling that emerged from the speaker as he rotated the tuning dial. He found the Ave Maria Hour, frowned and continued turning the knob. "Irene, good night, Irene, good night . . ." came the voice of Nat King Cole.

He switched off the radio and slouched in the chair, reviewing the penitent's arguments. He had not come to confession for forgiveness for himself but for the confessor to help him find forgiveness of his enemies. His speech had been lucid, though Father Lyons was convinced that the man's ordeal had somehow unbalanced or at least disoriented him. Still, he had made a strong case for his decision . . .

Father Lyons pounded his gnarled fist on the desk. That was the Devil's cant—the ends justified the means. Like most of Satan's rationales it had logical appeal, even a certain charm. But it was wrong.

Wasn't it?

The old priest scratched his head. The penitent had sorely tested his feeble skill at theological tap dancing. He had asked whether Christ hadn't, in effect, committed suicide by not invoking his almighty powers to stop his executioners. Wasn't the crucifixion really an act of self-immolation designed for the higher purpose of saving souls? And wasn't Christ the model we were born to emulate?

Father Lyons growled to himself in disgust. He was clumsy at rhetorical footwork. But some of the arguments sounded familiar, echoing the tempter in the desert. What would his own penance be for failing to talk the young priest out of it?

He went over to the window. The day was brightening. There had been a short sudden storm last night, or had he just dreamed it? His sleep had been fitful, disturbed by scruples and regrets. He yawned and checked his watch. It was time to prepare for mass.

Earlier that morning, before the sun had risen, Father Trapani was already reciting the Divine Office in his room. He was scheduled to say the first mass at San Gennaro on the day before Easter. Now he shut the book, ran a hand over his smooth face. The docile curate was ready to start the day.

He kissed the breviary, brushed the wreath of curls that circled his bald head and walked downstairs to the side door that led through the garden to the church. The ground exuded the lingering vapors of an overnight storm. He heard a symphony of crepuscular insects and birds. His step was buoyant as usual as he followed the flagstone path. Father Trapani was a guilelessly happy person.

Suddenly he stopped in mid-stride. Did he see what he was seeing? Was it some sleight-of-hand of nature caused by the dim light of dawn? Gathering up the folds of his cassock, he rushed over to the olive tree.

With one hand he covered his mouth to stifle a cry. With the other he made the sign of the cross.

The marionette that once contained the spirit of Angelo Falcone danced against the chiaroscuro sky at the end of the rubber hose that was tied to the bough of the tree.

Father Trapani turned away, burying his face in the crook of his arm and weeping. He staggered over to the bench to sit down and collect the shards of his emotions. In a minute or two he was able to cross himself repeatedly, still hardly crediting his senses.

Should he cut the body down?

No, he'd better not touch anything. He ran back to the rectory to wake up the pastor.

As soon as he recovered from the shock of the news Father Martin Meara told the curate to help him down the stairs and outside so he could see it with his own eyes. Then, with Father Trapani supporting him by the elbow, he went back inside the rectory to telephone the police. After that, his bony fingers dialed the phone again.

The Godmother was there when they cut him down from the tree. As she sat on the concrete bench a cop lay the body of the dead priest in the lap of his mother. She wore a black lace mantilla on her bowed head, shielding the tears that streamed down her cheeks and contrasted with her blank expression. Her eyes traced the lines of his thin lifeless form, naked except for undershorts. His flesh felt cool and smooth as marble.

His eyes were closed, his expression serene.

Was this God's ultimate punishment for the life she had led? La Cumare didn't accept it. Maybe she was deceiving herself to salve a guilty conscience, but she couldn't help feeling an eerie presence in the spring air, something beyond her understanding, but something strong enough to penetrate even her grief.

The body was soon taken away in a police van. Maria stayed in the garden, now bathed in sunlight. The organ sounded inside the church where mass was being celebrated. Claudio and Chip stood a few feet away, watching her.

Now Claudio came over and draped his arm over her shoulder, but his face was hard. "It was that Koenig," Claudio said. "First he kills my son, then he kills yours. I say, let's take out the bastard."

Maria shook her head. "No more killing," she said.

He seemed about to argue but the note of finality in her voice silenced him. He stood there, anchored to this woman by an enduring fealty of respect, loyalty and love.

After mass Father Trapani approached La Cumare. "*Signora*," he said with an air of deference, looking around to make sure nobody was spying on them, "I found these in your son's room. I told nobody, not even the police."

The curate handed over two envelopes, both addressed in Angelo's hand, one to Simon Fisher and the other jointly to herself and Cesare.

"Thank you," she said.

"Will you make sure Mr. Fisher gets his?" the curate managed to ask.

"I will," she promised.

"I pray to God I've done the right thing by not telling the police about this," the priest said.

She placed her hand on his arm. "You've done a kindness to a grieving mother. God will bless you for preserving our privacy."

"I know very little about theology," he said, and tapped his chest. "I try to follow what my heart says. And my heart said the letters were meant to be given to you."

She nodded. "Thank you again, from the depths of *my* heart."

Red-faced, eyes on the ground, he added, "I will take care of his garden."

She kissed him on the cheek.

In Claudio's Cadillac on the way home Maria burned to open the letter but she had decided to wait for a time when Cesare and she were alone. She thought that it was the way Angelo would have wanted it.

The time came at noon, after Claudio had left to carry out her instructions about the police investigation and other matters that had to do with Angelo's death. She had also told him to deliver the letter to Simon Fisher.

Now she and Chip faced each other across the living room coffee table. They sat in armchairs, neither speaking. Finally she took the letter from the pocket of her sweater.

"He left a note," she said. "For you and me."

A startled look crossed Chip's face. "Then it was suicide?"

La Cumare bit her lower lip, resisting this evident conclusion. "Maybe they made him write something before they killed him. A warning . . ." But she doubted it.

Chip, lines of grief in his face, looked healthier than usual since he had quit drinking and carousing, thanks to Maria Petri's influence. "Did he leave two notes? One for each of us?"

She shook her head. "The envelope is addressed to both of us."

Silence. Finally Chip said, "Well? Why don't you open it?"

Hands shaking, she produced the letter from her pocket. She thrust the letter toward him. "You open it."

He took the letter and opened it. As he read, Maria tried to decipher his expression. What she saw was a tear form in the corner of his eye.

"Well?" she said, at the edge of the chair.

He handed the letter to her. The script on the plain white paper was shockingly brief.

It read: "Woman, behold thy son! Behold thy mother!"

The sermon of her first-born son from beyond the grave brought a smile of self-recrimination to her face. She gripped the scrolled-wood arms of the chair. He had used the words of Saint John's gospel to remind her that Cesare was all she had left. She had been badly neglectful for so many years. Maybe now she could find a way to make it up to him.

Without a word, mother and son embraced each other.

Simon Fisher sat in the two-room bachelor apartment that he rented above a candy store on Houston Street. The place, which doubled as his office, was dark and untidy. He sat on a swivel chair in front of a rolltop desk buried in a politician's blizzard of paperwork. Among the clutter was the letter addressed to him by Father Angelo just before his death.

Fingering his scruffy beard, Fisher eyed the letter as the blood slowly seeped back into his face. He was recovering from the shock of the news he had heard from the priest's uncle, Claudio Falcone, who had delivered the letter. He had progressed from shock far enough to calculate the note's contents and the commission Angelo had given him.

He picked up the letter and read it a third time, shook his head, then reached over for a pint of Scotch stored in a pigeonhole of the desk and poured two fingers into a shot glass. He downed the whiskey in one gulp. He grimaced at the handwriting before his red-veined eyes.

But why shouldn't the plan work? First, it was hard for many to believe that a priest would risk damnation by taking his own life. And since no suicide note had been found and no evidence to the contrary existed, people naturally would conclude that Father Angelo Falcone probably had been executed by La Cumare's gangster rivals, who in the past had shown they favored melodramatic assassinations, maybe supported by political enemies threatened by the priest's popular championing of the poor and apparent cooperation with radical groups like the American Labor Party. The "Red Scare" was raging on the current political landscape.

At least it was a credible enough playbook for Fisher to sell to the columnists he had cultivated on the local newspapers. Portraying Father Angelo as the martyred victim of a gangland vendetta and political fanaticism made good copy. It also would help, Fisher observed to himself in a less ironic vein, to keep alive the flame of his client's good works, which he had promised to do.

He downed another shot of whiskey before thumbing through his dog-eared pocket phone directory and scribbling down likely names. Some reporters, in fact, would probably soon be calling him, since by now word of Angelo's death must have reached police reporters, who would alert their city and political desks. He decided to restrict himself to off-the-record comments that he could more easily mold. The gospel according to Saint Simon was that his newspaper cronies would strike the themes he coached them to write. They owed him, didn't they?

Wetting his thumb with his tongue, he traced the names on the list: Matt Heckmann of the *Journal-American*, Marco Pingi of the *Brooklyn Eagle*, Luke Wentworth of the *Herald-Tribune* and John Eagleton of the *Post*. These scribes would surely spread the news, Simon Fisher decided as he reached for the black telephone.

With minor variations dictated by the editorial policy of the particular paper, the published columns pretty well reflected the angles he had promoted. But then two sensational events occurred prompting more news stories and sidebars that fueled a movement to depict the dead priest as a martyred victim and champion of the people. The day after Father Angelo's death a rumor got started that the body bore the five wounds of the crucifixion. (Some observers traced the story to a leak in the medical examiner's office.) As was reputed to have happened in the case of Saint Catherine of Siena, the stigmata were said to have appeared on the body after death. The New York *Mirror* published the stigmata story, causing quite a stir.

"Cataleptic hysteria," said medical and psychiatric experts. But many, for their own reasons, seemed to believe otherwise. Especially when Father Angelo's body disappeared from the morgue the next day.

Junior Scario couldn't believe it when he read the news. The gum he was chewing as he stood on the corner of Madison and Catherine streets seemed to freeze in his mouth. He spat it out onto the sidewalk, gave a shudder of disbelief and reread the article, then threw the newspaper to the ground as if the printed words were crawling lice.

Looking over both shoulders, he began walking toward the river, telling himself that La Cumare must have spent a small fortune to bribe somebody to take the body from the morgue. But such speculation didn't exorcise his fear.

He continued walking east toward the viaduct. He had had hardly any sleep since Angelo's death, and what he managed to get had been full of nightmares featuring his dead ex-friend whom he had betrayed. The only friend he'd ever had, come to think of it.

Junior crossed South Street and stood under the structure of the East Side Highway listening to the sloshing of the river. On the north shore he could see the garland of lights on the Manhattan Bridge, a display mirrored in the south by the Brooklyn Bridge. He was startled by an unknown sound. Peering into the darkness, he saw that it came from a nearby trash heap where a rat rummaged in the tin cans. Was he going off the deep end, scared of his own shadow? Except he had good reason to be scared. Would La Cumare discover his treachery and settle the score? Or would the Koenig mob beat her to it, figuring he knew too much? Anything was possible when a guy was caught in the maze of mob rivalries. He felt like throwing the Mexican silver mine shares back into Albano's fat face.

He glanced across the pavement at the trash heap, where the rat emerged and then moved toward the pier. Junior pulled back at the sight of it. A rat, just like him. Like his father before him.

But how could he have known that the deal with Albano would end up in Angelo's death? Thinking that didn't help. He lifted his head and stared at the Brooklyn Bridge. The lights winked real pretty . . . if only he could get some sleep. What the hell was the matter with him? Why did he feel so bad? It wasn't like him, he'd never really cared a damn for anybody but himself. Now he looked at the Manhattan Bridge. Eeny-meeny-miney-mo. Sleep, that was the ticket.

He couldn't stand it any more.

He walked back to a liquor store on Madison Street and bought a fifth of bourbon, then sat by the highway and drank the bottle to the dregs. He threw the empty bottle into the river and watched it sink, then got to his feet and staggered over deserted streets until he came to the entrance of the Brooklyn Bridge. He went onto the walkway, now and then looking over his shoulder. Was an army of rats following him, like the fucking pied piper? The alcohol was making his head reel. He stopped and looked down. A big red moon was reflected on the water below. His mouth was dry, his breath short. He needed air. A lot of air. He was at the middle of the bridge when he climbed over the guard rail, then dropped down onto a steel girder. He inhaled the briny air deeply. His body hurtled into the field of blood.

Did he stumble? Who could say? Nobody was there to witness.

The chancery on Fifth Avenue was deluged with requests that Father Angelo be promoted to sainthood. Officials of the so-called Powerhouse that screened the requests took no action in spite of the ground swell of support. Proposing persons for public veneration was a rare and serious step. Father Angelo Falcone was disqualified for consideration on many counts, not the least being the reputation of his mother and the blasphemous way the corpse had vanished. Yet in the court of public opinion he was already declared a saint by some. The Archdiocese of New York signaled by its silence a decision to let the sainthood campaign wither on the vine.

But in such a climate it was hardly surprising that the district attorney was inclined to let the case against Father Angelo Falcone fade into oblivion. Prosecutors were also politicians. There was little point, after all, in alienating potential voters for no good reason. The death of the defendant made the case moot. What purpose would be served by publicizing the charges against him? More to the point, what public officeholder would be so foolhardy and undiplomatic as to smear the name of a dead Robin Hood? Case dismissed.

Likewise, the ammunition he'd hoped for against Maria Falcone.

One sunny morning a few weeks later Maria Falcone brought an envelope of lily seeds to the rectory and asked Father Trapani to plant them under the olive tree. As the curate troweled the earth she stood by. What did the parable say about sowing and reaping? The soil was rich in this spot, nourished by decay. The lilies would grow gaudy and fragrant here, she thought as she made the sign of the cross and kissed her thumb and knuckle.

She sat on the concrete bench that her son had favored and watched the curate cover the seeds with soil. Bury the seeds, was the way she saw it. Burial before birth. Before rebirth.

The remains of the son for whom she had had such high hopes

now rested somewhere within the tentacles of the olive tree and the radicles of the lily plants yet to come. Had the hopes she'd first known on the bluffs of Miseno been destroyed by her on the asphalt of Manhattan? What an idea! She had no say in the matter. It was beyond her, way beyond her.

The bodies of her parents moldered in Campania in consecrated ground. At least she had seen to that. Maria Falcone, peasant girl, gangster boss. The sins of the mother were visited on herself. The body of the son would not rest in the suburban mausoleum purchased with bullets and blood, but here in the neighborhood churchyard beside the bones of the lewd padrone. Okay. She would write a will stipulating that she be buried here too.

Meanwhile she intended to use whatever money and power she had left to help carry out her son's projects. She would build the children's hospital, pay for Joey's heart operation, finance a neighborhood old-age home, do whatever she could to make sure that he hadn't died in vain . . .

Father Trapani got up now from a squatting position, brushed off his cassock and slapped the dirt from his hands. "There," he said with his pleasant smile. "Now I'll give it some water."

La Cumare nodded.

Lilies also had banked the altar a few days earlier on Easter Sunday as Lena Morales entered the Church of San Gennaro to hear mass. Her lush red hair was covered by a black kerchief. She went to the altar rail to light a candle and kneel in prayer for the soul of Father Angelo. Would he (and later she) be condemned for the sin they had committed that day? She hoped that he had gone to confession. In any event, as she watched the flickering flame in the red glass she couldn't imagine such a good man enduring everlasting penalties. Maybe he would just suffer for a while, until God stretched out His finger. That, at least, was the prayer whispered by a woman who did not know that she carried in her womb the fruit of this man's seed.